Blossoming of Truth

SUSAN GRAY

 UK Book Publishing.com

Editing, design, typesetting and publishing by UK Book Publishing

www.ukbookpublishing.com

ISBN: 978-1-916572-72-0

Blossoming of Truth

To *Charlotte* and *Georgia*...believe in your dreams

Love is patient; love is kind...
It blossoms in truth.

1 Corinthians Chapter 13 (adapted)
The Bible

Prologue

November 1926

"Thomas Ezra Smallwood, I am arresting you on suspicion of causing the death of Jonathan William Smallwood on the 27th of August 1926 at Lasham Cragg in the county of Durham." The police officer paused. "You do not have to say anything, but it may harm your defence if you do not mention, when questioned, something which you later rely on in court. Anything you do say may be given in evidence."

The colour drained from Tom's face. The hairs bristled on the back of his neck. His tall, well-built body stiffened, as he stared into the eyes of the rotund police sergeant Sid Jones – a man he had been acquainted with all of his twenty-seven years.

"Wh…wh…what did you say?" he asked croakily, in total bewilderment.

"You heard me, lad," the policeman responded, stroking the handlebars of his greying moustache, then turning to the lanky young constable, he motioned towards the coat rack adjacent to the door.

"Best be putting your overcoat and hat on, Mr Smallwood…it's parky out there," he indicated as the constable handed Tom his grey Crombie overcoat and trilby hat. Once adorned in his outer clothing, Tom's hands were pulled behind his back and his wrists were secured with a distinct 'click' in the metal handcuffs.

Tom was numb…frozen…this was unbelievable! He was being arrested for causing his beloved Jonty's death. He was led out of the house to the waiting police car.

Thirty minutes later Tom was seated on a hard structure, deemed to be a bed, in a cold, white tiled cell in the town's police station. His coat, hat and handcuffs had been removed and taken away.

"Sorry about all this, Mr Smallwood," explained the police sergeant. "But I'm only obeying orders. The inspector from Durham is on his way and should be here within the hour to interview you. In the meantime, I suggest we contact a solicitor for you…will that be Gregory, Thompson and Porter solicitors?"

Tom was roused from his stupor by the question. "Er… oh…yes, I suppose so," the stilted reply emerged from his lips. Who else would it be? It was a small town, barely more than a village – there was only one firm of solicitors in Malhaven.

Tom lost track of time. The chilly, dismal November day slid into evening darkness…at least he assumed that fact, gazing up at the high barred window in the bleak cell. He vaguely remembered being offered a cup of weak, milky tea, which did little to hydrate his dry, parched throat, or quell the fear clutching at his stomach.

The awaited inspector duly arrived, preceded by the young solicitor Gregory Porter, who told Tom to say he was innocent of the charge levelled against him. The interview room was small and stark. Tom sat on a hard wooden chair, looked across the wooden table, into the eyes of Inspector Ramshaw. He was a smart chap, in his forties, Tom guessed. His sleek black hair and moustache were neatly trimmed. He asked Tom his name, date of birth and address, then repeated the charge – the reason he was being held.

"Do you have anything to say, Mr Smallwood?" he asked.

Tom pulled himself straight.

"I am totally innocent of the charge, Inspector. I loved my brother," Tom declared.

The inspector raised his eyebrows. "Mmmm...well that is to be proved, Mr Smallwood. But I must inform you we have a reliable witness who says otherwise!"

Tom stared back at the inspector in utter amazement.

***

Chapter 1

Nearly two years earlier
– January 1925

B ang! Crunch! Tom flung down his pen, scraped back his chair, rounded his desk and strode over to the window. 'What on earth was that?' he asked himself out loud. He gazed out into a swirling winter scene. The wind was howling; the sleet was bleaching against the windowpane, making it almost impossible to recognise the outline of the garden and grounds, in the fading twilight of the early January day. He shivered. Despite wearing thick tweed trousers, a twill shirt and a chunky knit jumper – one look outside made him feel cold!

The storm had set in about an hour earlier and already the ground resembled a white, winter blanket. Tom ran his fingers through his blond hair, sighed, closed the blind and pulled the heavy drapes. Pleased I'm not going out in that tonight, he mused as he ambled back to study the figures laid out in the ledgers on his desk.

Thump! Thump! Thump! Three loud bangs rattled on the front door of the large house.

'Good grief,' Tom uttered, 'what kind of idiot is hammering on our door in the middle of this storm?' As he spoke, he made his way out of his office, along the landing and down the creaking staircase in time to see Mrs Jenkins, the housekeeper, sliding back the bolts in the heavy wooden door. He stopped and stared across the square hallway at the bedraggled figure of a woman silhouetted against the white backdrop of the open door. Snow was sticking to her long, dark coat, and a hat and scarf encased her face.

"Quick, quick, whoever you are, come on in," urged Winnie Jenkins. "What on earth are you doing out in this storm?" She questioned the lone figure as the penetrating snow tried to invade the hallway.

"I...I...broke down," stuttered the stranger. "My car is stuck. Do you have a telephone I could use please?"

Tom walked over to greet the visitor. "Mrs Jenkins... please make a hot drink for our guest," he suggested. "Now, miss...let me take your coat." A large Bassett hound lumbered along the corridor into the reception area to observe the new arrival. "You can rest awhile in comfort while I make a telephone call."

Mrs Jenkins eyed the pool of water collecting at the stranger's feet, then turned and walked towards the rear of the house.

The stranger disentangled herself from her sodden garments and, bending, unfastened and stepped out of her black ankle boots.

"Stop it, Humph!" Tom chastised the dog trying to lick the growing puddle. "This way," he beckoned, and led the way down the passageway the housekeeper had taken, followed by the new arrival and a curious dog.

They entered a small cosy lounge, heated by a roaring log fire. "Here...warm yourself by the fire. I'll fetch you a towel," indicated Tom, disappearing into the adjoining kitchen. Handing the towel to the soaking guest, Tom watched and noted the petite woman appeared to be in her mid-twenties. She dabbed at her face and then rubbed her blonde hair, which was a mass of curls.

The housekeeper bustled into the room carrying a tray. "The tea's just brewing," she announced chirpily, placing the tray on a table underneath the window, which was obliterated by the heavy, burgundy drapes.

"Oh...thank you so much," acknowledged the young woman with chattering teeth.

"So...what are you doing travelling on such a treacherous day?" questioned Tom, fascinated to know the reasoning behind this attractive young woman's arrival in his home.

The stranger stopped drying her hair and looked up.

Tom stared and was momentarily unnerved...there was a familiarity about the movement. "Oh, forgive me please, where are my manners," he remarked, blinking away the thought. "I'm Tom, Tom Smallwood," he added, introducing himself and, reaching out, shook her hand. The stranger's hair was now a mound of bouncy, blonde curls.

"Er...pleased to meet you, Mr Smallwood. I'm Rachel Brooks," she replied, shaking his hand. "I'm so sorry to descend upon you like this, but my car just stopped…out there somewhere," she indicated, pointing vaguely into the distance. "If I could telephone a local garage then perhaps a mechanic could see what's wrong with it," she added.

The kitchen door sprang open at the behest of Winnie Jenkins' foot.

"Here we are," announced the housekeeper, pouring the tea into the cups on the tray. "Have a seat, miss," she said, pointing to one of the winged chairs beside the fireplace, then handing her a cup and saucer.

"Splendid, Mrs Jenkins," commented Tom. "This is Miss Brooks."

Winnie nodded to the young lady then asked, "Milk and sugar?"

"No thanks…just black," Miss Brooks replied.

Tom realised he was staring again.

"I'll go and telephone Jim Johnson at the garage," announced Tom and speedily left the room.

By the time he returned, he noticed their guest looked calmer, sitting on the edge of the chair, sipping her tea and eating one of Winnie's delicious fruit scones.

"Sorry, Miss Brooks, but you're out of luck. I'm afraid your car will have to stay where it is, until this storm blows itself out. Jim, our local mechanic, says it's too dangerous to venture out – apparently there's a tree down on the low road." Panic and fear struck the young woman's face. She opened her mouth to speak, but Tom interjected. "It's a good thing you knocked on our door, Miss Brooks. Meckleridge House is a hotel, so we have plenty of guest rooms, although we are currently closed for the winter break. I'm sure we can rustle up a room for the night," he said, then turning to the housekeeper asked, "That's possible, isn't it, Winnie?"

Winnie Jenkins took her final mouthful of tea, then stood.

"Yes, of course, Mr Smallwood. The bed's made up in the Lavender room and the fire is already laid. I'll go and put a match to it then fill a hot water bottle for the bed. It'll be cosy in no time," she added, disappearing into the kitchen.

Tom picked up his cup and began drinking his beverage.

"This is very kind of you, Mr Smallwood, I hope I'm not causing you any problems with my unexpected arrival," remarked the young woman.

Tom sat down opposite and scrutinised her curiously.

"So...back to my original question," Tom began. "What are you doing travelling in a car in such treacherous conditions?" Once again Tom sensed a familiarity in this stranger's demeanour – but he knew no Rachel Brooks to his knowledge.

Rachel took her last sip of tea and looked across at her host.

"I'm travelling to take up a new position," she replied. "I'm to be the new governess at Gilberta House in Malhaven. I think I missed the turning and then my car just...spluttered and died! I walked until I saw your house – I'm not used to the countryside," she explained.

Tom looked thoughtful. A governess indeed...how did she come to be in possession of a motor car, he wondered.

"Ah yes...Gilberta House – a governess to Dr Rossiter's boys...a task I don't envy." He chuckled, as visions of his friends Henry and Blanche Rossiter's mischievous offspring, came to mind. Their antics during the Sunday morning service were infamous.

Rachel stared at Tom.

"Well, we'll see about that," she added. "If they are in need of careful management...then I can provide that!" she declared.

Yes, thought Tom raising his eyebrows – he didn't doubt that – there was something quite formidable about this young governess.

The Bassett hound looked up and ambled towards her, sniffing at her stockinged feet. She bent to stroke him. "Hello there, you're a lovely boy...he is a boy?" she questioned.

Tom smiled down at the family pet, who was enjoying the attention.

"Yes...meet Humphrey – Humph for short," he chuckled. "So, how far have you travelled today?" he enquired, keen to know more about this attractive young woman.

She hesitated briefly. "I left Darlington this morning. It was a beautiful crisp winter's day – no hint of a storm," she replied.

Tom smiled. "The rolling hills of northwest Durham provide their own weather patterns. The terrain is almost a thousand feet above sea level, so we are often battered with snowstorms at this time of the year," he remarked. "I don't detect a northern accent – where do you hail from?"

Rachel dropped her eyes and picked at a few crumbs on her skirt, then she straightened her back. "Er...no, Mr Smallwood. I'm a southerner, hence my lack of a northern accent."

Tom was sure he sensed a discomfort in his guest's demeanour, but he pressed on with his questioning. "The south, eh? Which part?"

Rachel stood and walked over to place her cup and saucer on the table. "Oh, I've lived in many places. I was born in London, but I've lived in the southwest, on the south coast and the Bristol area, before moving to Newcastle, then Darlington."

Tom stood and placed his cup on the mantel shelf. "My, my, you are well travelled," he remarked, grinning.

Rachel lifted her eyes…and there it was again…he'd met this young woman before; he was sure of it.

"It's the nature of my work," she continued. "A year here, a couple of years there. I'm used to it."

The door from the hallway opened as Mrs Jenkins returned. "Now, miss – the fire's lit in the Lavender room and I've put a hot water bottle in the bed. It should warm up soon. I've also taken the liberty of putting some clothing on the bed, seeing as you have no baggage, and a pair of slippers. Miss Peggy always leaves a closet full of clothing for use in between her travels."

The guest looked surprised, and Tom noticed.

"My sister Peg works abroad and comes home occasionally," he explained. "Your luggage will be quite safe, I'm sure, until we can retrieve it."

"Are you taking dinner at the usual time, seven o'clock, Mr Smallwood?" Winnie addressed Tom.

"Yes, Mrs Jenkins – seven o'clock will be fine. It will give Miss Brooks a chance to rest after her ordeal."

Winnie nodded. "Now, miss, follow me and I'll show you to your room," suggested Winnie.

Rachel followed.

"The Lavender room...what a delightful name," Rachel remarked as they climbed the stairs.

"All the rooms are named after flowers – a botanical quirk of Mr Tom," the housekeeper commented.

Tom listened as the female voices faded. There was something quite disconcerting about the arrival of this young woman.

***

By half past seven that evening, Tom and Winnie were already eating their meal when Rachel entered the kitchen, full of apologies.

"I'm so sorry, Mr Smallwood. I lay down on the bed... and the room was so cosy...I fell asleep," she explained.

Tom stood. The refectory table in the large kitchen was a throwback to the days when Meckleridge House belonged to a wealthy businessman and employed many household staff. Tom pulled out a chair for Miss Brooks and she sat while Winnie placed a plate of comforting lamb hot pot in front of her.

"Mmm...this looks delicious," she commented, anticipating the food.

"I'm pleased you managed to get some rest," added Tom, sitting down. "Do you have experience of driving in snowy conditions?" he asked.

The guest shook her head. "I don't...in fact today is the first time I've driven in snow. I've only had the car for a few months," she remarked. Tom eyed her inquisitively, and she continued. "I was given the car as a gift. It belonged to a former employer's mother. Sadly, she passed away quite suddenly last summer. I had befriended the old lady while I was governess to her granddaughters, and I was bequeathed the car in her will. I still can't believe her generosity. But the family were happy for me to receive it."

Tom raised his eyebrows. "My...you were fortunate. You must have impressed the lady in question."

Rachel smiled and began to eat, as Tom observed her previously bedraggled hair now pulled back into a tight roll at the back of her neck. Her cheeks were rosy, and Tom recognised the cardigan she was wearing as one belonging to his sister. Then turning to the housekeeper, he said, "Winnie, why don't you stay the night? The paths will be slippery."

"Yes, Mr Tom...I was going to suggest it. I've prepared the Cyclamen room on the off-chance I would need to stay over." Winnie lived a short walk away from the hotel, but as she was a widow, she often stayed overnight at the hotel if circumstances required her to do so.

Rachel finished her plate of food in silence, then beamed with delight when the housekeeper produced a dish of rice pudding and jam. "Oh, Mrs Jenkins...pudding as well. I'm so grateful to you both for disrupting your evening like this," she declared.

Tom raised his hand to halt her flow of conversation. "Miss Brooks, please stop apologising. You are welcome to some northeastern hospitality. We are pleased to assist you. Now...do you think you should telephone your new employers – they may be concerned for your welfare?"

Rachel put down her spoon and clasped her hand to her mouth. Tom noticed the gesture.

"Oh, gosh, of course. I totally forgot. I said I would be arriving in the late afternoon…but I don't have their telephone number – it's in my suitcase in the car."

Tom reached across the table and patted Rachel's arm. "No problem. Henry is a friend I'll go and call him and explain, while you finish your food." Tom went to make the call. When he returned Rachel was helping Winnie by drying the dishes. "All sorted, Miss Brooks…no panic – they assumed you'd been delayed with the storm. Now, tomorrow morning we'll go to retrieve your car."

Half an hour later, Rachel Brooks was climbing the stairs to go back to her room. She left a bewildered Tom Smallwood warming his back beside the cosy fire in the rear lounge. He cupped his chin in his hand, rubbed his fingers across it and sighed. This 'déjà vu' sensation was uncanny. He was sure he'd met this young woman before. How could he find out without making a fool of himself?

***

The town of Malhaven was really an overgrown village. It lay in a basin with the river Meckle running through it. Originally created to accommodate the workers in various light industries, then gaining popularity as a spa resort during Victorian days. Now, it had become a tourist attraction causing some hotels and guests houses to emerge. Meckleridge House Hotel was one such establishment. It was stone built and stood in extensive grounds. It boasted ten spacious bedrooms, a residents' lounge, dining room, library and conservatory. At the rear of the house was a small lounge and a large kitchen, pantry, larder and wash house. The property was originally built as a family home in the 1860s. The former owner, a businessman, had been blessed with the foresight to install bathrooms on the first floor, making its conversion from a family home into a hotel quite straightforward.

As a small town, Malhaven now benefited from three churches; a bank; school; police station; garage; post office and various shops including a Co-operative departmental store. The town itself lacked an industry as such these days, but in the nearby town of Malsett a large iron works existed and coupled with many coal mines around the area, it was a thriving locality. From early Spring to late Autumn, many tourists and businessmen took delight in the offerings of this comfortable hotel.

By ten o'clock the next morning, Rachel Brooks and Tom Smallwood were standing on the doorstep of a large, detached house, just off the main street in the town.

"No wonder I drove straight past the turning," remarked Rachel as the housekeeper answered the door and invited them inside.

"Quite understandable, given the weather conditions yesterday," Tom replied.

The morning was crisp, bright and dry but the remnants of the storm were very evident on the paths, roads and gardens. After trudging through the snow to retrieve Rachel's Morris Cowley motor car, Tom was unable to bring it to life, so returning to the hotel with her luggage he telephoned the garage. Using his own car he drove carefully down the winding drive, and back into the town to Dr Rossiter's residence, Gilberta House.

"Good morning, Tom," Dr Rossiter greeted the couple standing in the hallway as he emerged from his surgery.

Rachel immediately stretched out her hand and introduced herself. "Hello, Dr Rossiter. I'm Rachel Brooks, your new governess. Sorry for my late arrival. I encountered difficulties in the snow with my car and Mr Smallwood kindly offered me overnight hospitality."

"Welcome, Miss Brooks...my wife, Blanche, will be with you shortly," replied the doctor.

Just then two young boys flew down the stairs, intent on hitting one another.

"Boys, boys...behave yourselves – this is your new governess Miss Brooks," he attempted to say. The two boys fled past their father, the guests and the housekeeper out of the door and into the winter wonderland – totally underdressed for the chilly reception awaiting them. Tom stood and watched as Rachel jumped into action, following the boys outside.

"I guess she's going to have her hands full," he remarked, chuckling, then explained to the doctor about his call to the garage concerning Miss Brooks' car. Moments later, Rachel and the boys returned to the hallway.

"Alasdair and Duncan have agreed to meet me for a snowball fight in one hour's time, when they are suitably attired for the weather," announced Rachel.

Tom decided this was his cue to take his leave. As he walked to the door Rachel followed and reached out to shake his hand.

"Again, many, many thanks for your kind hospitality, Mr Smallwood," she said.

Tom took her hand and stared into her blue grey eyes. He was aware of a sensation within him, as the feeling of familiarity resurfaced. "It's Tom, Miss Brooks, and it's been a pleasure to assist you, goodbye," he uttered. He called farewell to his friend and stepped out of the door.

***

"All people that on earth do dwell,
Sing to the Lord with cheerful voice."

Tom glanced around the congregation as he sang the words from memory on a cold Sunday morning in January. He was standing in a pew, halfway down the aisle of the church of St. Cuthbert's in Malhaven. His deep, baritone voice sounded cheerful enough to anyone listening, but it belied his true feelings. In a few minutes his aging father the Reverend Jonathan Smallwood, would deliver his final sermon as the rector. Next week his parents were moving out of the vicarage, his childhood home, which stood alongside the stone-built church. They were to move into a small cottage in the centre of Malhaven. After thirty-five years, Jonathan Smallwood had finally decided to hang up his cassock. The new vicar would be arriving any day.

This fact, however, was not the cause of Tom's lack of cheer...no, far from it. Tom, along with his mother Lilian, brother Jonty and sister Peg, had been urging their father to retire since the sudden death of Jonathan's sister Isadora, a few years earlier.

"Heart attacks run in the family," his mother had declared. "If hale and hearty Dora could drop down dead from a heart attack without warning, then you, Jonathan Smallwood, could do the same!" But Jonathan continued, not believing 'such twaddle'.

No...Tom was cheerful regarding his parents' retirement. The source of his 'non cheerfulness' lay in the lot life seemed to have dealt him. On their Aunt Isadora's death, Tom and his older brother Jonty had inherited her estate...her substantial estate. Meckleridge House Hotel stood in large grounds and was adjoined by Meckleridge Farm – 198 acres of farmland utilised for grazing. On this land stood a modest farmhouse and outbuildings.

At the time of Isadora's death, Tom had recently graduated from Cambridge University with a degree in Botany and was following his chosen career path in the study of botanical science. He had secured a temporary position at Kew Gardens in London, thanks to his good friend Fred, who worked there, and was anticipating the possibility of a permanent position. However, with his aunt's demise he was forced to leave it all behind and return to Malhaven, in northeast England. He'd been devastated, begging Jonty, his senior by almost a year, to consider 'selling up' so they could both pursue their individual careers; but Jonty was adamant. He was relieved to end his teaching role in a grammar school in Durham. He concluded that Tom could study as many plants as he wished in the grounds of Meckleridge.

So, the brothers became joint owners of the estate, and it was proving to be a consuming occupation. Now three years later, their hard work was being rewarded. Yet somehow Tom felt cheated...unfulfilled and longed to return to his former dream career.

Chapter 1

As the hymn ended and his father's voice began to drone, Tom switched off. He was adept at this, having drowned out his father's voice during the weekly sermon for most of his life. His eyes drifted around the congregation – a fair mix of residents…Anglicans of course – the Methodists and the Roman Catholics attended their own places of worship.

Then his eyes alighted on the Rossiter family and their new governess. From his sitting position he observed the Rossiter twins sitting either side of Miss Brooks – they seemed surprisingly docile this morning. I wonder what bribes she has offered the normally restless youngsters, he mused, smirking. Rachel Brooks intrigued him.

It was five days since Rachel Brooks' surprising arrival in Malhaven and he'd only spoken to her briefly on the telephone, enquiring about her car. As the service ended, the congregation filed out of the church. Tom was standing outside the church door as the Rossiter family departed.

"Good morning, Miss Brooks," he greeted the governess. "How are you settling?"

Rachel held hands with the two boys…firmly. "Fine, thank you, Mr Smallwood. Pleased to see we've had no further snowstorms," she commented, cheerfully.

Tom stared at her…then asked the question which had troubled him for days. "Excuse me for asking, Miss Brooks…but have we met before?"

Rachel looked directly into Tom's eyes…he detected a steeliness in hers.

"No, Mr Smallwood…you are mistaken – we have not met before," she replied quite definitely.

Tom felt embarrassed. "Sorry for asking, Miss Brooks, but you remind me of someone I met many years ago," he added.

Rachel smiled then turned, walking down the church path, swinging the arms of her two young charges. It was then, as Tom watched the receding figure of Rachel Brooks...he remembered where he'd seen that movement before.

Chapter 2

Easter 1914

The wailing penetrated Tom's ears...loud shrieking, gasping. It was heart wrenching and Tom knew the reason. He pulled the pillow over his ears and snuggled down under the blankets and counterpane – anything to block out the sound. Investigating seemed futile, because he knew...without being told, he knew... without hearing the words...he knew. He stuffed his fist into his jaw and bit down hard...it hurt – but surely self-inflicted pain was better and helped to distract him from hearing his mother suffer. How long he lay there he was unsure, but it was his sister Peg who roused him.

"To-To, To-To...what are you doing?" she demanded, shaking him. "To-To...wake up, you're scaring me," she begged.

Slowly, he pulled the pillow from his head and poked his nose out from under the covers. His young sister was standing in her nightgown, her fair hair woven into a long plait hanging down her back. By now he could hear the urgency in her voice against the background of incessant

21

wailing. She continued to demand his attention using the ridiculous name she'd called him since she was a toddler.

"To-To...PLEASE," she urged, stamping her foot.

"Calm down, Peg. Here...get in beside me," he replied, throwing back the covers and moving closer to the wall. Peg acted promptly and jumped in beside her big brother...he was warm...and solid. She snuggled up against his back. Tom listened as he heard her breathing gradually regulating.

The background wailing still pierced the darkness. Tom figured they were better off up here in his bedroom, away from the scene he imagined being played out downstairs.

It had been nearly midnight when a loud knock on the front door woke Tom from his slumbers. He crept out of his room and peered through the rails at the top of the stairs. His brother Jonty was halfway down the stairs, standing still. He motioned to Tom to go back to bed as his father opened the front door. It was Bertha Turner, the district nurse; Tom recognised her voice, as he slunk away.

"I'm ever so sorry, Reverend Smallwood," she began, her voice faltering. "But I've been asked to give you the message from the fever hospital, seeing as I was on my way home." She hesitated and her husband Bill put his arm around her shoulders. "Little Hermione passed away earlier this evening."

Jonathan Smallwood invited them to come in, but Bertha wisely declined the invitation. Steeling himself for the inevitable, Jonathan Smallwood walked towards the drawing room to give his distraught wife Lilian the devastating news. He looked briefly at his fifteen-year-old son Jonty, standing on the stairs and shook his head...

minutes later the wailing began.

Eight-year-old Hermione Smallwood had only been taken into the fever hospital earlier that day. Tom and Jonty stood watching from the landing window as a stretcher carrying their youngest sister was carried into the black van... Hermione Smallwood was a victim of typhoid fever.

When Tom ventured downstairs hours later it was daylight. He could still hear sobbing coming from his parents' bedroom – but thankfully the wailing had ceased. He'd left Peg asleep in his bed. Putting on his dressing gown and slippers, he descended the stairs to the kitchen. Jonty was busy stirring a pan of porridge. The kitchen stove was warm as Tom crouched down on the floor beside it.

"Did you hear?" Jonty asked, his voice sounding deep and manly.

Tom nodded. "I thought it best to stay out of the way and Peg was upset so she slept in my bed," Tom answered.

"Yes," replied Jonty, placing Tom's steaming bowl of porridge on the kitchen table. "I looked in on you before I went back to bed. There didn't seem any point in disturbing you."

Tom walked over to the table, sat down and began to stir his porridge, as Jonty poured cold milk onto it.

"How's Mother?" Tom asked.

Jonty shrugged his shoulders. "I got no sleep...she howled all night."

The two teenagers ate their breakfast in silence, full of remorse for the mischievous little sister, who would never again annoy them with her silly pranks. It was hard to believe it was only last Sunday morning she'd put a worm into Tom's jacket pocket, which he discovered when he was sitting in the pew, trying to listen to his father's sermon. She'd been full of mischief and adorable with it. Would the Smallwood household ever be the same again?

***

The tragic events of Easter 1914 caused the Smallwood children to be taken to stay with their aunt in Llandudno. The day after Hermione Smallwood's funeral, Jonty, Tom and Peg accompanied their father's sister, Isadora Soames, on a train journey to North Wales.

"Well now," remarked their Aunt Dora, as they finished their breakfast the following morning in the finely appointed dining room. "I think we should go on a picnic today."

Tom raised his eyebrows in surprise; Peg jumped up and down in her chair and Jonty ran his fingers through his blond hair. Then acting as spokesman for his siblings replied, "Yes, Aunt Dora...that sounds like a splendid idea," looking at his brother and sister for confirmation. They nodded their agreement.

"Good," announced their portly aunt, "I'll get Cook to pack us a basket of provisions. Make sure you wear warm clothing. The sea breezes here in Wales can be quite cold. We'll take a towel in case you want to go plodging in the sea."

Jonty rolled his eyes at his brother, obviously thinking he was too old for such childish pastimes.

Dora continued. "Uncle Bart will be going to the station after lunch to collect our other guest...so you'll meet her when we get back. She will be sharing your room, Peg – she's called Darcy and is about your age."

The children eyed each other suspiciously – they were a tight bunch and were unsure about making friends with a newcomer.

The outing to the beach was a huge success. Tom and Jonty spent hours rock pooling and messing about in the sea. Aunt Dora and Peg collected shells and used them to decorate sandcastles.

"I think you'll like Darcy," Aunt Dora commented to Peg. "She's an only child so you can pretend to be her family for the week."

Young Peg stared at her aunt in disbelief. "You mean she has no brothers and sisters…at all?"

Dora nodded.

"So, who does she play with?" asked Peg, struggling to comprehend this Darcy girl was the only child in her family.

"Well, I expect she will have friends at school and maybe her parents play with her…but they often travel abroad, which is why she is visiting us."

Peg continued to fill her tin bucket with shells totally flummoxed – there was no way her parents would play with her. Aunt Dora was so unlike her mother…she was always playing games and was good fun!

Isadora Smallwood had married Bartholomew Soames when she was in her late forties. Until then she had lived at the vicarage with her brother, his wife and their children. She'd been more of a mother than an aunt to the family. She was full of life and the children adored her. They'd been heartbroken when, upon meeting an older widower, who was visiting the vicarage, the jaunty Isadora formed an association with Bart Soames and within three months she married him and moved to Wales! However, the Smallwood children had enjoyed several school holidays with their aunt and uncle and after the tragic death of little Hermione, it was deemed wise to whisk them away from the house of mourning.

Darcy Shackleton was Bart's sister's godchild. His sister was also called Darcy and she lived a flamboyant lifestyle. She often made promises to her godchild which she failed to fulfil. This Easter was one such time. A frantic phone call from his sister, with some garbled explanation as to why she was unable to look after her friend's daughter, caused Dora to urge Bart to invite the child to Llandudno. Dora was in her element. "The more the merrier," she declared. If ever a woman should have borne a brood of children of her own…it was Dora Soames! But her childbearing years were passed by the time she married Bart.

The arrival of the extra guest worked well. The holiday week was splendid. Each day Dora and the youngsters went out on an adventure – seashore or countryside... no matter the venue, Dora organised games and adventures. Even Jonty at fifteen, thinking himself too old for such escapades, engaged in the fun. Evenings were spent playing parlour games and Tom's fiercely competitive nature caused many a laugh.

Peg and Darcy 'hit it off' immediately and enjoyed getting to know each other. Although only six months separated them in age, Darcy, the elder, was very mature, and Peg, used to the companionship of brothers, had her eyes well and truly opened during that week in Wales.

Chapter 2

Dora foresaw future holidays involving the four young people. Both the girls were outgoing. Darcy enjoyed poking fun at the shy Tom, who tended to be in a world of his own, quite happy to be picking flowers and looking at plants. But unknown to Darcy Shackleton, Tom was quietly observing this girl.

At twelve years old, Darcy acted and looked much older than his sister. Her bouncy blonde curls and pale blue eyes intrigued him. For the first time in his fourteen years, he noticed the beauty of the female form. Until now girls were just…girls – mostly a nuisance; often shrieking; asking stupid questions; demanding answers; generally annoying; frequently odious and prone to crying, if they couldn't get their own way! But there was something different about Darcy Shackleton.

Tom was an awkward, self-conscious teenager. He was uncomfortable with his maturing body, bashful and shy. He spent most of his time hiding behind his more confident, older, handsome brother. Not that Darcy Shackleton gave Tom a second glance – unless it was to poke fun at him and make him feel stupid. She was too focused on making eyes at the older Jonty, giggling in an irritating way and passing whispered comments to Peg. One night as Tom was returning from the bathroom he passed the girls' bedroom – the door was open. He heard peals of laughter coming from the room. He halted and looked at the reflection through the mirror on the wardrobe door. Darcy, scantily clad, was preening herself. Her loose, bouncy curls falling over her bare shoulders. Tom gasped…overcome by the beauty of this fascinating creature…a girl…who was causing his body to react inappropriately.

January 1925

Tom pulled himself from his reminiscences. Could Rachel Brooks be Darcy Shackleton? Or was his mind playing tricks? That holiday was years ago – just after his sister Hermione died. It was the Easter before the Great War began. Darcy Shackleton...well, well, well. The girl who awakened him to the beauties of the fairer sex. Darcy Shackleton...the girl who disappeared into thin air.

Being a Sunday during the hotel's winter break, Tom took lunch with his parents. He finished his plate of roast beef, Yorkshire pudding and all the trimmings and sat back.

"Mother, that was delicious as always," he declared. He looked around the dining room. Boxes were piled up in a corner ready for his parents' imminent house move. "This is a momentous occasion – our last Sunday lunch in the vicarage," he remarked as his mother placed a dish of fruit trifle in front of him.

"Shame it's only you who's here," commented Lilian Smallwood. "Just typical of Jonty to be galivanting, when we're moving...and as for Peg – well she's hardly ever around these days. I'm so glad you inherited your father's reliability, Tom," she added, smiling lovingly at him.

Tom felt embarrassed. His mother had a happy knack of pointing out his siblings' shortcomings. He finished his dessert and decided to take his leave, as his father excused himself from the table.

"Now, Mother, I must be going, but I'll be here bright and early on Tuesday morning to help with the move," he announced, bending to kiss his mother on the cheek.

"Oh, don't fret, Tom. Bill Frazer is bringing his wagon and his two young sons are lined up to help carry the stuff. We're not taking any big items of furniture – that cottage is far too small to house them. So, it's only the boxes and I'm well on with the packing." Lilian Smallwood blinked back tears. "It's the memories I'm going to miss…but I can take the happy ones with me. You were all born in this house, and we were happy, very happy…until."

Tom sensed his mother's anguish and put his arm around her. "Yes, Mother, it was a happy home, but you and Father are entering a new season of life now… retirement. Embrace it…look forward to making new memories. Now, I must be off, so see you on Tuesday."

During the twenty-minute walk from the vicarage to the hotel, Tom recalled the time he 'left' home. After Hermione's death things were never the same. He and Jonty were sent away to boarding school, the following autumn – paid for by his aunt and uncle, Dora and Bart Soames. Lilian Smallwood 'took to her bed' after her youngest daughter's death. The boys were attending the village school and whilst their father did his best for his children, there was a great deal lacking.

Jonty and Tom started boarding school much later than their counterparts, but they were both academically gifted and it soon became apparent the decision had been wise. Little Peg, however, remained at the local school and resented it! She couldn't wait to leave home.

Dora Soames was in despair of her sister-in-law, Lilian. So, she persuaded her husband to sell his property in Llandudno and move to Malhaven, in northeast England.

This was prompted by a large house becoming available to buy in Dora's former hometown – Meckleridge House. Dora knew the property well, having spent many hours there as a young girl with her friends – the daughters of the owners.

"It would make an ideal hotel," remarked Dora to her brother, the vicar, who thought she had taken leave of her senses. But Dora knew if she came to live close to her family, she could see to the wellbeing of little Peg, and care for the boys during their school vacations. Bart Soames doted on his boisterous wife and being a man of substantial means, the idea soon became a reality. Bart and Dora Soames moved north in the summer of 1914, shortly before the onset of the Great War. When the farmlands adjoining Meckleridge House came up for sale, Bart Soames saw a business opportunity and made the purchase.

When Jonty and Tom returned during their school vacations, they spent most of their time with their aunt and uncle. It took Lilian many months to recover, but eventually she overcame her problems and became the vicar's wife once again. During the war Dora began her hotel venture, initially providing accommodation for nurses at the nearby hospital, which was expanding its facilities due to the demands of much needed medical establishments. Once the war was over, however, she adapted its use to accommodate the tourism market.

Just as Tom was walking up the driveway to the hotel, a car pulled up...it was Rachel Brooks. He opened the passenger door.

"Hello again, Miss Brooks...twice in one day, but nevertheless a pleasure," he remarked. Rachel looked very attractive – certainly not the typical governess by any stretch of the imagination. Her blonde hair was pulled back from her face and tucked beneath a small brown cloche hat which toned beautifully with her long camel-coloured coat. Little wisps of blonde curls had escaped and framed her face in an alluring manner. Her looks had already made an impression on Tom Smallwood.

"I found myself with a free afternoon," explained Miss Brooks. "I thought I'd put it to good use and return your sister's items of clothing which I borrowed, the day of the snowstorm." She indicated a brown paper parcel tied with string, lying on the passenger seat.

"Oh, goodness me…no hurry for them. It could be months before my sister turns up. Would you like to come in for some refreshment…that is, if you have no other plans?" Tom asked.

Rachel was hesitant for a moment, then replied. "Why not…I was only going back to attend to some correspondence."

Tom smiled. "Good…just continue up the driveway, I'll be there in a jiffy. No tasty scones today though. Sunday is Winnie's day off."

Thirty minutes later Tom and Rachel were sitting opposite each other in the rear lounge of the hotel. Rachel was much more relaxed than she had been the previous time. Tom engaged her in conversation regarding her governess role and the antics of her young charges.

Then Rachel changed the subject. "How long have you lived here, Mr Smallwood?" she enquired. "I understand you are the vicar's son."

Tom smiled and replied. "Yes. Today was my father's last sermon…next week the new rector will be here.

He's young and unmarried – quite a change for the congregation," Tom remarked. "It's off with the old and on with the new." He paused. "I've lived here for about three years now. The hotel belonged to my aunt and uncle. My uncle died five years ago and when my aunt died two years later, my brother and I inherited the hotel and the adjoining farm." Tom watched Rachel carefully.

"Oh, my," she remarked. "Was that an opportunity... or a problem?"

Tom offered Rachel a top up of tea before replying.

"Both really. I was working as a botanist in London and my brother was teaching in a grammar school in Durham. Jonty was delighted at the prospect – he wasn't enjoying teaching. I, on the other hand, loved my work and resented being forced back here," Tom explained, looking thoughtful.

"I see," nodded Rachel. "You drew the short straw."

"Yes," remarked Tom. "It's my dream to return...but as time goes by, it seems less likely."

They were silent for a few minutes.

"Where is your brother at present?" Rachel asked, looking around as if he might pop out of a cupboard at any moment.

"Jonty is on holiday visiting friends in Liverpool," Tom explained. "The hotel is closed from New Year until Easter, so we each take a month's holiday. Jonty takes January and I take February, because neither of us can be away during the summer. Then we join forces and do maintenance work before the hotel re-opens for Easter."

"And is it working out for you both?" Rachel enquired, leaning her head to the side, a movement Tom found endearing.

"I suppose so, all things considered. Jonty carries the responsibility for the farm estate...and I do the same for the hotel, but it's a joint enterprise," he commented.

Rachel became aware of the fading daylight and looked at her watch in the glow of the fire. "Oh gosh, is that the time – I must make haste. This room is so cosy and relaxing. I'm due back to supervise the boys' tea."

Tom suddenly felt sad. He'd enjoyed chatting to Rachel Brooks. Tom walked her to the door and helped her on with her coat.

"Do you get much free time, Miss Brooks?" he enquired, cautiously.

She smiled. "Please, call me Rachel...and then I can call you Tom?"

A big grin spread across his face.

"Of course. I was wondering if you would like to go out for lunch sometime?" he asked tentatively. He watched as she put on her kid gloves.

"That would be lovely, Tom. I'm not sure of my time off yet, but I could telephone when I find out."

Tom opened the door to an icy blast of air and Rachel hurried out to her car.

"I'll wait to hear from you, Rachel," he remarked as she climbed into her car. He watched her reverse and drive away, feeling quite pleased with himself. At least he had made a move before his womanising brother returned. But one thing he was sure about...the more time he spent in Rachel Brooks' company...the more convinced he was that she was Darcy Shackleton!

Chapter 3

"Oooo...that was a treat," declared Rachel, wiping her mouth daintily and sitting back after finishing her lunch. She looked around... it was a cosy coaching inn, warmed by a roaring log fire and not too busy considering it was a Saturday. Tom crossed his legs as he relaxed, twisting his signet ring and smiling across at his attractive companion.

"I thought you'd like it...a bit of time away from the Rossiter boys," Tom chuckled and raised his eyebrows.

"Er...yes. They are delightful but so exhausting. A complete contrast to my last position – a studious boy and girl."

Tom signalled for the waiter to bring a pot of tea to their table. They'd driven about a half an hour out of Malhaven through the undulating hills of northwest Durham, to a historical village, and were dining in The Crofter's Arms.

"Have you known Dr Rossiter long?" Rachel asked.

"All my life," replied Tom. "Henry, another friend, Zac Proctor and I were inseparable as boys, but Henry was the first to settle down and marry. When he returned to Malhaven to take over his father's practice, he brought his new bride with him and wasted no time producing the scallywags!"

Rachel groaned. "That's a good description!" she laughed, then began to drink her tea.

Tom looked on – he was hoping he could use this occasion to dig into Rachel's background, but so far, she always managed to turn the topic of conversation back around to him. He had so many questions and hardly knew where to start.

"Did you always want to be a governess?" he asked.

As usual, Rachel weighed up the question carefully, before answering.

"No...not really but I wanted to leave home and this kind of work involves living in with a family, so it suited me."

Tom sensed an unhappiness in her past. "Why did you want to leave home...if I may ask?" Tom probed.

Rachel stiffened and Tom knew he'd touched a nerve. She shook back her bouncy curls, which were flowing freely today.

"My mother and I were...shall we say, not good together. She was strict and my father was much older and left her to discipline me. We 'tolerated' each other. My mother's friend heard of a governess position in Bristol and although I was young and had no formal training, I jumped at the chance. I was just a 'live in nanny', but I was bright and began to tutor the children. I made a good impression and was recommended for my next position."

Tom noted her vivaciousness as she talked – she fascinated him.

"Do you secure your positions through recommendation?" he asked.

She nodded and seemed to relax again.

"Yes…that's the way it's worked, and it suits me. I enjoy new challenges."

Tom moved to another question. "Where do your parents live?"

Again, Rachel looked uncomfortable at the question. "They lived in Cornwall…but they are both dead now," she replied, dropping her eyes and fidgeting with the tablecloth. Tom felt awkward for raising the question.

"Oh, I'm sorry, Rachel…forgive me, that was insensitive," he commented.

She looked up and their eyes connected… momentarily locking.

"It's alright, Tom…it's life…you move on." She gazed into the distance as if locked in a memory. She blinked. "Would you excuse me please, I need to visit the powder room." She stood and left the table. Tom observed her elegance as she walked across the dining room – she was attired in a deep-red woollen dress and black belt. She was stunning. When she returned, they chatted about general topics, then Tom tried again.

"Have you ever visited North Wales, Rachel?"

She looked surprised at his question. "I don't think so… why do you ask?"

Here goes, thought Tom. "This might sound strange, but as I've said, I'm sure we've met before. Many years ago, my brother, sister and I stayed with my aunt and uncle in Llandudno, North Wales. While we were there a girl came to stay…she was so like you, Rachel…was it you? She was called by a different name – Darcy Shackleton."

Tom stared at his companion, hoping for a reaction –
not a flinch!

"No, Tom, sorry to disappoint you. The only place
I've visited in Wales is Cardiff…my godmother used to
live there, before moving to Bristol. I must have a double
somewhere," she added, smiling.

So, thought Tom…that was it…a flat denial.

"Er, yes…you must, excuse me for asking, but the
similarities are uncanny."

They left the inn and walked back to the car chatting
easily. But as Tom left Rachel that day, he was far from
satisfied and hoped when his brother returned, he would
spot the likeness.

***

The new vicar was a 'wow' with the parishioners of
Malhaven. Having observed the slow decline of Jonathan
Smallwood, the youthful rector Greg made a refreshing
change. The congregation gathered around the church
door after the service the following Sunday, keen and eager
to shake the hand of the newcomer and wish him well.
Tom stood to the side with his mother, having already
been introduced during the moving day. Rachel exited
the church holding hands with each Rossiter twin. He
overheard her firm remark.

"Straight back here," she instructed, as the youngsters
ran over to greet some friends.

He smiled at her. "Said with an air of authority,
Miss Brooks," Tom chuckled, as Rachel lifted her
eyebrows. Then he turned towards his mother, who was

watching the boys.

"Mother...may I introduce Rachel Brooks, the Rossiters' new governess."

The two women shook hands.

"How delightful to see so much young life in the church," remarked Lilian, smiling. "I'm hoping for some grandchildren soon, now we are retired."

Quickly changing the subject, Tom asked Rachel, "Are you by any chance free this afternoon?"

She looked at him coyly. "Yes, Tom, I am. I was thinking of wrapping up well and taking a brisk walk."

"Splendid," remarked Tom. "I love hiking, but it's rare to be able to do that at this time of the year. However, I could show you around the town...if you fancy that?"

They parted, agreeing to meet after lunch.

"Now that's what I call a charming young lady, Tom Smallwood," his mother commented as Rachel took her two young charges and walked away.

"Yes, Mother," smirked Tom, knowing exactly what was passing through his mother's mind.

Tom met Rachel outside Gilberta House at two o'clock. It was bright and chilly, and all the remnants of the recent snowfall had disappeared. Tom explained their route. They walked through the main thoroughfare of the town and Rachel was given a blow-by-blow account of the various business premises, plus a few anecdotes concerning the proprietors. They passed the school, the police station, the garage and post office, ending up in the local park, which was quite small.

"Too cold to sit and chat today," added Tom, as they walked past the bowling green surrounded by wooden benches. "Do you like hiking, Rachel?" he asked.

"I love it, but rarely get the chance – are there many places around here to go hiking?"

Tom nodded. "Mostly a car journey is needed, but my friend Zac and I are going over to Channington next Saturday…if you would like to join us?"

"Oh, Tom, that would be splendid, but won't your friend mind me tagging along? I wouldn't want to hold you back," she added demurely.

"Nonsense, Zac often brings a lady friend with him. He works in London and tends to take his holiday up here visiting his widowed father…I think he's single at present." Tom noticed Rachel blushing – had he caused offence using the term 'lady friend'? "No offence, Rachel…but you're a lady and I hope by now we are friends…aren't we?"

Rachel's face lit up, her gaze never leaving Tom's.

"Of course, Tom, we are friends and I'd love to join you – but I'll have to let you know – I may be needed for the boys."

Tom escorted Rachel back to the Rossiters' abode. There was a spring in his step as he walked back to the hotel. It was a while since a young woman had wheedled her way into Tom's fancy…but Rachel Brooks was doing just that.

***

From the moment he opened his eyes he knew the day would be special. He felt a lightness in his step and a tranquillity in his soul, which accelerated as he thought of Rachel's pale blue eyes and bouncy blonde curls. Even Zac's phone call excusing himself, because of a heavy cold, did little to steal his bliss – instead, it enhanced it.

The dynamics could have caused a potential awkwardness, but it was dawning on Tom that Rachel Brooks was important to him. He'd only known her for three weeks, but he was spending copious amounts of time thinking about her. She'd telephoned mid-week confirming she was free on Saturday, as the Rossiter children were going to visit their grandparents. Tom was excited – he checked Rachel knew the basic requirements for hiking, especially in wintertime.

"Do you have appropriate outdoor clothing? Sturdy waterproof footwear? Bring a rucksack containing a torch, change of socks, hat, scarf, gloves, a drink and a snack." He listed the essentials and Rachel laughed.

"I'm not a novice, Tom," she responded. He felt a bit of a 'mother hen' but experience had taught him to be over prepared. They chatted easily and Tom anticipated the outing.

They set off at ten o'clock. It took an hour to drive into the Pennine hills. The weather was unseasonably mild for late January.

"Don't be fooled," warned Tom, "the weather can change unannounced."

They made a slow steady climb over rocky terrain but were sheltered by trees. Eventually, they arrived at a flat open area with outstanding views of the surrounding countryside. Tom entertained Rachel with his hiking escapades over many years. They ate their lunch snack. "There's a local ramblers' group in the town…which might be something you could consider," he informed Rachel. "But Zac and I prefer to do our own thing."

"What about your brother – did you say he was called Jonty – does he like hiking?" asked Rachel.

"Yes, Jonty – it's a shortened version of Jonathan, our father's name. He does like hiking, but we rarely get a chance to go together these days with the demands of the hotel and the farm."

The countryside was beautiful, even in the winter. Snow still lay along the hedgerows. "My aunt used to say…'snow in the hollow, more to follow' – and it was usually true – so I guess there's another snowstorm due in the next couple of weeks."

They were standing side by side, Tom pointing out various visible landmarks, when suddenly Rachel turned and their eyes locked. Tom sensed an immediate connection between them. It was Rachel who broke the connection. "This feels so good…open spaces…freedom, at moments like this it feels so good to be alive." Tom reached out and took her gloved hand, squeezing it gently.

"Alive and in good company," he added.

She turned and smiled and made no attempt to pull her hand away. For a few minutes they gazed into one another's eyes…spellbound.

"I guess we should make our way back," Tom added grudgingly.

They turned and retraced their steps. The day felt magical, and Tom was reluctant for it to end – so he suggested stopping for some food on the drive back.

Sitting in a local tavern beside a cosy fire, they enjoyed the speciality of the house – meat pie with mashed potato and peas – warm, comforting food.

"You haven't told me about your time in London?" Rachel asked, as they ate.

"Well, it was brief." Tom grinned. "Less than a year. It was only a temporary post, but it had the potential to be more. There's something satisfying about receiving remuneration for doing a job you enjoy. I would love to return...but it's a dream," he added, looking wistful. "How about you, any unfulfilled dreams?" he enquired.

It was Rachel's turn to look thoughtful.

"Not really...except I would love to settle somewhere eventually – and call it home. I envy people like you with family ties. I'd love to 'belong' to a place."

Tom watched her...she was growing on him. The connection they'd shared after lunch gave him hope... maybe Rachel Brooks could become more than a friend.

"I'm going away at the end of next week," he announced, breaking the spell. "I'm off to visit some friends in London. My brother is returning in a couple of days' time." He thought he noticed a look of disappointment in Rachel's expression. "Here's a suggestion – why don't we plan to meet for another hike when I get back...something to look forward to?"

Rachel smiled as they stood to leave the cosy tavern. Spontaneously, she slid her hand into Tom's as they walked to the car. He experienced a wave of joy engulfing him.

"I'm looking forward to our next outing already. Have a good holiday," she remarked, as Tom dropped her at the Rossiters' home.

He put his hand on her arm. "I've enjoyed our time together today, Rachel...until we meet again," he uttered, squeezing her arm. By now he was wishing he could cancel his trip to London…his heart was tugging at him to stay at home.

★★★

"Tom, thank goodness," shouted Jonty Smallwood, running along the platform in Durham station. Tom was a few minutes late. He reached out to hug his brother and relieve him of one of his bags. The two young men left the station. They could easily have been mistaken for twins. Only twelve months separated them – or eleven months and twenty-three days to be precise – Jonty loved to recite this fact when reminding his brother of his seniority.

"Have you had a good time?" Tom asked as he placed the luggage in the Austin car – an item they owned jointly. Not an ideal arrangement, but until their business became more profitable, they'd decided two vehicles were an extravagance. Before Jonty could answer, he was given a resounding welcome by the occupant of the back seat.

"Humph, old boy…what a sight," he declared, patting and stroking the large Bassett hound sprawling across the rear seat, thumping his tail. Moments later Jonty was sat beside Tom, in the passenger seat.

"Oh, I'll say…a splendid time indeed," replied Jonty. "Lots of socialising…and lots of female company to enjoy… if you follow my drift," Jonty chuckled.

Yes, Tom followed his brother's drift. Jonty Smallwood possessed a roving eye. Tom failed to keep track of the number of girls his brother had courted or corresponded with, in the last few years. Jonty loved his women…and they loved him – but he was reluctant to settle down.

44

"Too much fun to be enjoyed!" Jonty would say when his mother moaned at her handsome son that she wanted grandchildren. "Don't expect them from me," he quipped, "I think my sensible, young brother will fulfil that objective for you, Mother," he replied.

The Smallwood brothers shared the same handsome looks. Both were tall and broad with a shock of blond hair. Jonty preferred a neat beard and moustache, but Tom was clean shaven. Temperament also divided the brothers. Jonty was outgoing and charismatic – a restless soul, full of energy, preferring to work on the farm. Tom was quiet...a thinker and a good organiser, ideally suited to the 'hands-on' hotel management side of the business, taking care of the guests.

"Well, I've been gone for nearly four weeks...what have I missed?" enquired Jonty, as they drove the twelve miles back to Malhaven from Durham.

"Oh, nothing much," replied Tom. "Apart from a heavy snowstorm; Father's last sermon; our parents' house moving. I finished the decoration in the Tulip Room; got that rattling window fixed in the Primrose Room; and I've prepared the walls for you to paint in the Foxglove Room."

Jonty digested his brother's comments with a huge sigh, knowing he would have to pull his weight in the maintenance programme at the hotel, over the next month.

"Also, we had an unexpected guest, who stayed the night of the snowstorm," Tom remarked.

"Really? How did that happen?" Jonty asked, surprised.

"Well...technically speaking she didn't pay – so she wasn't a guest," remarked Tom.

"She?" queried Jonty, his curiosity rising.

Might have guessed, thought Tom, smiling to himself. How long before Jonty Smallwood would be calling on the newcomer to the town?

"Yes...she...and before you go getting any ideas – I've already formed an attachment with her."

Jonty leaned forward and placed his hand on his brother's arm. "Ooooo, little brother...tell me more," he demanded, with a glint in his eye.

Tom chuckled. "Not your type of attachment, Jonty," he was quick to comment. "We are...sort of...friends. I've met her a few times and taken her out for a meal...twice."

Jonty sat back. "Come on...I want details. Who is she? What age? Where does she belong? What's she doing in Malhaven? How does she kiss?"

Tom burst out laughing. Jonty's curiosity was piqued. For a moment Tom wondered if he should share his suspicions about Rachel Brooks...but something stopped him. If Rachel's resemblance to Darcy Shackleton was obvious, then Jonty would see it for himself.

"I'm waiting, little brother...I want details," requested Jonty, tapping his fingers on the dashboard impatiently.

Tom took a breath.

"She's called Rachel Brooks; she's in her mid-twenties – I guess about our Peg's age; she's the new governess for Henry's twins and I haven't kissed her...yet...not that it's any of your business," he replied.

"Oh, my, she must be insane to take on the Rossiter twins," Jonty remarked. "And you, Tom Smallwood, are too slow – kissing is allowed on a first date, you know, and is essential on a second date!"

Tom grinned at his brother's directness.

"One further detail...how does she rate on the looks scale?"

Tom smiled, visions of Rachel dancing before his eyes. "Scores highly, Jonty boy...very high!"

Chapter 4

Tom placed the last of his items in his battered old suitcase, fastened it and left his room. As he was donning his overcoat, he heard Jonty talking to the postie outside. Mrs Jenkins appeared in the hallway, carrying a greaseproof paper package.

"Some sandwiches and cake for your train journey, Mr Tom," she remarked. She always referred to Tom as 'Mr Tom' when Jonty was around.

"Oh, thanks, Winnie...you're an angel. I would have been starving by the time I got there." Saying goodbye, he stepped out to be greeted by a brisk northerly breeze.

"Brrrr...bet there's snow behind that," he muttered, placing his luggage in the back seat. Humph, the dog, looked 'put out' at the prospect of sharing the bench seat with the luggage and rested his head on it with a sigh. Tom stroked his head. "Cheer up, old boy – I won't be gone for long," he said to the dog, who seemed to sense his master's departure. Humphrey was Tom's dog. One of the benefits of moving back to Malhaven and taking over the hotel, meant Tom could have the dog he'd always desired but was not allowed to have when he was living at the vicarage.

"Yes, it feels like snow," commented Jonty, climbing into the driver's seat. "But I doubt it will affect you in London."

Tom picked up the large brown envelope lying on the passenger seat and sat down. It was addressed to '*The Indians*', *Meckleridge House Hotel, Malhaven, County Durham.*

"Ah ha – our errant sister has deigned to communicate with us at long last," Tom remarked, as Jonty drove down the drive to take Tom to the train station in Durham. Tom opened the large envelope. It contained a general letter...'To all' and three smaller envelopes bearing the names 'Ma and Pa; 'Jo-Jo' and 'To-To'. "When will that girl grow up?" smirked Tom.

"Read the general letter while I'm driving," suggested Jonty. It was written in Peg's characteristic style – full of descriptions with lots of details. It referred to her activities over Christmas and New Year and her forthcoming trips in the Spring and Summer. Tom read the letter.

"Sounds like she's not planning on visiting home for the foreseeable future," commented Jonty.

It was disappointing but not unexpected.

Tom looked at his watch then declared, "Step on it, Jonty...my train leaves in twenty minutes."

Jonty laughed. His style of driving was always fast compared to his brother's...he was a risk taker by nature. Tom stuffed his personal letter from Peg into his pocket. He held his seat tightly as the car journeyed on, then screeched to a halt outside the station. Tom jumped out, patted the dog and retrieved his suitcase. "I'll telephone about my return train," he shouted. "Bye."

Having found his seat on the train, stowed his luggage and removed his coat, Tom settled back for the long journey south. After a few minutes he retrieved Peg's letter from his pocket, smiling as he noticed the words 'To-To' in her bold script. Peg had called Jonty 'Jo-Jo' and himself 'To-To' as soon as she could speak – it fell into the same pattern as Da-da and Mama, he supposed. One day his father had commented "They sound like Red Indians," and from that point they were collectively referred to as *The Indians*. Why Peg chose to pen separate letters to her brothers was never revealed, but her relationship with each brother was different and it heartened him to think she had a special word for each of them.

He read through the two-page letter – she didn't waste pen and ink talking generalities. The letter was specific, almost as if she were sitting opposite to him in the carriage. *'Keep at it, Tom,'* she instructed. *'Your life dreams will still be there when this phase is over. Aunt Dora would be so proud of you. The way you keep the hotel and farm accounts so meticulously, is a credit to you. You have the brain and inclination for it – you always look for detail. A daisy is a daisy to me…but you see a collection of minute parts! Jonty would be lost without you – but he excels in his own way. You would be so awkward tending to sheep, goats, hens and horses, attending farm auctions and riding the perimeter of the land, checking for damaged fences and walls – but Jonty loves it…it's his escape. Aunt Dora saw the potential in both her nephews and as a bystander I can see it all coming together, the way she envisaged you two working. So, persevere, my dear To-To. Don't give up. The time spent now will pay off for you in the future. Soon, you will each meet your 'life partners'. Now, I have something for your ears only. I have met someone, and his name is Pierre. He works for the local gendarmerie as a detective. We met last Autumn, and we have become close…very close…we are lovers. Please don't be shocked. We have talked about a future together and if all goes well, I will make my home in France permanently. I will tell Jonty and our parents in my own time…not yet. So, I ask if you will keep my confidence. I hope to visit Malhaven in the summer and hopefully Pierre will accompany me – but our plans are 'up in the air' at present. If we don't manage to visit – please keep my secret. Lots of love Peg xxx.'*

Tom felt a lump forming in his throat. This was an unexpected turn of events. He shouldn't be surprised – Peg was an attractive girl…it was only natural she would meet a young man. Oh, gosh, he thought, looks like I'm destined to have a French brother-in-law! He was torn between happiness and sadness, joy and regret. He was pleased his sister had found happiness but regretted that she would cease to be around. Somehow, he'd always expected Peg would return to the northeast once she'd got this 'thing' out of her system.

Peg Smallwood had always resented the fact that Tom and Jonty went to boarding school and then attended university. She was expected to 'stay at home', in training for taking over the management of the family home as her parents became less able. This mantle should have fallen on the shoulders of the youngest Smallwood sister, Hermione, if she had not been taken from them. Yes, Peg always held a grudge, so when she attained the age of twenty-one…she escaped! It was a holiday at first – a visit to a pen pal in France. But once Peg was 'released' there was no going back and, on her return from holiday, she announced she was to become the companion of a French lady called Madame Medec. The role saw her travelling widely to many areas of France, Switzerland and Italy. It was a marvellous opportunity for her, and she embraced it. Tom always hoped his sister would enjoy her travels, then return to take over his role at the hotel. Peg had received a monetary inheritance from her aunt, which gave her independence. But each time the subject of her return surfaced; she was evasive. 'Just give me some more time…I can't let Madame down, she has plans,' she insisted. So, it had continued and gradually it dawned on Tom his sister was not interested in returning to Malhaven to live.

Tom put the letter in his pocket, stood and stretched, turning his mind to his vacation. He was to stay with his old chum Fred Broadbent and his new wife Mabel – he'd attended their wedding the previous summer. He and Fred met at university, both studying Botanical Science, but Fred was a year ahead of Tom. When Tom graduated, Fred was influential in gaining him a temporary position where he worked at Kew Gardens, in London, which could have led to a permanent post had his presence in Malhaven not been required. The two young men had shared rooms in London and although Fred became engaged to his childhood sweetheart during that time, he was never made to feel the 'odd one out'.

Mabel was an effervescent character and possessed many friends, so Tom frequently found himself in the company of attractive young women during his time in London. Inevitably, thinking of London his mind drifted to Angela Rochester – mmmmm. Tom rubbed his chin – no, he didn't want to dwell on Angela, so he rummaged in his suitcase and found his book – 'A Passage to India'; reading would take his mind off Angela.

***

As the fogginess of sleep ebbed away and the trickle of reality penetrated his mind, Tom blinked and reluctantly opened his eyes. It was obviously morning, but the dark winter day did little to beckon Tom from his cosy bed. The only window in the room was a skylight. He was three floors above street level, but even so he could hear noises – clattering, rustling, clanging, ringing, whistling, shouting, droning, clopping…the sounds of early morning London life. Unlike the peace and tranquillity he was used to back home. No audible birdsong, no bleating sheep, no crowing cockerel. He wasn't sure, if truth be told, which scenario he preferred. In his present state of mind, the peacefulness of the countryside helped to form his prison bars – a prison of his own making, born out of his inability to pursue his chosen profession here in London.

Deep down Tom knew he had much to be thankful for – but now was not the time to dwell on the 'what ifs' of life. He reached for his watch, struggling to read the time, so, switching on the lamp he realised he needed to make haste. Today he was accompanying Fred to his workplace… Tom's former workplace. It would be good to see familiar faces, enjoy a 'catch up' and learn about new discoveries in Kew Gardens. He would only stay for a few hours, then he would wander around London before meeting Fred and Mabel at a restaurant later.

Tom felt nostalgic as he walked around Kew Gardens. In some respects, he felt a stranger and wondered if he'd been wise to visit at all. There were many new faces, but he enjoyed chatting with some of the people he recognised.

Chapter 4

He was waiting outside the restaurant later in the day, when he spotted Fred and Mabel approaching arm in arm. Tom felt a pang of wistfulness…how long before he would share his life with a special woman? They looked so happy, smiling and laughing at some comment. He missed female companionship. These last three years, since leaving London, had seen a 'famine' in that area of his life. He greeted his friends, and they went inside. During the meal he noticed Mabel appeared distracted, frequently turning towards the entrance. By the time they were eating their dessert the reason became apparent. Mabel looked up and lifted her hand waving at the couple emerging through the doorway. Tom turned and his heart sank.

A tall, willowy brunette approached their table.

"Oh, my darlings…fancy seeing you here," boomed an all too familiar voice…Angela Rochester! Ever the gentleman, Tom stood and kissed Angela on the cheek, noting her distinctive perfume.

"Angela…delighted to see you again," he remarked – his well-bred English manners coming to the fore, masking his true feelings. She fixed him with a penetrating stare from her brown eyes.

"Tom…you look well – the northerly climate must suit you. You remember my brother, James," she added, introducing the tall man standing to the side. Tom shook hands with James, who'd been Angela's companion when they met at his hosts' wedding the previous year. He wasn't enthusiastic about the man…in Tom's estimation the man was a creep. Mabel fussed over Angela as if the pair had not met for weeks. Somehow Tom suspected they'd been in touch quite recently…perhaps earlier that day?

After exchanging pleasantries Mabel jumped in with an invitation for Angela and James to come to their flat for dinner on Saturday evening.

"You two will be able to catch up on 'old times'," she added, looking at Tom who was not pleased at the prospect of dinner with Angela and her brother. But he felt unable to object as he was a guest in their home. Angela and James left to find their table in another part of the restaurant.

"How fortuitous to meet Angela, of all people," remarked Mabel, then placing her hand on Tom's arm she dropped her voice and leaned in close. "Be nice to her, Tom – she took your breakup badly, suffered a kind of nervous breakdown. It's left her...vulnerable, but she seems to be recovering now. I'm sure you two could easily re-kindle the spark which used to exist between you. Perhaps your visit to London was 'meant to be'. I don't believe in coincidences. James is trying so hard to lift her spirits by accompanying her to dinner and the theatre."

Tom glared at his friend's wife. He'd been 'set up'... well and truly. It was almost like emotional blackmail. How dare she put him in this position. He opened his mouth to give her a piece of his mind, but Fred, sensing friction between them, interjected in the conversation. Shortly after, the threesome left the restaurant.

***

After young Darcy Shackleton awakened Tom to the mysterious beauty of women, he found himself drawn to meet and make female friends. However, that was not an easy task – boys' boarding school saw to that! It was another two years, just after turning sixteen, when Tom felt confident enough to approach a girl romantically. Ethel Chambers lived locally – Tom vaguely remembered her from elementary school, but one morning at the start of the summer vacation, he literally 'bumped' into her as he went into the dining room at his aunt's hotel. She was polishing the silver cutlery. The hotel was mostly utilised by nurses from the local hospital, but occasionally some other guests would require accommodation. Tom was taken aback at how attractive Ethel looked and struck up a conversation. He found himself inviting her to go for a stroll on her 'day off'. For six weeks that summer Tom enjoyed his first romance. Come the autumn he was back at school and by the time he returned at Christmas, Tom was devastated to find Ethel was 'walking out' with the butcher's son!

Not to be daunted, Tom soon found a replacement... and so a pattern developed. On each school vacation Tom managed to befriend a local girl – partly because there was a dearth of young men around due to the war and secondly because of his good looks. By the time he went off to university Tom was quite experienced in 'affairs of the heart'.

However, seeking female companionship at university proved more of a challenge. Women students were in the minority, especially on his course. So, he joined the college choral society. He possessed a pleasing baritone singing voice and enjoyed choral music. He also joined a ramblers' group, having spent many hours walking around the hills and vales of County Durham, with his brother and aunt.

It was nearing the end of the final semester of his first year when he befriended Millicent Simpson – a soprano in the choral society. The end of year concert was in the throes of rehearsals, and they struck up a platonic friendship, which resumed when they returned to commence their second year. But no matter how hard Tom tried, Millie was reluctant to let their friendship become romantic – she was too focused on her studies. Tom loved a challenge and eventually he was rewarded just as their finals loomed; they'd spent hours studying together, testing one another in their chosen subjects and it sort of happened...totally unexpected by both. That summer Tom was invited to stay at Millie's family home in Norfolk, and she spent two weeks in Malhaven. Both families seemed pleased, but as they both took up their respective careers, the cracks began to develop, and the romance failed to survive the hurdles of a long-distance relationship and they agreed to go their separate ways amicably. It was during this vulnerable period in Tom's life that Angela Rochester surfaced.

***

Tom was thrilled to have secured his temporary job at Kew Gardens, the autumn after leaving university. He was working and rooming alongside his friend Fred, who was now courting Mabel, seriously. Mabel was in her first year as a teacher and they were in no hurry to marry. Mabel and Fred enjoyed socialising. It was the 1920s and young people were embracing life to the full after the Great War. Tom was soon drawn into a group of young academics, who knew how to party. Within weeks Tom found himself paired off with Angela, Mabel's friend, who was working as a secretary in a law firm in London. The pair were compatible in many respects…except one – Angela wanted to 'settle down'. This was the last thing on Tom's mind. He was young, recently numbed from his broken romance with Millie – all he wanted was to be carefree and enjoy himself.

Tom handled the pressing nature of Angela's behaviour carefully, keeping it light-hearted and 'above board', avoiding any temptation to deepen their relationship. When the shocking news of Tom's Aunt Dora's death came – Angela was less than supportive. Tom made the decision to end their friendship before he returned to Malhaven.

"It's not fair, Tom," she'd objected, pouting. "It's only your aunt, for goodness' sake. Go to the funeral and then come back…I'll be waiting for you," she purred. That comment proved to Tom he was right to end things there and then. He returned to London to collect his belongings after hearing the news of his inheritance – he did not contact Angela. As far as he was concerned, he had ended their friendship in an appropriate way. But during the ensuing months, she plagued him with letters which he refused to answer. Finally, he parcelled them up, included a curt letter asking her to stop corresponding and sent them back to her. The only time he had seen her since was at Fred and Mabel's wedding…and he kept his distance.

***

Tom was dressing, not relishing the prospect of the evening lying ahead. The day after meeting Angela in the restaurant Tom spoke to Fred.

"This is supposed to be a holiday for me, Fred – and it's turning into a nightmare! I can see what Mabel is trying to achieve, but it's over, Fred, and has been for three years. I am being placed in a difficult situation."

Fred listened sympathetically to Tom's account of Angela's refusal to accept the fact that their friendship was over. "Mabel has a good, caring heart and I know she means well. It's not in my nature to snub people – please can you help in some way?"

The following evening Fred informed Tom that another couple would be joining them for dinner on Saturday – Mabel's brother and his current girlfriend.

"You'll like Oliver, he's a barrister," added Fred.

"Well, just make sure I'm not left alone with Angela," Tom asked imploringly.

Fred smiled. "I'll do my best, Tom. But remember, Angela has suffered a nervous breakdown since you finished with her and there's never been anyone else – so try to see it from her point of view as well."

The evening began and the atmosphere was tense. The seating was arranged so Tom was at the opposite end of the table to Angela. Oliver, Mabel's brother, was a lively chap and Tom found his conversation interesting. Angela made several mentions during the evening of her former friendship with Tom, but he remained aloof, and Fred was tactful, steering the conversation topics in another direction. Thankfully, the evening passed over pleasantly.

As Tom boarded his train home at the end of his trip, he gave a sigh of relief. Somehow his time spent in London caused emotions to surface, which had been bubbling underneath for quite some time. As the train headed north, Tom realised that for the first time since Aunt Dora's death, he felt his life at Meckleridge House Hotel was a blessing and not a burden. It was as if he'd turned a corner.

He was involved in a successful business and maybe, just maybe, his career as a botanist was never meant to be. He also felt ready to engage with a possible romantic element in his life. Observing the 'wedded bliss' enjoyed by his friend Fred and his bride, stirred at the embers of Tom's heart. The encounter with Angela was difficult, but it reinforced his desire to 'move on'. Tom Smallwood needed a woman in his life...and he knew just the right woman.

Chapter 5

Easter 1925

"Are we nearly ready, Winnie?" Tom enquired, sighing, as the housekeeper flopped into one of the fireside chairs in the rear lounge. Mrs Jenkins took a drink from her cup of tea. Tom was standing by the window watching a young housemaid carrying a pile of bedding over to the stable block.

"Just about, Mr Tom," she replied. "The fires are lit in the stable bedrooms, and I've instructed the maids to make up the beds – so all should be cosy and ready to go by tomorrow."

It was the run up to the Easter weekend, which fell in April this year and the hotel was expected to be full. They were blessed with returning guests once again. Aunt Dora had encouraged an Easter house party after the war and it gained momentum, so by the time Tom took up the reins of the hotel management, Easter, Christmas and New Year bookings were always at full capacity. The renovation of the stable block the previous summer, meant they now had extra bedrooms, including rooms for Tom and Jonty.

Until this year they used to 'rough it' in the attics, when the hotel was full. The renovation was a costly project, but one both brothers deemed necessary.

"Bookings are looking good well into the summer," Tom informed Winnie. "How's the new cook shaping up?" he asked.

A new cook had been appointed for this season relieving Winnie and the kitchen maid – another expense the brothers agreed upon. It would allow Winnie to concentrate on the housekeeping side of the hotel.

"She's great, Mr Tom…at least so far. It's still early days but I'm so grateful you've engaged her – I found it heavy going last summer."

Tom smiled and turned to face Winnie Jenkins – she was a valuable staff member and since her husband passed away, she'd spent more time at the hotel taking on extra duties, but Tom did not want to overload her, as she was now in her late sixties.

"You do a splendid job keeping the house shipshape, Winnie, we are grateful for all your efforts," he remarked, then glancing at his watch, realised he must make haste. Today, he was taking Rachel on the long-promised hike. After his return from London, he'd been unable to free up a whole day to visit Lasham Cragg, so they'd only met for short outings and a couple of evenings at a local inn for a meal.

Over the last few weeks Tom felt positive about the direction his life had taken and it was partly due to his friendship with Rachel Brooks. Each time they met he felt more attracted to her. He was learning the duties of a governess were demanding. Rachel's leisure time was firmly in the hands of the Rossiter family. Twice, arrangements were cancelled at the last minute, but this week the family were away on holiday, not returning until after Easter.

"I thought you might have taken the opportunity to go away and visit friends," he commented to Rachel, as they made their way on the hour's drive to Lasham Cragg, a renowned beauty spot.

As usual Rachel paused before answering. "No...just being in this delightful part of the world is holiday enough for me," she responded.

Once again Tom sensed her reluctance to talk about her past. Surely, she had friends and other family to visit?

"I know you told me your parents were dead...but do you have extended family?" He dared to probe again.

"No...no one to visit. I was an only child and I have no other relatives," she answered.

Tom felt so sad for her. It still rankled him, this resemblance to Darcy Shackleton. He felt sure Jonty would have noticed, but to his knowledge they'd only met after the church service – hardly the circumstances in which to notice a familiarity. Tom was still trying to convince himself the similarity was just a figment of his imagination. He would be interested to see his sister's reaction when she visited in the summer.

"Where did your parents live?" he asked, looking out of the window on this sparkling Spring morning.

"The southwest," she replied.

"Where in the southwest?" Tom enquired, once again sensing a hesitancy.

"Oh, a little village...nothing more than a hamlet," she hesitated. "It's called...Marets," she offered.

"That's a strange name...is it on the coast?" he enquired.

"No...it's near to Truro," she revealed.

Tom detected a hint of nervousness in her voice.

"And your father was a doctor, am I correct?" This fact had been alluded to on a previous occasion.

"Yes," she replied abruptly.

Tom concluded he'd interrogated his companion enough and changed the subject, making a mental note to locate this village with the strange name on a map.

As if sensing Tom's decision, Rachel requested, "Tell me about this place we are visiting?"

Tom smiled. "It's called Lasham Cragg. It's a waterfall in the North Pennines. I think I would say it's my favourite place," proclaimed Tom. "I hope you like it as much as I do."

They continued to converse with ease.

Driving for about an hour, they arrived at their destination. After parking, donning their hiking gear and carrying their rucksacks, they set out. Tom explained the geography of the area.

"We're on the boundary between Yorkshire and County Durham. This river is the river Tees. We are going to take a slow climb, across bridges and past waterfalls, until we reach a high point, where the river plunges over a precipice into a gorge...it's quite spectacular. The river begins as a trickle, high up on the fells amongst the heather, after which it gathers size and speed. We are taking a five-mile round trip...is that okay?"

Rachel nodded.

Tom had been eager to bring Rachel to this spot since they'd met, but knew they needed plenty of time and if possible fine weather to do it justice.

"This will be my last full day off for a while," Tom commented. "Once the guests arrive, I can only snatch a few hours here and there."

"I didn't realise how demanding hotel management could be," observed Rachel as they followed a path beside the river.

"Demanding is good, because it means we are successful. We did a lot of advertising in the press over the winter, and I think it's paying off," Tom remarked.

"I wondered about that, I suppose a walking holiday in the country is a relaxing kind of holiday for people who live in a city," Rachel suggested.

"If you are free over the weekend, come over to the hotel, meet the guests and see for yourself. You can help, but we'll be eating in the kitchen," Tom chortled.

Rachel stopped and stared at Tom.

"Oh, yes please, I'd love that. I'm willing to help and I promise not to be a nuisance. I was wondering what I could do over the weekend...now you've solved my problem," she replied excitedly.

They continued to climb, pausing occasionally to admire the view. Rachel had brought a map with her, explaining she liked to see her location, in case she wanted to repeat the route.

"You won't get lost with me as your guide," Tom jibed, then peered over her shoulder and pointed to various places. Their proximity caused Tom's heart to quicken, as he placed his arm around her shoulders. She turned slightly and without thinking Tom gave her a gentle peck on the cheek. She leaned in towards him and he hugged her – it felt so natural. "Not far now to the top," he encouraged as they continued. Turning sharply through some large boulders, they arrived. The thunderous roar of the water became evident as they carefully peered over the edge. "Careful," warned Tom…"it's a long way down."

"Oh, my…this is stunning," Rachel declared, overawed by the sight and sound of the water cascading onto the rocks far below and sending up a spray. "It's spectacular… breathtaking…what a beautiful place, Tom. Thank you so much for bringing me here." The sun was at its full height for the April day and was now shedding its warmth.

"Yes. I never cease to be moved by the beauty of this place when I visit…I'm so pleased you like it, Rachel." They were standing side by side and Tom slid his hand into Rachel's and squeezed it. He turned, noticing some of her crazy curls being blown by the gentle breeze. He was transfixed…she was beautiful. He felt a stirring sensation and reached out to push the stray hairs from her eyes. Suddenly, her stomach rumbled audibly, and they both began to laugh.

"Sorry," Rachel reacted, dropping her eyes, feeling embarrassed. "All this exercise has made me hungry."

"Me too!" exclaimed Tom, releasing her hand and motioning to some flattish rocks. They walked over and sat down to eat their lunch. They ate their picnic, chatting generally.

"Why is this your favourite place?" Rachel asked.

Tom swallowed his food and wiped his mouth, before answering.

"Because it reminds me of my Aunt Dora – the one who left the estate to Jonty and me," he explained. "She used to bring us here as children, before she moved away to Wales. Do you have a favourite place, Rachel?" Rachel put the remnants of her picnic in her rucksack, then stood and walked over to admire the view. Tom was becoming used to these 'delays' before she answered a question.

Gazing into the distance she replied. "My favourite place is a theatre. A place I visited in London when I was a child. My godmother was a performer…a singer and dancer. The glamour and splendour of it all overwhelmed me as a child…I've never been back…but I'll always remember it. Sometimes in my dreams I see myself performing on a stage. The curtain rises and…" Rachel stopped. The remembrance was obviously painful. She lifted her hand to wipe her eyes. Tom sprang to attention. He was behind her in seconds, placing his arm around her shoulders. She turned and rested her head on his chest. "It was all a fantasy…a dream." She began to laugh – a deep, hysterical laugh. Tom was perplexed at the range in her emotions, as he continued to hold her. Then she lifted her head and stared into his eyes…his deep, blue eyes. The moment was charged, and Tom bent down and placed a feather light kiss on her brow. He felt her body tense, but she didn't pull away, continuing to gaze at him.

"You are beautiful, Rachel…may I kiss you?" he asked. Receiving no objection, he lowered his lips to hers. This time his kiss was firm. A bird squawked, startling them. They broke away, embarrassment overtaking the moment. "I'm sorry, Rachel…perhaps I shouldn't have done that," Tom spluttered.

But Rachel reached out her cold hand touching his cheek. "Don't apologise, Tom…it was a special moment," she added.

He took both her hands in his. "You're cold...we need to get moving again." They stepped back beside their rucksacks. "Rachel," he paused as they retrieved their belongings. "It's mutual...it was a special moment."

Voices heralded the arrival of fellow hikers, so they turned and continued their walk. The encounter at Lasham Cragg lingered in both their minds as they journeyed home that day.

***

"Well, well, well – the wanderer returns." Tom was greeted by a familiar voice as he entered the hallway of the hotel after dropping Rachel off at Gilberta House.

"Zac, my old pal...what a delightful surprise," he cheered, embracing his life-long friend Isacc Proctor. "When did you arrive?"

"About an hour ago. Mrs Jenkins said you were due back anytime, so I thought I'd just wait."

"Come on through," Tom invited, taking off his boots and carrying them into the rear lounge as Zac followed. Dumping his hiking gear, he popped his head into the kitchen.

"The kettle's on, Mr Tom. You sit yourself down and catch up with your friend - I'll bring a cuppa through when it's ready."

Tom rejoined his pal.

"So, Zac...how long are you here?"

Zac lived in London but visited his father in Malhaven quite often.

"Only for the Easter weekend," he explained.

The two friends began catching up, drinking the cups of tea Winnie supplied. Tom and Zac had been friends since school days. When Tom went off to boarding school they missed their friendship, but somehow always reconnected along with Henry Rossiter, during the school vacations. Gaps in time never seemed to detract from their close bond. When Tom went to Cambridge, Zac began working as a reporter for the Northern Echo newspaper in Durham. After a few years he landed a job as an investigative journalist in London. Most of his work tended to be 'hush hush', but from time-to-time Zac sent cuttings from the newspaper of cases he'd been working on. Tom admired his friend's exploits.

"That was quite a scoop, on that kidnapping case – did you receive any 'pats on the back' for that?" Tom asked, referring to some cuttings Zac had sent recently.

Zac shook his head. "No way...it's all in a day's work. But tell me, Tom...are you any nearer returning to London? Last time we had a 'heart to heart' you were determined to get back by next year."

Tom finished his tea and stretched.

"I think I've changed my mind, Zac...but you are the first person to know this, so keep it to yourself." He stood and checked that the kitchen door was closed.

Zac understandably looked puzzled. He'd listened to Tom bemoaning his enforced stay at the hotel for over three years now. Tom hesitated; although he'd decided to settle at Meckleridge in his own mind after his recent trip down to London, he hadn't voiced it to anyone...yet.

"What's changed?" enquired Zac.

"Me...I guess...listen, let's go up to the office, then we can speak privately, without risk of any interruption." Once seated in Tom's office, he continued.

"This place has got under my skin. I no longer see it as a hindrance or an obstacle in my life...I see it as an opportunity...a challenge." Zac remained silent. "It's been hard work, but at the same time it's rewarding. I can't describe the euphoric feeling I have when a guest writes a thank you letter highlighting some aspect of their stay or passes on a word of praise. I head up a team and it's equally pleasing to pass on these compliments to the staff. But it's only recently that I've realised all this. I went down to stay with Fred and Mabel in February...I knew you were abroad then. I visited the old haunts...and something was missing, yet I failed to identify it. Then I met Angela again...remember her?"

Zac nodded. "The one who stuck like glue and wouldn't take 'no' for an answer," he remarked, grinning.

"Exactly," confirmed Tom. "I couldn't wait to get back north and on the journey home it hit me...I like my life here. There is no way I could leave Jonty now. I run this place – do the accounts; take the bookings; order supplies; manage the day-to-day staffing; act as host...and I enjoy it. My heart is here. I think it will be a relief to Jonty. I know for a fact that Peg is not going to return...so who would run the place? The two businesses are separate – but we pool the profits, each taking a small salary. We've ploughed all the profit back into the business since we started. We're beginning to see 'light at the end of the tunnel'." Tom sighed, feeling he had just delivered an important speech... perhaps he had!

Chapter 5

Zac had listened intently. "You and Jonty make a good team...you are partners. I often wish I had siblings to help. My father hasn't been well for months and I've only just managed to persuade him to seek medical advice. It's such a responsibility being an only child. But what will happen when one or both of you decide to marry? A woman in the mix could change the dynamics," he chuckled. A broad grin spread across Tom's face; the two young men knew each other too well. "Come on, spit it out, Tom Smallwood...you've met someone, haven't you?"

Tom's face was a picture. "There's nothing to tell...yet," he responded truthfully. "It's early days – but yes, I've met a certain young lady by the name of Rachel Brooks. She's a governess to Henry and Blanche's twins. We met in January when she took up her position. If you come to the hotel over the weekend, you can meet her...and give me your opinion."

Zac smiled. "Yes, I'll do that!" he replied.

***

Rachel was enjoying her 'time off'. Since arriving in Malhaven three months earlier, her young charges had proved a challenge...but she was resourceful and entertained them far beyond her remit. Any spare time was usually spent in lesson preparation, but each evening she allowed herself a least half an hour to become 'lost' in a book – mainly a classic. She loved Pride and Prejudice and had read it many times. But this acquaintance with Tom Smallwood was providing pleasant interludes and this holiday week was promising to be interesting. The hike up Lasham Cragg the previous day was uppermost in her mind. She felt happy and tingly as she recalled his kiss. It was a pleasing romantic interlude and she hoped they could build on it. As she mused over Tom's invitation to help at the hotel over the Easter weekend, a few ideas started to form in her mind. So, spurred on by her desire to be in Tom's company again, she decided to telephone him.

"Rachel, how delightful to hear from you," he exclaimed, answering the telephone after breakfast. "Can I assist you in any way?"

Just hearing his light-hearted tone sent Rachel's pulse racing.

"No, Tom, it's me who hopes to assist you," she replied. "Do you have activities planned for your guests over Easter?"

"Well, I suggest various walks or hikes they can take, and we do some general knowledge quizzes…is that what you mean?" he asked.

"No, not really," Rachel chuckled. "Tom…shoot me down if this sounds mad…but what about some fun, silly games and activities?"

"I'm listening," Tom replied, his curiosity growing.

"What about things like an Easter Egg Hunt; egg rolling competition; egg and spoon race; an egg decoration competition; an Easter Bonnet parade?"

Tom was silent absorbing her comments.

"Tom…are you still there? I won't be offended if you don't like my ideas. It's only a suggestion…and probably a ridiculous one…" Her voice tailed off as she doubted herself.

"Rachel," Tom's voice sounded alluring, "you are amazing. Your suggestions sound brilliant. Can you come over this evening and we'll discuss it further...and Rachel... go out and buy whatever you need – I'll reimburse you!" Rachel breathed a sigh of relief and excitement engulfed Tom. "See you later," he added.

***

"Plonk, plink, plonk, plink...arrrrg!"

Rachel followed the sound of voices. Having spent the afternoon amalgamating a pile of equipment and jotting down a timetable of events, she'd eventually made it over to Meckleridge House Hotel around six o'clock. Winnie Jenkins answered the door and explained Tom and Jonty were over in one of the garages playing table tennis.

"It's their way of letting off some steam," she explained, grinning. "They're just a couple of big kids when they play ping pong...hugely competitive," she chuckled. "Here, leave your bags, you look heavy laden, pop around to the garage, turn right out the front door and head for the noise. Oh, and remind them dinner is at seven o'clock please. They get carried away and lose track of time."

The doors to the garage were open as Rachel approached.

Plink, plonk, plink, plonk, plink, plonk...onk...onk... onk..."Ahhhh – you win again!" Tom's voice shrieked.

Rachel peeped through the open doors. Tom had his back to her and at the opposite end of the green topped trestle table, his opponent picked up the small white ball, turned and looked up.

"Hellooo...good timing," Jonty Smallwood's deep voice crooned. "Just in time to see my victorious achievement... whiff whaff champion, Jonty Smallwood at your service," he added, raising his small bat in the air in triumph.

Tom looked around. Both men were dressed casually in trousers and shirts with rolled up sleeves and open necks, revealing hairy arms. Perspiration beads were visible on each of their faces.

"Rachel, welcome...excuse our attire...gets a bit vigorous in here. Can you stay for dinner? I should have asked you earlier," Tom beamed at Rachel.

"Well, if you're sure...I'd love to, but I've come to work, I'm not a guest!" she remarked.

"Even the workers get fed around here, Miss Brooks," commented Jonty as he made his way past Rachel and winked at her.

An hour later, suitably attired, fed and watered, Tom and Rachel sat down in the rear lounge with a cup of tea. Jonty had excused himself earlier. Tom listened carefully, watching an animated Rachel describing the proposed guest activities. Then she unloaded the boxes she had brought with her, unveiling an Easter basket, decorated with green foliage and yellow, daffodil heads. Inside the basket lay a piece of crumpled white satin, covered with an array of neatly painted hard boiled eggs.

"Wow...that must have taken some planning...when did you do all that?" Tom enquired, wide-eyed.

"Today," she remarked. He jumped up and walked over to where Rachel was sitting, to view the items closely. "I've spent all day since our telephone conversation sorting things. It's amazing what people discard. Blanche has some old hampers in the storeroom, and she told me I could use the stuff in them, whenever I wanted. I did go out and buy some items, as well." Tom was amazed. "Now, I could bring a small blackboard and easel and write the daily activities on it...it could be displayed in a corner of the hall...if that's okay? We must make it clear it's voluntary and is just for fun." She stopped and gazed at Tom...his face was a picture, like a child on Christmas morning.

He reached out and cupped her chin with both his hands. "You are a little wonder, Rachel Brooks. Let's seal your suggestions in an appropriate manner." He reached out and, taking both her hands, pulled her to her feet then promptly kissed her firmly on the lips. Pulling away, he noticed Rachel looked flustered.

"Oh...er...thanks for your seal of approval, Tom," she added coyly. Tom was elated and hugged her.

"This is just the kind of personal touch I was hoping to extend to our guests, but I lacked the ideas, the organisation and skills. Mrs Jenkins is great at baking Easter goodies and decorating the house with Spring flowers. But these suggestions are splendid...just splendid."

Rachel felt embarrassed. "It's nothing original, Tom. If the children had been at home over Easter, I'd have done this sort of thing with them."

Tom reached out and took Rachel's hands in his. "Thank you so much, Rachel, for your assistance. Can you be here each day...after all, it's your plan?"

"Yes, of course. I'll do some baking as well...if that will meet with Mrs Jenkins' approval. Now, can I look at the gardens to choose an appropriate place for the outdoor activities?"

"Certainly," replied Tom, leading Rachel out into the gardens where the sun was just beginning to set. He indicated gentle slopes, leading to a wider, flat, grassed area which would be ideal for the races. The Rose Garden and Walled Garden could be utilised for the egg hunt.

As Rachel left the hotel that evening Tom felt happy. Things were looking up for him and it was enhanced by the presence of this delightful young woman, who was occupying his thoughts more and more.

Chapter 6

"Your new friend is attractive," commented Jonty Smallwood to Tom, as they ate their breakfast the next morning.

Later that day the guests for the Easter house party were due to arrive. While eating Tom had outlined Rachel's suggestions for activities.

"Thanks for your approval, big brother," Tom added cynically. "Always good to know!" Tom was surprised Jonty had made no attempt to befriend the young governess – knowing his reputation. The two brothers were often attracted to the same girls. Tom could recall two occasions in the past, when 'Tom's girl' became 'Jonty's girl' after the smooth talking, older brother, wangled his way into Tom's attempts at courtship. But that was all 'water under the bridge' and these days the two brothers issued a warning to each other, when eyeing up a potential girlfriend.

"Sounds like she's experienced in adult frivolity," remarked Jonty smirking, placing his knife and fork on his plate.

Tom looked warily at him. "I don't think its frivolity, Jonty – I think it's a splendid idea. A family-friendly touch I'd call it. She's very organised…you don't know her – so leave off the comments until you see her in action."

Jonty sensed he was being reprimanded. "Well, anything's better than your general knowledge quizzes," he laughed. "And may I remind you, little brother – the day you collected me from the station, I got the distinct impression you were staking your claim over a certain Rachel Brooks – I was being 'warned off'...am I correct?"

Tom pushed back his chair and took his plate over to the sink, as the new cook came bustling into the kitchen.

He greeted her, then turning to his brother added, "Too right, Jonty...the message is...steer clear, okay?"

Jonty nodded. The brothers left the kitchen together.

"Perhaps you could suggest to your events co-ordinator, that a trip over to the farmyard might be of interest. I could make a tractor and trailer available, and they could trundle over to see some newly hatched chicks and some pet lambs. I could put some bales of straw in one of the barns for the guests to sit on and they could have a shot at feeding a pet lamb with a bottle," Jonty added, jovially.

Tom looked at his brother. "And who's being frivolous now?" he jibed.

"Only trying to be helpful and score points with your girlfriend," he exclaimed, dodging a playful punch from Tom.

***

Rachel arrived the next morning with a mountain of hardboiled eggs. Winnie eyed her suspiciously, then went to locate some folding card tables for her to set up her display in a corner of the library, a small room accessed behind the reception area. Rachel was busy covering the tables with some oilcloth when Tom found her.

"Good morning, Rachel…how are you today? I see you've brought the supplies." He observed her working meticulously, totally absorbed in her task.

"I'm raring to go, Tom. This little corner is ideal – if your guests want to partake in the activities, they'll need to seek them out."

Tom continued to watch her…a pastime he could lose himself in all day, but duty called.

"I was telling Jonty about your plans. He came up with an idea for a tractor and trailer ride over to the farm, to see some newborn lambs and chicks…maybe on Saturday morning, if the weather is suitable?"

Rachel's eyes widened. "Oooo, that sounds great. Can I go over to the farm to see the layout, when I've finished setting up?" Rachel enquired.

"Of course," replied Tom. "But you'll have to make your own way there. I need to be on hand in case of early arrivals." Just then Winnie called from the hallway and Tom turned to see the reason. "Staff lunch at midday in the kitchen, Rachel…you are part of the team, now," he added as he left the library.

A while later Rachel walked over to the farm, having borrowed Tom's sister's wellington boots. Winnie had given her instructions, and it took about ten minutes to reach the farm buildings. The farmhouse was occupied by the farm hand and his mother. Winnie told Rachel to knock on the door, if none of the men were around. The farmhouse was attached to single storey barns, forming a U-shape around the farmyard. Rachel was alerted to voices emanating from one of the barns and walked over to investigate.

The rough, wooden door was open, and she could just make out the shape of two men in the dim, dusty interior. "Good morning," she chirped, as the two men stopped moving the straw bales and looked up. Jonty Smallwood looked handsome and rugged as he lifted his flat cap off his head with dirty hands. His shirt sleeves were rolled up, revealing bare, hairy arms.

"Miss Brooks...we meet again, welcome to Meckleridge Farm," he announced. "Bennie," he said indicating to the man standing beside him. "Meet Rachel Brooks, the mastermind behind these activities." He smirked as the other man greeted her.

"Pleased to meet you, miss. Me Ma's in the cottage, just go in, she's always got a brew ready."

Before Rachel could speak, Jonty interrupted. "Will this suit your requirements, Miss Brooks?" he asked, pointing to a six-foot square area, surrounded by straw bales.

"Er...yes, Mr Smallwood, it's fine, but is there any way we could have a lamp in here – it's a bit dark."

Bennie coughed. "I can sort that, Mr Jonty. There are lamps in the cottage we can use."

Jonty walked over to where Rachel was standing. He stood with his arms folded and looked her up and down. Rachel felt a trifle uncomfortable under his glare.

"So...it meets with your approval," he remarked sarcastically.

Rachel bristled at his manner...and his stance. "I don't want to put you out in any way, Mr Smallwood. I understood from Tom, this was your suggestion," she remarked defensively.

Jonty began to laugh.

"Relax, Miss Brooks...of course it was my idea...and the name is Jonty, we don't stand on ceremony around here...do we, Bennie? Now we were just about to take a break – so let's head over for that cuppa."

Rachel sighed inwardly...what was it about this man that made her skin prickle? He led the way out of the barn, and she followed, without answering.

As she entered the farmhouse kitchen, a buxom woman was lifting a large, blackened kettle off the range fire. Rachel could immediately see the likeness between mother and son. Both were heavily set with large shoulders and hands like shovels. Yet their faces were round and open, with weather beaten complexions, sharp angular noses and tiny eyes.

Jonty bent over and whispered into Rachel's ear. She felt tiny beside his bulky frame. "Go and say hello to Ma Barker, she won't bite," he instructed.

She turned and looked at him. "Oh,...er...yes," she replied obligingly.

Ma Barker was a cheery soul, with a plentiful bosom and two arthritic hips. Rachel greeted the older lady, introducing herself.

"Sit thee down, lass," she said, handing Rachel a large mug of sweetened, milky tea – not to Rachel's taste, but she accepted it. "Now, where ye be from?" she asked.

"Oh, I've lived in many places, but more recently in Darlington," Rachel replied.

"A townie is ye?" Bennie's mother continued.

Rachel pretended to sip her brew.

"Er...yes, I suppose I am, but I lived in a country village when I was a child. I'm loving this area, and everyone is so welcoming," she responded.

Jonty explained Rachel's plans for the hotel guests over Easter, to Ma Barker, and the proposed farmyard visit.

"I'll make a batch of cookies and a pot of tea for them to enjoy, after they've seen the animals," Ma Barker offered.

Rachel wasn't too sure about this but felt obliged to agree. After struggling to drink half the mugful of tea, Rachel stood to leave, and the older woman patted her back. "Come and see me again, miss, I like your face." Rachel almost burst out laughing, but Jonty interjected.

"You best be getting on, Bennie, and I'm sure Miss Brooks has other things demanding her attention."

Rachel followed Jonty outside after saying goodbye to Ma Barker. As she followed Jonty across the farmyard, she observed how similar the two Smallwood brothers were. If it hadn't been for the scruffy work clothes and flat cap, Rachel could have easily mistaken Jonty for Tom. Their bodily form and walking gait were identical.

Jonty stopped and turned, looking directly at Rachel. "I'll walk you back," he suggested with a twinkle in his eye.

Rachel nodded in agreement and struggled to keep in step with Jonty's stride but found his conversation easy going. By the time they reached the hotel she felt herself warming to Jonty Smallwood.

⁂

The Easter weekend was a huge success. The warm Spring sunshine graced Meckleridge House Hotel with its presence each day. The hotel grounds looked so seasonal with wavering, yellow daffodils and cushions of purple crocuses. The grounds were dry, making the egg rolling and egg and spoon races easy to manage. The egg hunt and the Easter Bonnet making activities were a hoot. Rachel was in attendance from early morning until late at night each day. All the guests except for an elderly couple, Mr and Mrs Carruthers, joined in the games, but they spectated with enthusiasm.

On Saturday morning the tractor and trailer arrived to pick up the guests in two groups and Rachel accompanied them, with Jonty driving the tractor. The newly born animals were a hit and much admired. Ma Barker's cookies and tea served in China cups, kindly provided by Winnie, were the 'icing on the cake'. Back at the hotel the new cook prepared appetising meals throughout the weekend. Rachel baked her speciality – 'canelé cakes'.

"These are different," Tom remarked, devouring one. "And delicious!" he added.

On Saturday evening the guests were invited to take to the floor, as Tom provided 'dance music' on the gramophone player. Rachel found herself being swung around the conservatory floor by both brothers and admired their skills at dancing. There was a 'party' atmosphere to the proceedings.

Zac made two appearances…on Good Friday evening and Monday afternoon. Rachel asked Tom if his friend would like to judge the egg decoration and the Easter bonnet competition, and he agreed to do the honours. A fuss was made over the winners and a box of chocolates was presented as a prize.

By Tuesday lunchtime all the guests had departed, and Tom, Jonty and Rachel sat around the kitchen table discussing and reliving the events of the weekend. "I think we can declare this weekend a huge success," announced Tom as they finished eating. "A vote of thanks to Rachel in particular."

Jonty started to clap. "Here, here." Jonty smiled broadly at an embarrassed Rachel. "You've set a standard now, my girl...what will we do next year if you've moved on?" he queried, raising his eyebrows.

"Oh, you'd manage...it's not complicated stuff. Anyway, a lot can happen in a year." Her eyes met Tom's and locked. Yes, thought Tom...who knows? The way I'm feeling about you, Miss Brooks...a lot could happen before this time next year, as a warm cosy feeling descended upon him.

***

"So, Zac...what did you think of Rachel?" Tom asked as he gave his friend a lift to the station in Durham on Wednesday morning.

Zac glanced across at his friend. "I don't think you need my opinion, Tom...I'd say you are well and truly smitten!" Tom laughed. "But a word of warning, my friend."

"Oh," responded Tom, the smile slipping from his face and his eyes narrowing. "And what's that?"

"I was watching your brother...watching your girl...and..."

Tom interjected. "No, Zac, no...he wouldn't dare...we have this 'code of respect' between us. He'd hardly spoken to her before last weekend, apart from pleasantries."

Zac lifted his eyebrows. "Just an observation, Tom… remember he's done it before. Be aware. You don't see it, and you are too trusting."

The car pulled into the train station.

"When will you be back?" Tom asked.

"Soon," replied Zac. "My father is unwell. I can't leave too long between my visits. Thanks for the lift. Bye." Zac climbed out of the car.

On the way back to Malhaven, Tom pondered over Zac's remark about Jonty…surely not. He'd told Jonty he and Rachel were friends…good friends. Perhaps he should show Rachel just how interested he really was. I know, he thought, I'll take her out to dinner – somewhere special, to show my appreciation for her help over Easter…and perhaps…I might…maybe…I could send a clear message to Rachel and my brother just how much I value Rachel's friendship. Satisfied with this thought he began to work out when 'said dinner' could take place.

It proved a difficult task and took three weeks to arrange, but at seven o'clock on the first Saturday in May he arrived at the Rossiter residence to collect his dinner companion. When Rachel had asked where they were dining it meant little to her, but, when she mentioned it to Blanche – her employer's face lit up.

"Rachel – that is a very posh hotel. You must dress up for the occasion," she remarked.

The evening air was balmy. Tom was smartly dressed in a black suit, white shirt, burgundy waistcoat and matching bowtie. As Rachel appeared at the door, Tom gasped…she looked amazing. Her dress was deep blue satin, long and fitted. She wore tiny heeled black shoes, and a black lace cape was draped over her shoulders. Around her neck was a diamante necklace. Tom leapt out of the car to open the passenger door.

"Rachel...you look amazing," he exclaimed as she approached. He took her black gloved hand, lifted it to his lips and placed a gentle kiss on it.

"Oh, Tom, stop making me blush," she quipped. "I hope I'm dressed appropriately. When I told Blanche the venue, she insisted I dressed up," she protested.

She would have looked wonderful wearing an old raincoat, thought Tom, as his companion slid into the passenger seat.

The venue lived up to its reputation. It was a hotel in the centre of Durham, which had retained an ambience of class. Looking around the decorative dining room, Rachel felt her choice of attire matched the other clientele. The waiters were attentive as the menu of fine dining was delivered and they enjoyed a delightful array of inspiring cuisine.

"I didn't think places like this survived after the war," Rachel commented, as they worked their way through the six courses.

"Oh, there are plenty still around, if you know where to look. The war didn't affect the tastes of the nobility. I've only been here a few times...for special events – our twenty-first birthdays," Tom replied smiling.

"I'm honoured, Tom, thank you so much for treating me in this manner. When is your birthday?"

"My birthday is third of July. When's yours?"

"Fourth of April," she replied.

"Oh, I wish I'd known, we could have celebrated," Tom declared, realising how recently the date had been.

"I'm not one for celebrating birthdays," Rachel admitted.

The subject changed and their conversation was peppered with anecdotes of the Rossiter boys' behaviour and humorous antics of hotel guests. There were many references to the Easter weekend activities at the hotel.

"I guess we both enjoy our respective work lives," crooned Tom as they finished their wine. "Tonight, I wanted to arrange something special to say 'thank you' for two reasons."

Rachel looked puzzled. "Two?" she queried.

"Yes – one to say thank you for all your splendid ideas and involvement over the Easter weekend – I've received some positive letters praising the entertainment."

Rachel bowed her head sheepishly and spoke softly. "It was a pleasure, Tom. I wanted to be helpful and I'm so happy it was appreciated."

Tom stared at his companion. There it was again. Tom was watching Rachel carefully...that action...dipping her head...placing her chin close to her chest...it sent a chill rushing through him. She must be Darcy Shackleton! No two people could share so many resemblances.

"Tom...the second reason?" Her voice jolted him back to reality.

Oh gosh, he blinked. He'd thought to use this opportunity to speak up and make their friendship more official...but that moment before...that doubt...he couldn't...not yet. He had to know – he was a stickler for honesty, a throwback to his religious upbringing as a vicar's son, he guessed. He sat up straight.

"The second reason…is to thank you for being such a special friend, Rachel." It was only a repeat of words he'd spoken before – that day at Lasham Cragg, a month previously. They raised their glasses.

"Yes…I'm enjoying our friendship too," she remarked, smiling, as the small band struck up.

"Shall we?" invited Tom.

For the next half hour Tom swirled his attractive dinner guest around the dance floor – they made a handsome pair.

The evening ended pleasantly. Tom kissed his glamorous companion goodbye as they parted. He wanted so much more from this friendship, but before he took that step, he needed information, and he knew someone who might be able to help him.

***

Three weeks later

Tom pushed open the door of The Jug and Hare, situated on Front Street. It had been a frequent watering hole for Zac and Tom over the years, when they were both at home. Zac was already seated in a corner booth. He stood as his friend arrived and went over to the bar to order their drinks.

After taking a long gulp of his beer Tom asked, "How's your father?"

Joe Proctor had recently retired as the local postmaster and undergone surgery for a stomach ulcer, prompting

Zac's speedy return to Malhaven.

Zac shook his head. "The operation was successful, but the recovery time is going to be slow. The bottom line is he needs someone to look after him. I'm due back in London the day after tomorrow – so this is a fleeting visit." Zac's father lived in a small cottage not far from Tom's parents.

"I'll ask my mother to look in on him, when he gets out of hospital," Tom commented.

"Thanks, Tom – that would be great. His sister lives up in Malsett and her daughters live in Bronhill – so there's plenty of folk around to keep an eye on him. But long term...I have my doubts. I need to visit frequently. When you wrote to say you wanted to speak to me, I knew this would be my only chance – he's being discharged tomorrow." He paused to take a drink. "So, Tom...what's up?"

Tom sighed and looked uncomfortable. "How easy is it for you to trace a person's birth record, address and possibly death record?"

Zac shrugged, then pursed his lips – it was 'bread and butter' stuff in his line of work.

"It depends on age, whereabouts and remember we've had a world war – many records were destroyed or mislaid or not reported accurately. But give me some details and I'll advise."

Again, Tom looked concerned. "This is a delicate issue, Zac, but I trust you. You know I've become attached to Rachel Brooks."

Zac's eyes lit up. "How attached?"

"No...nothing official, but I care for her, Zac. We've only known each other since January, but there's something there between us," he explained.

Zac grinned. "You're smitten, Tom. I told you that at Easter…it's all over your face."

Tom felt his face flushing. "I've courted many girls over the years, Zac, but I've never experienced anything like this before."

"Just how involved are you?" asked Zac.

Tom shrugged his shoulders. "Not involved…like that. I mean we're affectionate towards each other…but she's special, Zac, and I don't want to make a mistake. So, here's my problem." Pausing to take a drink, he rubbed his forehead. "Before I take the next step…I need to know something about her – you see, I'm sure I've met her before, when she was about twelve years old."

Zac's eyes widened. "Really…where?" he enquired.

"In Wales after my little sister died. Jonty, Peg and I went to stay with Aunt Dora and Uncle Bart after Hermione's funeral. While we were there, Uncle Bart's sister sent her godchild, called Darcy, to stay for the week. She was a bonny young thing and she and Peg hit if off immediately. Mind you, she was quite mature, unlike our Peg. Well, you know how I observe details – probably why I ended up studying botany. I noticed things about her…looks; mannerisms; gestures; tone of voice – lots of stuff other people don't bother with. When this 'stranger' Rachel turned up at our door in a snowstorm, we gave her refuge, and I was alerted to her strong resemblance to this Darcy girl I'd met all those years ago and it's plagued me ever since. I spot the similarities every time I'm with her. Jonty mustn't have seen them, because he's made no mention of it. Peg isn't around so I can't ask her."

Zac leaned forward. "Why don't you ask her?" he suggested.

"Oh, I've already done that, and she says I am mistaken, and most people have doubles. But Zac...it's uncanny. The more I'm with her...the more curious I become." He stopped and looked thoughtful, rubbing his chin. "It's more than curiosity, Zac. If I'm going to deepen our relationship – I want to know she is being honest with me and so far, not believing her is holding me back. So, I'm asking you with your reporter's nose to trace a Darcy Shackleton, born in London in 1902."

Zac was quiet. "Okay...that's easily checked. Do you know the district of London?"

Tom shook his head.

"Census records might be useful as well, but I would need a father's name...although 'Shackleton' might not be too difficult to find. Does she have any brothers or sisters?"

"No, she was an only child...but then so is Rachel and her parents are dead. But there's something else. She says she was born in London but grew up in Cornwall, a village called Marets, near Truro. However, I can't find a Marets, near Truro in Cornwall on the map. Her father, who was quite a bit older than her mother, from what she told me, was a doctor."

Zac pulled a small notebook and pencil out of his jacket pocket and scribbled down some notes. The two young men sat in silence.

"Right...that's a starting point – but remember what I said about the war. Also...it's not a crime to change your name, although it needs to be done by deed poll if you want to do something like apply for a passport. I'll do my best, Tom, and let you know what I find."

Tom and Zac stood. Tom slapped his old friend on the back.

"In the meantime, I'll try to curb my ardour, until I hear from you, Zac," chuckled Tom, as they left the public house.

Chapter 7

Tom climbed into bed. He'd not seen Rachel since church last Sunday and they currently had no plans to meet. Oh, what was wrong with him? Their 'dinner date' in early May was so special – he really should have built on it, but this stupid business of her likeness to Darcy Shackleton was bugging him. Hopefully, Zac would find something positive, and he could lay his suspicions to rest for good and 'court' the girl, with a view to building a future together.

He sat propped up against his pillows, not feeling in the least sleepy. His faithful dog Humph was snoring loudly, on his mattress in the corner. Until now he'd resisted asking Jonty if he saw any likeness in Rachel, to the young girl they'd met in Wales – he was waiting for Peg to visit. He still had no idea if his sister and her boyfriend were going to make a summer visit to Malhaven.

He linked his hands behind his head and made two decisions – one, he would arrange a meeting with Rachel when he saw her after church the next day; and two, he would look for an opportunity to ask Jonty about Rachel and her similarity to Darcy Shackleton. Decisions made, he reached over to his bedside table and picked up a book… Aunt Dora's gift to him. It was a part of the Bible – the

New Testament. He flicked to the inside cover and read the words scribed in her neat handwriting.

"Charity suffereth long and is kind, Charity envieth not. Charity vaunteth not itself, is not puffed up, Doth not believe itself unseemly; Seeketh not her own, is not easily provoked. Thinketh no evil, rejoiceth not in iniquity, but rejoices in truth. Beareth all things, believeth all things, hopeth all things." (1 Corinthians chapter 13 verses 4-7)

Tom smiled at the terminology – old fashioned English, almost a foreign language. Tom had read these words many times; somehow, they made him feel close to his aunt, the woman who in many respects had been his mother – certainly, his mentor and guide...until her untimely death. He turned to the back of the book and on the inside cover were more words penned in Dora Soames' beautiful hand. He vividly remembered the day she had sat with him in the parlour at the vicarage.

"Tom," she said, "let's unpick these old-fashioned words – what do they really mean?" So, phrase by phrase, Aunt Dora made suggestions and eventually when she was satisfied that it read in a way it could be understood, she wrote it out in the back of the book.

"Love is patient, love is kind. It doesn't envy or boast. It's not rude, proud or selfish – not easily angered. It doesn't think the worst in others or keep a tally of their wrongdoings. It blossoms in truth; puts up with anything; always trusts God; looks for the best;

keeps going to the end; love never dies. (I Corinthians chapter 13 verses 4-7 according to Aunt Dora.)

Tom sat and stared at the writing – he knew it from memory. He knew from his father's sermons there were many different forms of love, but at this point in his life he was only concerned with one kind of love…the love of a man for a woman. How does love manifest itself, he mused. In his present state of mind these verses caused him to realise that his past experiences with women had not come close to the way he felt about Rachel Brooks. Here he was, almost twenty-six years of age and for the first time in his life he felt he was 'falling in love'.

How did the different forms of love separate themselves? Oh, if he thought long and hard about it, he could probably define them…but surely love in essence was love. His eyes homed in on the phrase *'it blossoms in truth'*. And that, he felt, was his starting point. Forget Rachel's outstanding looks; the way his heart skipped a beat when he saw her; the strange sensations he experienced when he kissed her. No, he needed to focus on this important aspect…truth. Until he was convinced Rachel Brooks was telling the truth, he needed to tread cautiously. He extinguished the lamp and fell asleep.

***

Jonty jogged down the stairs, whistling, walked over to the doormat and picked up the post – a large brown envelope addressed to *'The Indians'* and five smaller envelopes… bookings he guessed. Sauntering through to the rear lounge, he threw the post on the table. "Correspondence from Peg and other stuff," he announced.

Tom was sitting enjoying a cuppa. "Oh, good," he remarked. "There's tea in the pot, if you want one." He stood and picked up the post. As usual Peg's presence oozed through her letters and never ceased to bring him joy. He was scanning the family letter as Jonty returned from the kitchen with his mug of tea and biscuits.

"Has she got much to say?" Jonty enquired, sitting in the chair opposite his brother.

"She's been away a lot – South of France in April; a week in Paris in March; when she wrote this, she was going to Switzerland for the month of June...oh...guess what...she's hoping to visit Malhaven at the end of July! Wow! Peg returns – we are honoured." Tom was excited but Jonty seemed aloof. "And she's bringing a friend with her," Tom added.

"Hope she realises the hotel is full in July – but Peg will rough it in the attic, rather than stay with Mother and Father," Jonty commented, picking up his personal letter from his sister as he left the room.

Tom opened his letter from Peg. When he wrote to her weeks ago, he asked if she remembered Darcy Shackleton and if she knew what became of her...he hoped Peg remembered something about her.

'Dear To-To,

As you will know from the family letter, I plan to visit Malhaven at the end of July. Madame's youngest sister is visiting from Cherbourg – so I will not be needed. Don't worry about accommodation, Pierre and I will sleep in the attic – if you still have a mattress up there...we will NOT stay with Ma and Pa! I'll let you into a secret, Tom – Pierre and I are engaged! It's unofficial at present, until Pierre asks my father formally, so I am wearing my beautiful ring on a chain around my neck. Now, To-To, your letter was rather vague – what made you think of Darcy Shackleton after all these years? You wanted to know when I last heard from her...honestly, To-To, it's so long ago, I can't remember. We became pen pals after that holiday in Wales. She lived in London and was quite lonely as I recall – her parents often went away and left her with her aunt. She idolised her godmother, also called Darcy – she was Uncle Bart's sister and I think she was on the stage, or something like that. Anyway, after a few weeks her letters stopped. Aunt Dora told me she had moved away and that's all I remember apart from the big crush she had on our Jonty!'

Tom read the remainder of her letter – it was full of bits and pieces about Madame and Pierre. He would put the letter in the old shoe box when he went up to his bedroom; he always kept Peg's letters. But first he needed to exercise Humph. He whistled for his dog and went out into the grounds for a walk, mulling over the contents of his sister's letter.

So, Bart Soames, his aunt's husband, had a sister called Darcy and she was on the stage...a comment Rachel had made about her godmother being a performer, sprang to mind…a definite connection there. Was this Darcy Soames still alive? Quite possibly – and if the Darcy he knew idolised her godmother, then perhaps they were still in touch – maybe his mother might know something about Bart's sister…he must ask her. Born in London, an only child, moved away, a godmother on the stage…he was sure he was on to something.

He picked up a stick and threw it, chuckling as Humph attempted to 'run' after it. A bright green hue adorned the gardens. The last vestiges of blossom were cascading to the ground in the gentle breeze. Tom sighed, remembering his decisions a few nights ago…perhaps now would be a good time to ask Jonty if he saw any likeness in Rachel, to the girl they'd met in Wales.

***

Jonty and Tom Smallwood had always shared a sense of humour. In their own sweet way, they'd amused each other with their joking, jibes and pranks during their formative years. But these days the realities of business life tended to cloud their conversations. Tom entered the house and headed for the rear lounge. It was Jonty's 'day off' and he guessed his brother would be relaxing – he knew he was going out later. Most of the guests were out and about at this time of day, so sensing an uninterrupted opportunity, Tom took the plunge. Jonty looked up from reading the newspaper.

"Jonty…do you recall that time we went to Wales after Hermione died?"

Chapter 7

"Er…yes, I think so…why? Mother was in meltdown and Aunt Dora whisked us away."

Tom sat down facing his brother. "Do you recall the girl who joined us…Darcy Shackleton, she was about Peg's age?" Tom could almost see the wheels whirring in Jonty's brain.

"Do you mean that annoying little squirt, who used to follow us around, making googly eyes at me?"

Tom nodded.

"She was a 'pain' as far as I recall – far too old for her years. I wonder what became of her. Peg used to write to her, I think."

It appeared as if Jonty had failed to spot any resemblances in Rachel…maybe Tom was just mistaken. He coughed.

"What brought her to mind?" asked Jonty.

"Well. I'm probably wrong…but ever since Rachel Brooks arrived in Malhaven, I'm convinced she is the grown-up Darcy Shackleton."

Jonty folded the newspaper and sat on the edge of his chair. "No way, Tom…whatever makes you think that? She's got the right colour hair and I seem to remember curls…but honestly, I tried not to engage with the girl, so I guess I didn't take much notice of her looks."

"It's not so much her looks," Tom added. "It's the small gestures; eye movements, mannerisms; tone of voice…that sort of thing. I know comparing a young girl to a grown woman is difficult – but I sense it all the time."

Jonty was silent observing his brother. "You're quite taken with her…aren't you?" A slow smile spread across his face. "My, my, I do believe my little brother is love-struck!"

101

he exclaimed, smirking.

Tom could feel colour rising in his cheeks. "I wouldn't go that far, Jonty…but we are enjoying our friendship and who knows where it will lead? I asked her if we'd met before, but she was adamant we hadn't…so it remains a mystery. Maybe Peg will recognise her when she visits – if she is Darcy."

Jonty looked thoughtful. "I haven't seen any similarities, but as I said she was a kind of leech, and I wanted to avoid her as much as possible."

Jonty had answered Tom's question - so why did he always need to be so convinced about things…he should wear his heart on his sleeve like Jonty!

"It's my night off, so I won't be around for dinner," Jonty announced. "I'm meeting the guys over at The Falstaff Inn and I'm getting a lift…okay?"

Tom nodded, then an idea floated into his mind – I wonder if Rachel is free this evening. Before he could convince himself not to call, he walked into the hallway and picked up the telephone.

"Hello Rachel," he greeted her, after chatting for a few minutes to Henry Rossiter while Rachel came to the phone. He heard her gasp in surprise. Tom gulped, trying to swallow down the surge of delight he felt hearing her voice. "Is there a remote chance you could come over to the hotel tonight?" he asked, suddenly thinking how stupid it sounded.

"Tonight? I'm not sure, Tom…is something wrong?" she enquired.

"No, nothing's wrong…do I need a reason to spend an impromptu hour with a beautiful girl?" Tom could almost sense her blushing through the telephone receiver. He heard a muffled voice and guessed she was speaking to her employer.

"Yes, Tom…that's okay. Blanche says she'll do the bedtime duties, so I'll be there later…is that convenient?"

"Perfect," he responded, and finished the call.

Dinner was over, the kitchen was tidy, and Tom had performed his host duties when Rachel arrived. Being the height of summer, the sun was still shining. One maid, Sally, remained on duty until eleven o'clock to attend to any guest requests.

"Fancy a walk around the grounds?" Tom asked, noting how pretty Rachel looked in a pale lemon, cotton dress and white cardigan. They left the house – Humph following. The grounds around the hotel were extensive. As they walked and chatted, Rachel stopped frequently to admire a flower or a garden border. The beds were kept in pristine condition, thanks to the two gardeners. Tom took delight in relaying the names of the plants – both their Latin and common names. "Sorry, Rachel – you must think me a bore," he added, realising how he must sound to her.

"Of course, I don't, Tom. It's not every day I get to walk around a beautiful garden and have my education extended. Before I met you, I could name a daisy, a dandelion, a buttercup – perhaps a few others…and of course, a rose."

"Roses…eh…let me show you something," he commented, then taking her hand, led the way past the greenhouse; the kitchen garden; the walled garden, stocked with fruit and vegetables, behind some neat trellis to a path leading to the Rose Garden.

"Oh my...a secret garden, I remember we used this for the egg hunt at Easter...but it didn't look like this," marvelled Rachel, standing in awe at the sight in front of her. Her eyes scanned the rectangular shaped area boarded by three hedges and a wall. A trellis covered the wall, interwoven with pink climbing rose bushes. Three wooden bench seats were placed at intervals along the wall. "Tom...this is spectacular...it's like being in a park. Who tends this?"

Tom indicated a bench, as Humph wandered off to sniff. They sat down, enjoying the warmth of the fading rays of the June sunshine. The garden faced southwest. It was sheltered and benefited from sunshine from late morning until evening.

"We employ two gardeners, but I was instrumental, along with my uncle, for most of the design." Tom recalled the area when his aunt and uncle first bought the property, just before the Great War. It had shape but had been neglected for many years. "When my aunt and uncle bought the house, the gardens were rather bland. They employed two old gardeners, and the grounds were soon sorted. Uncle Bart loved roses and had a vision for this area, backing onto the walled garden. I was a youngster at the time and when I was here on my vacations from school, I spent hours with him in here, helping to bring the bushes to fruition. It's a haven. I often bring a book and sit in here on a summer evening."

Tom could sense Rachel relaxing as she lifted her head to feel the warmth of the sun.

"It's beautiful and the aroma of the roses is delightful. I love their old-fashioned charm and rich fragrance," she commented.

Tom stretched out his long legs and crossed his ankles. "Did you know that the rose is one of the world's oldest and most popular flowers?" Rachel nodded with a faraway look in her eyes, as Tom slid his arm around the back of the seat. "Roses are mentioned in the Bible, and they have become a timeless gift of love." As he spoke his fingers grazed the edge of Rachel's shoulders.

"How's this for some fun facts about roses," he announced, chuckling. Rachel turned and looked at him. "In 1492 when Columbus was sailing on an expedition, some crew pulled a rose branch out of the sea, indicating land must be nearby. The next day...he discovered America!"

Rachel stared in amazement. "Really? That's fascinating. I must tell the boys," she remarked.

Tom stood and walked over to a beautiful red rose, gently cupping its bloom in his hand.

"Did you know that most roses have five petals, but many new ones are being cultivated now with multiple petals." He beckoned for her to join him. He carefully stroked a petal of the rose. "On each petal are minute perfume glands which produce the scent."

"That's incredible," she exclaimed, sensing Tom's passion for the plants. "Was this garden instrumental in your choosing to become a botanist, Tom?"

Tom pursed his lips. "I don't know...I was always fascinated by plants – their details intrigue me. I guess helping to create this Rose Garden did shape my choice of study." Tom moved over to a bed containing some yellow roses. "The colour of a rose is significant to their meaning.

Red symbolises love; yellow – friendship, joy and warmth". He reached into his jacket pocket and produced a penknife. Carefully opening it, he cut a short stem – a perfect yellow rosebud. He lifted it to his nose, its fragrance penetrating his nostrils. He held it out for Rachel to smell, then lifted it and gently placed it in her hair. "Friendship, joy and warmth, Rachel…my gift to you." She lifted her eyes to his – they became transfixed. He reached out and placed his finger under her chin, tilting it upwards. Then bending forwards, he placed a gentle whisper of a kiss on her lips. She was so beautiful. Placing his hand on the back of her head, he pulled her close and kissed her again…a deep, lingering kiss.

As they pulled apart, he added, "The name of this rose is 'Souvenir de Claudius Pernet' – it's a hybrid rose created in France. Joseph Pernet Ducher cultivated it and named it after his son who was killed in the war. When it blossoms it has many, many petals." He took her hand and they moved on to another rose bed.

"What do pink roses signify?" Rachel asked, still reeling from their moment of intimacy. They were standing, looking at the various shades of pink roses.

"Pink speaks of elegance and sweetness," he replied. Then walking on to a bed adorned with white roses, he commented, "And white speaks of innocence, grace and purity."

Rachel surveyed the whole garden. Their hands were still entwined.

"This is tranquil, Tom – thank you so much for showing it to me. I guess you know all the different names in Latin as well as the different varieties."

He smiled. "A lesson for another time – we have Damask; Centifolia; China; Tea; Bourbon; Noisette...they are some of the species, but many have fascinating names as well." They continued to walk through the rose beds, pausing at intervals to admire the buds and blooms and inhale the perfume. Slowly, they made their way out of the garden and back over to the house, the dog followed. "If you're interested, I can show you our kitchen garden, orchard and greenhouse another time – we are quite self-sufficient in fruit and vegetables."

"Yes, Tom...I'd love that," she responded.

Later, after Rachel left, he was locking up when the words of some lines penned by the poet Robert Burns came to his mind: *'My love is like a red, red rose that's newly sprung in June'*. It was June and as Tom thought about the red roses they had seen in the garden on that beautiful evening, he felt he could agree with the poet – his love... Rachel Brooks or perhaps, Darcy Shackleton, was his red, red, rose. An urgency to know the truth swept over him.

Chapter 8

The next morning Tom woke early. As sleep eluded him the previous night, he'd replayed his interaction with Rachel in the Rose Garden. Jumping out of bed, he quickly donned his clothes and grabbing a trug and some secateurs from Winnie's cupboard in the hall, he wandered out into the Rose Garden. It was an idyllic morning. Although still early, the June sunshine was already casting its yellow glow over the peaceful garden, causing the dewdrops to sparkle like silver on the rosebuds.

Carefully, Tom made his selection and cut mostly yellow and pink rosebuds. Then he walked around, searching for a red rose in full bloom. Adding a few white rosebuds, he placed them in the trug and made his way to the greenhouse. It was too early for the gardeners. He trimmed the stalks to an even length, then delicately arranged them until he achieved the desired effect. Cutting some twine he found on a shelf, he tied the bouquet to hold its shape.

"Oh, Mr Tom...they look delightful. I'll get a vase and put them in reception," announced Winnie as he entered the back door into the kitchen.

"Sorry to disappoint, Winnie...but they are a gift for someone special."

Realisation dawned upon the elderly housekeeper, and she raised her eyebrows. "Ahhh, but you'll still be needing a vase then...I'm sure she will return it," commented Winnie, reaching up to a wall cupboard to locate a suitable vase.

Tom placed the flowers in the vase. He went through to the bureau in the rear lounge and wrote a note on some paper. *'Dear Rachel – a belated birthday gift. May the fragrance of these rosebuds enhance your day. With affection, Tom.'* Placing the note in an envelope, he sealed it and positioned it down the side of the vase. Standing back to view his handiwork he felt pleased. The design featured a central full bloom red rose, surrounded by a ring of alternate pink, yellow and white rosebuds. It was a statement – he hoped she would understand its meaning.

It was lunchtime when the telephone rang.

"Tom...thank you so much for the bouquet. It was so kind and thoughtful of you, especially so long after my birthday."

He smiled down the phone, imagining her face. He'd left the gift with the Rossiters' housekeeper earlier, instructing her to add water and pass them on to Miss Brooks.

"When is your next free time, Rachel?" he asked, knowing he was acting like a lovesick boy...but he couldn't help himself. They arranged to meet the following week. "It won't be a grand occasion this time, Rachel," he informed her. "Just some homely food at a local tavern."

A roast dinner followed by treacle sponge was grand enough for Rachel. "That was delicious, Tom...do you know it's been one of the nicest 'birthday treats' I've had…and it's way past my birthday," she remarked as they finished eating. Tom noticed a sadness clouding her visage. "It's a long time since anyone bought me a gift and pampered me," she added.

"A long time?" he dared to ask, hoping she would be open and reveal something of her past.

Rachel was obviously struggling to formulate her words.

"Someone very special gave me a gift on my birthday, which I still treasure…it was many years ago, I was only a child," she divulged, then reaching for her handkerchief she dabbed her eyes. "I'm sorry, Tom…I'm spoiling this lovely occasion and I'm being stupid – many people lose a loved one…it's life…we soldier on," she remarked, tossing back her hair, reminding him of Darcy, but at the same time he sensed a determination, a grim determination to hide her true feelings. A switch flicked and suddenly the controlled Rachel was turning the tables and asking Tom a personal question.

"Do you have a painful memory, Tom?" she enquired.

"More than one," he confessed. "I was a young boy when my maternal grandfather died – this was his ring–" he indicated the signet ring on his right hand. "He was called Ezra and as my middle name is Ezra, I was bequeathed his ring – it's inscribed with the letter 'E'. Then when I was fourteen my youngest sister died. My mother was distraught. Peg, my other sister and I are close…we clung to each other all night." Even now he could still feel the sadness of that night. "Then years later, when I was working in London, I received a telegram informing me my aunt had died suddenly – I never want to see a telegram again." Tom rubbed his brow; he felt a lump forming in his throat with the memories.

"I sense you were very fond of your aunt…am I correct?" Rachel asked.

Tom looked at Rachel intently. "I know this sounds insensitive of me…but Aunt Dora showed me more love than my real mother ever did…please keep my confidence, Rachel, it's very personal. I must really trust you to share that – neither Jonty nor Peg knows the way I felt about Aunt Dora."

Their meal continued and Tom felt so at ease with Rachel. The act of sharing confidences seemed to underline their deepening attraction for each other.

Rachel told Tom the Rossiter family were going to be away the following weekend. Tom saw a window of opportunity. "Rachel…does that mean you are free on Monday? It's my birthday next week – I'll see if I can arrange a day off and we could go to Lasham Cragg again?"

Rachel gasped. "I'd love that, Tom – the spot was glorious in the spring…I imagine it will be spectacular in the height of summer…a lovely spot for a birthday outing."

They made their plans.

The day was blissful. Tom was waved on his way by his brother and Winnie.

"Enjoy yourselves…the hotel will still be here when you get back," joked Jonty.

Rachel and Tom followed the same route they had taken back in April…their relationship seemed so much more established in the intervening months. Reaching the top they enjoyed their lunch, sharing the space with many passing visitors. Packing up, they walked towards the edge – it was a splendid view.

"A force of nature," Rachel commented, mesmerised by the gushing waterfall.

"My aunt used to recount a poem when we looked at this view as youngsters," Tom mused, obviously lost in a memory. "I think she was the author."

'There is a place 'twixt heaven and earth,
That fills me with such joyful mirth.
With bright blue sky and rolling hills,
My singing voice begins its trills.
The Maker of this universe created such a wide diverse.
My heart cries out, yes in this place,
I'm overwhelmed by love and grace'.

Rachel nodded her head slowly. "That's so beautiful, Tom…I almost feel I know her."

They turned and gazed into each other's eyes. The words were special…the place was special…the day was special…the moment was special. Tom bent forward and kissed Rachel in a way that sent a definite message – but their moment was whisked away as a group of walkers interrupted their bliss.

***

Three weeks later

The telephone rang. Tom raced to answer it but was beaten by a maid.

"Good morning, Meckleridge House Hotel...how may I help you?" The young maid repeated her well-rehearsed phrase with an air of accomplishment.

Tom took the phone from her mouthing 'thank you'.

"Tom," shrieked his excited sister.

"Peg...where are you?" he responded.

"London...about to board a train to Durham."

Tom had known Peg's visit was imminent, but in her usual fashion, details of the arrival date and time were non-existent. Fortunately, he'd anticipated this scenario and made sure one of the attic rooms was as tidy and comfortable as possible.

Tom was so looking forward to seeing his sister – it was nearly a year since her last visit. So much seemed to have happened in the intervening months, not changes other people would notice but changes in himself. He was a different person to the one who waved goodbye to Peg last year. At that point he'd been a restless soul, counting the months until he could return to his chosen profession, but now...he was at peace with himself. He was settled in his role as a hotel manager. He set about his daily tasks with enthusiasm and the reward was evident. Added to this, his growing affection for Rachel Brooks enhanced his daily walk.

The feelings he held for Rachel were unlike any he'd experienced before...he could deny it no longer – he was in love! Outwardly their relationship remained unchanged. They snatched a few hours together here and there – a walk, a drink after their demanding days, an impromptu lunch. They were comfortable holding hands and sharing a kiss when they parted...but Tom was still hesitant. Was she lying to him? The enquiries Zac had promised to make seemed to have been forgotten. He'd seen him a couple of times when he'd visited his father, but no mention was made of his request. Tom sighed as he entered the station carpark to meet his sister. Why was this 'truth' thing so important to him anyway? Deep down he knew the answer. The mantra he'd built his adult life around would be breached if he deepened a friendship with someone untruthful. So, it really hinged on Peg's 'take' on Rachel Brooks. If Peg dismissed it as coincidence, then Tom thought that would be his answer…but if not?

***

Peg's visit to Malhaven was almost over before she met Rachel Brooks. The Rossiter boys developed chicken pox and Rachel opted to stay with them until they had both fully recovered. Tom shared his observations concerning Rachel with Peg soon after her arrival.

"By the way, Peg, you remember I asked you about Darcy Shackleton?" he asked when they were alone.

"Yes…what brought her to mind after all this time?"

Tom placed his hand on his sister's shoulder. "In a nutshell, Peg, I think Henry Rossiter's new governess is the same girl we knew as Darcy Shackleton – but she denies it and is called Rachel Brooks."

Peg's eyes widened. "Really…what makes you think that?"

"Gestures, mannerisms, tone of voice, physical appearance – as much as you can compare a young teenage girl to a grown woman."

115

Peg pursed her lips. "What does Jonty think?"

Tom shrugged his shoulders. "He reckons it's coincidence and everyone has a double. Chooses to believe what she says," he sighed. "So, I'm looking for an honest answer from you Peg," he added.

"Why is it so important to you, Tom?" Peg enquired, sensing a determination in her brother.

"Because, dear sister…and this is for your ears only… I've fallen for her – big time!"

Peg stared in disbelief. "When do I get to meet her?" she asked with excitement.

"Soon…I hope. Normally she's over here at least once a week, but her young charges have chickenpox, so she's confined to barracks. But if Mother organises an engagement party for you and Pierre before your holiday ends, I can invite her to come along, so you'll be able to see for yourself."

Tom and Pierre hit it off immediately. They shared a wicked sense of humour and Tom found Pierre's tales of his detective experiences fascinating. Pierre was everything Tom had hoped for in a future brother-in-law. He was tall, dark haired and well built. His eyes were brown. His face was kind. When he spoke, he gave you his full attention. His broken English was good with an attractive accent. Tom knew from the moment he clasped his hand in the station – Pierre was a man of character. It was evident to Tom – Pierre and his sister were besotted with one other. Pierre, like all the Smallwood siblings, was a keen hiker, so halfway through the holiday Tom, Peg and Pierre visited Lasham Cragg. Reaching the top, they sat down to eat their picnic.

"Tell Pierre about your suspicions regarding this Rachel person, Tom," Peg commented.

Tom gave Pierre an overview of his observations.

The handsome French detective stroked his beard. "How long eez it since you met her?" Pierre asked.

"About seven months now – and I see the similarities every time we meet. What I can't understand is…if she is the same person - why she would deny it."

Pierre looked thoughtful. "Perhaps she az no choice, Tom. You say she seemed to vanish at the start of ze war?"

Tom nodded.

"Perhaps she was forced to disappear because of her family."

Tom looked at Pierre in bewilderment.

"Ze war, Tom, ze war…many strange things happened in ze war."

Tom had never thought of that angle before.

**

Lilian and Jonathan Smallwood were delighted with their daughter's news and welcomed the tall, dark Frenchman with open arms. As Tom suspected, his mother was determined to arrange a celebration dinner in honour of Peg and Pierre's engagement and although the little cottage was small, Lilian made sure her culinary skills were put to good use.

An invitation was extended to Rachel. She was dubious at first, pointing out it was a small family occasion, and she was an outsider.

"Rachel, I want you to meet my sister. This would have happened sooner if your duties had permitted...please say you will attend," Tom begged when he telephoned her.

"Well, if you are sure...I don't want to be an interloper. The boys have recovered now so I can be free," she commented.

The Smallwoods' cottage was cosy and welcoming. Tom introduced Rachel to his sister and future brother-in-law with a degree of trepidation. Rachel was smartly attired in a dark green wool dress. Her hair was pulled back from her face, but her curls were in evidence bouncing around the rear of her neck. Tom experienced a wave of pleasure as he observed her making conversation with Peg and admiring the engagement ring which was finally released from its chain around Peg's neck. At no point was there an inkling of recognition between Peg and Rachel. Lilian excelled herself, producing a delicious dinner. Jonathan gave a fine speech welcoming Pierre to the family.

"Now our daughter is embracing matrimony...it's about time our two sons did likewise," he chuckled, dropping a broad hint.

"Not much chance of that with me – I'm sorry to disappoint, Father. I only meet farm animals on a regular basis," joked Jonty, as everyone laughed.

Most of the evening was spent sitting around the table which took up most of the space in the tiny cottage dining room. Unfortunately, Peg and Pierre ended up sitting at the opposite end of the table to Rachel, affording little opportunity for small talk.

At the close of the evening Tom was assisting Rachel with her jacket in the hallway, before escorting her along to the Rossiters' house, when Peg and Pierre appeared.

"Rachel, it's been a delight to meet you, my brother has mentioned you many times during our visit and it's good to finally put a face to a name."

"Yes, likewise, Peg," Rachel replied buttoning her jacket. Peg watched Rachel closely.

"I can't help feeling we've met somewhere before. You bear a strong resemblance to someone I knew when I was a teenager," Peg remarked.

Rachel stiffened and Pierre noticed, watching her carefully.

"No, Peg…we've never met before. I obviously look like someone else…your brother made the same mistake. Now, if you'll excuse me, I must dash." She turned, rather abruptly, and grabbed the doorknob to open the door.

Tom followed her outside. He put his arm around Rachel as they walked the short distance along Front Street to Gilberta House. "I'm so pleased you were able to join us tonight, Rachel…now you've met all of my family," Tom commented as they stopped outside the gateway. He pulled her into an embrace.

"I like Peg," she remarked. "I can see why you two are so close. Thanks for including me in such a private celebration." They kissed, with a promise to meet the following week.

"Nightcap?" asked Tom as Jonty, Peg, Pierre and he arrived back at the hotel. Winnie had agreed to stay overnight and 'hold the fort'. They sat down in the conservatory while Jonty went for some drinks, as all the guests seemed to be elsewhere.

"Well?" Tom asked, looking imploringly at his sister.

"I agree, Tom. The mannerisms and gestures are quite convincing. It's a shame we were seated at the opposite end of the table preventing me from engaging her in conversation. But she's a good liar – not one indication of recognition."

Jonty entered the room carrying a tray of drinks.

"Oh, he's not interrogating you as well…is he?" Jonty asked, picking up on the last sentence Peg spoke. After handing out the drinks he stood in the centre of the room. "Listen, 'they', whoever 'they' may be, contend we all have a double. You just happen to have met two people who resemble each other strongly. Anyway, what if she is Darcy…it's not a crime to change your name. She's Rachel Brooks now, Tom…just accept it. She's a fine-looking woman…and if you're planning on vacating your position as her beau, give me a 'heads up' so I can step in to replace you," he added, chuckling. "Well folks, I've got an early rise in the morning, so I'm off to my bed." He bent to hug his sister and shake hands with Pierre, as he would be gone when they left for the station the following morning.

The threesome sat in silence after Jonty left, then Peg asked her fiancé, "What did you think of Rachel, Pierre?" Turning to Tom she added, "Pierre is experienced in interviewing techniques – he notices facial expressions and body language," she explained.

Pierre looked at Tom. "I observed someone who was tense and uncomfortable. How do ze British say…shifty. Her eyes showed a hint of alarm. I think Mademoiselle Brooks…she az something to hide."

Tom's jaw dropped.

Chapter 8

Peg and Pierre's visit unsettled Tom. He'd thoroughly enjoyed seeing his sister again, coupled with the pleasure of meeting her future husband. It was sad though – they would live so far away. At best he could only hope to see them once a year. Peg's 'take' on Rachel unsettled him also, along with Pierre's comments. He reasoned with himself daily...everyone has flaws...no-one is perfect. At other times phrases kept jumping into his mind – 'an honest answer is like a kiss of friendship'...'speak the truth in love'. He would shake his head – all this he was sure was the by-product of being a vicar's son. But she couldn't be a true friend to him if they glossed over an important issue like this...they must be truthful with each other.

The week after Peg and Pierre returned to France, Zac contacted Tom unexpectedly. "I have some information for you, Tom...meet me in the pub tonight."

Tom's heart sank, panic clutched at his stomach...what had Zac discovered?

Chapter 9

Tom took a long gulp of his beer – it should have been something stiffer to calm his nerves, but he needed to face whatever revelations Zac was about to make, with a sober mind. He looked expectantly at his friend. He'd spent the last ten minutes catching up on his friend's news – his father's progress was very slow, causing Zac to pay a 'flying visit' north every other week.

"Perhaps I should look for work in the northeast again," Zac commented. "But I like the buzz of London and there's not much call for investigative assignments round here." He sighed, obviously facing some tough personal decisions. "Anyway…I'll get to the point." He reached into his pocket for his notebook and flicked some pages.

"Right. I've located a birth record for a Darcy Ann Shackleton on July 5th, 1902."

Tom's jaw dropped – that was not Rachel's birthdate.

"She was born in the district of Hackney, East London. The father's name was Percival known as Percy, aged 35 years; mother's name was Philomena, known as Philly, aged 26 years. Father's occupation was given as wood craftsman. I checked for death records for all three – none exist, so that probably just means they are still alive." He turned a page in his notebook.

"Next, I looked for a marriage record. Percival Shackleton, widower, wood craftsman married Philomena Brooks, midwife, in Hackney, East London on 29th May 1901."

Tom lifted his hand. "Did you say Philomena Brooks? Now there's a link, Zac." Tom sat forward.

"Percy's father was also called Percival, a wood craftsman and Philly's father was Henry Brooks, a physician," continued Zac.

Tom's eyes were almost popping out of his head. "Whoa, Zac…Rachel's father was a doctor…more links." Zac pursed his lips.

"The witnesses on the marriage certificate were Sydney Cartwright and Darcy Ann Soames."

Tom let out a low whistle. "Uncle Bart's sister was called Darcy Soames – so it's the correct family. The Darcy I knew was named after her godmother – that would fit… Philomena Brooks and Darcy Soames must have been friends. Anything else?"

"Yes…the 1911 census. The name Percival Shackleton wasn't too difficult to locate, once I had an area of London. However, it wasn't Hackney but Islington – so they had not moved too far away. I went to look for the property listed but it had been demolished and flats built in its place. The entry showed Percival Shackleton aged 44 years, was a salesman now; Philomena Shackleton 35, still a midwife; Darcy Shackleton, daughter aged nine years – so no further children at this point." Zac sat back and finished his drink, then tore the page from his notebook and handed it to Tom. He looked at the facts on the paper.

"So, this confirms Darcy's existence…but I'm interested in this surname Brooks. The birthdate for Rachel doesn't match Darcy's…a close relative perhaps?"

Zac looked thoughtful. "Quite possibly – family resemblances can be close. Listen, I'll check a birth record for Rachel Brooks when I get some time. What is your Rachel's birthdate?"

"Fourth of April 1902."

Zac made a note. "Did she indicate where she was born?"

Tom shook his head. "Only London…it's a big place."

"I'll start with Hackney, then Islington – if she's a close relative they probably lived nearby." He put his notebook in his pocket. "Meanwhile, you could try to find out about Bart Soames' sister – Darcy Soames. She will be in her fifties. If she was a friend of Philly Shackleton, there's a chance your mother might remember her." He swallowed down the last of his drink and stood. "Cheer up, Tom – high probability your Rachel is a close relative of this Darcy girl and may never have met her or even known of her existence. Must dash – can't leave the old man too long. I'll be back in a couple of weeks – hopefully I'll have more information."

Tom slapped his pal on the back. "I'm indebted to you, Zac – and it does look more hopeful. Rachel might be telling the truth after all!" Tom set off to walk back to the hotel feeling quite positive but this connection with the name Brooks intrigued him…how could he further this enquiry, he pondered.

The following day after paying the butcher's bill, he walked along to his parents' cottage.

"Well, well – look what the wind's blown in," remarked Lilian Smallwood as he stepped into the cottage.

"I had some errands to do, so I couldn't walk down Front Street and not pop around the corner to see you," Tom quipped, bending to kiss his mother.

"Your father is at a meeting," she informed her son, pouring him a cup of tea.

Tom sat down. "That was a fine celebration you put on for Peg and Pierre's engagement, Mother. I'm so pleased you like Pierre – it's a joy to see Peg so happy," Tom commented, sipping his tea.

"Yes, we approve of her choice but wish she lived a bit nearer. I'm determined we are going to go to France to see her after they are married," Lilian commented. "But you and Jonty better stay local – so you can look after us in our old age!" she joked. "Now…something I want to know, Thomas Ezra Smallwood," she chuckled. Tom braced himself, when his mother used his full name, she meant business. "Do I hear wedding bells in the distance with you and this governess?"

Tom blushed. "Far too soon for that, Mother…let's just say we are good friends."

Lilian raised her eyebrows.

"What's wrong with young people these days? She's a lovely girl; you've known her several months now and I see the way you look at her in church on a Sunday morning… what's stopping you, Tom – you're just the age to be settling down – not like your lothario brother."

Tom nearly choked on his tea – his mother did not approve of Jonty's dalliances and was not shy about making her opinion known! He swiftly changed the subject.

"Mother – do you remember Uncle Bart's sister, Darcy Soames?"

Lilian looked thoughtful for a few minutes.

"Yes, I do. A flashy sort of lady – always dressed to kill, wore paint on her fingernails – tut, tut!"

Tom smiled at his mother's description.

"I think she lived in London and was an actress, or a singer or a dancer, or some such thing. Only met her a couple of times – but she didn't come to Bart's funeral, and that upset your Aunt Dora. I mean, not attending your only brother's funeral – that's very bad behaviour. She didn't come to visit after, either. We didn't let her know when Dora died – wouldn't have known where to find her anyway. Why are you curious about her?"

Tom stood and put his cup on the table. "Her name cropped up in a conversation I had with Peg. Do you recall the three of us going to Wales after Hermione passed away? We met Darcy's goddaughter, also called Darcy." Tom saw a cloud of anguish pass over his mother's face… better leave it, he thought. "Well, I must be going, Mother, thanks for the tea. Tell Father I was sorry to miss him."

Lilian blinked away her memories. "Aye, I will. He's concerned about his old friend, Anthony, you remember him, he lives in Edinburgh. He wrote a few weeks ago saying he was ill and now his housekeeper has written to say he's in hospital – it doesn't sound good."

Tom nodded; Anthony Black was his father's oldest friend, they trained for the clergy together. "Oh, dear… that will be upsetting for him if anything happens."

Tom took his leave feeling somewhat dejected – it looked like the Darcy Soames lead was a dead end.

***

After a bit of effort on Tom's behalf, he managed to free up some time to meet Rachel for another full day outing. August was peak season at the hotel, but by the beginning of September the 'rush' had ebbed. Technically, the Rossiter boys were still on their summer break and Rachel was enjoying the first week in September as 'holiday'. She came over to the hotel to help Tom with various bits of paperwork. They made a good team and Tom was hopeful it was a sign of things to come.

The planned outing was to Durham – not a hike. "It's a beautiful city, not big but a lovely cathedral and pleasant walks along the River Wear." Rachel was excited. She had only been to the station and a hotel in Durham. They took a picnic lunch. After visiting the cathedral with its connections to St Cuthbert and St Bede, they wandered through the town and down to the riverside.

They found a spot to sit using a rug Tom had packed in his rucksack and ate their lunch. As usual their conversation was easy, and mention was made of Peg and Pierre's recent visit.

"When do you think they will be married?" Rachel asked.

"I've no idea," replied Tom. "But I doubt if it will be at Malhaven. They are both busy people and holiday time is rare. I imagine we'll get a letter to say 'the deed is done', knowing Peg," he chuckled.

"I like Pierre – his accent is quite alluring."

Tom bent over, placed his head on one side and grinned at Rachel. "And I suppose that means my northern accent isn't alluring...does it?" he joked, pretending to sound offended.

She wafted him away, her eyes sparkling. "You, on the other hand, have other attributes, Mr Smallwood," she teased.

The moment was charged. Tom reached out and cupped her chin.

"Like this?" he questioned and brought his lips to hers gently. Then he shuffled over and took her in his arms, pulling her into a tight embrace. His whole being was alive...gosh she did things to him...good things.

"Exactly, Mr Smallwood – that certainly makes up for not having an alluring French accent."

They sat back, Rachel resting her head on Tom's lap. It was a warm September day – the gentle sound of the river rippling over the rocks, coupled with the sounds of insects and the distant noise of the city made them both feel euphoric.

"I don't want this day to end," murmured Rachel.

Tom reached over and snapped a grass stalk, then waited until Rachel closed her eyes. Carefully he trailed it across her ear – she flapped it away thinking it was an insect. He grinned to himself, then repeated the action under her chin. She opened her eyes, he looked nonchalantly into the distance. Once again, she closed her eyes and once again, he tickled her face. This time she guessed. "Tom Smallwood...is that you?" she asked. Their lips met in answer...their kiss was firm and deep.

Pulling back, they gazed into each other's eyes. Tom's throat felt dry, but sensing the preciousness of the moment he stroked her face gently. "I love you, Darcy," he whispered. Immediately he realised what he had said. He regretted it instantly! If only he could swallow the words. She pulled away and sat up. He placed his hand on her shoulder, but she shrugged it off. "Rachel...forgive me...I'm sorry...it was a slip of the tongue."

But by now Rachel was on her feet, dusting down her skirt. Tom jumped to his feet pulling her back, but she squirmed out of his grasp.

He lifted his hands in surrender. "Rachel...please... please forgive me," he pleaded.

She turned and faced him. Then he saw it...the look of doubt...mistrust. Her eyes were cold. Her body stiffened.

"Please, please forgive me Rachel...I love you."

She straightened and answered calmly. "No, you don't, Tom...you love this 'Darcy' person. Take me home please. Our friendship is over."

***

What had he done? If he could have kicked himself, he would have received a severe beating, no matter how hard he tried on the return journey home, Rachel refused to be drawn into conversation. Arriving at Gilberta House he jumped out of the car and ran round to open the door, hoping to sort the issue before she went into the house. It was her calmness that shocked him.

"Thank you, Tom. It was an enjoyable day...until the end. I want to thank you for all the kindness you have extended towards me, since my arrival in Malhaven. But...I can't continue our relationship any longer...so please respect my decision. We will no doubt see each other at church – goodbye." She turned and walked through the gate.

He stared after her, his mind in a state of despair and disbelief.

He was utterly and hopelessly in love with this woman, no matter what her name. Why, why, why had he said Darcy instead of Rachel? Was it a subconscious thing? Why did she react so negatively?

He drove home…an emotional wreck. He replayed those moments at the riverside repeatedly. Had his declaration of love frightened her? Had she used his 'slip' of the tongue to end a relationship she wasn't ready to embark upon? The rebuff hurt…no matter which way he tried to analyse it.

Thankfully, Tom's occupation made demands upon him daily, so it was easier to distract himself with legitimate business over the ensuing weeks. At church he made a point of speaking to Rachel – she returned his greeting politely but stiffly. It didn't take Jonty long to apprise the situation. One evening while playing table tennis, Tom was playing somewhat aggressively.

"What's up with you, Tom…do I detect a cooling in your relationship with Miss Brooks?" Jonty enquired.

Tom knew Jonty would notice eventually, but he tried to be vague. "Just pressure of work with both of us…you know how it is," he remarked.

But Jonty guessed.

The following week Tom's father telephoned.

"Tom…I have a favour to ask. My friend Anthony has passed away. I have been asked to take the funeral in Edinburgh. I would like you to accompany me. I will be away for a week. Your mother has offered to take up residence at the hotel and I expect Winnie Jenkins will help. So, can I rely on your companionship?"

Tom was torn – support his father or hide behind his demanding hotel duties.

He knew his loyalty to his father would win the day.

However, it also afforded an unexpected window of opportunity for Jonty Smallwood.

***

Christmas 1925

Tom looked out of his office window – a heavy frost coated the scene. Trees almost bare of their leaves stood dark and silent, covered with a silvery sheen. It was Christmas Eve. The hotel was open and beautifully decorated thanks to Winnie and her team of helpers. The Christmas house party was already underway – the final four guests were due to arrive this afternoon. The event was well established, started by Dora Soames a year after the Great War ended. Many of the guests had been at the inaugural event. Ultimately, the atmosphere took on a 'family' feel. Children had been at the heart of the activities in past years – but not this year and somehow it suited Tom. He was struggling to engage with the spirit of Christmas.

Tom and Jonty's parents would arrive in the evening along with the carol singers from the church. This highlight involved a group of children from the Sunday

School whose rendition of 'Away in a manger,' guaranteed to bring tears to the eyes of the guests. I wonder if Rachel will attend, Tom mused – the Rossiter twins were members of the Sunday School. It was almost a year since she had swept into his life in the middle of a snowstorm. For most of the year he'd found himself falling blissfully in love with the attractive governess…until it ended so abruptly that day in Durham. Would she give him a second chance? He'd deliberated this possibility for weeks and was determined to act cheerfully.

It was tradition to give the children little gifts as a thank you for their singing. He walked over to the Christmas tree to distribute them, as they ended their performance. He was dressed smartly – wearing the burgundy waistcoat and bowtie he'd last donned for that special dinner with Rachel back in the Spring. He'd been watching her all evening, as he stood at the back of the conservatory and as the guests made their way into the dining room to partake of the Christmas delicacies Winnie and the cook had prepared, he ambled over to her.

"Merry Christmas, Rachel," he said chirpily. "I hope you have enjoyed the evening so far – please enjoy the refreshments," he added, indicating the way to the dining room, and patting the head of one of twins.

She looked up and their eyes met. They'd spoken formally, after church, since their friendship ended but there was a homeliness to the proceedings tonight. "Merry Christmas to you, Tom. The hotel looks splendid, and the singing has been delightful."

He followed as they stepped into the hallway. "By the way, we are holding a New Year's Celebration next week.

Would you like to attend…if your duties allow?" he asked jovially – it was worth a try.

She stopped and told the boys to find their mother, then turned to face Tom. "I've already been invited, Tom," she responded. "Did Jonty not mention it?"

Tom felt the ground beneath his feet starting to sway. His jaw dropped. "Jonty?" he asked as the realisation kicked in – it felt like a punch in his gut. He should have known.

"Jonty asked me last week," she continued, "I have accepted – I trust it won't cause any unpleasantness between us or between you and your brother…we are all adults, and these things happen."

There was an ominous buzz inside his head…this couldn't be happening. Her manner was confident and cool. He straightened his back…somehow finding the words to reply.

"No…it won't. As long as you have been invited, that's what's important, Henry and Blanche usually attend. So, we'll see you next week on New Year's Eve."

Rachel turned and he watched as she made her way to join the others. Tom managed to plaster a smile on his face for the rest of the evening. It wasn't until he shut his bedroom door that he stifled a cry of anguish, as he flung himself onto his bed. He was heartbroken.

***

Christmas week passed in a blur. Tom performed his duties in a perfunctory manner – but at least his mind was occupied. He observed his brother carefully and gave him plenty of opportunities to talk about his friendship with

Rachel Brooks – if one existed. Maybe he'd only asked her out of courtesy – was he being paranoid thinking they had formed a relationship? He'd spent the week trying to think back for any tell-tale signs…but none came to mind. Maybe he should ignore Rachel's comment and blasé his way through the impending celebrations.

Like Easter and Christmas, the New Year house party was a tradition at Meckleridge House Hotel, but with one difference – the guests were personal friends of the family. It was a mix of Jonty, Peg and Tom's friends…the ambience was casual and friendly. The festivities began with a buffet lunch followed by an afternoon of hilarious parlour games. The brothers always enjoyed this event – it was the beginning of their 'down time'. After New Year the hotel was closed and each brother took a month's holiday, catching up with friends and relaxing.

Fred and Mabel were in attendance, as was Zac. The guests weighed heavily in Jonty's favour, but over the years everyone became friendly. The new addition this year was Rachel, who was free to attend along with Henry and Blanche as Blanche's parents were looking after the boys.

A formal dinner was served at eight o'clock preceded by a sherry reception at seven-thirty. The dress code was formal – so it was an evening to shine. Rachel looked elegant wearing the deep blue evening gown she had worn when she dined with Tom last Spring. The menu was… parsnip soup, roast beef and all the trimmings, followed by an old English trifle – cook excelled herself.

Dance music played on the gramophone in the conservatory, for those who wished to partake; otherwise, the guests sat around talking, playing cards and drinking, until just before midnight. Then the assembled group formed a circle, joined hands and sang 'Auld Lang Syne'. As the clock struck midnight the guests lifted a glass as a toast was served to welcome in 1926. Then as tradition deemed it, the guests put on coats, hats, scarves, gloves and sensible footwear and traversed the half mile along to the town. Their mission was to 'first foot' various homes, whose residents were awaiting them – a Scottish tradition held in the northeast and embraced by the southerners who thrived on the escapades. Finally, the group returned to the hotel in the early hours of the morning to be greeted with hot drinks. The following day after a late breakfast the guests would take their leave.

Tom was light-hearted throughout the festivities, even whisking Rachel around the dance floor for one dance. He observed no particular connection between his brother and his former girlfriend. She spent her time sitting with Henry and Blanche – perhaps he was mistaken about a friendship between the pair. Jonty always assumed the 'host' role at New Year and treated the guests to endless jokes.

It fell to Tom to do the final 'sweep' in the early hours of the morning, checking all the doors, windows, lights, candles and fires. "That's it, Humph," he said to his faithful dog as they climbed the stairs to his bedroom. He was tired but pleased...it had been another successful house party. Just as he was about to shut his bedroom door, he heard a noise coming from the far end of the corridor. Curious, he peeped out...just in time to observe his brother and Rachel tip-toeing into Jonty's bedroom.

Chapter 10

February 1926

Chugga...chugga...chugga...chugga. Hisssss...
hisssss...hisssss...hisssss. The rhythm and the
sounds of the steam train carried Tom out of
London to his destination in Truro, Cornwall. Tom was
no stranger to rail travel. His years spent in Cambridge
and London often saw him taking train journeys to and
from his home in northeast England. But today he was
travelling in a new direction – southwest.

It was mid-February, six weeks since the bottom
dropped out of Tom's world. His annual holiday in
London held no appeal to him this year, but after Zac
suggested they take a walking holiday in Cornwall, he
managed to stir some enthusiasm. It was a risky time of
year for weather and the southwest was known for heavy
snowfalls, but Tom had no choice in his holiday time and
Zac was able to be free at short notice. It would be cold,
but the two young men were hardy and used to wrapping
up, having taken many hiking holidays together over the
years. Just being in each other's company would be good

fun and hopefully allow Tom to 'forget' his heartache for a few days. Why Zac suggested Cornwall was a mystery – but all would be revealed, and it was a totally unknown part of the world for Tom.

He spent the weekend with Fred and Mabel, insisting Mabel did not invite Angela Rochester for dinner, as she had done the previous year. Fred assured him that would not happen, and the weekend proved both enjoyable and relaxing. He was due to meet Zac at Paddington Station on Monday morning, but his friend telephoned Fred's flat on Sunday, to say he was needed at an important meeting on Monday afternoon and suggested Tom go on ahead and he would follow on Tuesday.

So, Tom travelled alone. In a way it helped to clear his mind. The weeks since New Year had been unsettling, and he fancied a bit of solitude. However, the solitude only led to reflection.

After his devastating discovery at New Year, Tom confronted his brother.

"Just when did you plan on telling me about your relationship with Rachel?" Tom asked as they ate their evening meal the night following the discovery.

Jonty eyed his brother solemnly. "There was no requirement to seek your approval, Tom. Rachel and I met by chance that week you accompanied father to Edinburgh. During our conversation, she told me there was nothing going on between you two anymore. I got the impression you had offended her."

Tom dropped his knife and fork on his plate with a clatter. "Just hang on…I offended her…how come?"

Jonty sat back and sighed. "She didn't give details, Tom, and it was none of my business – all she said was that you wanted her to be someone else. I surmised it was that Darcy Shackleton stuff. Now…you know me…if I fancy a girl and the coast is clear, then I take what's on offer."

Tom had been incensed at his brother's attitude.

Jonty chuckled and resumed eating. "Mind you – she's a hard nut to crack. That stupid governess job has her at the Rossiters' beck and call. Chances to meet her have been few and far between. But suffice it to say we have established a cosy relationship. Not sure where it will lead but remember, Tom…'all's fair in love and war'. You had your chance, and you blew it. I had nothing to do with that." Jonty had continued eating.

Tom left his food – his appetite had vanished. "It was a bit below the belt, Jonty, to see you two sneaking around after hours."

Jonty had pointed his fork at Tom. "Come on, Tom, this was bound to happen one day – you and I falling for the same woman!"

Tom was angry, an emotion he rarely showed. "There was no need to invite her to your room in our home, last night…that was hardly subtle." By this stage Tom's normally quiet voice was raised, alarming Humph, who came over to his master to see what was wrong.

That comment silenced Jonty who was totally unaware his nocturnal antics had been observed. He had stiffened and shovelled the remaining mouthfuls of food into his mouth, then standing, bent over Tom.

"I told you years ago, Tom – 'you are not your brother's keeper'. It's my business how I conduct my love life…

not yours. I see no point in continuing this topic of conversation. Let's agree to make it a taboo subject; after all, we must live and work together." He walked over to the sink with his plate. "Rachel may or may not visit the hotel – our home, remember – from time to time as my guest. I expect you to treat her with courtesy as my friend... is that understood?"

There was little Tom could say to such a dismissive comment and it was true. He'd had his chance with Rachel Brooks and through his own stupidity he had thrown it away.

Fortunately, in the intervening period since that conversation, Jonty had been away for a couple of weeks and now Tom was away. During that time, he had been spared any signs of affection between his brother and Rachel. Looking back, Tom was thankful the hotel was empty that night, so no-one heard their raised voices – except Humph!

The suggestion from Zac to visit Cornwall was a surprise. It was quite some time since they'd holidayed together. He'd been unsure how to spend his free time and a long weekend in London with Fred and Mabel was all he had planned.

"I've been doing a bit more digging," Zac informed Tom over the telephone a week ago. "Do you fancy a trip to Cornwall? I could arrange a few days off in the middle of February. I'll book the accommodation."

Tom found himself agreeing, then asked, "Why Cornwall?"

"I don't want to discuss my findings over the telephone, Tom. I'll drop you a note with the hotel details and the train time," his friend replied.

So, here was Tom heading to the southwest for a mystery few days with Zac.

***

Later that afternoon Tom was standing in the foyer of The Albert Inn in Truro. It was situated on the High Street and was an old coaching Inn. The proprietor checked his booking and handed him his large, wooden fobbed room key. Tom explained his travelling companion had been delayed and would be joining him the next day.

Looking around he noted it was a well-established lodging house, which appeared to be well maintained. He walked into the lounge bar. Heat radiated from a roaring log fire in an inglenook fireplace. A pile of logs lay to the side on a stone slabbed floor. There were beams on the ceiling and the stonework on the walls was exposed and adorned with prints of hunting scenes and brass hunting horns. Overall, it gave off a comfortable, cosy feel.

He was drawn to the fireplace to warm his chilly body on the cold February afternoon.

"You be visiting then," mumbled a voice from behind a newspaper.

Tom looked in the direction of the voice and saw an elderly gentleman with a long grey beard and mop of grey hair. "Er...yes, I am, a few days of holiday," he replied, rubbing his hands together.

The man put his paper on the table in front of him. "Strange time o' year for holiday," he remarked, pulling a pipe from his pocket and proceeding to fill it with tobacco.

Tom watched as the old man lit his pipe.

"It's the only free time I've got – so I have to make the most of it," Tom remarked. "Only hope the weather stays fine – my friend and I plan to go walking."

Taking a few puffs and sending a distinct aroma across the room, the elderly gent then tapped his nose. "Aww ye be alright…my nose tells me it be fair," he commented, then picked up his newspaper again.

Tom smiled – Cornish hospitality, he guessed.

Entering his bedroom, Tom was pleasantly surprised. A fire was lit in the grate, although he guessed only recently, as the air in the room felt chilly. At either side of the fireplace were two armchairs and adjacent to one chair stood a small table. A carafe of water, two upturned glasses and a local map lay on the table – nice touch, noted Tom. On the opposite wall were two single beds with wooden headboards. A small, curtained window looked out onto a small courtyard and underneath the window was a set of drawers. On the opposite wall, next to the door, was a double wardrobe. All the furniture was mahogany and relatively scratch-free. The hotelier in Tom noted the shabby rug between the two beds and the mis-matching bedcovers, but it was clean, and the drapes looked new. Tom unpacked and visited the bathroom along the hallway.

Returning to the lounge, he enjoyed a tankard of local ale before eating a welcoming, home cooked meal by himself in the dining room. The bar was populated with local men enjoying their beverages as he emerged from his solo dining experience. A couple of older men nodded a welcome to him. Some younger, rather loud men eyed him with curiosity. Tom found their accent alien, so decided to retreat to the comfort of his room to read.

He stepped out of the inn the next morning to explore his surroundings. As expected, it was very cold but dry and bright. He was well wrapped up in his Crombie overcoat, trilby hat, scarf and gloves to combat the chilly breeze, and walked around the town to get a feel for the place. He watched people busying themselves in their daily tasks – no different to any other town in England. Eventually, he found a little café and partook of a warming bowl of vegetable soup, a slice of fruitcake and a pot of tea. He estimated Zac's train would arrive in the late afternoon, so returned to his accommodation and settled himself with his book, near the fireplace in the lounge. He became so absorbed in his reading material, he was surprised when he heard a familiar voice.

"Tom...so good to see you. My, that fire's a sight for sore eyes," remarked Zac, walking over to the crackling fire. "It's mighty cold out there...pleased I brought extra layers!"

The two friends greeted each other heartily and Tom ordered a pot of tea.

***

Later that evening, fed and watered, the two young men found a quiet corner in the lounge.

"Cornwall?" queried Tom, raising his eyebrows in expectation.

Zac smiled and pulled out his notebook.

"Thought we could both do with a change of scenery, but don't let on to my father," Zac chuckled.

Tom had already informed Zac about Jonty and Rachel's friendship, which he was not surprised about.

"Okay, down to business. The family name for your Darcy's mother was Brooks, as I found out on her marriage certificate. So, I looked up a birth certificate for Philomena Brooks. She was born in 1876 in Islington, London and her father was called Henry Brooks – he was a physician. Her mother was called...Rachel."

Tom's eyes widened but he remained silent.

"I checked for Henry's marriage record...Henry Brooks, born in 1849, a physician, married Rachel Black, born 1851, a nurse, in 1874.

"Next, I looked up the census for 1881." He paused.

Tom shook his head. "How do you know where to look?"

"Investigative journalism, Tom. Looking up records is all in a day's work to me. Anyway, census records are very useful. In 1881 Henry and his wife Rachel have two daughters...Jemima aged six years and Philomena aged five years. They are living in Islington, London."

Tom nodded.

"Skip forward ten years to 1891 census...no change. But by the 1901 census Henry is now a widower, living with his two daughters Jemima aged 26 years and Philomena aged 25 years. The census was in March, and we know Philomena got married in May that year."

Tom was starting to look bewildered.

Zac tore a sheet from his notebook and passed it to Tom. "Here, jot these facts down, because there's more and you need to study them carefully."

Zac repeated the dates and names, and Tom made a note of them – this was Darcy's grandfather, mother and aunt, Zac was talking about…but still there was a mystery about his Rachel…did she fit into all this somewhere?

Tom finished writing and yawned. "I can't help feeling this is all hypothetical, Zac, now Rachel and I are no longer together…but my curiosity is piqued, and I want to know what all this has to do with this holiday in Cornwall?"

"Are your brother and Rachel still friendly?" Zac asked.

A sadness spread across Tom's face.

"I don't really know…Jonty and I had 'words' over the subject and it's never been mentioned since. Then Jonty was away and now I'm away. I assume they are still together, but I care about her deeply, Zac and I can't bear the thoughts of Jonty touching her, it makes me feel angry and you know me…I'm not prone to anger. I'm trying to convince myself if we are meant to be together, then some miracle will take place and she'll come back to me…but I'm probably living in a fool's paradise." Tom looked dejected.

"Come on, Tom…the rest can wait. I feel my bed calling."

Tom and Zac retired to their bedroom.

***

Tom was wide awake at his usual hour of six o'clock. He'd spent the night tossing and turning longing for the kind of deep sleep he'd enjoyed the first night. There was no point lying in bed, so he got up, put some coal on the fire and visited the bathroom. On his return Zac was still 'in the land of nod', so after dressing he sat down by the cosy fire, switched on the lamp and studied his notes from the previous evening.

Darcy's grandfather, Henry, trained as a physician and married Rachel Black, a nurse, when he was 25 years old – two daughters followed in quick succession. All normal stuff. However, by 1901 his wife, Rachel, had died and he continued to live with his two daughters Jemima and Philomena. Tom thought back to the information Zac had given him last Autumn and rummaged in his wallet for the dates he scribbled on a piece of paper back then. He added them to his notes – Percy and Philly Shackleton were married in May 1901 and Darcy was born the following year in July 1902. Again, nothing unusual.

He sat back and stared into the glowing fire. The girl who had stolen his heart last year was called Rachel Brooks…and he was convinced she was the same girl he'd met in Wales, who was called Darcy Shackleton. He was perplexed.

"What time is it?" Zac asked, sitting up and looking at Tom with bleary eyes.

Tom consulted his watch. "Just gone seven o'clock. Plenty of time – breakfast is served at eight o'clock," Tom replied.

Zac lay back.

"Birth, marriage and death records are a fascinating source of information, aren't they? Also census records. We are fortunate to live in such an organised country." Tom voiced his thoughts aloud, not expecting Zac to be listening.

Then Zac spoke. "Did you know the 1901 census was referred to as the centennial census? It was the eleventh census to be collected and was held less than two months after Queen Victoria was buried."

Tom looked across at his friend. "My, my…you're a mine of information at this early hour of the day," he remarked, then stood and, folding his notes, put them in his jacket pocket. "While you're getting ready, I think I'll stretch my legs and go out to buy a newspaper. I'll meet you downstairs for breakfast."

After consuming a full English breakfast, Tom and Zac went to sit in the lounge by the fire. They shared the newspaper, making observations to one another on various news items. Finally, Tom reassembled the newspaper and sat back. "So, Zac…what else did you find – I still have no idea why I am sitting in a hotel in Truro in the southwest of England," he chortled.

Zac reached for his trusty notepad and Tom pulled out his notes.

"Okay…I guess you've digested the facts I gave you last night?" Zac asked, looking questioningly at Tom, who nodded.

"Yes, it's fairly normal stuff and proves Darcy's background but her grandmother's name – Rachel Brooks, that's got to be significant and connected to my Rachel… somehow, but how?" Tom looked imploringly at Zac, who raised his eyebrows.

"Next, I checked the 1911 census," he continued, as Tom sat poised with his pencil. "Percy, Philly and Darcy are living at an address in Islington, London. Percy's occupation had previously been listed on his marriage record as a wood craftsman…but now he is a salesman."

Tom shrugged – was that relevant, he pondered, but made notes.

"And this is where the trail ends, I'm afraid. By the next census, 1921, there are no records for Percy, Philly or Darcy Shackleton living in London. The 1921 census was a comprehensive census return. It listed the individuals who survived The Great War."

Tom looked up. "Yes, but that could just mean the Shackleton family had moved out of London because of the war," Tom suggested.

Zac flicked over a page in his notepad. "Now I come to the information Rachel gave you. She told you she was born in London and moved to Cornwall...correct?"

Tom nodded.

"So, I checked for a birth record for Rachel Brooks in 1902, and sure enough I found one...fourth of April 1902. Mother was Jemima Brooks aged 27 years; father was listed as 'unknown'."

Tom's scribbling ceased, as he looked at what he'd written and frowned.

"Birth date is correct, but Rachel said her father was a doctor," he reminded Zac, then stretched out his long legs and put his pencil down. "Where's all this going, Zac...Cornwall?"

Zac nodded. "Exactly. You said Rachel commented she lived in a small village in Cornwall called Marets, which you could not locate on the map. She also told you her father was much older than her mother and both parents were deceased. So, I took a punt and checked for a death record for a Henry Brooks in Cornwall...and eureka...I was rewarded. Henry Brooks, born in London in 1849 died in St. Eram near Truro, Cornwall in December 1921, aged 72 years."

Tom looked thoughtful, absorbing the information. "Do you think when Rachel talked about her father...she meant her grandfather?"

Zac raised his eyebrows and pursed his lips. "Write down Marets on your paper...then look at it."

Tom did as Zac indicated.

"What do you see?"

Tom continued to stare at the word, shaking his head.

"Spell it backwards, Tom," said Zac, so he did and blinked back in surprise...It spelt Steram. "The name of the place where Henry Brooks died was...?" Realisation crept over Tom's face.

"It's St. Eram spelt backwards...cunning!"

"I'd call it deceitful – done to hide something, Tom. Your girl Rachel set out to deceive you when she told you her home village was called Marets! Anyway, that aside, I checked the 1921 census record for Henry Brooks in St. Eram. He is listed as living with...Jemima Brooks aged 46 years. No mention of anyone else."

Tom stood up and walked to stand in front of the fire. The lounge was devoid of other guests or staff.

"I'm confused, Zac. I feel like we're digging a hole and sinking into it with all this information."

Zac crossed his legs and looked back at his notes.

"In my line of work there's nearly always another route to explore. This time I looked for a death record for Rachel Brooks, born fourth of April 1902."

Tom returned to his seat. "A death record...why?" he exclaimed, mystified.

Zac smiled. "I had a hunch...and it paid off. Rachel Brooks, daughter of Jemima Brooks, died as an infant in

March 1903 aged 11 months."

Tom resumed his jottings, then sat back. He was utterly confused. He waited for Zac's rationale on this fact.

"So, here goes my theory, Tom...and remember that's all it is – but it's convincing. Darcy Shackleton had a cousin, Rachel, who died as a baby. There was only three months between them. For some unknown reason, Darcy took over the identity of her dead cousin and became Rachel Brooks. I suggest we leave theses dates alone for now and set out on a walk – after all, that's why we've come to Cornwall."

***

In less than two hours the two young men had donned their walking gear, consulted a local map and traversed five miles of Cornish country lanes. The lanes were narrow, winding and bordered by high hedges, but they led to the village of St. Eram. Spying a public house halfway down the street, they headed there. It was a typical local hostelry, with a stone flagged floor and a cheery fire.

"Two pints of your local ale, please," asked Tom, rummaging for some coins.

"With pleasure," replied the burly man behind the bar. "Would ye be fancying some pork pie to go with that?" he added.

Tom looked at Zac who nodded.

"Then sit ye down and I'll bring them over," he answered in a strong dialect.

While they ate, a few local men entered, looking warily at the strangers. Hunger and thirst satisfied, Zac and Tom left the pub to explore. Zac had warned Tom not to discuss the purpose of their visit while they were eating. "Say little, but listen a lot, Tom," he advised.

St. Eram was situated on a road not much bigger than a wide track, although there was evidence of motor vehicles. It sported two public houses; two shops; a blacksmith; a bicycle repair yard; a police house; numerous small cottages with thatched roofs; a park; a small school and a church – St Augusta's. In the centre of the village was a war memorial and beside it a village hall with a water pump in front.

"Neat little village," remarked Tom, imagining Rachel as a girl wandering around.

As if reading his mind, Zac spoke.

"This, I think, is where your Rachel spent her teenage years. Round here are people who knew her...it's not that long ago. But you must be subtle in your mode of enquiry. People are naturally suspicious of strangers – especially those asking questions, so leave the talking to me Tom...okay?"

Tom agreed.

They meandered down the road and entered the churchyard. It was small, surrounded by tidy grounds forming a cemetery. There was a clock tower which sounded its presence by striking two resounding 'boings'.

"I reckon we've got an hour of decent daylight. Then we need to walk back."

"What are we looking for?" enquired Tom.

"A gravestone for Henry Brooks – should be easy to find, he's only been dead for a few years."

Chapter 11

Although it was only early afternoon the light was fading on that February day, making it almost impossible to decipher the lettering on the headstones. There was a dampness in the air and as the two young men stepped between the gravestones a chill seemed to wrap around them.

"It's the wrong time of year to be doing this," remarked Zac, after a fruitless half-hour search. The pair assessed they'd only covered about a third of the cemetery, so they decided to leave.

"Tomorrow, I suggest we leave earlier and come to the churchyard first. And we need to bring a torch," commented Tom.

"Have you got one with you?" enquired Zac.

Tom chuckled as they made their way out of the church grounds and back up the main street. "Always, and I've got a penknife. Remember we were boy scouts, Zac…be prepared and all that."

They laughed remembering their days in the boy scouts in the church hall in Malhaven. "We learned some useful skills…oh, look over there," Tom stopped and pointed to a sign on the door of an ivy clad cottage. It read *Dr Sutton*. "Might be worth a try knocking on the door, tomorrow. If

Henry Brooks was still a practising doctor when he died, he might have known Dr Sutton."

"Well spotted, Mr Smallwood," Zac joked. "It's also worth engaging that barman in conversation or some older customer at the inn – these people are a mine of information, especially if you buy them a pint of ale!"

They stepped out on the open road and made good time arriving back in Truro as twilight descended.

A clear blue sky and bright sunshine greeted Tom and Zac as they retraced their steps to the village of St. Eram the following day. This time they had avoided the temptation to loiter by the warming fire, reading the daily newspaper. They'd also brought edible provisions and a beverage. Their plan was to eat their snack as soon as they arrived, then visit the graveyard. After that they would go to the public house and see if they could engage the barman in conversation.

"What are we going to ask about?" Tom pondered as they ate their snack.

Zac took a drink.

"I can't be specific, Tom…it all depends on the character and who else is around. You get a feel for this sort of thing. In my early days as a journalist, I used to jump in showing my 'press' card, but I soon learned to stay anonymous and ask non-pointed questions. As I said yesterday, do more listening than talking and don't be afraid to be vague – also be on the lookout for people's reactions, they often speak louder than words! The bottom line is – we want to find out about the Brooks family when they lived in St. Eram."

Day two of the graveyard search was more successful. In less than an hour they had located the gravestone. It read:

'Henry Brooks died 3rd December 1921, aged 72 years, beloved father and grandfather. Greatly missed.'

The two young men stood back.

"So, what does this tell us, Zac?" Tom asked.

Zac stood assessing the inscription. "Three things, Tom. First, there's a headstone – so someone cared enough to pay for one to be erected; secondly, it says 'beloved father and grandfather' – so there was a daughter – we assume Jemima and maybe Philly. And grandchildren – maybe Rachel and Darcy; third, it says, 'greatly missed' so he was appreciated and loved."

A crunching noise alerted them to someone approaching up the gravel path.

"Good day gentleman," called a voice.

Zac and Tom turned simultaneously to come face to face with a clergyman dressed in his cassock.

"Hello," they said in unison.

"May I be of assistance?" the clergyman asked, pushing his spectacles onto the bridge of his nose.

Zac spoke, "Er…yes, possibly. Did you know Henry Brooks?" He pointed to the headstone.

"Yes – I did," he replied. "He was a regular attender at our Sunday morning services…a lovely man, our village doctor. Are you a relative?" he enquired.

"No," responded Zac. "But we are acquainted with one of his granddaughters."

Momentarily the vicar looked bemused. "I only knew Rachel – a bonny girl, blonde curls as I recall. She moved away before her grandfather and mother passed away," he added, looking thoughtful.

Zac jumped in. "Mother – was that Jemima or Philomena?"

Once more the vicar looked puzzled. "I only knew Jemima, Rachel's mother," he replied.

Zac immediately asked another question. "Oh, dear – so Jemima has passed away also?"

The vicar nodded.

"Is she buried in this graveyard?"

"Yes – right there with her father–" he indicated the same headstone, which gave no mention of Jemima. The vicar shook his head and rubbed his jaw. "Jemima died suddenly – less than two years after her father. Rachel's whereabouts were unknown, so we were unable to contact her. As Jemima's vicar I deemed it appropriate she should be laid to rest alongside her father – hence the reason there is no inscription on the headstone. If you two gentlemen know the whereabouts of Rachel Brooks…there are several private items belonging to her mother, in the safekeeping of one of my parishioners. It would be most helpful if you could inform her about this."

Tom and Zac stared at each other.

Tom spoke. "We will see if we can help." he replied, keeping vague and knowing they would not be informing Rachel of this visit. Voices could be heard and, turning, they saw two elderly ladies approaching.

"Ahh, the flower committee are arriving, you must excuse me. It has been interesting talking to you, gentlemen. By the way I'm Godfrey, Godfrey Irwin. My address is The Manse, St Eram, Truro…if you need to contact me." The vicar bade farewell and shook hands with Tom and Zac, who then headed for the public house.

***

"The plot thickens," remarked Tom as they walked out of the graveyard.

"Yes indeed – so it was no secret that Henry Brooks was Rachel's grandfather and not her father. When she told you her 'parents' were dead she was referring to Jemima and Henry. Did you notice the vicar's reaction when I mentioned 'granddaughters' and then Philomena? I don't think Percy, Philomena or Darcy were ever associated with this place."

"But it doesn't make sense, Zac…Jemima's daughter Rachel Brooks - died as an infant."

Zac stopped and turned to face his friend. "It makes perfect sense, Tom. I'm beginning to think your Darcy Shackleton became Rachel Brooks when she moved to Cornwall. It's been done many times before. A person takes over the identity of a dead infant, usually about the same age, in order to get a new birth certificate. In this case, Jemima would still possess the birth certificate of her own deceased baby."

Tom was amazed. "But…there's a death record, Zac – you viewed it."

Zac placed his hand on Tom's arm. "Not many people join up the dots, and check for a death record of an infant – just folks like us who are curious! Moving away to

Cornwall – nobody knew anything different. Your Darcy, I think, became Rachel Brooks – complete with a birth certificate and a mother who was really her aunt."

Tom let this fact sink in, as they made their way to the public house. His voice was despondent as he remarked, "So, looks like I've been correct all along and Rachel is Darcy Shackleton…but that leaves us with another mystery…why would Darcy take over her dead cousin's identity?"

As they pushed open the door, Zac cautioned his friend. "A puzzle yet to be solved, my friend…now remember – general chat."

The visit to the public house offered nothing other than a hefty piece of pork pie and a pint of local ale.

"You gents back again, I see," remarked the publican. Zac was poised to ask if he remembered the former doctor, when he said, "It's a strange little place, St. Eram – I've been here three years now and the locals still treat me like an intruder." He turned to answer someone calling from the kitchen, so Zac returned to his seat.

"No point pursuing any chat with the publican," he announced.

"Yes, I overheard," remarked Tom. "Why don't we try the other pub tomorrow?"

Zac agreed.

On the third and final day of their Cornish visit, Tom and Zac arrived in St. Eram about eleven o'clock. They began by knocking on the door of the doctor's cottage – but there was no answer. Undeterred, they went into one of the shops – a general dealers' store. Several customers were waiting to be served. Zac weighed them up carefully.

They consisted of a young mother with a child; two elderly ladies and an older gentleman. Zac prompted Tom to look around the store, while he joined the queue behind the young lady. He made eye contact with the toddler and smiled.

"Sweet face," he commented to the young mother.

"Oh, aye...looks can be deceitful – he's a little terror in the 'ouse," she remarked, grinning. "Are ye visiting? I've not seen ye around these parts before?"

Just the opening Zac was anticipating. "No, I don't live around here – do you?"

The young woman bent down to wipe the toddler's face. "Oh, I've lived here all my life," she chuckled. "Wedded the blacksmith's son, I did," she announced.

"Ahh," replied Zac. "I wonder if you might be able to help me. I'm trying to locate the whereabouts of a young lady who used to live in this village – we lost touch a while ago."

The ladies at the front of the queue left the store and the young mother moved up behind the elderly gentleman.

"Oh, and who be that now?" she asked, her Cornish drawl a confirmation of a lifetime spent in the village.

"Her name was Rachel Brooks," Zac informed her.

The young woman's face looked startled. "Oh, my... now there's a blast from the past! She be gone a long-time, mister. We were in the same class at school – the big school in Truro. We used to walk there together with some others. She wasn't at the elementary school, though. Her father – but we all know he was 'er grandad – he was the local doc." She paused. "Not for a while mind, he took over after Dr Symmonds went off to the war. No, Rachel's been

159

gone years, mister – didn't even come back for her ma's funeral." She made the last comment shaking her head in disapproval. She seemed lost in her remembrances and was shocked to realise it was her turn to be served. Soon, it was Zac's turn to buy some sweets and some fruit.

As they stepped out of the shop, the young woman was waiting for them. "I just 'ad a thought, mister. Old Annie Thomas in that cottage o'er there with the green door, she was friendly with Rachel's mother – she might know where she went."

Zac thanked her, checking which cottage she'd indicated. She walked off along the road holding the toddler's hand tightly.

"Well done," remarked Tom to his friend. "I would never have thought to engage that young woman in conversation."

Zac grinned. "In that shop we had someone Rachel's age, older ladies probably about Jemima's age and an elderly gentleman around Henry Brooks' age. In a small village like this, you have residents who love to share memories."

Arriving at the cottage the young woman had pointed out, Zac opened the gate and knocked on the door. A portly lady in her sixties, who looked as if she might have been a headmistress or a nursing matron in a former life, answered the door.

"Mrs Thomas?" asked Zac.

"Miss Thomas," the lady replied indignantly, emphasising the 'Miss', her jaw set firm.

"Pardon me, ma'am," apologised Zac. "I was wondering if you could assist my friend and me. We are trying to locate Jemima Brooks, who we understand used to live in this village."

The elderly lady eyed Zac and Tom suspiciously. "And why are you trying to do that?" she asked formidably.

Tom noted Annie Thomas' defensive reaction – he doubted they would glean any information here.

"We have a message for her...from a relative," Zac replied.

The older lady stiffened. "I think you better be on your way, young man; Jemima Brooks is no longer of this world, and she had no relatives – so I'll bid you good day!" With that she slammed the door in Zac's face.

Tom and Zac stared wide-eyed at the closed door, then walked back through the gate.

"She was rude," commented Tom, pulling a face.

Zac grinned. "Yes, but her demeanour told us quite a bit," Zac implied.

"Really?" questioned Tom.

"Annie Thomas has lived elsewhere – her dialect gave that away. I guess she was very friendly with Jemima Brooks and may well be the parishioner keeping Jemima's personal effects safe. She was also keeping whatever she knew to herself, she was on her guard. She did not like our line of inquiry."

They greeted a couple of residents enroute, then arrived at the other public house, The Waggon Way.

After enjoying a pint of ale and a sorry excuse for a plate pie, the pair were surprised when an older gentleman walked over to their table. Tom recognised him as the elderly man in the shop earlier.

"Excuse me, gents, but I couldn't help overhearing when you asked young Sally about Rachel Brooks in the store earlier."

Zac moved along the bench seat, making room for the old man. "Ah, yes, Mr?" Zac queried.

"I be Seth…Seth Stokes," he replied, sitting down. "Now I might know a bit about the Brooks family that young Sally didn't know."

Zac and Tom's eyes lit up.

"Can we buy you a drink, Mr Stokes?" asked Tom, rising to go over to the bar.

A few minutes later Seth was enjoying a pint, courtesy of the two young strangers.

"I knew Henry Brooks quite well," he began.

Zac nodded encouragingly.

"Henry wasn't a practising doctor as such. He lived here with his daughter Jemima and granddaughter Rachel. He loved to 'help people' with their ailments. I once asked him why he wasn't a proper doctor and he told me he had been, when he lived in London, before they had to move away. I always thought there was a story behind that…but he never told me. Anyway, folk liked him and when Dr Symmonds went off to the war, we were expected to go into Truro for our medical needs. That's when Henry became the doctor, unofficially, of course. Jemima had been a nurse, so she was a great help to him. Then young Rachel took off – went to be a live-in nanny to some posh folk in Bristol. Jemima was real 'put out' when she didn't come back for Henry's funeral, so sad," he exclaimed, stroking his beard. "She didn't show up for Jemima's funeral either. Annie Thomas has some boxes of stuff belonging to the family…if Rachel ever returns. It was a right 'rum do' she just disappeared after she left

Bristol apparently." Seth took a drink.

"Did you say the family came from London?" Tom asked.

Seth nodded, continuing to drink.

"When would that be...can you remember?"

Seth finished his drink, wiping the froth from his mouth.

"Oh, that's easy...it was just before the war started, summer 1914."

Zac asked Seth if he would like another drink, which he affirmed.

While Zac went over to the bar Tom asked, "Did Henry mention if he had any other family?"

Seth shook his head. "He never mentioned any."

Tom asked another question. "Can you recall when Rachel left St. Eram?"

Seth looked thoughtful. "Eeeeh now, I'm not sure. She was a youngster when they arrived – not quite a woman, if you follow my drift. She was here until after the war, and she was certainly a woman, a pretty woman, when she left," he added, his eyes twinkling.

Tom mused – probably 1919 or 1920, he guessed, certainly before the 1921 census.

Tom and Zac continued to chat to Seth, learning how Henry Brooks had cured him of various ailments with his pills and potions. He'd often played dominoes with him in this pub. The only other information they learned was that Jemima kept herself to herself; her only friend was Annie Thomas. She died suddenly from a heart attack, less than two years after her father. The vicar and Annie organised the funeral, as no other relatives attended.

Zac and Tom left the pub and began their final trek back to their hotel in Truro.

***

Spending a restless night on Zac's couch, in his tiny living room in North London, Tom was ready to be on his way north. They'd mulled over their findings on the train journey back from Cornwall. In one respect Tom felt informed, satisfied that Rachel's time spent in Cornwall was, to all intents and purposes, exactly what she'd indicated – but he hoped she never found out he'd visited her former home village. On the other hand, Tom was disappointed…he was no further forward in identifying Rachel Brooks as Darcy Shackleton

"Something happened for Darcy to take over her cousin's identity, Tom. So, I'll keep poking about," Zac commented. "Old newspapers from just before the war might prove informative. If I find anything…I'll let you know."

A thought struck Tom as he journeyed north – Darcy had 'disappeared' as a young teenager, becoming Rachel. When Rachel left Cornwall she effectively 'disappeared' again…was there a pattern here? And if so…why? He tried to turn his mind to the next few weeks and the Easter house party. Somehow, he needed to find a way to live with his brother, who was by now enjoying a relationship with the woman he, Tom Smallwood, adored…and that was going to be tough!

It certainly was tough. As Jonty collected Tom from the station in Durham he commented, "Rachel is willing to organise the Easter guest activities again, so...can you be 'adult' in your behaviour and accept the fact that the better man won?" he smirked.

Tom struggled with the prospect, but he knew many of their returning guests were expecting a repeat performance, so he gritted his teeth and put on a steel façade.

As Easter approached, Rachel's visits to the hotel became frequent. As hotel manager he was responsible for all hotel-related business. He found himself meeting with Rachel in a business-like fashion. She was in his mind all the time. He began to doubt himself, feeling he couldn't rely on his own judgement anymore. Had he been the one at fault? In their few months together he'd opened himself up to her, divulging things he'd never told a soul before...but he'd thought he was confiding in his future life partner...so, why wouldn't he? He'd trusted her – but this identity thing had broken that trust. Surely, surely if she really was Darcy Shackleton, which his recent inquiries were telling him was the case...she could have told him – without telling others – he would have kept her secret.

She acted stiffly, almost like a stranger, when she was in his company. Oh, how he missed her – the easy banter they'd established; the playfulness which led to affection; the remembrances of it all pulled at his heart strings as they discussed the forthcoming arrangements. Was our friendship of no value to her? He thought back to the night in the Rose Garden – that was the night he knew she was special; he'd felt himself falling for her...and he was sure it had been mutual.

Was she ever the friend he thought she was? Perhaps he'd been gullible, taken in from the outset. Her strong resemblance to the young girl from Wales...had it tricked him into believing he loved her? He'd always been so trusting of others; always saw their good points; always expected them to be truthful.

What he would give to go back to that afternoon in Durham, by the riverside. At that point he'd already started to accept the 'Darcy' thing was all in his imagination...and then he let the name slip out, just at that crucial point... when he declared his love audibly. Why did it offend her so much? He'd asked this question countless times. Why did she end their friendship so abruptly? Did their friendship mean so little to her she could 'jump' her affection from one brother to another – so quickly?

Jonty and I are poles apart – except in our looks, he reasoned. Jonty liked to be Mr Popular and look good in the eyes of others, whereas he was usually the one behind the scenes, happy to be invisible. How could Rachel drop me and turn to Jonty...it baffled him. But she'd made her decision and because he loved her, he accepted it.

***

A few days after another successful Easter house party, Tom heard raised voices in the hallway downstairs. He walked to the door of the office and opened it...listening. The voices belonged to Jonty and Rachel. Jonty was speaking calmly, trying to pacify an outraged Rachel. What's up? He pondered, deciding to stay out of the way. Then he heard heavy, stomping footsteps on the stairs and watched as a red faced, irate Rachel approached him, as he stood outside his office door.

"How dare you!" she growled, from halfway along the corridor.

Suddenly he realised...he was the focus of her vengeance. Quickly, he signalled for her to enter his office and closed the door after her. There were some guests still in residence and a maid dusting the picture frames on the landing. He did not want any of them to be privy to this outburst...whatever the cause.

She turned and faced him. There was anger in her body stance – her fists were clenched, but in her eyes, he thought he saw fear.

"Rachel...what's wrong? Please...calm down, I'm sure we can help you," he said in a soothing manner.

But Rachel Brooks was on a mission. "I will not calm down," she declared at full blast. Then lifting her finger, she pointed at him. "How dare you go poking your nose into my past, Tom Smallwood. I know all about your visit to Cornwall...and I demand an explanation and an apology...NOW!" she yelled.

Chapter 12

T om took a deep breath. Every muscle in his body seemed to tighten. He viewed the woman standing before him. All five foot two inches of her was raging. Anger oozed from every pore in her body. Her threatening stance; red face; perspiration beaded brow; flaming eyes and clenched fists, demanded his response. They eyeballed one another for what seemed like an age, and Tom's hesitation to speak only served to incense the fire burning within Rachel Brooks.

"Are you deaf? Did you hear me? I demand an apology, Tom Smallwood." She almost spat the words at him with pent up venom.

He pointed to a chair. "Please sit down, Rachel, and try to calm yourself," he said softly, attempting to quell the wrath still threatening to erupt – but it was to no avail.

"I will not sit. I will not calm myself," she insisted. "You have violated my privacy. You had no right to travel to Cornwall asking questions and prying into my business. Surely my word was enough?" Her voice was slightly quieter.

Tom had hoped she would never find out about his trip to Cornwall – which begged the question…who told her? Now she knew – he owed her an explanation.

"Well, I'm going to sit, if you don't mind…and can I ask you to lower your tone of voice please – we have guests in the hotel," he remarked.

Rachel snorted as Tom walked over from the door, across the room and took the seat behind his desk. He was attempting to formulate his words of explanation.

"Rachel…I'm sorry my visit to Cornwall has offended you so much and to that end I apologise. However, I need to give you the reasoning behind my action." He paused and fingered some papers on his desk. Then placing his elbows on the arms of his chair he sat back. "It was never my intention to hurt you or as you put it 'pry' into your business…so let me explain."

Rachel stiffened, sighed with indignation and reluctantly sat down on the edge of the chair opposite the desk. Tom watched her, noting a slight relaxation in her tense body. As usual she was dressed smartly, wearing a straight, brown pencil skirt and cream, high necked blouse and short brown jacket. Tom waited then resumed.

"Since our friendship ended, I have done a great deal of thinking and soul searching. I'm sure it will come as no surprise to you that I still care about you deeply. The words I spoke to you that day in Durham beside the river, still apply. I firmly believe if we are meant to be together, then somehow, we will overcome our differences. It will take time…but I am a patient man."

Rachel sat back in the chair and tilted her head. A smirk spread across her face, followed by a sarcastic chuckle. "You are so sure of yourself…aren't you, Tom Smallwood?" she said, sneering.

Tom looked at her sternly. Then continued.

"Your likeness to the girl I knew as Darcy Shackleton troubled me. Every time I was with you, I saw the strong resemblances. I value honesty, Rachel, always have. If we were ever to resume our friendship, I needed to convince myself that you are a different person. So, to that end Zac offered to check birth and death records for Darcy and her parents. If you are telling me the truth…then my line of questioning should have caused you no offence." He stopped to gauge her reaction.

She sat staring out of the window, deep in thought. Then she lifted her hands questioningly and looked at Tom.

"Let me explain further," he said, surprising himself at the cool determined manner with which he spoke. "Zac's findings showed that Darcy and her family were living in London at the time of the 1911 census. I met her during Easter 1914…but after that the Shackleton family seemed to vanish. No death records or future census records exist for them." Again, he observed her closely, but he detected a faint smugness in her demeanour.

"That is where my search should have ended, until Zac checked the marriage record for Darcy's parents."

Rachel looked down at her hands and smoothed her skirt…this time he sensed anxiety in her movement.

"Zac, as you know, is an investigative journalist and he leaves no stone unturned. The marriage record stated that Darcy's mother, Philomena, was called Brooks before her marriage. Her father was called Henry Brooks and one of the witnesses to the marriage was a Darcy Soames. Now, I knew of a Darcy Soames – not a common name – she was my uncle Bart's sister."

Rachel stood, placed her hands on the desk and glowered at Tom. "Brooks is a very common surname ...so what took you off to Cornwall?" Her voice was demanding again, but he sensed she was nervous. She stood back and resumed her seating position.

"You told me you were born in London then moved to Cornwall," he remarked. "Zac also checked for a marriage record for Henry Brooks and his wife was called...Rachel, Rachel Brooks." He watched as Rachel lifted her hands in exasperation.

"Oh, Zac has been a busy little bee...hasn't he? There must be hundreds of Rachel Brooks living in England!" she commented with disdain.

Tom waited, then continued. "Checking the census records for Darcy's grandfather, Henry Brooks, Zac found he was listed as a widower, living in Islington, London on the 1901 census return, with his two daughters Jemima and Philomena." Rachel's stare was penetrating. "A further investigation found a death record for Henry Brooks in December 1921 in St. Eram, near Truro in Cornwall – the date of birth matched." They were both silent for a few minutes.

A smile spread across Tom's face. "I liked the anagram, Rachel...Marets was really St. Eram...wasn't it?" How would she respond to this discovery, he wondered. A vague flicker passed across Rachel's face, but she said nothing, so he spoke again.

"I was due to take my holiday...I had no plans so, Zac suggested joining me on a walking trip in Cornwall – an area I had not visited before."

Rachel's face was blank, but at least she was calm. He'd deliberately made no mention of his knowledge of the death of Jemima Brooks' daughter.

"The rest I think you know – although I'm unsure how you do know, as we were led to believe no one in St. Eram knew of your whereabouts. The vicar asked us if we were in contact with you, to inform you of Henry and Jemima's deaths. You'd already told me your parents were deceased." Tom paused expecting another flat denial – but none came so he asked another pertinent question. "Who is your informant, Rachel…Annie Thomas?"

Rachel looked totally composed – a far cry from the woman who had entered his office earlier. She straightened her back. "Well, Mr Busy Body," she declared. "Your detective skills have rewarded you with the information that Rachel Brooks did in fact live in Cornwall with her mother and grandfather, who are now deceased…so what? People move; people choose to leave their family behind. My little attempt to muddle up the name of the village is hardly a crime, nor is the fact that I regarded my grandfather as my father," she sighed. "I hope you are satisfied this 'Darcy' person has nothing to do with me. But the damage is done, Tom Smallwood. I resent your interference into my background. I care nothing for your feelings towards me. I only wish I didn't have to lay eyes on you again, but my friendship with your brother makes that impossible. However, I declare we are enemies and I do not wish to converse with you again. You brought this on yourself – we could have remained acquaintances. I trust I have made myself clear." She stood and walked over to the door, then turned to face him. Tom was stunned.

"I'm waiting for your response, Tom."

He stood, lifted his hands in resignation and declared, "It's as clear as crystal, Rachel."

She left the office.

A mighty chasm had opened between them, and he was helpless to bridge it.

***

During the weeks following Rachel's outburst, Tom felt numb. On the surface no one guessed. He was still the jovial host of Meckleridge House Hotel. His handsome looks, neat appearance and competent manner were quite deceiving. His days were full running his successful business. Rooms were in high demand and there was little chance of a would-be guest acquiring a room at short notice. The nights, however, were a different story. Sleep evaded him until the early hours. Closing his eyes, he saw Rachel's bouncy curls, petite round face and chubby cheeks drawing him into her grey blue eyes, which were always smiling in his vision – so unlike the irate woman in his office that day. He tortured himself replaying the events leading up to their separation and finally the heartbreaking wrench after her discovery of his visit to Cornwall. Thankfully, he saw little of his brother with Rachel. They did not choose to conduct their courtship near him. Apart from mealtimes and business meetings, Jonty was conspicuous by his absence.

Jonty's reaction to Rachel's dramatic entry that day, left Tom in no doubt where his brother's support lay. "I can't believe how underhand and sneaky you were going off to Cornwall with Zac to check out Rachel's background. You've got exactly what you deserve, little brother. You couldn't trust her word and now she despises you – was that what you set out to achieve?"

In defence Tom retaliated, "There's still unanswered questions, Jonty. Zac's findings were more comprehensive than what I told Rachel. Suffice it to say, I'm even more convinced she is Darcy Shackleton, after that trip to Cornwall – but it's all hypothetical now. I'm the brother who lost. I still care for her, and I hope you appreciate her and treat her well." But Jonty's reaction that morning incensed Tom.

Jonty picked up his dishes and walked over to the sink. "She's a sweet little thing and she's keeping me occupied. I find her attractive – a bit fiery at times – but that enhances the chase!" Then he turned and left the kitchen.

Tom felt so helpless – his brother was using Rachel for his own ends. It did not surprise him – he was sure Jonty was incapable of deep love. In time, Jonty would cast her off and move on. At that point he should have been there to pick up the pieces and help to heal Rachel's broken heart. But this rift between them made that a highly unlikely prospect.

***

Not only did Rachel despise Tom, but he was astounded when she was openly hostile towards him. At first, she ignored him; cut him dead; but then given the opportunity she began to ridicule him publicly. At times her behaviour was almost childlike. It was Blanche Rossiter who alerted him to this unexpected aspect of behaviour.

"What have you done to our governess, Tom Smallwood?" she whispered to him one morning after church. Tom shrugged his shoulders, unsure how to respond. "She told me you were a despicable man and a non-person in her eyes, and we were not to include her in any events where you would be present."

Tom stared at Blanche in disbelief – how could Rachel speak so derogatively about him?

"It's her choice, Blanche," he replied, refraining from satisfying Blanche's obvious curiosity. It was none of her business and he was not about to give explanations. But he didn't expect to feel so vulnerable. It was a shock to his system. Inwardly he tried to make excuses for her, but then he began to doubt himself – after all, everybody was entitled to their privacy.

As spring gave way to summer, Tom found his behaviour becoming irrational. One day he overreacted and shouted at a young maid who accidently tripped on a rug and sent a trayful of crockery crashing to the floor. Normally, he would have comforted the maid, telling her not to worry – these things happened. Instead, after reprimanding her regarding her footwear, he stormed out of the room, leaving her in floods of tears.

The following week he found himself thumping the wall in the rear lounge when a supplier sent the wrong order. His usual reaction would have been to contact the supplier and calmly negotiate a replacement. Winnie noticed his changed behaviour and confided in Lilian Smallwood.

"I don't know what's got into you, Tom Smallwood," his mother said one morning when he called in to see his parents. "Betty Simmons in the Post Office told me you were rude to her the other day, all because you missed the last collection. It's so unlike you. I heard from Winnie she's concerned about you also...shouting at a maid and thumping walls. You've always been so placid and patient... what's wrong with you?"

Tom made some excuse about not feeling well and blamed the pressure of a heavy workload.

"Get yourself along to see the doctor...he'll prescribe you some pills," she remarked...but there were no pills to heal a broken heart.

He took a regular 'day off', usually a Thursday, and sought refuge in the hills and vales of northeast England. The long, solo hikes he took became his tonic. Fortunately, he knew the less trodden paths and rarely met any other hikers. It was on these occasions he missed his brother's companionship...and latterly Rachel's. He walked for miles come rain or shine, his mind frequently analysing the Rachel predicament.

They'd fit like a hand in a glove. It had been such a comfortable friendship progressing so easily to romance. He longed to talk about it with someone...but there was only Zac, who was far too busy. He felt he was becoming a different person. Even Aunt Dora's little book at his bedside failed to comfort him these days. He read the words out of habit, before extinguishing the bedside lamp, trying to let the words slip into his unconsciousness as he drifted off to sleep...*love never fails...love always looks for the best...love keeps going to the end...love never dies.*

***

August 1926

Tom drove to Durham station. He checked his watch: he was running late – Peg and Pierre would have to wait. His sister's letters had been infrequent of late and he was hoping all was well with her. He had resisted telling his sister about the situation with Rachel in his correspondence – wanting to do it face to face, although she knew they were no longer an item. Two days ago, a letter had arrived addressed to him – no large brown envelope containing other letters.

Dear To-To,

Surprise, surprise! Monsieur and Madame Thibault will be arriving in London on the 7th of August. I'll ring with the train time. NOT A WORD to anyone. Love Peg.

Tom had stared at the letter and re-read it. His sister and her fiancé were already married! He shook his head and jumped into action. Being the height of the season, all the guest rooms were occupied. Last year Peg and Pierre had 'roughed it' in the attic, but somehow that didn't seem appropriate this time. He guessed this visit would be their 'honeymoon' so, taking Winnie into his confidence he organised for his bedroom in the stable block to be put at their disposal...he would sleep in the attic. Jonty was rarely around at bedtime these days and Tom was

Chapter 12

always up and about before his brother came downstairs in a morning – so he doubted Jonty would notice the preparations being made.

Peg telephoned from London with the train time. He was eagerly anticipating her arrival and looking forward to unburdening himself. It was a year since she'd last been home and they'd held an engagement party for her – and now she was already married. Tom smiled to himself – Mother would not be a 'happy bunny'. But no doubt his parents would shower the newlyweds with love and perhaps another celebration meal.

In the event the London train was ten minutes late, so Tom was standing on the platform when the train pulled to a halt. His sister looked so attractive and excited as she raced along the platform to greet him. He took her in his arms and swung her around, she looked so pretty, her skin was glowing, and she possessed a radiance Tom could only guess emanated from her marital bliss. He hugged Pierre who followed, weighed down with luggage.

"Tom," she exclaimed. "It's so good to see you."

He held her arms out. "So, you two are already married...fancy doing me out of making a speech at your wedding."

Peg clasped her husband's arm. "Yes, it all happened so quickly, there was little time to plan." As they journeyed back to Malhaven Peg explained that her employer had been called away to stay with her older sister in Switzerland. Peg had accompanied her, as it was her job, but three weeks into the visit, Madame announced to Peg she would have to terminate her employment as she intended to move permanently to live with her sister. "Madame knew Pierre

179

and I were engaged and realised it would be unfair to expect me to move from Lyon. So, we were married one week ago – all Pierre's family were present and now we have travelled to England for our honeymoon. Pierre has three weeks' leave from his work. I'm hoping my parents can organise a blessing ceremony for us at the church, as we had a civil ceremony in France."

Tom listened with delight, so pleased for his sister and new brother-in-law.

"I'm sure Mother will whip up a celebration, Peg. It was always unlikely everyone could have been together for your wedding."

It was two days before Tom found an opportunity to talk to Peg and Pierre in private. Jonty seemed to be around most of the time, equally pleased to see his sister, but thankfully made no mention to them of his friendship with Rachel.

Hearing their daughter's news caused initial disappointment for Lilian and Jonathan. But they soon accepted the pressing circumstances surrounding the hasty decision and as Tom predicted, their mother began to plan. The church hall was booked; a wedding cake baked; a guest list drawn up and a visit to the dressmaker arranged. Lilian's organisational skills were exemplary. Peg and Pierre were in Tom's office sorting a seating plan for the reception, when he joined them. He closed the door.

"Good," he declared. "At last, I've managed to find you two alone." He pointed to the seating plan. "You need to place Jonty next to Rachel and put me at the other end of the table."

Peg looked perplexed. During the next fifteen minutes, Tom brought Peg and Pierre up to date with the situation concerning the hostility with Rachel and its cause. They listened intently. As he finished, Peg stood and walked across to her brother and enveloped him in a big hug.

"Oh, Tom, that's so distressing for you," she exclaimed.

"It's such a relief to be able to talk about it openly. Jonty and I rarely converse these days. I've been bottling it all up for months," he sighed.

Pierre stood and placed a hand on Tom's shoulder. "We are with you, Tom. We will speak further on this issue. I agree with you. Miss Brooks has something to hide."

***

"Ladies and gentlemen, please be upstanding in a toast to Monsieur and Madame Thibault." Jonathan Smallwood raised his glass and the assembled guests stood to toast the bride and groom.

The belated wedding reception was amazingly well attended, given the short notice – but most of the Smallwood family and friends lived in the northeast, so did not have far to travel. Peg and Pierre were showered with gifts and good wishes. Lilian had cracked the whip and produced a banquet fit for royalty, calling on her army of helpers from the church. The church hall was decorated delightfully with fresh flowers. Rachel was in attendance but ignored Tom.

Jonathan insisted on walking his only daughter down the aisle. The new rector gave a blessing on the marriage which had already taken place in France, almost a month earlier. Both Jonty and Tom gave hilarious speeches concerning their little sister and the bride looked so pretty in her hastily made cream satin gown.

"You must come to France to meet my family," Pierre offered the invitation to the Smallwoods. Tom was astounded when his parents promised they would.

With only a few more days left before their return to France, Peg asked her brothers if they could arrange a day off to go for a hike.

"Let's go to Lasham Cragg," suggested Peg.

"Is Rachel invited?" Jonty asked.

Tom froze. Peg looked warily at each of her brothers.

"She's my friend, Peg. I want her to feel welcome at family occasions and it's about time Tom accepted this situation."

Peg looked at Tom for approval. He shrugged his shoulders in resignation.

"I hope there will be no unpleasantness," remarked Peg.

As the Smallwood siblings made their plans, no one could have envisaged the devastating outcome of this family hike.

Chapter 13

Daylight penetrated the attic bedroom through the skylight. Tom blinked and rubbed the sleepy fuzz from his eyes. He groaned, longing to be back in the comfort of his double bed – that would be a reality in a couple of days, when Peg and Pierre returned to France. He made a mental note to sort a decent bed in this attic. For years it had only been used for storage, but in recent times, as the hotel became busier, the old attic had often been utilised as sleeping accommodation – a decent bed was needed, he decided.

Today was Peg and Pierre's final day of holiday – tomorrow they were leaving Malhaven. Tom placed his hands behind his neck and thought back over the last three weeks. It was such a relief to 'talk out' the Rachel situation with his sister and her husband. They each brought a different perspective to the facts. Peg considered it was natural for Tom to want to discover if Rachel was being truthful about her early years in Cornwall. She saw no reason why he should feel guilty for making these enquiries. Pierre agreed, but considered Rachel's outburst showed she had something to hide…something of importance…something she was still running from as her 'second' disappearance would indicate. "You demonstrated she was still able to be 'found', Tom, and that, I am sure, is why she was so angry and upset."

Peg had sought him out one day just before the wedding celebration. "Tom…I've remembered something about Darcy," she said in a low voice.

They went out into the grounds for some privacy.

"Darcy had a yearning to become a performer. Her godmother was a singer and dancer. During that holiday she would pretend to be on the stage dancing and singing, as we were playing in the bedroom."

Tom smiled…he'd witnessed it through a long mirror, but he kept quiet.

"Another thing – but this will be of no help… she has a birthmark at the base of her spine, like two overlapping circles."

Tom burst out laughing. "No, Peg…that piece of evidence will not help, especially now!" Peg's remembrances were useless.

Tom stretched. He was looking forward to their family hike. His parents were coming over to assist at the hotel, if needed. It was kind of them to offer, but Winnie was organised. Only one cloud hung over the day…the possibility of Rachel showing up. She'd been vague about joining them apparently, according to Jonty, saying she would make her own way there and meet them at the top. But if she did show up, he would have to grin and bear it. He prayed there would be no unpleasantness to mar Peg and Pierre's last day.

It was such a rare event for the brothers to take time off together during the summer. Peg's suggestion coincided with the news that the farm and hotel business had turned a profit for the first time since Tom and Jonty took over. That was a cause for a celebration – their hard work and dedication was paying off at long last. So, all round it was going to be a special day doing something the Smallwoods enjoyed…a hike up to Lasham Cragg.

Just before ten o'clock the family assembled in the hallway. Humph was getting excited. "Not today, boy – it's too far for you." Tom tickled the ears of his beloved dog.

"I'll take him for a walk in the grounds, when you've gone," Tom's father suggested.

Peg was sharing out the provisions, so everyone had an equal load in their rucksacks.

"All set?" asked Jonty, striding into the hallway and heading for the front door. Just then the telephone began to ring. Tom answered it and after a pause his expression turned serious. He covered the receiver with his hand and called to Pierre.

"Pierre…It's a call for you from France." Passing the telephone to his brother-in-law, he joined the others to help load the car. Minutes later, Pierre appeared at the door and beckoned for Peg. After listening to her husband, she turned to her brothers.

"Sorry, boys, Pierre must wait for a telephone call from France. It's unfortunate but it's very important. He's unsure how long it will be so perhaps you two can go on ahead and Father…would you take Pierre and I over to Lasham Cragg after his call?"

Jonathan agreed. Tom's face showed disappointment.

"Seems a shame to hang back after we've made all the arrangements," Jonty commented to Tom, who nodded.

"Let's go," agreed Tom. "We'll meet you at the top."

The brothers set off on the hour-long journey over to Lasham Cragg. It was a warm day, but a gentle breeze took the edge off the temperatures. High, passing cloud gave spasmodic shade from the sun…a perfect day for a hike!

Tom and Jonty took the walk steadily – they had plenty of time, they would all meet eventually at the top, beside the thundering gorge of the waterfall. Circumstances had worked in the favour of the two brothers that morning, allowing them to spend bonus time together. After dispensing with current hotel and farm chat, they began to reminisce. 'Do you remember that time when…?' 'Can you recall when we…?' 'I was thinking about…' The rapport between them was good; the tensions of recent months seemed to ease away as they lost themselves in a brotherly harmony. Time evaporated and they stopped twice to take refreshment.

Tom looked at his watch as they neared the top, almost half past noon. Peg and Pierre would be here soon. The path was well worn and familiar to the two young men. Surprisingly, there were not many other hikers around today – it was spectacularly perfect and amazingly quiet, except for some birds. A fluttering breeze provided a refreshing coolness.

Jonty quickened his step. "I'm the winner," he called, laughing – it was a game they'd played as boys…who was the first to reach the viewing point.

"Couldn't have picked a better day – it's stunning," remarked Tom as he walked up behind Jonty, watching and listening to the force of nature, as the water pounded the rocks below.

"What's that old ditty Aunt Dora used to quote when she brought us up here as boys?" asked Jonty.

"There is a place 'twixt heaven and earth, that fills me with such joyful mirth," Tom recited.

"Yes, that's it...gosh it's a long time since I heard that," Jonty answered, turning. His back was to the edge, then looking over Tom's shoulder, his face lit up in surprise. "Aah, good...you came," Jonty began...then...'arrrrrrrrg'... he lost his footing...and fell backwards.

Tom reached out to grab his brother and froze as he clutched at fresh air...

Tom heard a shriek from behind as he dropped to his knees and peered over the edge of the Cragg. Horror struck him as he took in the scene...Jonty was lying spread out, on his back, on a ledge of rock about ten feet below. His eyes were closed, and he was very still.

The howl behind him intensified: "Jonty, Jonty... no...no. Help him, Tom...help him." It was Rachel. Somewhere in the back of Tom's mind, it registered it had been Rachel Jonty had seen over his shoulder, but he was focused on how he could reach his brother. He quickly assessed his options – to scale down the rocks was risky – but he must try.

"Get help, Rachel!" he cried out to the hysterical form behind him, already swinging his long body around to scramble down to reach his injured brother. "We need rope...quick, Rachel...go now," he urged.

"I'm...not...leaving," Rachel spluttered, sobbing, her voice gulping – but less high pitched. Tom's legs were already dangling over the edge as he grasped at grass stumps and imbedded stones.

"GET HELP, RACHEL," he commanded, emphatically. "Ropes, police, ambulance...get help." He desperately felt for a foot hold to steady himself. Three or four more feet should do it. He didn't want to jump down – it might cause a jolt...the ledge might give way. He heard sounds from above. He found one foot hold then another. He heard Peg's voice, calm and reassuring, above the rushing water. "Pierre, grab his hands, I'll grab you...Rachel, go for help."

A strong arm clasped his wrist. "Got you, Tom," said the Frenchman.

Tom let go of the ledge as Pierre, lying on his stomach, took Tom's weight. The extra inches allowed Tom's feet to reach the jagged ledge. Tom recalled his rock-climbing skills, learned as a boy scout, grappling with tiny jutting rocks, as he carefully lowered himself...leaving Pierre's strong grasp. He carefully slithered down onto his knees. Peg and Pierre held their collective breath as Tom turned slowly – he was unsure how secure this ledge would be; he could take no chances. Cautiously, keeping close to the rock fascia, he assessed his position. The ledge was about eight feet long and three feet wide. Dismissing any thoughts for his own safety he lay down on his stomach and slowly propelled his body inch by inch until he was touching his brother's feet.

"Carefully, Tom...that's it...you're there," encouraged Peg from above.

Feeling up Jonty's body...his ankles...his calf...his knee...his thigh – he detected no movement.

"Jonty, it's me. I'm here, help is coming," he reassured the still form. He continued to feel his way up Jonty's long body, inch by inch, pausing then resuming – aware that any second the ledge could collapse under their weight. As he reached Jonty's neck, he gasped…under his brother's head a pool of blood was forming.

He moved his fingers to touch Jonty's face, vaguely aware of the sound of voices up above. His brother's face felt warm…he felt on his neck for a pulse…phew…he was rewarded with a pulsating sensation!

"He's alive," he called out, desperately thinking of his next move, when a stranger's voice spoke.

"We're lowering a rope…can you grasp it and tie it around his armpit," instructed the stranger.

The events of the next few minutes were a blur for Tom – but after several attempts he grasped the dangling ropes and somehow attached them under each of his brother's armpits. Then reaching over he finally secured a rope around his ankles. Tom dreaded to think what further injuries they were inflicting as the strong men on the other end of the ropes hauled the lifeless form of Jonty Smallwood's body up the rock fascia to the viewing point.

Hours later, Tom sat in the waiting room of the emergency department in the Infirmary in Newcastle. He was flanked on either side by his sister and brother-in-law. He was being urged to sip a cup of disgusting sweet tea, to aid his state of shock, as they waited for the hospital consultant to deliver his findings.

A doctor had arrived at the scene of the accident, by the time Tom was pulled back up from the ledge. He vaguely recalled seeing two police officers and hearing Rachel's voice as he stood over Jonty, Peg clutching his arm. The doctor administered first aid, assessing his fractures were multiple but the concern was for the injury to the back of his head, which thankfully had stopped bleeding. The doctor had applied a large bandage to the wound. Slowly, the assembled group had followed the stretcher, as Jonty was carried the two miles to the waiting ambulance. Somewhere along the way his parents, as Jonty's next of kin, had arrived, and along with Rachel the Smallwood family sat in silence, dreading the arrival of the doctor. Time seemed to stand still. Peg attempted to console her mother, who had begun to whimper – fearful of the full-scale wailing that occurred when Hermione passed away all those years ago. The group of six waited…and waited…and waited.

***

Almost twelve hours after the accident, Lilian and Jonathan Smallwood were allowed into a side room to see their oldest son. Wires, tubes and monitors attached to his body bleeped. After five minutes Tom and Rachel entered the room to replace Jonty's parents. Tom looked at the motionless body of his beloved brother. He appeared peaceful. His head was shaved and bandaged. Each arm was encased in plaster. A metal cage had been placed over his legs and covered with a sheet. Each leg was broken in several places. He'd also sustained a spinal injury. Rachel stepped forward and kissed Jonty gently on the cheek.

Tom reached out and touched the motionless hand, peeping out from under the plaster. "We're all here, Jonty… we're praying for you," he whispered, bending forward. "Hang in there and get better, we need you." His voice sounded calm and controlled, belying his true feelings – inside he was quaking, fearing the prognosis.

After a few minutes Tom and Rachel were replaced by Peg and Pierre.

Following the visits, the group were ushered into the doctor's office. A tall man in his sixties greeted the group. "Hello, I am Mr West, an orthopaedic surgeon. Along with my colleagues we have assessed Mr Smallwood's injuries, which I am sorry to say are complex. However, his broken bones will heal. I am confident the spinal injury has caused no nerve damage, but he has received a serious trauma to his head. We have no idea how much internal brain damage has been sustained. It will take time. We will monitor his functions carefully…but I need to warn you, the outlook is grave."

***

'The outlook is grave'. Those words haunted Tom in the ensuing weeks. One month on from the accident there was no change in Jonty's condition. Pierre returned to France by himself, after a few days and Peg followed three weeks later. She was reluctant to leave but Tom persuaded her to rejoin her husband. "Jonty could be like this for months, Peg. You can be here in twenty-four hours. We'll let you know when you are needed."

Since the accident a routine had developed – Tom accompanied his father one day; Peg took her mother the next. Rachel visited on a weekend. Now with Peg returning to France, Tom visited alternate days to his parents. It was a lonely vigil for him, compounded by

Rachel's apparent indifference to him. Surely the severity of the circumstances should have helped her to overcome her antagonism towards him, he reasoned. But Rachel continued to avoid Tom, cutting him dead whenever she met him. Her attitude towards him was hurtful.

They were all missing Jonty. They'd all questioned themselves repeatedly as to what else they could have done to help him. The police were satisfied from their inquiries – it had been an accidental fall. The emotional burden was hard, but the physical burden was also difficult. Both the farm and the hotel needed to function. Tom was so relieved when Bennie Barker at the farm stepped into the managerial role. He was well experienced and more than willing to take over Jonty's duties alongside his own. The farmhand was given more duties and appeared to be shaping up well. Tom suggested another lad be employed to enable Bennie to man the farm office, as needed. Tom knew even if Jonty did recover, it would be a long time before he could resume his duties.

Peg was a tremendous help at the hotel in the days following the accident. She helped take some of the paperwork from Tom, as some days he found it hard to focus. As she prepared to go back to France, she suggested Tom should engage a part-time secretary-cum-bookkeeper. An older spinster lady in the church, who used to work in the post office, was approached and it was agreed that Ada Beck would work three mornings a week to help with the administrative tasks.

Day after day; week after week – the vigil continued. Adrenalin kept Tom going and, somehow, he managed to retain a pleasant manner for the sake of the guests. The summer ended and the autumnal days began. A numbness settled upon Tom; he resigned himself to a changed future. As the days shortened, it seemed impossible to imagine Jonty Smallwood's condition would improve. The word 'disabled' was spoken frequently...but only if he regained consciousness. One by one the plasters were removed, and his limbs were manually exercised. Lilian and Jonathan became hopeful at this sign of progress. Each time he visited, Tom would shave his brother Jonty's face and talk about the daily business of the farm and hotel.

At the end of October Jonty was moved to a rehabilitation ward. "We don't know when...or if Mr Smallwood will regain consciousness," the new doctor on the ward declared. It was a pleasant ward – but it made no difference to Jonty's condition.

One dark, murky morning in mid-November, almost three months after the accident, the telephone rang. Ada Beck answered. "For you, Mr Smallwood – it's the hospital," she informed him.

"Can you bring your parents to the hospital this morning please," the ward sister requested.

Tom froze. There were two likely reasons for a request such as this...but Tom sensed which one it would be.

Lilian, Jonathan and Tom stared in disbelief at the motionless body of Jonathan Smallwood, now relieved of its wires, tubes and monitors. As the sheet was removed from his brother's face his mother's wailing began – he wanted to scream, but instead he reached out and touched Jonty's face...this time it was cold. A short stubble covered his chin – Tom would have shaved him later that day. Jonathan William Smallwood aged 28 years had passed away early that morning without regaining consciousness.

"It was probably for the best," proclaimed the nursing sister with her arm around Lilian. "His brain injuries were possibly severe."

Tom stared blankly at her...how did she know? He'd been praying for a miracle. Where there was life there was always hope. But now life had gone and with it all hope for his beloved brother Jonty.

As soon as the formalities were attended to, and Jonty's personal effects bagged, Tom took his parents home. Then he drove around to the Rossiter residence. He waited in the drawing room as Blanche went to fetch Rachel. She entered the room with an expectant look on her face.

"Tom?" she questioned.

He stood and shook his head. "I'm sorry to inform you, Rachel, but Jonty passed away early this morning without regaining consciousness." Rachel lifted a hand to her mouth to stifle a gasp, then turned and fled the room, banging the door in her wake. Tom gazed after her in bewilderment.

***

Three months after the family outing to Lasham Cragg, Jonty Smallwood was laid to rest in a grave alongside his youngest sister, Hermione. Lilian, his mother, was absent from the group standing around the grave. She had refused to see her youngest daughter's body put in the ground and she refused to see her oldest son join her. "A mother should not have to see her children buried," she insisted.

Tom stood alongside his father, sister, brother-in-law and Rachel. Everyone seemed to accept Rachel's right to stand with the family – although nothing official had been indicated between Rachel and the deceased. She stood next to Peg and as had been her manner for many months…she totally ignored Tom.

"Has Rachel spoken to you yet?" Peg enquired when she arrived the day after Jonty's death. He told Peg about Rachel's reaction to the news. "Pay no attention to her, Tom – she would be in shock."

"It hurts, Peg. We could have supported each other, through our shared grief, but her whole attitude towards me is hostile. I wish she would just move away and leave us to grieve in peace."

Peg walked over to her brother and gave him a hug. "You still care for her…don't you?"

Tom pulled back and wiped a stray tear away from his eye.

"I love her, Peg. No matter how harshly she treats me…I still love her…but it's futile, so it would be better if she moved away and let me get on with my life."

There was a loud rap on the front door. It was the afternoon after the funeral and no guests were in residence, having been asked to change their booking due to the family bereavement. Tom left his office and sauntered down the stairs as Winnie answered the door. It was just after two o'clock.

He was greeted by the presence of the local police sergeant Sid Jones and a young constable. Reaching the bottom of the stairs he looked across at the two police officers and opened his mouth to speak, then stopped as

Sergeant Jones said in a commanding voice:

"Thomas Ezra Smallwood, I am arresting you on suspicion of causing the death of Jonathan William Smallwood."

Chapter 14

Swish, swish, swish, swish. The wipers on the windscreen swept the heavy rain to the side of the glass to cascade in torrents down the metal framework of Tom's Austin 7 motorcar. Peg was driving – a bit too fast for Tom's liking.

"Careful, Peg – watch those puddles…don't brake too fast," he urged.

"Calm down, Tom – I can drive, you know. It was one of the first things Madame insisted I did, when I first went to work for her."

Tom swallowed, resigned to the fact there were many things he was not privy to, since his young sister went to live abroad. Anyway, he wanted to be quiet – conversation was of no interest to him. He needed to reflect and come to terms with the bombshell, which had hit him almost twenty-four hours earlier.

He was tired, very tired. He'd had virtually no sleep, lying on the wooden structure, supposedly a bed, in the police cell in Malhaven. The thin blanket and lumpy pillow given later in the evening did little to ward off the cold chill of the November night. Tom shivered throughout the night hours – whether from fear or cold temperatures he was unsure, but he had welcomed the frequent tin mugs of milky tea the custody officer provided at intervals. Tonight, thank God – he could sleep in his own bed.

Earlier that morning, he'd been transported to the Magistrates Court in Durham. After a brief hearing concerning the charge of manslaughter, to which he had pleaded 'not guilty' – it was decided Thomas Ezra Smallwood could be freed on bail, pending his court appearance at some future date in the New Year.

The whole episode was still a nightmare. Coping with the death of his brother Jonty and the ensuing grief, was ordeal enough, without this 'trumped up' charge of manslaughter to handle. How on earth could he possibly be to blame for Jonty's accident? Although the name of his accuser was anonymous – the allegation could only have been made by one person...Rachel Brooks. She was the only person present and if truth be told she was the one who had distracted Jonty, causing him to lose his footing!

Oh, he felt helpless – he stared unseeing into the driving rain as his sister drove the twelve miles back home. During the long, lonely hours of the night he replayed the events of the accident over...and over...and over again. He did not, as the charge indicated, cause the accident which led to the death of his brother from his injuries three months later.

"Don't fret," the young solicitor, Hugh Porter, was at pains to point out. "This case will be dropped long before it comes to court. From your account of the day of the accident, your accuser would be unable to see, because you were blocking the view." This was encouraging to hear, but standing in the dock at the Magistrate's Court, the blood had drained from Tom's face. It was a terrifying experience to have a charge read out against you, knowing if you were tried and found guilty...a custodial sentence would follow. He shuddered at the prospect.

Peg was the only family member to attend the court. His parents were too distraught – it being two days after the funeral. His friends Zac, Fred and Mabel had travelled north from London to attend Jonty's funeral and returned the morning of the day Tom was arrested, along with Pierre who was travelling back home to France. As yet, none of them knew he'd been arrested yesterday afternoon.

It was so ill timed...why...why...why had Rachel made such a serious allegation? What could she possibly hope to achieve by it? As if reading his mind Peg spoke.

"I think Rachel wants someone to blame."

Tom swallowed and turned to look at his sister. "But why? What good will it do? Nothing can bring Jonty back," he said in despair. "Honestly, Peg...it's farcical...she must be deranged...no...I take that back...she's upset, she's not seeing things logically. Surely when she's calmed down – she'll withdraw the allegation. That's what the solicitor thinks – but until then he suggests we prepare a case."

Peg sighed. "I'll telephone Pierre tonight. I hope he will be able to come over again soon...he'll know the best way forward."

Thankfully, there were no guests in residence at the hotel. Ada Beck had cancelled the remaining bookings stretching into December at Peg's request. The Christmas and New Year house parties, however, were still in place... although Tom couldn't get his head around fulfilling those obligations, but neither did he want to disappoint their regular guests.

Winnie had left a beef stew in the range cooker, so after telephoning his parents to let them know he'd been bailed, he and Peg sat down to eat their meal at the kitchen table. The hotel was strangely quiet. Humph was snuggled up next to the cooker.

"Pleased to see you haven't lost your appetite, To-To," remarked Peg, grinning.

Tom forced a smile. "First food I've eaten since lunchtime yesterday," he replied. "I couldn't face the stuff they offered me in that cell." Suddenly, from nowhere tears gushed from Tom's eyes, chasing down his face. Jonty his big brother...his boyhood protector...Jonty was gone!

"S-o-r-r-y," he stuttered. He dropped his knife and fork, pulled his handkerchief from his trouser pocket and sobbed. Jonty...his boyhood idol...his sparring partner... Jonty was gone!

"No more, Jo-Jo, Peg," he gulped.

Peg stared at her brother, chiding herself for her insensitivity regarding the use of her brother's childhood name. She watched as he wiped his tears and calmed.

"How can I go from being a law-abiding citizen to being a criminal in handcuffs...in the space of an hour?" he asked, pleadingly.

Peg laid her hand on his arm.

"Don't stress yourself, Tom, come on, eat up – you're going to need every ounce of strength you can muster to fight this."

He began eating again. As they finished their food, Tom looked at Peg, his face blotchy.

"I'm so grateful you were still here, Peg...if you'd gone back home with Pierre, I'd have been facing all this with

Mother and Father." Peg had decided to stay on for another week after the funeral to help Tom with office work, but she'd been at her parents' home, when the police arrived to arrest him. Peg thought back to the scenario the previous afternoon. Winnie telephoned to let Jonathan, Lilian and Peg know about the arrest. Peg, accompanied by her father, had immediately gone to the police station but they were denied visiting Tom. It was the kindness of the sergeant, later in the evening, who called to tell them about the court hearing the following morning. Peg insisted on attending and persuaded her father to stay with his distraught wife.

"Now," said Peg rising from the table, "I'm going to telephone Pierre. Are you going to phone Zac and Fred?"

Tom nodded. "Yes, I will when you've finished. It will help to talk about it. Mabel's brother is a barrister… he might be able to help, offer advice…if it comes to a court case. I've met him – I think he'll be good at his job," he commented, then remembering added, "I've got an appointment with the solicitor in the morning."

Peg went through to the hallway.

Two hours after climbing into his bed, Tom was still wide awake. He felt sure weariness and the stress of the situation would have caused him to collapse into a deep sleep, plus the hot bath he'd taken to rid himself of the memories of the cell bed. He tossed and turned, and his head began to ache. The annoying thing was…every time he closed his eyes, he saw Rachel Brooks – her flawless face, grey-blue eyes and bouncy blonde curls. The day he told her about Jonty's death – she'd looked so beautiful. Even in the tragedy of that moment, he'd wanted to reach out, envelop her in his arms and let them share their grief together...but she'd turned, and fled.

"Oh, Rachel, Rachel," he said aloud into the stillness of the night. "What happened to us?" For a few minutes he allowed himself the luxury of memories...the intimate moments they'd shared. Why did it turn so sour? Was he to blame? Could he have fought harder to win her back? Why did he stand back and let Jonty take his place? He'd been so sure she would have returned...eventually, when Jonty grew tired of her. She must dislike him with a passion to make such a false accusation. He sobbed with regret...for what might have been. At some point in the early hours, exhaustion won the day...until loud thudding on his door woke him.

"Tom...are you awake...it's after nine o'clock," called Peg.

He rubbed his eyes and stared at the window...it still looked dark. Remembering his solicitor's appointment, he thanked Peg and hurriedly dressed. As he dashed towards the stairs, he heard voices from the front door. Winnie raised her hand to stop him descending the stairs. He waited, stood back, trying to work out what was happening. A few minutes later, Peg shut the front door with a bang... and sighed loudly.

"Of all the cheek," she declared in outrage. "I've just had my photograph taken by two reporters. They wanted to speak to you...but I told them you were not available, and I added for good measure – 'my brother is totally innocent of this ridiculous allegation. Go away and don't come back'!"

Tom ran his hand across his face, and smirked. "I bet that's in the newspaper tomorrow morning, Peg. It's typical – you're regarded as guilty until you can prove your innocence – not the other way around. We need advice from the solicitor. Come on, or I'll be late for my appointment."

Tom grabbed his coat.

***

Tom listened to the conditions of his bail – a repetition of the words spoken by the magistrate the previous day. He would abide by the rules...what else could he do? However, he needed some legal advice. The young solicitor closed the file on his desk.

"Now, Mr Smallwood...before we turn to the charge and how we will proceed, there is the matter of your brother's will."

Tom looked across as Mr Porter stood and walked over to the adjoining door.

"I'll pass you over to Mr Gregory."

With all the kerfuffle of the arrest, Tom had forgotten about his brother's will. After the funeral the older solicitor had asked him to visit his office at his earliest convenience, but understandably it had slipped his mind.

Mr Gregory was a man in his sixties – someone Tom had known all his life. He was a staunch member of the church. He walked into the room and shook hands with Tom.

"Tom...this is a dreadful business, but I have every confidence in my colleague – he will give you excellent advice. Now, to the matter of your brother's will." Mr Gregory sat behind the desk and opened a file.

Tom watched him, recalling a similar event, in this same room, a few years earlier, when he'd sat with Jonty and Peg and listened to his Aunt Dora's will being read.

The solicitor read out Jonty's will. "As you know you are the only beneficiary in Mr Jonathan William Smallwood's estate."

Tom nodded and listened. It was straightforward. In the event of his death, Jonty's share in the farm and estate, plus any monetary assets, would pass solely to Tom.

Their father had insisted the boys made a will after they inherited Dora's estate. They were young and inexperienced – will-making was for old people – but Jonathan Smallwood knew life was unpredictable...and how right he had been.

"Make a will. As soon as you settle down and marry – you can make new wills," he'd advised his sons. So, they each reluctantly made wills. They owned the farm, hotel and adjoining lands jointly. In the event of one of them dying, the other would inherit their share. There was a small monetary amount left in Jonty's account.

"So, Tom," Mr Gregory concluded, "you are the sole owner of Meckleridge House Hotel and Meckleridge Farm Estate. I'll draw up new deeds of ownership, but it now means you need to make a new will."

Tom coughed and rubbed his brow, then sat twisting his ring. When did life become so complicated? Who would he leave the estate to?

"Yes, I'll need to give that some serious thought," he replied.

After making a future appointment, the older solicitor left the room and Hugh Porter returned. Tom outlined his sister's encounter with the reporters earlier that morning. The solicitor listened attentively.

"I will prepare a statement on your behalf, Mr Smallwood and if they return – which they will – stay away from the door and the telephone. They'll print what they want anyway, but don't give them a chance to twist your words."

Tom felt relieved.

Opening his file, Mr Porter handed Tom a sheet of paper. "The matter of your defence...I have prepared some questions. I want you to take them home and study them carefully. Then, when you are ready, write down your responses. I suggest we meet again in a week. Think long and hard about your answers. Include every detail, no matter how small or trivial they seem." He folded the sheet, placed it in an envelope and handed it to Tom. "Now if you take a seat in the waiting room, I'll prepare that statement for you."

***

A false state of euphoria descended upon Tom, throughout the remainder of that day. After the grimness of the last two weeks – Jonty's death; the funeral; the arrest; the night in the cell; the court appearance and the visit to the solicitors – he suddenly felt a wave of relief. Relief at being allowed home...sleep in his own bed...eat in his own kitchen. Relief in handing his predicament into the hands of a capable young solicitor who seemed determined to cross every 't' and dot every 'i'. Relief in knowing his future finances were secure. He was a wealthy young man with a thriving business and a secure future – if his innocence was proved.

However, Tom's state of euphoria was short lived. Peg walked into the rear lounge after supper. Tom was sitting in front of a cosy fire reading, Humph was snoring at his feet.

"I've been speaking to Pierre," she began. Something in her tone of voice alerted Tom.

"What?" he asked, looking at his sister expectantly.

She sat down. "Pierre has just made a disturbing observation," she announced. Tom looked puzzled. "He pointed out that now you have inherited Jonty's share of the business…a clever prosecution barrister could use that as a motive for you causing Jonty's death."

Tom flung down his book and jumped up, scaring the dog.

"That's preposterous, Peg," he cried out in alarm, grabbing his sister's shoulder. "You know that's not true!"

Peg looked at her outraged brother. "Yes, Tom, I know it…but what about a jury? Twelve strangers, who don't know you. A clever barrister could use that piece of information…to work against you."

Tom sat down again and buried his head in his hands. "Then we will need to hire a better barrister…won't we?" He was incensed. As a result, he spent another restless night, wanting to hurl Rachel Brooks over the edge of the viewpoint at Lasham Cragg. It was so out of character for him to wish harm against another person. He felt vulnerable…so helpless…but he knew he must fight.

The headlines in the local newspaper next morning did little to pacify Tom. He'd risen early, as was his usual pattern, washed, dressed and was making breakfast when Peg entered the kitchen carrying the Northern Echo. She handed it to him.

'LOCAL HOTELIER ARRESTED' stated the headline. Under the headline was a grainy photograph of Peg, standing at the front door looking startled and wide-eyed. The caption read.

The suspect's sister commented,

'My brother is totally innocent of these ridiculous charges'.

Beneath it stated:

'Thomas Ezra Smallwood, hotelier in Malhaven, has been arrested on a charge of manslaughter for causing the accident, which led to the death of his brother Jonathan William Smallwood, at a local beauty spot three months earlier.'

Also printed was the brief statement issued by the solicitor –

'My client has no comment to make about this alleged accusation. A court date is yet to be decided. Meanwhile, Mr Smallwood, an upstanding businessman in the local community, has been released on bail.'

Tom's hands were shaking as he placed the newspaper on the table. "Let's hope they leave us alone now," Tom remarked. "Although Zac indicated the story might attract the national press – so, be aware. Leave the door answering to the staff." Tom walked over to the sink. "You look like a frightened rabbit, caught in the headlamps," he chuckled.

Peg looked at the photograph again. "At least I was up and dressed – imagine if I'd answered the door in my nightgown!" Peg exclaimed. The pair giggled at the thought. "Oh, just listen to us, laughing when things are so serious," spluttered Peg.

Tom walked over and placed an arm around his sister.

"It's good to have a lighter moment, in the midst of all this gloom," he commented.

***

Winnie and Ada formed a formidable team over the next few days, taking charge of answering the front door, back door and telephone. As Zac predicted, the story came to the attention of the national newspapers, but thankfully their curiosity soon waned, without further incident.

Pierre rang each evening. He helped Tom to formulate his answers to the solicitor's questions. By the time Tom returned to keep his appointment with Hugh Porter, every minute and detail of the ordeal – before, during and after – was crystal clear in Tom's mind.

"Good, Mr Smallwood – that's an excellent start. Now, over the next two weeks, I want you to record everything you know about your accuser. I understand you met her less than two years ago, when she came to take up her position as a governess for Dr Rossiter's children. I am also aware you were romantically involved with Miss Brooks for a short time. I want you to include your relationship with her...how close were you? When did your friendship begin? When did you become more than friends? Why did your friendship end? How did you feel when it ended? How did you react when your brother started a friendship with Miss Brooks?" Hugh Porter paused and watched Tom – his face was ashen. Tom was astounded his brief relationship with Rachel was public knowledge...but it was a small town!

"I know this is personal stuff, Mr Smallwood, but believe me, the prosecution will probe and probe, trying to trip you up. You must adjust your thinking to accept the level of detail they will try to uncover."

Tom was bewildered. "I don't understand...why do they need so much detail?" Tom asked, perplexed.

"Look at this from the prosecution perspective, Mr Smallwood...rejected lover seeks revenge against his brother. The prosecution will make the most of that scenario."

Tom gulped. "We were not lovers," Tom whispered.

"That's as maybe, Mr Smallwood, but the prosecution could try to convey that you were. You must be prepared. It's going to be painful but write it down...read it...digest it...write it down again. Give us, your defence team, all the details – then we won't be faced with any surprises. It might not be needed, but to be forewarned is to be forearmed. We have several weeks at our disposal – we must make good use of them."

As Peg drove Tom home that afternoon, his heart was heavy. This was a minefield. How could he possibly withhold the fact that he'd met Rachel Brooks before, when she was a teenager? Or, that he made that visit to Cornwall? On and on his mind went. He didn't know where to start...all he wanted to do was prove his innocence. Why did these personal facts need to be considered? He was confused. He needed help.

Peg walked into the rear lounge after supper. She'd been speaking to Pierre. Tom looked up. His sister should have been back home with her husband by now, but she'd insisted on staying in Malhaven.

"Guess what, Tom, Pierre has arranged ten days' leave, in exchange for agreeing to be on duty over the Christmas and New Year period...he will be arriving here next week," she announced, excitedly.

Tom stood up and hugged her. "Oh, Peg, that's such good news. I trust Pierre's judgement. He sees things from different angles and in different ways. He will help me with the dilemma I have. But this was to be your first Christmas as man and wife...It's not fair on you two," Tom objected.

"It's worth the sacrifice, Tom, if he can help you put together your defence...and prove your innocence."

Chapter 15

Christmas came early to Meckleridge. Peg was determined to show Pierre how a northeast England Christmas felt. Winnie decided they all needed a bit of festive cheer, so, before Pierre arrived the decorations were up; a tree was sourced from the woodland on the farm and the Christmas goodies were prepared well in advance.

"You're giving yourself extra work," Tom protested to Winnie, but he could have saved his breath…Winnie was on a mission. He didn't feel inclined to help, he did not feel festive. However, he tried to brighten up when Pierre arrived. His sister and her husband were hopelessly in love…it filled him with joy and pain to watch them. They were spending precious time together each day. Tom insisted Peg did not do office work, while Pierre was around. Where would he be spending next Christmas, he pondered. No…he refused to dwell on the possibility of a custodial sentence.

He turned his mind to the Christmas house party – the guests were all known to him, but he intended to excuse himself as much as possible, his involvement would be minimal because of the circumstances. He was beginning to feel imprisoned in his own house. His bail terms allowed him to leave the hotel if he wished, but since the court hearing he'd ventured no further than the hotel grounds and over to the farm. Today, however...he was going on a hike. He went in search of Peg.

"Tom, don't be daft. It's cold and damp...you'll freeze," she pointed out.

"Peg...I want to escape, by myself. I want solitude...I'll be fine." Within half an hour he was dressed appropriately and carrying supplies in his rucksack; he was prepared for whatever the weather might throw at him. He drove to a flat area beside the river Meckle, about two miles away, and set off. He did want solitude. Maybe it was a self-protection thing – he'd been aware he was building walls around himself. He'd started to let conversation pass over his head. His mother was the most challenging. She'd taken to visiting the hotel every day. She'd sit and drink the cup of tea he made for her, then without fail, she would begin...singing Jonty's praises over this, that and the other. In essence – she was driving him mad. It was her way of grieving, he assumed. But they were all grieving and they each had their own special memories of Jonty.

Jonty had always been Tom's protector – until they went their separate ways to university. Tom had 'hidden' behind Jonty in his formative years. Although less than a year separated them, Jonty reached all the milestones first and delighted in showing his little brother how to behave. In stature they'd always struck a similar pose – possibly why they were often mistaken for twins. But Jonty was always the independent one, the larger-than-life character – Tom was gentle and more sensitive. Jonty oozed confidence, strength and masculinity. Tom tended to be bashful, yet comfortable in his own skin. He always felt 'second best' when in his brother's company, but they could fight physically and often Tom emerged the victor! He smiled as he recalled Jonty's protectiveness.

They went to boarding school at the same time, but the school bully, a boy called Arthur Digby, picked on Tom until Jonty taught him a lesson and sent him packing. Jonty could always be counted on to see the funny side of things – often turning a serious situation into a light-hearted one with a timely quip. As boys they'd embarked on many adventures – building camps, raiding orchards. Reaching their late teens, girls threatened to force a wedge between them, but they found common ground. Tom's engaging manner could easily charm the girls, so quite often he was the one to make the initial move and set up a romantic encounter for his brother. Tom could 'connect' with the girls, and it amused him when Jonty found this challenging in those early years. He recalled Eugenie Swift – Jonty was sweet on her but failed to organise a meeting with her. Tom did it with ease then graciously slipped into the background – yes, they'd looked out for one another.

He trudged along the riverbank, stopping to admire some birds and take a drink, before continuing his reminiscences. University taught Tom to stand on his own feet and amazingly he coped well. He met and kept his girlfriends, unlike Jonty, and he discovered he could pull himself out of his own scrapes. He sighed...how would he pull himself out of this scrape? Suddenly, a choking sensation of despair engulfed him. He felt his throat tighten, as tears erupted – he coughed and spluttered. Wiping them away he took another drink. Then raising his cup, he toasted his loving brother with gulping words "J -J...on...ty, old boy...th...th...ank you...for...be...ing the best...ever...brother." Slowly his breathing calmed, and his tight throat eased.

He'd experienced a few episodes like this now and was accepting they were part of the grieving process. He'd been crushed with a deep anguish and distress, when he left his brother's lifeless body at the hospital the morning he passed away. The stream of condolence letters he received felt like an insurmountable mountain – but he'd tackled them in batches, eventually managing to reply to them. And now he was facing guilt and fear, brought on by Rachel's bitter betrayal. Even as her name fluttered into his mind, he held no ill will towards her...was he a fool? All these feelings, emotions and actions were going to take time to heal. Would he be forever changed by the loss of his brother? Definitely...he would. But as he realised this, he saw Jonty in his mind...encouraging him...urging him...to prove his innocence. At that moment he knew he would fight this charge and he also knew Jonty would want him to live again.

As Tom returned to the hotel hours later, he was cold and chilled to the bone. His face was red, his eyes were puffy and stinging, but...he knew he'd experienced a decisiveness which emerged from his solitary hike. The hours spent by himself had been therapeutic. He was caught up in a process – mental and physical. He vowed to take each day as it came. He'd handle the new emotions which would undoubtedly surface one by one; he'd push through, striving to prove his innocence and...he'd live his life once again. He refused to curl up in a ball and wallow in self-pity. He was Thomas Ezra Smallwood, who'd lost a loving brother, and this would give him the strength to face whatever lay ahead.

***

Tom attempted to give Peg and Pierre as much space as possible. As he watched their interaction, he longed to share his life with another…a sweetheart and ultimately a spouse. Visions of Rachel flashed through his mind alongside a deep, gnawing feeling which swept over him, knowing their friendship was not meant to happen. One morning about halfway through Pierre's visit, his brother-in-law popped into the office.

"Today, 'mon frère'…we talk about your defence and each day…until I return," Pierre said.

Tom was grateful for his help and showed him the initial responses he'd shared with Hugh Porter. It was the account of the first meeting when Rachel turned up on the doorstep in a snowstorm, their 'summer of romance' and the way it came so abruptly to an end after eight months. Pierre made a few minor adjustments, but agreed it was a satisfying account.

"Now," considered Pierre, stroking his beard, "we must look carefully at your reactions. Go back to your recollections of the day Rachel ended your friendship…tell me how you felt, and I will make the notes."

Somehow, with Pierre's presence Tom was able to articulate his reactions. How he was sure she would realise he had made a mistake, in calling her Darcy – and forgive him. But when that didn't happen, he thought she'd been frightened off by his declaration of love and was hiding behind this 'Darcy' thing.

"Pierre...I was hoping the fact I knew Rachel, as Darcy, would not need to be mentioned to anyone," he stated.

Pierre looked solemn. "I'm not sure that can be achieved, Tom. If the prosecution discovers your visit to Cornwall...then it will be revealed. You need to keep an open mind and your legal representatives must be told, even if they do not use this information, they must be made aware of it."

They moved on to Rachel and Tom's contact over the festive season.

"By then, I was ready to ask Rachel for a second chance. We'd spoken briefly, albeit stiffly on her behalf, at church. I was sure the intervening months would have softened her approach towards me, but I was wrong and when she informed me Jonty had already invited her to the New Year event, I guessed they were friendly."

"How did you feel, Tom?"

"Annoyed...frustrated...hurt," Tom replied.

Pierre looked at him intently. "You must not display this emotion, Tom. The prosecution will goad you and use it to their advantage. You must answer that you were sad and upset...do not use words like...annoyed or frustrated, mon frère."

Tom nodded, understanding the implications.

"Now how did you feel when you discovered your brother and Rachel were more than friends?"

"I was mad...gutted," Tom replied. "We had words, the next day, in the kitchen over a meal. Jonty told me I'd had my chance and blown it. He told me to get over it and accept his friendship with Rachel, because we had to live and work together."

Pierre finished jotting his notes and looked up. "Did anyone hear these 'words' you had with Jonty?"

Tom shook his head. "No...we were alone," he responded.

"Good, no one needs to know about that." Pierre added: "You must put these emotions out of your mind, Tom – otherwise if they are spoken it will lead to an assumption that you had a motive to see Jonty dead."

Tom put his head in his hands...this was going to be hard, very hard.

"So, Tom, the prosecution will ask how you felt when you learned that your brother and Miss Brooks had formed an attachment?"

Tom could see how Pierre was preparing him.

"I was disappointed, but at the same time I was pleased that my brother was finding happiness," he responded, and Pierre nodded encouragingly.

"The prosecution will try to trip you up...asking – were you angry? Did you feel resentful? Did you try to win her back?"

Tom shook his head. "Pierre...the reason Rachel and I split up was because she was being untruthful and wouldn't admit it. That is a fact I cannot divulge – that I knew Rachel Brooks before!"

Pierre looked solemn. "I need to dwell on this, Tom... you might have to make this disclosure – better to come from you than for the prosecution to find out and hit you with it in the courtroom. But that will suffice for today. We will continue tomorrow."

Pierre left Tom in his office.

The gravity of Pierre's words struck an anxious chord with Tom. He could keep this information to himself; Rachel was unlikely to disclose it, having spent many years trying to hide her Cornish upbringing...but would someone else uncover it? He doubted it. It was later that night as he was dozing off to sleep when he remembered something!

The day Rachel arrived at the hotel after learning of Tom and Zac's visit to Cornwall – she was enraged. Jonty was trying to calm her, but she pushed past him and stormed the stairs in search of himself. Her voice was raised; her stance was angry. He recalled her opening words as she stomped up the stairs...'How dare you, Tom Smallwood'. The ensuing conversation had taken place behind a closed door...but walls had ears! Did the young housemaid, Jenny Flynn, who was dusting the picture frames with her feather duster, hear Rachel's accusation? Rachel's voice was loud...very loud. If this titbit came to the attention of the prosecution, then Tom knew his endeavour to keep Cornwall a secret was futile.

The following day he told Pierre about his nocturnal remembrance. This time Peg joined them.

"This confirms what I was about to suggest to you, Tom. You must make this aspect of your association with Rachel known to your solicitor."

Tom shook his head. "I don't think I can," he told his brother-in-law.

Pierre looked thoughtful. "Would your friend Zac be willing to testify? Zac was the one who unearthed the Cornwall connection, so, it would make sense if he was the one to be questioned. This way it might be possible for you to keep your suspicion of Rachel being Darcy to yourself. Zac could say how you queried where Rachel grew up and as he was an investigative reporter, he looked up the census records. It may not be necessary to make the full disclosure about Rachel's birth certificate or Jemima being her aunt and not her mother. By disclosing these facts to your defence team, you will give yourself an advantage... just in case the young maid is questioned."

Tom was quiet, running Pierre's ideas through his mind...it might work – he was sure Zac would be willing to help in whatever way he could.

When Pierre was due to return to France, Tom had worded his statement carefully. Pierre had checked and double checked it. Zac was visiting over Christmas, giving Tom an opportunity to ask for his friend's help. It was a wrench to say farewell to the Frenchman – his assistance had been invaluable.

***

Peg was at Tom's side as the Christmas house party began. Together they faced the guests as they arrived and engaged in conversations surrounding the family tragedy and Tom's predicament. All offered their full support, convinced it was 'a dreadful mistake'. "You're a good man, Tom...a jury will sense it; we're right behind you praying your innocence will be proved," was the consensus. Tom thanked them all and hoped they would understand his lack of involvement during the festive period.

Fred and Mabel came for both Christmas and New Year. This was a bonus for Tom – they normally only travelled north for the New Year holiday. "Mabel's family are going abroad for Christmas," Fred explained a week before Christmas. "Can you squeeze us in so we can stay over both Christmas and New Year?"

Tom was delighted to offer his friends accommodation and it meant Tom was unable to 'hide away' as he'd originally intended. The extended time with them gave him the opportunity to 'sound out' the possibility of Mabel's brother, Oliver, being approached as Tom's defence barrister.

"He already knows about your case, Tom," Mabel confided. "And he offered his services, if your solicitor makes the request through the formal channels."

It was a relief to Tom. He'd liked Olly Bolton when he first met him at Fred and Mabel's wedding.

"He's very experienced. I've seen him in action," she added.

Tom thanked Mabel for the recommendation. The ramifications of British Law were something Tom had rarely thought about until recently, but as the New Year approached, he knew the trial date could not be too far away.

Zac came by the hotel twice over the Christmas season, giving Tom a chance to ask Zac for his support if required.

"I'll do anything to help, Tom...but let me get this clear. If called upon to testify, and I say you asked me to find out about Rachel's background before she came to Malhaven.... won't that appear strange to a jury?"

Tom pursed his lips. "No...remember I asked you to find out about Rachel's background before our friendship ended. I was hopeful things were going to develop between us and when she told me the name of the village...I couldn't find it on a map, so I asked for your help."

Zac looked unconvinced. "Don't get me wrong, Tom. I've given evidence like this before – I'll do whatever it takes to prove your innocence, but...I think approaching it from that angle will be misinterpreted. It will give rise to questions such as...why you didn't trust Rachel when she named her village. Do you see my concern?"

Tom was silent – he could see Zac's angle. But he needed to trust his legal representatives to know how to handle the facts.

A drop in the temperatures heralded in the New Year. It was unbelievable: it was only two years since Rachel Brooks stepped into his life in similar temperatures – it felt more like twenty years. Tom kept several appointments with Hugh Porter during January, giving him all the details Pierre had advised.

"This is sound stuff, Mr Smallwood. Your brother-in-law has prepared you well. I will digest it thoroughly – then we will wait for the trial date, after which I shall approach Mr Bolton. A London-based barrister will cause heads to turn and might encourage national press interest, but it's important you have every confidence in your defence team and if Mr Bolton is willing, then we will proceed with him and hopefully it will work out well for you."

Tom felt he was at a hiatus. He wanted to use his time wisely. So much needed to be done in the hotel by way of planned maintenance but he lacked the impetus to set it in motion. Peg took the opportunity to go to France to be with Pierre for a few weeks, but intended to be back at the beginning of February and was all geared up to make new curtains for some of the rooms.

Every week he met with Bennie Barker, the farm manager who had taken on the mantle with ease. There had been a few staffing issues, but Bennie had proved himself competent in sorting them. Tom increased his wages at this time. Sadly, Bennie's mother had passed away around the same time as Jonty died. Bennie informed Tom afterwards that he was intending to get married in the Spring. Tom smiled at the news. Obviously, old Ma Barker had resisted the idea of being usurped from her position in the farmhouse, hence Bennie's reluctance to name the date with his fiancée. Tom was pleased at the news. He'd known Nancy for years and hoped she would be an asset around the farm.

Tom was struggling with the problem that should he be convicted...what would happen to the management of the business? During Pierre's visit in early December, he had raised this concern with his sister and her husband. Eventually they decided to visit the solicitor, old Mr Gregory. He advised that Peg became a partner in the Meckleridge Estate. Tom had already made his will in favour of his sister, so it seemed the logical thing to do. Peg would only take a share in the annual profits, but the solicitor advised that if she was to work at the hotel, then she needed to draw a regular wage. So far, it had been unspoken, but it was decided if Tom were to serve a prison sentence, then Peg would oversee the hotel management. Tom struggled to see these plans taking shape, but he needed to be realistic.

The week before Peg returned to England, Hugh Porter telephoned. The trial date was set for the last week of March. Oliver Bolton accepted the brief, saying he would visit beforehand to become fully acquainted with the defence case. Tom was relieved the trial was to take place before the hotel opened at Easter.

As time grew closer, Tom found himself rehearsing his statements in all the areas of questioning. Olly Bolton visited twice. He stayed with his fiancée at the hotel, combining a weekend break with an opportunity to interview Tom and lay out his strategy. His trump card was to reveal Rachel as a liar…if the case appeared to be going the prosecution's way. Zac promised to attend the trial regardless of whether he was needed as a witness.

The night before the trial sleep evaded Tom – he was pent up! By the early hours he was weary of tossing and turning, so sat up and put on the lamp. He picked up the book Aunt Dora had given him. He read the words on the inside page, scribed in Dora's beautiful handwriting. The words were so familiar…then he turned to the inside cover at the back.

'Love blossoms in truth,
It puts up with anything; always trusts God.
Looks for the best; keeps going to the end…love never dies.'

He stared at the words…there it was in Dora's script…'love blossoms in truth'. His mind drifted back to the evening in the Rose Garden with Rachel…the yellow rosebud he'd cut and placed in her hair. At that moment he knew he loved her...but his love for her could not blossom...it was like a tight rosebud...it could only blossom if she told him the truth!

As he closed his book, he extinguished the lamp and lay back on the pillows. Closing his eyes, he saw Rachel... beautiful Rachel...he loved her. He knew the truth and he would put up with this accusation; put up with being found guilty; because he trusted God...he would keep going to the end...his love for Rachel Brooks would never die!

Chapter 16

Gilberta House

Rachel Brooks tried to sleep. She'd taken a hot bath, enjoyed a warm milky drink and read a chapter of her new Agatha Christie book. She stretched out, relaxing in the comfort of her bed in Gilberta House. Yet still she was wide awake. Normally these activities encouraged a blissful haze leading to deep, restorative slumbers – but not tonight. Tomorrow morning, she would not attend to her usual governess duties – rising early then waking her charges, the Rossiter twins, overseeing their morning routines, taking breakfast with them, and spending the morning in the schoolroom.

This pattern had shaped her days at Gilberta House for the last two years – days she had found enjoyable. Henry and Blanche Rossiter were more like friends than employers. Although she had not met them before taking up this position, they quickly found they shared many common interests – their conversations were friendly, often lively and she felt totally at ease in their company.

The boys proved to be challenging – each with their own style of learning, but she had adapted and encouraged each boy to achieve good standards in their basic skills. Soon, they would leave the protection of their home and move on to formal education…and she would move to her next position. But before that lay tomorrow.

Tomorrow, she would breakfast alone, then she would travel in her car to Durham. Her destination…a court of law. There she would meet her solicitor, Terence Pembroke. Over the last few weeks under his careful tutorage, she had perfected her prosecution case. It had proved a rewarding experience. From being a young child, she had longed to be an actress – and tomorrow she would star in her leading role!

Scarred by the instability of her childhood circumstances, she had grown up in an environment of lies and half-truths. As she developed through her adolescent years, she'd created a make-believe life. Her 'life' began when she was twelve years old…the day she became Rachel Brooks. Before then…her existence was erased from her mind. Except for one occasion – her twelfth birthday. That day was imprinted on her mind – the last time she saw her real parents.

"Your mother and I are going away," her father told her. He was so handsome – tall, smartly dressed, fine features, neat moustache and always to hand was his brown suitcase with the dirty cream borders. The suitcase appeared frequently and marked the beginning of yet another separation. He was a travelling salesman – it was his job to travel abroad, her mother told her. Often, Philomena, her mother, would accompany him…and then she was left with her aunt.

That day, her twelfth birthday, her father gave her a gift...a beautiful handmade box. It was one of his own designs. Before becoming a travelling salesman, he crafted beautiful wooden boxes. She had admired the box, inlaid with mother of pearl diamond shaped pieces – the carving was intricate. It was crafted from a piece of oak and measured about twelve inches by eight inches by six inches. The sides of the base were about an inch in thickness. It was large enough to hold a pair of her tiny shoes.

"A place to keep your precious things, my darling girl," her father said, cupping her face in his hand and gazing adoringly into her blue grey eyes added, "I love you, Darcy." The moment was poignant. Then he said, "And look...here is a secret drawer." Her eyes had widened – a secret drawer! She remembered with fascination how he had demonstrated the release process. It required pressure on two points simultaneously, before it would release. The space inside was long and thin. "Roll up any papers you wish to keep and slide them in there – they will be safe," he'd explained. Then after hugging and kissing her, her parents picked up their suitcases...and walked out of her life – although she failed to grasp the significance of their departure that day.

It was a few weeks later when she realised they were not returning. She'd spent a short time with her godmother, who lived in the west end of London; an interesting week with her godmother's brother in Wales and when she returned to London she went back to school. She loved school and enjoyed spending time with her friends. But one morning she was woken up early and told to dress. They took an early morning train, travelling to the southwest.

"We're going on an adventure," her aunt exclaimed, as they packed lots of suitcases with their belongings. "We are going to pretend to be a family. I will be your mama and your grandfather will be your papa." Rachel recalled how she had giggled...what fun...a game...a real-life game. "You will be our daughter, and your name will be Rachel Brooks." Her eyes had lit up as she repeated her new name several times.

"A new name," she declared. "How exciting!"

Still, sleep refused to come. Rachel got out of bed and put more coal on the fire. It was almost midnight – she should be asleep, but her mind was too active. She went downstairs to the kitchen and made herself a cup of tea. Returning to her room, the fire was burning brightly, and she sat, sipping her tea in its warming glow. After finishing her drink, she walked over to her drawers and pulled out her special box from its storage place underneath her nightgowns. She sat down and opened it.

It contained memories of her life...a long strand of blonde hair which she pulled out and watched as it bounced back into a curl. She'd tried to cut her hair one day...unsuccessfully. Her aunt caught her before she did much damage...but she kept the lock of hair as a reminder.

Photographs...a few – their cottage in Cornwall. She recalled the day they arrived. The name of the village was St. Eram...but in her make-believe world, she'd reversed the letters and called it Marets...she smiled. Life was a game, back then.

A photograph of her pretend 'parents'...her Aunt Jemima and her grandfather...Dr and Mrs Brooks. The folk in the village accepted it – why wouldn't they? She'd taken the photograph using her grandfather's camera, a prized possession. She looked at her mama's stern face. "Remember, Rachel…trust no one. You were born in London, then moved to Cornwall – never, never speak of your life before moving to Cornwall…we are your parents now."

She'd obeyed.

She glanced at various photographs of children she'd tutored over the years. She been fortunate – since leaving Cornwall behind, she'd always held a 'position' as a governess.

In the bottom of the box was a programme for a variety show in London. It was dated 1910. She opened it up to the third page and ran her finger down the listing until she found her godmother's name…Darcy Soames. Her one and only visit to a theatre to see her godmother perform… she'd been eight years old. It was magical. She dreamed that she too would become a performer – one day.

A shiny pebble, a pretty shell; a pen – a gift from her grandfather; a cheap necklace – a gift from her aunt – all reminders of a tangible life. But she'd grown up learning to be vague. She feared rejection and didn't trust people to keep their promises. She was suspicious of anyone with religious beliefs. Her 'parents' attended church and she'd accompanied them to keep them happy, but she regarded praying as a waste of time. She'd prayed fervently in those early days in Cornwall for her real parents to return – but that prayer remained unanswered. She'd turned her back on God, only attending church in her working life out of respect for her employers.

All these reminders...she was a 'surface' person; a person with no depth; always on the edge; antsy; always wanting to blame someone when things went wrong. Her mama's best friend Annie was a stiff, upper lip character – they became friends when Annie worked as a matron in a hospital in London. Annie was regarded as a tyrant in their village, but she'd admired Annie's no-nonsense approach to life and modelled herself on her. When she'd excelled in her Highers at school, it was Annie who advised her to step out into the world and she sourced her first position as a governess to a family in Bristol. Once she left home... there was no turning back. Annie Thomas was the only person who knew a forwarding address as she moved on. There were boxes of belongings stored with Annie from her 'parents'' home...but they were of no interest to her. She possessed all her treasures in this box...just two things remained.

She found the pressure points and released the secret drawer. Rolled up inside was a document. She unrolled it...her stolen identity. I wonder what my cousin would have been like – she mused, if she'd lived. Replacing the document, she lifted out the final item.

At the base of the box, were two sheets of heavy card. Sandwiched between the card lay a pressed flower...a yellow rosebud. She held its fragile stem and brought the tiny flower to her nose. A distant hint of fragrance filled her nostrils. She gasped...Tom! Fear clutched her stomach.

Rachel admired her reflection in the vanity mirror the following morning. Thankfully her nocturnal activities had not taken their toll on her flawless complexion or dulled her bright mind. She was ready and satisfied with her smart appearance. Presentation was key to the impression she would make. She'd selected a light grey two-piece suit, teamed with a high-necked white silk blouse and a dark grey cloche hat. Her accessories were black – small-heeled shoes, black handbag and black leather gloves. The shoes added height to her petite, trim figure. Her curls were loose but carefully held in place by her hat. She stood tall and erect as she left Gilberta House.

***

Durham

As she drove to Durham, the leading lady rehearsed her script. "On that tragic day last summer, I travelled to Lasham Cragg to meet my friend and his family at the viewing point. When I arrived, I saw Tom Smallwood push his brother Jonty over the edge. The deceased...my dear, dear Jonty never regained consciousness and his broken body eventually gave out three months later." She patted her pocket to check if her lace edged, white handkerchief was ready to use at the appropriate moment.

That was to be her statement...the basic facts. However, when she'd arrived at the viewing point that day...she'd panicked. Before her stood two handsome men – one facing her, the other with his back to her. Both men had showed her affection – she'd befriended and formed an attachment with each of them – but only one of them had found a pathway to her heart and Rachel's heart was a place she guarded fiercely!

For three months she'd travelled regularly to sit at Jonty's bedside, often transporting his distressed father. Occasionally, she'd meet Tom Smallwood on these visits, and when she did – she treated him with the contempt he deserved. Tom Smallwood had dared...yes dared, to unearth her background and in retaliation for what she perceived to be an insult, she had 'cut him off'. He'd become a non-person in her eyes. She'd ostracised him; snubbed him; spurned him; rebuffed him...why? The answer to that was simple – he deserved it...for daring to call her...Darcy!

Even now the use of that name brought a tsunami of hurt and abandonment, threatening to engulf her. Tom Smallwood had brought it all back that day at the riverside. He'd said those words...'I love you, Darcy'. They'd been the key – unlocking the buried memories she'd tried so hard to eradicate. Her retaliation was to avoid him, ignore him and reject him. So, when the charismatic, light-hearted, amusing Jonty charmed her...well...it was the perfect way to humiliate Tom. She'd fallen into the older brother's arms and enjoyed his advances and flirtations. It was an easy-going relationship, and they'd had fun...only for it to end so tragically, on that beautiful summer's day.

The news of Jonty's passing was devastating...so once more she lashed out, at the only person she could punish... Tom. The betrayal idea started small, but then it took on a life of its own. It grew...and grew...and grew. In her mind it became a conflict which spread like ripples in a pond, until the day after the funeral it reached its culmination. She walked into the police station in Malhaven.

"I want to report a crime," she'd told the duty sergeant, "I saw Tom Smallwood push his brother Jonty over Lasham Cragg edge."

The police officer had stared at her in amazement but was obliged to take her statement.

Rachel parked her car and looked down at her hands... they were trembling, visibly. What had she done? She knew it was retribution – but she'd always needed someone to blame when things went wrong in her life. She'd blamed her mama, Jemima Brooks, when her parents didn't return – but she'd stayed peaceful for the sake of her dear grandfather, never fully seeing her aunt's reaction...but there was no love lost between them.

And now...she was pouring out her vengeance on Tom Smallwood.

***

Tom looked around the courtroom. It was strange, but in all his imaginings since he was charged, he'd always thought he would be a crumbling wreck as he sat in the dock. Yet here he was feeling unusually calm. Probably living in a fool's paradise, he mused. His eyes scanned the public gallery – it was packed, but he only recognised Zac, Peg and Pierre. Zac was in conversation with another man, no doubt a journalist, Tom surmised. In fact, many of the spectators could be journalists, hoping for words to fill tomorrow's newspapers. Oliver Bolton sat at a desk alongside Hugh Porter, the solicitor.

Suddenly, his eyes were drawn to the door, as the legal team for the prosecution entered the courtroom, followed by Rachel Brooks. Tom swallowed. She looked elegant and poised, dressed to perfection – he'd not seen her since Jonty's funeral, four months ago. He focused on her face...the face he saw regularly in his dreams...the face of the woman he loved. Oh, Rachel...Rachel – how have we arrived here in this court of law? The only crime I've committed was to fall in love with you – he yearned to reach out and touch her.

Tom was physically present in that courtroom in Durham, but he felt absent...as if he were viewing the proceedings from afar. He stood along with everyone else, as the judge was announced. Then the jury was sworn in. He heard the prosecution barrister, Randolph Tate, make his opening statement – outlining the events of that summer's day at Lasham Cragg. He was an elderly gentleman, but eloquent. He described how Miss Brooks was invited on the outing but was delayed, so arranged to meet the rest of the party at the viewing point. On arrival she was greeted with the sight of the two brothers – Jonathan Smallwood standing with his back to the edge and his brother, Thomas, facing him. Jonathan noticed her and spoke, then she watched, shocked and stunned as Thomas Smallwood pushed Jonathan and he fell backwards. She ran to the edge to join Thomas but saw Jonathan lying still and silent on his back, on a ledge about ten feet below. Miss Brooks was so traumatised by the event; she did not summon the courage to speak out about it, until after Jonathan Smallwood's funeral. The prosecution barrister paused and addressed the jury.

"I shall endeavour to prove that Jonathan Smallwood's fall that day was an attempt by Thomas Smallwood to cause his brother's death, in order to reconcile himself to Miss Rachel Brooks by rekindling their former friendship."

A loud gasp reverberated around the courtroom.

Oliver Bolton waited until he had the courtroom's full attention, then he stood. He struck quite a contrast to the elderly prosecution barrister. His tall, erect, commanding stature caused all eyes to watch as he strolled across to stand in front of the jury – he was in no hurry.

"On a gorgeous summer's day last August, five individuals set out to meet up at the viewing point of Lasham Cragg, a renowned beauty spot. It was organised as a farewell outing for Monsieur and Madame Thibault, who as newlyweds were to return to their home in France the following day. Madame Thibault was the youngest member of the Smallwood family." Already Oliver Bolton's easy manner held the audience in his grasp. "However, circumstances dictated that Monsieur Thibault and his wife needed to wait for an important telephone call from France, causing their arrival to be delayed. Miss Brooks was also delayed, promising to meet the group later. So, the two brothers took the hike to the top by themselves." Again, he paused, walked towards Tom then turned, and walked back towards the jury. "After admiring the view, Jonathan Smallwood turned to face his brother, who was standing behind him. A movement from behind Tom distracted Jonathan…he looked over his brother's shoulder, began to speak, then lost his footing and toppled backwards, landing on a ledge some feet below. Thomas Smallwood, having reached out unsuccessfully to grab hold of his brother, looked over the edge to see the motionless body of Jonathan, lying with closed eyes. Within seconds

Miss Brooks appeared at his side. Thomas urged her to seek help while he attempted to scramble down to aid his brother. At no point did Thomas Smallwood push his brother – the pair were devoted to one another." He waited, then continued, "I shall endeavour to prove that what happened at Lasham Cragg on 27th August last year was a tragic...tragic...accident." A silence ensued during which Oliver Bolton returned to his seat and Tom hung his head in disbelief at the charge laid against him.

Slowly, he lifted his head and looked at the twelve men of the jury – total strangers...who possessed the power to alter the course of his life. The severity of it hit him. He knew from his conversations with Pierre that the prosecution could push for a murder charge, but Pierre thought it was unlikely and expected it would be manslaughter. Tom shook visibly and adjusted his seating position. The prosecution barrister called for his first character witness.

Blanche Rossiter took the stand. She sang Rachel's praises. "She is totally trustworthy and honest – a woman of her word. We have been delighted to hand the education and daily oversight of our two boys into Miss Brooks' care. We have no problems with her whatsoever." She then explained how she came to be employed. She was recommended by a friend of her husband, Dr Rossiter. This friend was also a doctor. Two further character witnesses followed – both former employers, one from Darlington and one from Newcastle. They both added to the glowing words concerning Rachel's character. All agreed Rachel Brooks was an excellent governess, never once giving any cause for them to doubt her word. Oliver Bolton declined the offer to cross examine these character witnesses. The court was adjourned for lunch.

Tom watched as Rachel walked to the stand and took the oath. Gently, her barrister asked what motive Thomas Smallwood would have to cause his brother harm. Her voice was quiet...so quiet the judge asked her to speak louder. She stiffened, paused then declared, "Tom resented his brother because Jonathan and I were in a romantic relationship."

The barrister paused then asked, "Why did Thomas Smallwood resent your relationship with his brother Jonathan, Miss Brooks?"

Rachel looked over at Tom...their eyes met. Then speaking with a superior air, she answered, "Tom Smallwood and I were friendly beforehand but when he wanted to deepen our relationship...I wasn't ready for that next step...so I terminated our association. He was obviously upset, but it was some time before Jonathan and I became friendly."

Rachel's barrister rubbed his chin. "So, Miss Brooks, Thomas Smallwood was jealous of your friendship with his brother. He was angry because you thwarted his romantic advances."

A loud voice boomed across the courtroom. "Objection, Your Honour – the witness did not use the words 'jealous' or 'angry'," Oliver Bolton exclaimed, rising to his feet.

The judge looked over his spectacles.

"Sustained," replied the judge, then addressed the jury. "Miss Brooks referred to Mr Smallwood's reaction as being resentful and upset...not otherwise. I wish to speak to learned counsel in my chambers. So, we shall adjourn the proceedings for today and reconvene at 10am in the morning."

Tom looked at his watch – it was only half past three.

***

Having eaten little of the tasty food Winnie had prepared for their meal, Tom sat in the rear lounge with Peg and Pierre. Before they left Durham, Oliver told Tom he was feeling upbeat, referring to the judge's reprimand. "Go home and relax, Tom – remember the saying 'you get your day in court'. Tomorrow the jury will see what a different person Tom Smallwood is…unlike the one portrayed today." His words were encouraging.

"I understand Mr Bolton visited Lasham Cragg," Pierre commented as they sipped their tea.

Tom nodded. "Yes, he visited me on two occasions and on the second visit he asked to see the scene of the accident. He took a tape measure and recorded measurements."

Pierre looked pleased. "I'm impressed with the man. Not many barristers would do that. You say he got you to 'act out' the order of events?"

Peg responded. "I think Oliver Bolton knows his stuff. I have every confidence in him – let's see what transpires tomorrow."

Sheer mental exhaustion caused Tom to sleep soundly – but he woke early, before daylight. As usual his mind drifted to Rachel. A different image – the way she looked in the courtroom the day before. He recalled the way she said, "Tom wanted to deepen our relationship, but I wasn't ready for that next step, so I terminated our association."

The words were cutting, slicing through the ripples of his heart. He hadn't expected to be ridiculed in such a public fashion. He began to question himself...back to those heady days when they'd held hands, cuddled, embraced and kissed...was she ever a sweetheart? Was he a gullible fool from the beginning? Was he too trusting? Hearing her words in the courtroom had a traumatic influence on him...he wanted to recoil like a snail into its shell. How could he ever trust his own judgement again?

He lay in the stillness of the morning and tried to make excuses for her – she's overwrought; the occasion has caused her to say things she doesn't really mean. But after all his deliberations he came back to one question... why was she doing this to him?

Today could be his turn in the dock. He would be facing whatever questions Randolph Tate threw at him. Before he climbed out of bed he sat up, put on the lamp and reached for Aunt Dora's little book. It was amazing how each time he read these words, one phrase would jump out at him.

'Love is not easily angered. It keeps no record of wrongs,' he read. Tom took comfort in the judge's closing remarks the previous day, saying he wasn't an angry man – he must hang on to that. "You're weak," Jonty often remarked when he failed to provoke Tom...but it wasn't weakness. It was not in Tom's nature to retaliate.

He continued to read:

'Love always hopes; always perseveres.' Why? He looked at the words, pondering. Because...love never stops loving. That was his understanding of those words...and that realisation would help him to face what lay ahead, during the remainder of the trial!

Chapter 17

"I call Miss Rachel Brooks," Randolph Tate requested. Tom was surprised Rachel's barrister was recalling her to the dock – but he was inexperienced in the workings of a court of law. She was faced with a barrage of questions…

When did your friendship with Jonathan Smallwood begin? How did Thomas Smallwood react to this association? Were the three of you in the same company at any time? Did Tom Smallwood display any signs of resentment?

Rachel was composed and steely faced as she responded to this line of questioning.

"Jonty and I became friendly a short while after I terminated my friendship with his brother. I visited Meckleridge House Hotel, their home, over the Christmas period and both brothers were present. Tom and I remained…courteous but distant. It was during this time that Tom became aware of my friendship with Jonty, but he seemed resigned to the way things had worked out."

Tom listened and watched, thinking back to the way Rachel had snubbed him and refused to engage in any kind of comment, let alone conversation. She was doing a good job of making it seem as if he'd been the one to alienate her.

Randolph Tate viewed the jury, assessing their response to Rachel's answers. Then he turned back towards her.

"How would you describe your relationship with Jonathan Smallwood, Miss Brooks?"

Rachel dropped her eyes and fidgeted with her hands, then in a whisper replied, "It was a romantic relationship."

Randolph Tate looked at her encouragingly.

"Can you speak a little louder please, Miss Brooks."

Rachel was obviously embarrassed. Tom's heart went out to her...this was cruel...for each of them. She coughed.

"It was a romantic relationship," she repeated, using a louder voice.

The barrister smiled, inclined his head towards her, and arched his brows. "Were you in love with Jonathan Smallwood, Miss Brooks?" he asked, smiling.

Rachel's face flushed as the judge interjected. "I think Miss Brooks has given her answer, Mr Tate."

The elderly barrister tapped his fingers on the front of the dock shelf beside Rachel and smiled sweetly at her.

"Then I will move on to an incident which took place in March last year...three months after your friendship with Jonathan Smallwood began. "You arrived at Meckleridge House Hotel in a state of agitation. You were upset and distressed. You needed to speak to Thomas Smallwood... not Jonathan...can you explain please, Miss Brooks?"

Tom's stomach clenched – he glanced over at Oliver Bolton...the prosecution must know about his visit to Cornwall. Rachel hesitated.

"Miss Brooks?" the barrister asked.

Her face was like stone as she responded.

"Tom Smallwood had done something to hurt me, and I wanted to know the reasoning behind it."

The barrister observed the jury. "And what was the nature of 'this something to hurt you', Miss Brooks?"

Again, Rachel paused before answering.

"He invaded my privacy, visiting Cornwall and making enquiries about my family."

The jury seemed to find this interesting, as twelve pairs of eyes stared at her.

"Ahh...so." The barrister paused for effect. "The acquiescent Thomas Smallwood–" he turned and looked at Tom. "The quiet Thomas Smallwood...who seemed resigned to the way things had worked out...or so we are led to believe – in fact he did not accept the termination of your friendship, quite so calmly." Mr Tate walked over to the jury. "Did he, Miss Brooks?"

Rachel looked pale. "No," she whispered.

Randolph Tate opened his arms in front of the jury. "Let me remind you, members of the jury. Six months have passed since Miss Brooks ended her friendship with Tom Smallwood...I repeat, six months – and what does he do? He goes off to Cornwall, where Miss Brooks grew up, to make enquiries about her family...a man with a grudge, I would say!" he smirked. "Is that true, Miss Brooks...Tom Smallwood was still carrying a grudge after six months?"

Rachel looked flustered. "I wouldn't say it was a grudge...it was more like curiosity. I told him I was offended, he apologised, and we agreed to let it drop. We met several times after that but didn't acknowledge one another."

The barrister turned. "That will be all, Miss Brooks," he said with a flourish, returning to his seat.

The judge addressed Oliver Bolton. "Do you wish to cross examine Miss Brooks, Mr Bolton?"

Oliver jumped to his feet. "I do, Your Honour," he responded eagerly. Adjusting his wig, Oliver walked across to the dock and smiled broadly at Rachel. Resting his thumbs in the top of his gown he turned to Rachel and asked politely, "Miss Brooks…I hope you don't mind this personal question," he began.

Rachel looked at him warily.

"Do you wear spectacles?"

Rachel looked perplexed. "Er…no…I don't," she replied.

Oliver smiled sweetly at her.

"Do you have any problems with your long vision – I understand you drive a motor car?"

Rachel straightened her back. "No, there is nothing wrong with my vision," she remarked sternly.

Oliver Bolton looked at the judge. "Your Honour, with your permission I would like to conduct a little experiment."

The judge eyed the young barrister. "Let me hear what it entails," he said, somewhat wearily.

The two barristers approached the judge's bench. After giving an explanation in hushed tones, Oliver Bolton signalled for two clerks to bring in a blackboard, easel, some chalk and an eraser.

"Now, Miss Brooks, would you stand over here, please." He directed Rachel where to stand. The board was angled for the judge and jury to see clearly. "Two weeks ago, I visited the beautiful Lasham Cragg and took some measurements." He then indicated on the board Rachel's position. "From the point at which Miss Brooks arrived here" – he marked it with an x – "to the point where the two brothers were standing was about ten feet." He drew two stick men. "Mr Porter and Mr Hicks – please will you assist me?" He spoke to the solicitor and the court clerk and used a tape measure to mark out ten feet. "These two gentlemen are a similar height to Thomas and Jonathan Smallwood." Hugh Porter and the clerk stood where Oliver indicated.

"Now, gentlemen of the jury, I wish to conduct a little experiment to demonstrate what Miss Brooks thought she saw, when she arrived at the viewing point. For the purpose of the demonstration Mr Porter will be Thomas Smallwood and Mr Hicks will be Jonathan Smallwood."

Most of the jury nodded.

"Action 1, gentlemen," Oliver said.

There was some movement between the two men.

"Miss Brooks, did Mr Porter push or grab Mr Hicks?"

"Er...push," she replied.

Oliver nodded and turned back to the two men.

"Action 2, gentlemen." Again there was a movement between Hugh Porter and the clerk. "Same question, Miss Brooks," he asked, smiling.

"Grab," Rachel answered confidently.

"Bear with me please, everyone...action 3, gentlemen." For the third time there was a movement between the two demonstrators. Arching a brow, Oliver asked, "Miss Brooks...push or grab?"

Rachel looked exasperated. "Push," she replied emphatically.

Oliver Bolton stared blankly at Rachel, then spoke. "Thank you, Miss Brooks...you may be seated. Gentlemen, thank you for your assistance."

Rachel returned to her seat, as did Mr Porter and Mr Hicks. Oliver Bolton walked over to his desk and turned.

"Miss Brooks...actions 1,2, and 3 were all 'grab' actions." He looked at Hugh Porter and Mr Hicks who both affirmed the type of action. "So, members of the jury, I have demonstrated that from a distance of ten feet with two men of similar height, facing each other...it was not clear for Miss Brooks to see if Thomas Smallwood pushed or reached out to grab his falling brother." He stared at the jury to make his point, then walked over to stand in front of Rachel.

"Now, Miss Brooks, the afternoon you arrived at the hotel last March you were, to quote your learned counsel... 'upset and distressed'...is that correct?"

"Yes," she replied, and Oliver nodded.

"Can you tell the jury why you wanted your background to remain private?"

Rachel appeared uncomfortable and took a sip of water.

"Think carefully, Miss Brooks...remember you are still under oath."

Rachel stared at her solicitor, then spoke. "My family life is private. I did not wish for anyone to ask questions about my life in Cornwall," she answered.

Oliver glanced around the room. "Please tell the court how you found out about Mr Smallwood's visit to Cornwall, Miss Brooks?"

Rachel swallowed. "A friend told me."

"Can you tell the court the name of this friend and where she resides?"

"She is called Annie Thomas and lives in St. Eram, near Truro in Cornwall."

"Is that the same village where you used to live?" Oliver asked.

"Yes," she affirmed.

Oliver Bolton walked over to the blackboard and picked up the chalk and eraser. Wiping it clean, he then wrote in capital letters, large enough for the jury to read... ST. ERAM and MARETS. "When you were friendly with Thomas Smallwood, you told him you lived in a village in Cornwall called MARETS. He tried to locate this village on a map – but was unsuccessful...because it doesn't exist!" Olly pointed to the other word. "It's a reversal of the letters...isn't it, Miss Brooks?"

Rachel flushed and shrugged her shoulders. "It was a game I played with my mama as a child. It came to my remembrance when Tom asked where I used to live in Cornwall."

Oliver Bolton smirked.

"Did you enjoy playing games as a child, Miss Brooks?"

"Of course...all children do," she replied, looking more composed. Oliver strode across the courtroom away from Rachel, then turned.

"Childish games are not conducive to adult relationships...are they? Is it any wonder that Mr Smallwood was curious to find this place near Truro and went there on a walking holiday with his friend? Quite understandable, I think...he had no ulterior motive. So, I want to ask, Miss Brooks...why were you upset and distressed about this visit...did you have something to hide?"

Rachel sat erect. "No," she replied indignantly.

Oliver Bolton walked over to his desk to consult his notes. "What was your relationship to Jemima and Henry Brooks?" he asked, spinning around to face her. "May I remind you...you are still under oath, Miss Brooks."

The jury became more attentive.

"They were my mama and papa," Rachel answered.

"Yes, Miss Brooks...that's what you called them.... but what was the physical relationship between you?"

Rachel was resigned as she answered. "Jemima was my aunt and Henry was my grandfather."

The jury gasped.

"Another childhood game, Miss Brooks?" Oliver asked.

Rachel bent her head, nodding.

"Now, members of the jury...what do we deduce from this? Eh? I suggest, Miss Brooks, you manipulate the facts when it suits your purpose. It's not a crime to call your aunt, Mama or your grandfather, Papa, or indeed to reverse the letters of the village where you grew up. But...given your propensity to manipulate facts and bearing in mind the demonstration carried out earlier...I ask you, members of the jury, to weigh up carefully the charge against Mr Thomas Smallwood. Did Miss Brooks see Thomas Smallwood push his brother?" Oliver stood and viewed the jury. "I have no further questions for this witness at this point, Your Honour."

Oliver Bolton returned to his seat.

The judge addressed Mr Tate. "Mr Tate, any further questions?"

Randolph Tate stood. "Yes, Your Honour." He addressed Rachel.

"Miss Brooks...why did you call your aunt and grandfather – Mama and Papa?"

Rachel's moment of glory had arrived. She pulled out her lace edged handkerchief and dabbed both of her eyes. Tom's heart lurched in affection for her.

Stumbling over her words, she spluttered, "My parents... my birth parents...abandoned me...as a young teenager... my aunt and grandfather took care of me. We moved to Cornwall." Rachel began to sob, her shoulders heaving...in essence it was the truth. All eyes in the courtroom watched her distress. Moments passed and she dried her eyes. Once she was composed, her barrister moved.

Randolph Tate faced the jury. "A family sadness which is obviously still painful for Miss Brooks...and the reason she wanted her family background to remain private." The barrister directed his comment to the jury. "This disclosure has no relevance to the charge against Thomas Smallwood." Then speaking to Rachel added, "Thank you for your honesty, Miss Brooks. No further questions, Your Honour," he stated and sat down.

The judge adjourned the court for lunch.

Tom was numb. One minute he thought the jury was on his side – the next minute, they seemed to be with Rachel; her clever dramatics appeared to have won them over. Her tearful 'disclosure' had won her a strike... for honesty!

During the lunch recess Oliver told Tom the character witnesses on his behalf would come next – so he doubted if he would be called today.

The afternoon session began with Tom's character witnesses – Winnie Jenkins, Roy Pitt, the bank manager, and Bennie Barker, the farm manager. All affirmed how calm, trustworthy and reliable Tom Smallwood had been in their dealings with them. Each testified to the devotion of the two brothers.

Peg was called to give her account of arriving at the scene of the accident. She described how she heard a woman shrieking as she rounded the corner to the viewing point, then saw her brother Tom and Miss Brooks peering over the edge. Her brother Tom was urging Miss Brooks to seek help as he turned onto his stomach and swung his legs over the edge, giving no heed to his own safety. She completed her statement describing how her husband, who was behind her, fell to the ground at the edge to grab hold of Tom's arms, while she held onto her husband to provide ballast. She urged Miss Brooks to seek help – which she did. Randolph Tate did not cross examine Peg Thibault.

Pierre took the stand next. He reiterated what his wife had seen and added how unselfish Tom's actions had been. "He put himself in grave danger – landing on the ledge was precarious – it could have given way at any moment," the Frenchman commented. His statement was straightforward and again the prosecution barrister did not cross examine. The court was adjourned until the following morning.

***

Tom experienced another restless night. Visions of Rachel standing in the dock wearing another two-piece suit, this time in navy, with a matching cloche hat and sky-blue blouse, tormented him. He guessed her outfits were specially made for her court appearances. She struck an elegant pose as she dabbed her eyes with her pristine white handkerchief, with its lace edges – a distressed damsel personified. Tom could recall the details perfectly.

Her words 'after my parents abandoned me' played on his mind. If he felt an outpouring of sympathy for her... then surely the jury would think likewise. She'd succeeded in portraying herself as a poor rejected child, taken in by her close relatives – so what if they played name changing games to cheer the youngster? Thankfully, no mention had been made of Rachel's former name...so far. That piece of information would open an intriguing can of worms, which the press would jump upon. Hopefully, it would not happen. Oliver Bolton had dismissed Rachel's performance as 'mere amateur dramatics' – all geared to win over the jury, into believing what she said she witnessed was true. But it did little to quell the fierce knot of foreboding in Tom's stomach, as he snatched erratic bouts of sleep.

With a sombre heart and a pale stone face, Tom Smallwood took the stand and swore the oath, the following morning. Oliver Bolton sensed his anxiety and attempted to put him at his ease asking him to describe his relationship with his brother. Tom referred to a happy childhood with a loving, protective older brother – mentioning they were often mistaken for twins. Moving on to their adult life, he told how they socialised together. Oliver then asked about the circumstances which brought about their taking over the hotel and farm, on the death of their aunt. Again, the jury were presented with two loyal brothers, giving up their chosen career paths to fulfil the wishes of their beloved aunt.

Oliver then asked about the subject of female companions – did their friendships give rise to arguments? Tom relayed occasions when they'd admired the same girl, but they developed a 'code of understanding' to step aside if a particular preference was shown.

"So, Mr Smallwood, when your friendship with Miss Brooks began – did Jonathan indicate that he also found her attractive?" Oliver asked.

"Jonty was away on holiday when Rachel and I met – he made no attempt to intrude on our friendship," Tom replied.

Oliver paused then continued. "Tell the court about your friendship with Miss Brooks, Mr Smallwood."

Tom was prepared for this question. "We became friends shortly after Miss Brooks arrived in Malhaven, just over two years ago," Tom began, briefly mentioning how she had arrived at his door after experiencing difficulties with her car in a snowstorm and had been accommodated in the hotel until the storm stopped the next day. "We enjoyed each other's company and met a few times for a walk and a couple of dinner engagements. Over the Easter period Miss Brooks helped at the hotel with some guest activities, and it was shortly afterwards that our friendship became romantic. By the summer my feelings for Rachel Brooks had deepened – I mistakenly thought it was mutual and when I expressed how I felt, she informed me she did not reciprocate this and suggested we ended our relationship at that point."

"When was this, Mr Smallwood?" Oliver enquired.

"The end of summer 1925," Tom answered.

Oliver tugged at his wig. "How did you react?"

Tom braced himself – both Oliver and Pierre had schooled him how to answer, but it was still embarrassing to have your feelings made so public. "I was saddened by her response, but hoped she would reflect further on it."

The young barrister stared at Tom.

"Did you retaliate in any way, Mr Smallwood?"

Tom shook his head. "No…I respected her decision – hoping she would reconsider. But her attitude towards me became cool and distant."

Oliver walked over to his desk, checked his notes and walked back. "How did you feel when your brother 'stepped into your shoes', so to speak, a few months later?"

Again, Tom was prepared. "Understandably I was sad and disappointed, but I did not do or say anything to make my brother and Miss Brooks feel awkward."

Olly smiled. "Now, Mr Smallwood…what about the event in March last year at the hotel, when Miss Brooks arrived upset and agitated over your visit to Cornwall. May I ask why you chose Cornwall?"

Tom glanced up at the gallery and his eyes rested on Zac.

"My friend and I enjoy walking. I had not visited Cornwall before, so my friend suggested visiting the county, particularly the area surrounding Truro, as I recalled Miss Brooks telling me about the village where she used to live – I suppose I was curious to see where she came from. When Miss Brooks found out about my visit, she saw it as an invasion of her privacy. So, I apologised for causing any offence…and she accepted my apology."

Tom braced himself for further questioning, but none came. He took a drink of water.

Oliver Bolton then asked Tom to give his account of the day of the accident at Lasham Cragg. Again, it was well rehearsed. He gave his account. It was painful when Olly asked Tom if there had been any tension between the brothers as they travelled to the beauty spot. "None whatsoever – it was good to be together away from our work environment." Then he was asked to clarify the expression on his brother's face as he turned from admiring the view. Tom was choked at this point.

"Take your time, Mr Smallwood, I understand this is poignant as it was the last time your brother spoke."

Tom swallowed and paused, then replied, "Jonty's expression was...surprised...but pleased. He said 'Oh, good, you came'." Tom's voice was crackling as he spoke these words, the significance of the moment hitting him afresh. He bowed his head trying hard to blink back tears. Oliver Bolton waited until Tom was composed.

"At that point, Mr Smallwood, did you realise who your brother was addressing?"

Tom shook his head. "No...it all happened so quickly... it could have been my sister and her husband. Then... then...Jonty just vanished...I reached out to grab him... but he'd gone." It was Tom's turn for dramatic effect – but this time it was genuine...he was visibly shaking as he relived those agonising moments. He lifted his head and gazed imploringly at the jury. "I loved my brother... dearly...I did not push him."

"Take a few minutes, Mr Smallwood," Oliver Bolton suggested.

Tom sighed, rubbed his brow and stared at the ceiling. After a pause the young barrister continued his questioning, asking Tom about the days after the accident – did he have any conversation with Miss Brooks?

"We met at the hospital on several occasions, but there was no conversation between us," Tom stated.

Oliver then asked, "Did Miss Brooks at any time, refer to having seen you push your brother…think carefully, Mr Smallwood?"

Tom shook his head. "Never, in my hearing," he said.

Oliver stared at Tom then walked over to the jury and repeated what Tom had just spoken.

"And after the accident – how would you describe Miss Brooks' attitude towards you?"

Again, Tom was prepared for this question.

"It was…as if I didn't exist," Tom replied.

"Tell the court about Miss Brooks' reaction when you went to tell her about your brother's subsequent death," Oliver requested.

Tom ran his finger around the inside edge of his shirt collar. "Miss Brooks was in the schoolroom when I arrived. She entered the drawing room at Gilberta House, her place of residence. She appeared surprised to see me and said 'Tom?'. I shook my head and told her Jonty had passed away that morning. She gasped, turned and fled the room, slamming the door behind her."

Oliver nodded and walked across the floor towards the jury.

"So, to summarise…from the ending of your friendship with Miss Brooks, she remained 'distant' and 'cool' towards you, except for the day she enquired about your visit to Cornwall, and from that incident she proceeded to treat you as if you did not exist…is that a fair assumption, Mr Smallwood?"

Tom replied, "Yes."

"No more questions, Your Honour," said Oliver Bolton and sat down.

The prosecution barrister eagerly accepted the invitation to cross-examine Tom.

Tom was weary and exhausted – he glanced at the courtroom clock…was it only one hour since he'd taken to the stand? It felt like a lifetime. The prosecution barrister wasted no time jumping into a vital question.

"Mr Smallwood, we have listened at length to how devoted you were to your brother. But the jury need to know a significant fact…with your brother's demise…who inherits your brother's share of the Meckleridge Estate?"

Tom was stunned. The jury held their collective breath.

"I do," Tom replied.

"In total?" Randolph Tate asked.

Tom nodded. "Yes."

The elderly barrister walked over to the jury. "My, my…you did fall on your feet that day, Mr Smallwood, didn't you?"

Oliver Bolton leapt out of his seat as if he'd been shot. "Objection, Your Honour. My learned friend's comment is most insensitive!"

The judge looked over his spectacles and announced, "Sustained."

Randolph Tate smirked – his intention was achieved. He walked back towards Tom.

"Mr Smallwood…your walking holiday in Cornwall – we've heard your explanation, but I want to ask…did you choose that location to 'dig up some dirt' on Miss Brooks, in retaliation for being made to feel like a 'jilted lover'?"

The jury gasped, but Tom remained calm.

"Miss Brooks and I were not lovers. No promises were made between us, so I could not be 'jilted', and I had no intention of 'digging up any dirt'. I was merely taking a holiday in an area of the country, which I had not visited previously."

Chapter 18

Tom stepped into the Rose Garden at Meckleridge House Hotel. Although it was only the end of March, there was a sense of Spring in the air and a pleasant warmth to the lowering sunlight. The court had adjourned early. Having established no further witnesses were to be called, the judge instructed the two barristers to prepare their 'closing arguments' and be ready to deliver them at 10 am the next day.

To Tom it seemed an endless stretch of dragging the procedure out but had to accept the ramifications of the legal system. Thankfully, it had not been necessary for Zac to be called as a witness. At least the early finish had afforded Tom some time to relax and take a walk around the hotel grounds in daylight, when he arrived back home. It could be his last opportunity for some time – if he was found guilty. He stood and admired the tidy beds of roses, still tightly budded. His mind drifted back to the day he and Rachel stood in this garden and shared their first gentle kiss – the moment he realised just how much she meant to him.

He rubbed the back of his hand across his brow. Since that day, almost two years ago, so much had transpired... so much had been lost...but one thing remained – his love for Rachel Brooks. He rotated his signet ring on his finger. Seeing her again this week in the courtroom setting, had only served to underline the strength of his feelings towards her...he knew he loved her...deeply. Her beauty was breathtaking. But he was a fool...an absolute fool...she cared nothing for him and only wanted to discredit him.

A tear trickled down his face and he wiped it away. He sighed – there was little point in thinking what might have been. Tomorrow – or the next day – he would learn his fate...guilty or not guilty. He refused to countenance the probability of a guilty verdict – his barrister was confident the jury would find him innocent of the charge. The tight knot in the base of his stomach was a permanent feature now.

He walked around the garden enjoying the sight of nature preparing itself for its burst into life...he loved Spring...its anticipation and potential. Would he see this Rose Garden blossom forth into life, this year...or the next...or the next – as the warming sun teased open the tight buds to enable the unfurling of each rosebud? Or would the summer days see him confined to some stone walled...no...'stop it, Tom' he shouted out aloud. But he was naïve to ignore the possibility.

Peg had been so supportive saying she would work something out, if he faced a custodial sentence – but he had dismissed her doubts. He should have been more proactive and made tentative arrangements...just in case. "Let's not face things that might not happen...let's remain positive," he'd commented, to which she'd replied, "Yes, let's stay positive, To-To!" But tomorrow he would leave the hotel with a bag in his hand...just in case. He straightened his back, took one last look, and left the Rose Garden.

Chapter 18

***

The occupants of the courtroom sat down after the Honourable Justice Herbert Smythe made his entrance. "Now, gentlemen are you ready to deliver your closing arguments?" He looked at the two barristers. Both men affirmed they were, and Randolph Tate stepped forward.

"Gentlemen of the jury, we have listened to the testimony of this young governess, Rachel Brooks. She was shocked and upset, as she arrived at the viewing point of Lasham Cragg that day and witnessed a dreadful scene. Picture her state of mind for a moment please. A smart, attractive young woman, who had won the affection of both these handsome young men, during her short time at Malhaven. She is a bright, alert, well-educated young lady who has been highly praised by her present and former employers. She is faced with a horrendous sight...the man she cares for being pushed by the man she used to care for – oh dear...oh, dear what a dreadful sight to behold. She runs forward...the volume of her voice is raised and alarmed because of the shocking circumstances – she is not hysterical, nor was she shrieking – as has been suggested. She quickly assesses the situation and on the arrival of Monsieur and Madame Thibault she leaves the scene and flees to seek assistance." He paused. "Gentlemen, why would Miss Brooks make a mistake...she saw what she saw." Again, Randolph Tate paused. "Now, my exuberant, learned friend, who deemed it necessary to take the time to view the layout at Lasham Cragg," he intimated, looking condescendingly at Oliver Bolton as he spoke. "He has demonstrated how in his opinion Miss

Brooks was mistaken in what she saw. Gentlemen, I think Miss Brooks possessed, like many members of the fairer sex...a sixth sense! She knew what she saw...just knew it. But oh, what a dilemma she faced...how could she tell anyone what she had witnessed...not at that point...or indeed during the long, agonising months when Jonathan Smallwood lay on a hospital bed. She kept her counsel out of respect and concern for the Smallwood family and indeed for Jonathan Smallwood himself, should he make a miraculous recovery." Randoph Tate paused yet again and walked over to stand in front of the jury.

"Tragically, as we know, Jonathan Smallwood did not make a recovery, but died from his injuries last November without regaining consciousness. He was laid to rest, and at that juncture, this brave young woman, out of civil duty, came forward to make her concerns known." He turned and walked away from the jury. "You see, gentlemen of the jury; Rachel Brooks knew the accused quite well. On their own admission we know Mr Smallwood and Miss Brooks had engaged in a romantic friendship – no doubt secrets were shared as the two sweethearts romanced." He turned and smiled. "Ah...young love," he commented, waiting for effect, then pulling himself to order continued.

"Rachel Brooks had seen the other side of the quiet, respectful, likeable Tom Smallwood...she'd seen the brother who wanted it all for himself...lock, stock and barrel...or farm, hotel and fair maiden! And that," he stopped his voice raised, his papers held high, "that...I suggest is the reason why Rachel Brooks terminated her friendship with Thomas Smallwood. She didn't trust his scheming – look no further than this walking holiday in

Cornwall...I ask you, was it with mere curiosity that he visited the very village where Miss Brooks grew up? No, gentlemen of the jury, you must ask yourselves if he was bent on raking up some hidden family secrets – like the schemer Rachel Brooks now knew him to be...he'd proved it by his own actions."

He hesitated briefly.

"We can excuse Miss Brooks' outburst of anger at discovering his nosiness. Tom Smallwood stood to gain a great deal – a substantial inheritance – and then he could swoop in and comfort the grieving damsel." Randolph Tate turned towards Rachel Brooks. "This selfless young woman saw through this schemer and allowed herself to be subjected to the scrutiny of this public court. So, I ask you to consider carefully just what kind of man Tom Smallwood really is...remember the old saying...'still waters run deep' – don't be deceived by how he appeared to others. I urge you, like Rachel Brooks did, to see this man in his true colours and put him where he belongs... behind bars! I rest my case, Your Honour." Randolph Tate turned, swept across the court room and took his seat.

Tom was in a state of shock – how could he be the person Randolph Tate had just described? He had never given any thought to inheriting all the Meckleridge estate – even after Jonty's death and visiting the solicitor...it was all hypothetical in his mind. He twisted his thumbs backwards and forwards in agitation. Then circling his signet ring, watched as Oliver Bolton stepped forward.

"Gentlemen of the jury," the young barrister declared, using a commanding voice. "Here we have an intelligent, well-educated young man." He opened an outstretched arm towards Tom. "Tom Smallwood has been described as gentle...kind...caring...upright...hard working... fair...blessed with a friendly manner and trustworthy. I could have called many more witnesses to the stand, who would repeat these platitudes, but I kept it to a minimum because...Tom Smallwood is genuine – you get what you see. He is confident, relaxed and until recently, he was happy and secure in his occupation as a hotelier. And then Rachel Brooks arrived in Malhaven. Within a short time, the pair became friendly, and it was no surprise when a romantic liaison began. The reason behind the breakup of this romantic liaison is not a question for this court." Oliver Bolton walked over to stand in front of the jury.

"Things happen...people change their minds...but my learned friend has suggested that Tom Smallwood embarked on a trail of revenge after their breakup. Pardon?" He paused. "Revenge and Tom Smallwood do not fit together. Tom Smallwood's character does not allow him to be revengeful – it's alien to him. Neither is he, as my learned friend suggests...greedy, wanting the Meckleridge Estate for himself!" Oliver walked back across the floor allowing his words to be absorbed.

"Tom Smallwood accepted the breakup – feeling as any man would – sad and disappointed. But at no point does he display any malice towards Miss Brooks, not even when his older brother swoops in to win her heart. No evidence exists of the brothers arguing over Miss Brooks – they remained as they had always been... devoted brothers. I urge you to consider carefully...why would Tom Smallwood wish to harm his beloved brother? The pair continued to work amicably together." He waited.

"Now, picture if you can, Rachel Brooks arriving at the scene of the accident. Understandably she emits a noise...a shriek...a cry of anguish...a call of alarm? It was a distraught young woman witnessing an accident and momentarily she was stunned by the spectacle she beheld...as her handsome beau falls backwards." Oliver Bolton rubbed his chin, then scratched the top of his wig. "She pulls herself together and goes to seek help after Madame and Monsieur Thibault arrive." Oliver Bolton paused. "But why did Miss Brooks take so long to report her misgivings?" He looked at the jury.

"Was Miss Brooks the one who wanted...retaliation? On her own admission, we know she grew up in an environment of 'make believe' – calling her aunt and grandfather, Mama and Papa. Abandoned as a young teenager by her parents, she learned to be devious – playing around with the letters of the village name, leaving her home and moving from place to place as her work demanded, only one person privy to her whereabouts. And now, the young man with whom she may have imagined spending her future...lies unconscious on a hospital bed and the prognosis is grave. Does she feel 'abandoned' again?" Mr Bolton pursed his lips and paced the floor for a few minutes.

"Did Rachel Brooks want to blame someone for yet another disappointment in her young life? There was no way Miss Brooks could see what action took place between the brothers that day...push or grab...the demonstration showed that. I put it to you, gentlemen of the jury...Miss Brooks wanted to blame someone for causing Jonathan's accident...and that 'someone' just happened to be

Tom Smallwood!" As Oliver Bolton spoke, he stared questioningly at the jury.

"I contend what Rachel Brooks observed that day at Lasham Cragg...was a tragic, tragic accident and Tom Smallwood has no charge to answer! I rest my case, Your Honour," he declared, taking his seat.

Tom's brain refused to focus...was that it? Were the closing arguments over? To Tom they seemed brief and succinct. He snapped to attention as the judge spoke.

"Gentlemen of the jury, we have heard the arguments from both learned counsels. You have heard two accounts about what might have happened that day. Your task is to decide...which one is true? Please bear in mind this was not a planned attempt to end Jonathan Smallwood's life – at best it was opportunistic – and if you deem him guilty, it would be a charge of manslaughter." The judge took a drink of water then continued.

"Did Tom Smallwood see the opportunity to rid himself of his older brother, allowing him to inherit his brother's share of the Meckleridge Estate and perhaps win the hand of his former girlfriend as a bonus? Or...could Miss Brooks have been wrong – mistaking Tom Smallwood's actions? Was it a push...or a pull? Did she want to blame him for the death of her boyfriend? Remember, you must decide... without any reasonable doubt, if what Miss Brooks says she witnessed did in fact occur? Was Jonathan Smallwood's accident and subsequent death an opportunistic attempt by his brother to cause his death...or was it a tragic accident? You are dismissed, gentlemen of the jury, to consider your verdict."

The occupants of the courtroom stood. The judge made his departure, followed by the jury.

Oliver Bolton approached Tom. "Chin up, Tom, I'm confident we made a good case. You've done well. Now the waiting begins. I suspect it won't be too long, then I can get back to my lodgings, collect my bag and be on my way south." Olly placed his hand on Tom's shoulder as he stepped down from the dock.

Tom shook Oliver Bolton's hand. "Thank you, Olly... whatever the verdict...you did your best."

Oliver smiled then walked over to his desk. Tom glanced over to where Rachel had been sitting...but she had vanished, along with her legal team.

Tom barely ate a morsel as he joined Peg, Pierre, Zac, Olly and Hugh Porter for an early lunch. His family, friend, barrister and solicitor all seemed to be in good spirits...but Tom just listened, as if he was miles away. His parents appeared after lunch. Peg had telephoned to let them know the jury had been dismissed to consider their verdict. Lilian was tearful and hugged her son tightly.

"We know you're innocent, Tom...let's pray justice will be done today." Tom's father was choked up and could only offer his son a tight two-handed handshake. The next two hours seemed unending. Then the court usher summoned them to return. Tom felt faint...this was it – the verdict!

"All rise," announced the court clerk. After the judge took his seat, he asked the foreman of the jury if they had reached a unanimous verdict. All eyes homed in on him.

"Yes, Your Honour, we have," came the reply. The middle-aged jury foreman stood tall and proud, enjoying his moment of importance. He looked at the judge, coughed, then declared, "We find the defendant Thomas Ezra Smallwood..." The courtroom stared with bated breath..."NOT GUILTY of the charge." The gallery erupted with joy.

"You are free to go, Mr Smallwood. Court dismissed," the judge announced.

Simultaneously, Rachel and Tom put their heads in their hands...but only Tom shed tears.

***

Peg, Pierre, Zac and Tom were sitting in the conservatory each with a newspaper in their hands. Zac had arrived a while earlier with copies of the national papers. Their regular newspaper was delivered by flat capped Timothy, son of the local newsagent. At breakfast the family had pored over the local papers' account of the trial verdict. The Northern Echo featured a front page, grainy photograph of Tom, surrounded by his family outside the court – he had no recollection of it being taken. 'LOCAL HOTELIER FOUND NOT GUILTY' – the headline declared. It was all a little macabre for Tom's fancy and having read the local account, he had little appetite to read more. But the others were picking over the finer details in each of the reports.

Tom wanted to escape...run away...far away... anywhere. But the first guests of the new season were due to arrive in two days' time and although everything was sorted, thanks to Winnie and Peg, Tom felt obliged to be around, now he was a free man.

"Just listen to this one," retorted Peg and began reading an account by a journalist, who obviously favoured Rachel.

"Probably fell for Rachel's good looks and hopes he's in with a chance," chuckled Zac, glancing over Peg's shoulder to see the reporter's name. "I know the guy – that's the sort of trick he'd try to pull."

The group laughed about it…except Tom. Peg noticed.

"Come on, Tom – snap out of it – remember Mother's holding a celebration dinner tonight…so try to be cheerful!"

Tom gave an empty smile; it was the best he could muster. His mother loved an excuse for a celebration so, he must try to be enthusiastic…after all he could have been spending his first day in jail today.

The celebration dinner had a dual purpose – Tom's 'not guilty' verdict and a farewell meal for Peg and Pierre. The next day, before any guests arrived, Tom would drive his sister and brother-in-law to the station in Durham. Peg had spent so much time in England since her wedding, she'd almost forgotten her little apartment in Lyon. Over dinner that evening she made it clear that they did not intend to visit England for the foreseeable future. She was looking forward to becoming a homemaker, getting to know her neighbours and familiarise herself with her locality. It would be a contrasting experience for Peg. In all her years in France, she'd lived an itinerant lifestyle and settling in one place for an extended time would be a challenge, but she owed it to her husband.

Earlier that day she had met with Ada Beck, the lady who worked as a part time secretary. Ada had been so helpful. But now Tom's case was over…it was time for changes. Unknown to Tom, Peg and Ada had interviewed a lady who came with excellent credentials from her previous employers. Peg's objective had been to seek out and secure someone to replace her role...whatever the outcome of the trial – she needed to return to France.

The office work for the hotel and farm needed more than one person to oversee. Peg knew her brother would be living in a fool's paradise, expecting to step back into his former role, and decided as a partner in the business, to find her replacement, before she left England. Deborah Hogarth was the ideal choice.

Tom was summoned to the office after the newspaper assessment. Peg and Ada laid out their proposition. In one respect it was an opportune time, considering Tom's state of mind – given a longer time he might have been harder to convince.

"She's ideal, Tom," Peg was saying, "Ada will work extra hours to train her, and she needs to give notice to her present employer." Tom looked through the paperwork listing Miss Hogarth's skills – she appeared well qualified for the role. "It will give you freedom from the office, Tom – you've been accustomed to spending a considerable amount of time behind that desk. You'll need to spend more time over at the farm. Bennie will welcome the help, now he has a little one on the way." Tom smiled, remembering the forthcoming event for his farm manager and his new wife. Peg was so organised and far seeing... where would he be without her?

He wished Peg and Pierre could move to England – but that was never going to happen.

"Do we have your agreement to hire the services of Deborah Hogarth?" Peg asked and Tom nodded. He wanted to be enthusiastic…but he was 'spent' – physically and mentally. "Right, I shall telephone her immediately," responded Peg. "Ada, will you prepare the job offer and I'll post it today?" she commented.

"Where will this lady live?" Tom asked.

"That's for Miss Hogarth to decide, Mr Smallwood," remarked Ada. "I understand her family live in London and she is working in Durham at present. How would you feel about offering her accommodation here in the hotel?"

Tom shrugged his shoulders and looked at his sister, as if she were the fountain of all knowledge.

Peg responded. "There is accommodation here…if she wants it, but she may prefer to keep her work life and private life separate. There are plenty of rooms to rent locally. Good gracious, we are jumping ahead of ourselves – she hasn't accepted the position yet," exclaimed Peg.

As the family and their friends sat around Lilian and Jonathan's table enjoying her fine cooking, Peg announced Deborah Hogarth had accepted the role of hotel secretary. She would tender her resignation to her present employer, when she received the written offer and expected to be able to take up her position after working a month's notice. Everyone agreed it was a good solution.

Tom drove Peg, Pierre and Zac to the train station the following morning. Zac promised to visit during the summer, as he was travelling overseas on his return "I've still got some enquiries to make regarding Rachel Brooks," he commented to Tom as the two friends hugged. "Now the case is over I can poke around freely."

Tom shook his head. "No, Zac…let it rest. There's no point pursuing it," he replied – but he knew his friend.

Pierre shook his brother-in-law's hand firmly. "A good result, mon frère," he remarked.

Peg pulled her brother into a tight hug. "Best foot forward, To-To. It's all over now," she said, staring intently into Tom's face.

"No, Peg...It's not over. I love her with all my heart, and I must win her back," he announced.

"Tom...are you crazy?" Peg asked in disbelief.

Chapter 19

Four weeks later

Tom took a day off. The season at the hotel was well under way. The Easter house party was a huge success. Many returning guests had enjoyed his hospitality, delighting in the news their young host had 'cleared his name'. He'd de-camped to the stable block and it looked likely he would be remaining there for some time as the bookings filled up. Tom suspected his recent notoriety had caused some new business, but he was delighted to accommodate new guests. He felt he was getting back into the 'swing' of things, and it was such a relief to know he was a 'free man'.

Yet, Tom had failed to factor in how much grieving he still needed to work through. From the time of his arrest until the moment the jury foreman said 'not guilty', he felt the grieving process was in suspense, but this post-trial period was proving to be a time of intense sorrow.

His solo hike took him up onto the moors beyond Malsett. He was kitted in hiking boots and waterproofs and faced the bracing breeze as he surveyed the bleak moorland. His only companions were sheep, which suited him just fine. Everyone around him – staff, family and friends agreed he was coping well...but Tom knew otherwise. 'Chin up' was a phrase he'd learned to hate. His heart was breaking...he felt in despair...he was a walking robot. The void created by his brother's death and Rachel's stinging betrayal caused him mental pain every day.

Yes, he functioned...but that was all. Without Peg's constant encouraging presence he felt bereft. He was in danger of becoming a recluse, if that was possible when you shared your home with twenty guests and several staff. He pushed people away when they tried to make conversation; avoided personal telephone calls; shelved personal letters to a 'needs a reply' pile; made excuses to not attend social events. Work was his excuse, and it was a legitimate one.

He strode out enjoying the invigorating call to his languid muscles. He must get back to a weekly hike – nothing helped his mental and physical wellbeing like hiking...it had always been that way. He found himself telling Jonty about the day-to-day trivia of the hotel – it was stupid, he knew that, but the sheep didn't seem to mind. Arriving back at the hotel, in time to freshen up and host the evening dinner guests, he felt the tight band around his head had eased, but the gnawing sensation in his stomach remained.

A loud knock on his bedroom door the following morning startled him.

"Mr Smallwood...are you awake...you have a visitor," Winnie called through the door.

He looked at the clock. Goodness, he thought, I've overslept – it was just after eight o'clock...he was normally up and about by six-thirty.

"Coming, Winnie, I'll be down shortly," he called and jumped out of bed. A visitor, he pondered...at eight o'clock in the morning – most unusual. Twenty minutes later he strode through the back door, kitchen and rear lounge into the hallway. Winnie gesticulated towards the conservatory which ran along the front of the house. She was using stage whispers, which Tom failed to understand. "Who? Why?" he attempted to ask but gave up and entered the conservatory.

Sunlight shone through the windows, highlighting the shiny hair of the tall red-head who stood to greet him. He walked across the black and white tiled floor and took in her appearance. She was slim built and attired smartly; her hair was tied back in a bun. "Good morning," he greeted the stranger, reaching out to shake her hand. "Er...you have me at a disadvantage," he uttered smiling, noting her firm handshake and brown eyes.

"Pleased to meet you, Mr Smallwood – I'm Deborah Hogarth," the visitor stated. "I apologise for arriving so early and without an appointment."

"Aah...Miss Hogarth," Tom stuttered, buying himself time to recollect. Then it dawned on him. "Oh, gosh... you're the new secretary – is that correct?"

The young woman smiled. "Yes, I am, sorry about the misunderstanding. I hope I haven't overstepped the mark by turning up so early."

All Peg and Ada's careful planning with regards to Deborah Hogarth's initiation into the hotel routines had been put on hold when she'd telephoned a few days after Peg had returned to France. The expected one month's notice had been rejected by her present employer and she was unable to give a starting date. Tom had told Ada to write back assuring her the position would be available whenever she was free. Tom was in no rush; he was beginning to think the appointment was unnecessary; so, in a nutshell, he had completely forgotten about Deborah Hogarth.

But here she was – not at all as he'd imagined. He'd pictured her as a lady in her mid-fifties – why, he had no idea, but looking at Deborah Hogarth he doubted if she had celebrated her thirtieth birthday.

"Miss Hogarth – delighted to make your acquaintance. Can we start again…I mean, no I wasn't expecting you and no, it's not too early…and oh, would you like some breakfast – I'm starving," he declared.

They both laughed and the formality seemed to evaporate as she followed Tom through to the rear lounge.

Within a short time, the ice, if any existed, had melted away as Tom and his new secretary were soon sharing their experiences of hotel life.

***

The arrival of Deborah Hogarth at the end of April marked a turning point for Tom. She was able to communicate with him in a quite unexpected way. Perhaps it was borne out of the fact that she was a fresh face, who had known nothing of Jonty or Rachel or the trial, although Tom suspected Ada and Winnie had given her the 'low down' on the recent events. She quickly became part of the fixtures and fittings and was highly efficient. Her arrival on that Saturday morning was as a result of having worked her month's notice, but her employer was reluctant to lose her services and was dilatory in finding her replacement. Deborah guessed this was deliberate and decided to leave as she had fulfilled her obligations.

Soon, Deborah's no-nonsense, 'jolly hockey sticks' persona was encouraging Tom. She possessed a dry sense of humour accompanied by a deep throaty laugh. Winnie shook her head in amazement at the notable difference in Tom's demeanour. She exchanged knowing looks with Ada Beck, when a month after Deborah's arrival, the pair could be heard laughing out loud at one of her pert comments. Deborah Hogarth was just the tonic the depressed Tom Smallwood needed.

***

Less than a mile away in Gilberta House, Rachel Brooks left the twins to settle down to sleep. She retreated to the sanctuary of her bedroom – a delightfully spacious room, with a southwesterly aspect. The evening was pleasant, the sun just dropping behind the trees casting a warm, golden glow over the large garden. Of all the places she'd lived and worked...this was by far the best. She sat down in the comfortable winged chair which she'd positioned beside the window so she could admire the rolling hills in the distance. She loved northeast England and hoped she could remain in this area.

She sat back, kicked off her shoes, wriggled her toes and sighed. That morning her employer, Henry Rossiter, had called her to his office, before her morning duties began. She'd been expecting this summons.

"Rachel, I thought it best to mention this sooner rather than later," he'd begun. The smartly dressed country doctor took a seat behind his desk. "You are aware that Blanche and I always intended to send the boys to boarding school and applied for them to attend Troughton Hall. Yesterday we received confirmation that a place for each boy is available from mid-September." He had paused and looked at the young governess who had surprisingly managed to 'tame' his two unruly sons. Rachel Brooks had been exemplary in her duties…the only unpleasantness had been this court case with his friend Tom Smallwood. It proved challenging, being torn between loyalty to his friend and loyalty to his employee. Eventually, he'd decided to write to Tom saying Blanche would give a statement concerning Rachel's character and work ethic, and they were not making a judgement either way.

Henry Rossiter continued, "So, Rachel, we will not be requiring your services after that time, but you are welcome to stay with us until you secure further employment. My wife and I regard you as a friend and want to thank you for the way you have worked with the boys. As a token of our appreciation, we are willing to make enquiries around the area to see if anyone needs a governess – with your permission, of course."

Rachel had smiled. "Thank you for the information, Dr Rossiter – I've been expecting this, it's the nature of my work. I'm grateful for the advanced notice and the offer to make enquiries on my behalf. I hope I can secure a new position by September and would like to remain in the northeast. It has been a challenge but also a pleasure to work with your children."

Her chat with her employer ended with his promise to approach two doctor friends, concerning her future employment.

Rachel was thankful her employer had made no mention of the court case and seemed willing to recommend her. She'd make her own enquiries, scouring the daily paper for a suitable vacancy but four months would pass quickly. The court case could easily damage her reputation locally, so she must be prepared to move to another area.

She glanced down at the small table under the window. On it lay the novel she was reading, selected from the extensive library in the Rossiters' house and a new Agatha Christie novel, recently purchased. Beside it lay her journal. She picked it up and read the entry from the previous day. It ended with a question…should I contact Tom? She flicked back through the entries, for the last few weeks. Each day the same question appeared – almost as if writing it down would provide an answer.

Since the trial ended, she had struggled to come to terms with her feelings of guilt. She knew her behaviour was unacceptable. She questioned herself frequently…why did she accuse Tom? That young barrister had 'knocked the nail on the head' saying she needed to blame someone. When that suggestion was voiced audibly…she'd felt ashamed. She'd been relieved when the jury returned a verdict of 'not guilty'. There would have been no triumph if Tom Smallwood had been found guilty – she shuddered to think how she could have lived with herself in that eventuality.

She was becoming irritable with herself – she'd accused Tom Smallwood because of a lifetime habit. A habit which caused her to find someone to blame when things went wrong. Blaming her Aunt Jemina when she said her parents would not be returning and it would be better to regard them as dead. 'Does that mean they are dead?' she'd asked. Her aunt had replied, 'No, my dear…it doesn't, but they are dead to you, and it will be easier for you to accept that as fact.' As a result, she'd kicked back at her Aunt Jemima…blamed her for the abandonment.

In a similar way, she'd betrayed Tom Smallwood in retribution for a perceived insult. She'd resented his prying into her background and when Jonty died, she needed to 'lash out' and blame someone and she chose Tom. She wanted to *hurt* someone and so she *blamed* him for the accident. Why? She was hurting and she needed someone else to suffer.

She'd treated her Aunt Jemima with disdain after learning about her parents and left home at the earliest opportunity. Once this retaliation took hold it resembled ripples in a pond after a stone is thrown…it spreads. Oh, she was annoyed with herself.

After she left St. Eram behind, she'd experienced regrets – especially when her grandfather died. She bore no malice towards him. When Annie informed her of his death, she almost…almost returned…but didn't. Then two years later when Jemima died…it was too late to make her peace. She would have to live with that for the rest of her life. But this time she must not make the same mistake. In order to live with herself she needed to seek Tom Smallwood's forgiveness. If she could hear his words, 'I forgive you Rachel', then she could leave Malhaven and begin the rest of her life in peace.

This was her dilemma – how could she contact him? Would he even agree to meet her? She only had a few weeks to achieve this before she moved away.

July 1927

The doorbell rang and Tom answered – it was the postie. After exchanging a few words Tom took the pile of post, waited while Humph the dog received his regular patting and headed back inside. He scanned the letters – he'd pass them over to Deborah. It was one of the tasks she was handling with efficiency. In the three months she'd been with them she'd become indispensable.

The telephone rang – it was Zac, up for a few days visiting his father. They greeted each other heartily and arranged to meet at their favourite watering hole the next evening. As Tom replaced the receiver the front door opened, and Deborah walked in. She'd asked for a late start that morning. Since arriving in Malhaven she'd been staying at a local boarding house. Tom had offered her a room at the hotel, but she declined, saying she preferred to draw a line between her living and working environments. The previous day Deborah informed Tom she needed a few hours the following morning to move into a rented flat.

"Good morning, Deborah," Tom greeted his secretary with a big smile. "Did you get moved?" he asked cheerily.

"Morning, Tom. Yes – it will take a few days to get sorted, but the flat comes with furniture, and I've already bought household linens and crockery, so it shouldn't take too long."

Tom smiled. "Deborah, take a couple of days off. It's three months since you arrived."

Deborah shook her head. "No thanks, Tom. There's not that much to sort. I'll save my holiday for visiting my family."

Tom nodded, realising he knew nothing of his secretary's background, other than she'd worked in Durham previously – he made a mental note to rectify that situation. Deborah started to climb the stairs to the office then suddenly turned back. "Oh, I almost forgot. The lady in the post office asked me to hand deliver this to you." Tom knew Deborah's new flat was above the post office. He handed her the pile of post, recently delivered, and took the envelope Deborah pulled from her handbag. He looked at the envelope and his heart began to thump. He thanked Deborah and walked through to the rear lounge.

Sitting down heavily in one of the armchairs he perused the cream envelope...what now? He recognised the handwriting. Slowly he opened the envelope and pulled out a card, resembling an invitation card – it read...

Date: 27th August
Venue: A place 'twixt heaven and earth
Time: 12.30pm
R.S.V.P. with your presence.

His blood ran cold. What was she doing? He turned it over – it was blank. The invitation, if it could be called such – felt more like a summons. It gave no clue to the sender...but he knew...it was Rachel Brooks.

The question was...why? The date was significant...the place was significant...the time was significant...but why? Why did Rachel Brooks want to meet him at the very place; on the very date; at the very time Jonty's accident had taken place one year previously?

The weather was experiencing a rather unseasonable spell of wind and rain for July. Tom was swept through the door of the local tavern.

"Oh, the good old British weather," boomed a voice from a corner booth, where Zac was sitting. Tom greeted the barman with a raised hand and walked over to sit beside his friend.

"Gosh, it's ridiculous," Tom responded. "It's warm enough, but that wind and the rain – it's like a monsoon." He shrugged off his wet raincoat and sat down.

"A beer?" queried Zac.

Tom shook his head.

"I'll have a cider instead," he remarked, as Zac walked over to the bar. Returning, he placed Tom's drink in front of him, slapped him on the back and sat down.

"Well, my friend...how are you?" he asked.

Tom took a gulp of his cider then lifted his hand and rocked it from side to side. He'd not seen Zac since the day he dropped him at the station two days after the trial.

"Good days and not so good days," he responded. "I won't say 'bad days' because they're not. Loads of folk are in a worst state than me...but some days I need motivating more than others."

Zac smiled. "It'll take time. How are you coping without Peg running the place? Did the new secretary materialise?"

Tom's eyes brightened. "Yes, Deborah arrived...and what an asset she's proving to be," Tom responded.

Zac raised an eyebrow. "Deborah? Tell me more, Tom Smallwood. Do I detect a liking on your behalf for this 'Deborah'?"

Tom spluttered over his drink. "Goodness me...no," he declared. "Not my type at all, Zac...but she might interest you," Tom remarked, knowing Zac's penchant for redheads. "Tall, slim, red hair, brown eyes and a cracking sense of humour," he added.

"Single?" asked Zac, his curiosity piqued.

Tom nodded, relaying the arrival and efficiency of Deborah Hogarth. Zac was intrigued and determined to meet this new addition to the staff at the hotel. "All sounds positive, so...is she diverting your mind away from Miss Brooks?"

Tom's expression turned serious at the mention of Rachel's name.

"What is it, Tom? Has she – 'who wanted to see you jailed for a crime you didn't commit', been up to something again?"

Tom sat back in his chair, placed his hands behind his head and let out a prolonged sigh.

"Well, yes...and no," Tom answered and reached into his jacket to retrieve the card. "I received this yesterday."

Zac took the card, read it, then let out a low whistle. "From Rachel? Lasham Cragg? Anniversary of the accident?"

Tom nodded. "I don't know what to do...I mean I would probably have visited Lasham Cragg that day in any case, but now receiving this...it feels weird, as if I'm being summoned."

Zac was silent, mulling it over. After a few minutes he spoke.

"I think you should go. If you don't, you'll always wonder what she wanted to say to you. If there's something she wants to say — let her say it without judge, jury and gallery of spectators to witness it."

It was Tom's turn to be silent. He knew deep down he wanted to go — if only just to see her face again...feel her presence.

"Well, it doesn't require a reply, so, I'll think about it and if I decide to go...I'll just show up on the day," Tom remarked.

The two friends changed the subject and chatted about other topics. As Zac indicated he needed to be going, he said, "Oh, I almost forgot. I double checked at Somerset House for death records for Darcy's parents and none exist. But it occurred to me they might have travelled abroad before the war and never returned or died abroad. What age would they be now?"

Tom rubbed his brow. "If I remember correctly Philly Shackleton, Darcy's mother, was born in 1877 so she'd be in her fifties and her father was a little older, so quite likely they are still alive."

Zac looked pensive. "I wonder if they did move abroad. And if so...why?"

Tom raised his hands in surrender. "Honestly, Zac, I wouldn't know, and I doubt if I'll ever know. This whole Darcy business has brought me nothing but grief and aggravation, and if I meet Rachel Brooks on the anniversary of Jonty's death, I'll listen to what she has to say, then I shall try to…forget her!"

Zac laughed out loud. "Come on, Tom – that's impossible and you know it. You're still in love with the woman. Just watch out she doesn't try to push you over the edge at Lasham Cragg!" he chuckled.

Tom's jaw dropped as he looked at his friend with incredulity.

Chapter 20

August 1927

Running his thumb carefully along the edge of the blade, Tom reached the pointed end of the knife. It was part of a letter opener and pen set, crafted in matt silver. It sat in a matching tray and had resided on his desk for many years. It had been a gift from his beloved Aunt Dora. Jonty had received one also, but Tom had no idea where it was now...come to think of it, where were Jonty's personal possessions? Between his mother, father and sister they'd disposed of Jonty's personal effects after the funeral – no doubt thinking it was better to get on with the task while Tom was caught up in the aftermath of the arrest. He would have liked something belonging to Jonty to keep as a remembrance – where was his watch? Both brothers had received a gold watch on their twenty-first birthdays...he must ask Mother about that.

He sorted through the letters waiting to be opened. Today the task was falling to him. Ada was on holiday and Deborah had taken the day off. Tomorrow was Tom's turn...a day he had an important appointment to keep.

He turned his attention to the task in hand and noted a letter with a French postmark. Gently, he slid the point and then the blade of the knife under the top edge of the ivory-coloured envelope bearing his name – he always looked forward to Peg's letters. These days she sent their parents' letter direct. He recalled with sadness receiving the large brown envelope with '*The Indians*' written on it.

For a few minutes he could imagine his young sister sitting opposite to him. Her letters were always so newsy and easy to read – they brought a smile to his face. He and Peg were always the closest of the four Smallwood siblings, but now with Jonty's passing, the bond he shared with Peg seemed tighter. He began reading and chuckled how Peg could make the most mundane tasks sound interesting. She had befriended a neighbour, an older lady, living on the floor above their apartment. Peg had a way with 'older' ladies, hence her work as a travelling companion. She seemed to have acquired a social connection with this lady – visiting the market together, taking a stroll around the nearby park and visiting a local café. Tom was pleased his sister was occupying her days, doing the things she enjoyed.

Moving to the second page, he sat bolt upright as he read,

'*To-To, you are to become an uncle! Yes, Pierre and I are so pleased to announce we are expecting our first child early in the New Year. We are so excited. Pierre cannot contain himself – he is oozing with joy and is spoiling me. This news means we will not be travelling to England for a long time – but I hope this means you will visit us in France instead. Get a*

passport, To-To, and come for the month of January,
when the hotel is closed...you may even be here for
the birth! I am posting a letter to Mother and Father
with the same news – hopefully you will be reading
it at the same time.'

She went on to write about other matters – the changes
they needed to make in the apartment for the impending
birth; Pierre's work commitments and finally she ended,
urging him to get out and make new friends.

'Put the past, painful months behind you, Tom.
Somewhere out there is the woman you are meant to
marry. Stop pining for Rachel Brooks, To-To...move
on with your life'.

Tom folded the letter...what would his sister say
if she knew who he was meeting tomorrow? No-one
knew...except Zac.

The telephone rang – it was his mother. She'd opened
her letter from Peg and was ecstatic. "Our first grandchild,
Tom. Oh, it's so exciting. Your father and I intend to travel
to France in the autumn."

Poor Peg, thought Tom, as he finished the call.
Peg won't relish that prospect...but he knew his
mother meant well.

***

The anniversary of Jonty's accident dawned every bit as
fine as it had been the previous year. The sun was bright,

the clouds were sparse, and a gentle breeze brought a pleasantness to the temperatures. Tom set off in good time, carrying only his rucksack with refreshments – he'd dared to leave his waterproofs behind...less to carry. Each step carried a memory. He paused at the same places, recalled the comments he'd shared with his brother on his final walk last year. He remembered how any tensions between them had quickly evaporated. Memories from boyhood, school days and those made in adult years peppered their conversation. His heart was thumping, and he stopped to take a drink.

He was pleased he'd made this outing...it was acting like a healing balm, forcing him to revisit that painful day in detail. With each step something was releasing, shedding pain and regret. Jonty would never have wanted him to avoid visiting this beautiful place. So, he promised himself after today...after whatever Rachel Brooks had to say to him...he would visit Lasham Cragg regularly and remember the happy times.

He approached the viewing point – listening to the water as it gushed over the edge and fell into the river gorge far below. The waterfall at Lasham Cragg never ceased to fascinate Tom. He was early but that was his plan – to share some uninterrupted moments of reflection. He surveyed the view – beautiful as always. Nothing seemed to have changed...but so much had changed for him and his family. An unseen hand gripped his stomach, reminiscent of the tight knot he'd experienced during the ordeal last year and its continuance until a few months ago.

It was a pain he must endure today. He must re-run those tragic, agonising moments – to dismiss them would be wrong. He looked down carefully at the ledge where Jonty had lain…no signs of the tragedy which had taken place remained. Fear gripped him afresh. It had all happened so quickly. Even now running the order of events in slow motion, he knew it was a tragic incident. If only Jonty had stepped forward as he turned…if only Rachel had not appeared at that precise moment…if only Peg and Pierre had not been delayed by that phone call. He could dredge up as many 'if only' scenarios as he could recall…but to what end? A set of circumstances brought together at a particular time with a devastating result. Tom sat down on a rock, back from the edge and the tears began to flow…he let them. Tears of grief; tears of regret; tears of thanks – for the brother he'd loved; tears of pain – for the years snatched from them.

He heard a crackle as a twig snapped and blinked back his tears. He felt her presence as she walked up behind him. He resisted the urge to turn around but was aware of a shadow…the shadow of a petite figure…Rachel Brooks.

"You accepted my invitation," Rachel spoke softly.

Tom continued to stare ahead. The sun was warm… strangely he felt peaceful, as if he'd come full circle, back to the place where his torment began a year ago. His eyes were dry now. He cleared his throat.

"Of course – I was intending to be here today, without your invitation," he replied, his voice calm.

Rachel moved to sit on the rock adjacent to Tom. It was the place they'd sat and eaten their picnic when he first brought her to this beautiful place. They sat in silence for a few minutes, Tom continuing to gaze ahead.

"Why are you here, Rachel?" He asked the question casually but calmly. He could so easily have regurgitated the many insults she had thrown at him over the last months – but they seemed to disappear like dirty water down a deep, dark drain.

His skin tingled at her closeness. He wanted her explanation…why she'd asked him to be here…but he would give her space…let her say her 'bit'…or give a reason for this rendezvous. A gentle breeze wafted, carrying the light fragrance of her perfume to his nostrils…evoking memories, happy memories. He tried to swallow them; they would serve no purpose.

Her voice was feeble as she spoke. "I…I…I've… come…to," she began, then coughed to clear her throat. "I've come to…apologise, Tom…to ask…ask…if…you can…possibly…possibly…find it in your heart…to…to forgive me?"

Tom struggled to hear her, not only because her voice was so feeble, but he couldn't believe what he was hearing. The words 'apologise' and 'forgive' seemed so alien, coming from her mouth. Even after receiving her invitation to meet him in this place, he'd failed to envisage a scenario where she would want to make her appeasement with him.

"Why should I do that?" he asked, keeping his eyes firmly focused on the view ahead. The rushing water, cascading into the gorge below seemed even louder than usual.

"I need some kind of peace, Tom, I'm looking for an armistice between us," she swallowed, her voice barely more than a whisper. "I can't live on this planet knowing I've hurt you so much. I need a resolution. I am so, so sorry I caused you all that hurt and pain. If I can hear your words of forgiveness for my cruel actions and attitudes, then maybe...just maybe I can step into my future in peace."

Tom shook his head and sighed deeply. His brain computing her words. She wanted resolution...how dare she suggest it. After the pain and anguish, she had caused him – how did she have the audacity to ask this of him?

She continued to speak. "I'm leaving Malhaven, Tom. The boys are going to boarding school in September, so my services are no longer required. I needed to see you before I left, to attempt to bring an end to this state of hostility between us."

A bee buzzed around Rachel's head, and she stood to lose it. Her sudden movement caused Tom to turn and look at her. His heart jumped a gear...she was beautiful: sunlight bounced off her blonde curls; her blue and white cotton dress fitted her figure perfectly – he swallowed hard. How could he hold animosity against this woman... it wasn't in his nature. No matter what she had said, done or intimated...he still loved her.

She looked up and their eyes met – they were different, somehow. Her eyes had appeared hard and unrelenting during those days in the courtroom; threatening in the days following their breakup and menacing in the months at the hospital...but now they held a softness, reminiscent of the early, carefree days of their friendship. Could there be pacification in them...they were drawing him in like a magnet.

She resumed her sitting position and he angled himself so he could continue to look at her.

"Where will you go?" he enquired.

She deviated her gaze. "I don't know. I like the northeast and would love to stay in this area – but I must go where my work takes me."

Tom's forehead puckered – it would be for the best, then he could try to forget her. She twisted her body to face him.

"I appreciate what I am asking is…huge, and I seek no answer today. I'll be in the area for a few more weeks. Henry and Blanche are happy for me to stay until I find a new position."

Would he feel any different in a few weeks, he pondered.

"You must miss Jonty so much," she continued. It was stating the obvious; no doubt it was an attempt to extend their conversation. How could she possibly know how much he missed Jonty?

"I miss him – but I want you to know something, Tom." She paused, straightened her skirt then looked up. Their eyes met again. "I didn't love him…I hope you realise that…I don't think he loved me either. We didn't speak in those terms. We were friends, good friends. We enjoyed spending time together – talking, debating, joking even flirting…but it was all shallow – there was no depth to our relationship. It would have ended in time, but it was good while it lasted, and I remember him fondly."

Tom was struggling to get his head around her declaration – he'd just assumed…knowing how his brother usually behaved, that they were lovers. "So, Rachel…why… if all this is true…why did you need to blame me?"

She raised her hands and cupped the sides of her face. He could tell she was struggling; his question having thrown her off kilter. She replaced her hands in her lap.

"In the weeks after the accident, I realised how shallow my relationship with Jonty had been, but it was good fun – it gave me something to look forward to. I enjoyed being pampered and being the girl on Jonty's arm. He flattered me and then...poof! He was gone. I was angry at myself; angry at Jonty and angry with you. I've always needed someone to blame when things go wrong, I need to 'take it out' on someone and you were the obvious target. I wanted to hurt someone...and that someone was you. By the time I realised what I was doing...it was too late. If I live until I'm a hundred, I'll never...never be able to say sorry enough...for all the pain I've caused you." Her voice was crackling, as she wiped tears from her eyes.

If Tom had followed his inclinations he would have reached out, taken her hand and told her she was forgiven... but he couldn't. He cleared his throat.

"You're asking a lot of me, Rachel. I need time. Time to grieve properly...time to heal mentally and time to process what you've told me. I'd assumed you and Jonty...were involved." He looked away and ran his fingers through his blond hair. He was unsure how to word his proposition. "Listen...I'm prepared to hold out an...an...olive branch. One year from now...same place...same date...same time... meet me. By then you will have moved away and found a new position and hopefully...I will have worked through my grief and be able to tell you what you want to hear."

He saw anguish in her eyes. She'd expected more from him. She'd come to this place seeking peace of mind. But he'd listened; he hadn't rejected her. Slowly, he saw a glimmer of a smile drift across her face – how long was it since he'd seen that?

"Yes, Tom…one year today, I'll meet you here. Before I go will you remind me of the rhyme your aunt used to say when she visited this spot…I can only remember the first line."

Tom chuckled and felt a release at the mention of his beloved aunt.

'There is a place 'twixt heaven and earth,
Which fills me with such joyful mirth,
With bright blue sky and rolling hills, my
singing voice begins its trills,
The maker of this universe created such a wide diverse.
My heart cries out…yet in this place,
I'm overwhelmed by love and grace.'

He glanced over at Rachel and saw a tear slowly make its path down her cheek – he longed to reach out and wipe it away, but his hands remained glued to his side.

"That's so moving, Tom. She must have been a very special lady," commented Rachel.

"She was…very special," he responded.

Rachel stood. "Thank you, Tom, for meeting me today and listening to my request. We may meet before I leave Malhaven and I trust we can be civil towards one another."

Tom didn't stand – Zac's words rang in his ears. "Of course, Rachel, we can always choose to be civil to each other."

She turned and took a step away, towards the path. "Until next year, Tom…goodbye."

Tom stood...now she was a distance from him. "Goodbye, Rachel...I hope to see you next year."

Then raising her hand towards the falls, she waved, saying, "Farewell Jonty," and walked away.

***

Being civil didn't raise its head. Tom heard, via Blanche Rossiter, a few weeks later, Rachel had moved to Durham to take up a new governess position, the same week the boys left for boarding school. Perhaps it was for the best, mulled Tom as he walked home from church that Sunday.

Her name wasn't mentioned again until the Christmas Carol Service, but she filled his thoughts at some point every day, especially at night. Tom was chatting to Henry Rossiter.

"How's Peg?" asked Henry.

"She's doing well, but is confined to bed since her collapse," Tom replied.

Henry nodded. "Yes, I heard. Blanche was talking to your mother yesterday. I gather they have just returned to be home in time for Christmas."

Tom nodded. "My parents went straight over to France when they heard the news about Peg and stayed for a few weeks. It was quite a panic, from what I understand."

Henry went on to explain the medical condition which Peg was experiencing, where the placenta presents first, and total bed rest is required for the remainder of the pregnancy.

"It was fortunate that when she collapsed two neighbours were on the stairway and one happened to be a retired midwife. Her prompt intervention saved the day. Mother and Father were intending to visit, but were called into action quicker than they'd expected," Tom added.

Blanche joined them as they were chatting. "We had a visitor last Sunday," Blanche remarked to Tom.

Tom looked at her questioningly.

"Rachel Brooks came over from Durham to bring the boys a Christmas present – it was so kind of her to remember them."

Tom froze initially, at the mention of her name, then asked, "Is she settling into her new role?"

Blanche laughed. "Yes, but quite a change from our boys – one girl who is quiet and an avid learner."

Tom smiled. "Not as challenging as your boys then," he remarked. Somehow Tom suspected Rachel would be bored. The Rossiter offspring had caused Rachel to dig deeply into the caverns of ingenuity to spark their interest. A brief flashback to the time she transformed the Easter activities at the hotel threatened to invade his mind. He quickly diverted his line of thinking.

"I'm off to France to stay with Peg and Pierre just after New Year. I'll be away for a month – I might even be there for the birth," he grinned, as the twins arrived to find their parents.

"Give our love to them, Tom," Henry said, ruffling his son's hair. "It's an exciting time for them, becoming parents."

Tom looked wistfully at the two youngsters – would parenthood be a path he would walk?

"We'll see you at New Year," Henry called, as the family walked out of the church.

Chapter 20

***

Foreign travel was an experience Tom was eager to embrace. For years he'd listened to Zac talking about his adventures into Europe. He'd always intended to traverse the distant lands beyond the shores of England, but sadly that dream was lost – another casualty of ambition sidetracked, when Aunt Dora died. Peg's descriptions of her tantalising escapades over the years, had whetted his appetite to explore, even more. Now, at last, he was setting foot in France.

An overnight stay at Zac's pokey flat in London and an early morning train to the port of Dover, heralded Tom's foray into Europe. After two further train journeys he arrived in Lyon, the town Peg had regarded as home since making her escape from Malhaven, a few years ago. It was late afternoon as he traversed the 'rues' from the station, carefully following Peg's detailed instructions to find himself outside a four-storey apartment block. Pushing open the large imposing entrance door, he found himself in a cold stone flagged foyer. A stark staircase led to the first floor. He knocked on the door of apartment 'cinq'. A portly lady in her sixties answered his knock.

"Bonjour, Monsieur," she greeted, then proceeded to speak in French.

Tom returned the greeting, but his schoolboy French was extremely rusty, and he failed to understand the older lady's comments.

"To-To, is that you?" A familiar voice called from a bedroom.

He followed the portly lady into the wide hallway, across a tiled floor into a spacious bedroom, to be enveloped in a bearhug, as he sat on the bed beside his sister.

"Oh, To-To, it's great to see you…it's been so long," waxed Peg, finally releasing him.

He stood and looked at his sister…was this his little Peg? Her pregnant condition had rendered her almost unrecognisable.

"Peg…it's great to see you…er, you look 'different'," he chuckled as Peg patted her large baby bump.

"Not long now, To-To. I can't wait to be up and about, it's been torturous sitting in this bed, day in day out for the last few weeks," she declared, her bright eyes scanning Tom's face. A movement from the doorway alerted Peg to the presence of the older lady. "Oh Tom, this is Madame Levigne, my lovely neighbour, who takes care of me when Pierre is at work."

Tom walked over and shook hands with the lady, who again spoke to him in French.

Peg translated. "She's pleased to meet you, Tom and she has prepared your evening meal. If you follow her, she will show you to your room."

Tom picked up his suitcase and followed. The apartment was surprisingly spacious, comprising three bedrooms, a bathroom, kitchen and a large lounge incorporating a dining room. Tom admired the substantial furnishings. His brother-in-law had provided his English bride with a delightful home – it oozed quality and the cosy touches were no doubt his sister's handiwork.

After settling in and enjoying his first taste of French cuisine, Tom re-joined his sister in the bedroom, sitting on one of the two armchairs in the cosy room, warmed by an open fire.

"Oh, To-To, I feel this bedroom is my prison. I long to be free. I am allowed to spend two hours lying on the chaise in the lounge in an afternoon and that is it. I crave fresh air and exercise."

Tom knew how much Peg loved the outdoors and sympathised with her. "Hang in there, Peg...it's all for the best. Was it Madame Levigne who found you when you collapsed?"

Peg gave Tom a detailed account of her mishap. "I owe my life, and the baby's life to the prompt attention I received from Madame Martin, who was staying with Madame Levigne. She is a retired midwife from Bordeaux and often travels here to stay with her friend. They take it in turns to look after me when Pierre is at work. At a time like this you need family. I was grateful for Mother and Father's extended visit, but...shall we say...pleased they were required to return for Christmas."

Tom and his sister exchanged a knowing look – Tom understood perfectly: his mother Lilian meant well, but her manner could be overpowering.

A noise in the hallway signalled the arrival of Pierre. "Tom, mon frère, how good to see you again,"

The two men hugged and greeted each other. After chatting for a while Tom's eyelids were almost closing, so he left his hosts and bid them 'bonne nuit'.

Being with Peg and Pierre was a treat for Tom. Not having seen them since the aftermath of the trial, there was much to discuss. Peg was concerned about her brother's mental state.

"I'm improving each day," he remarked. "The persistent knot in my stomach has gone and the tight band around my head. I'm sleeping and eating well, and I make sure I take a regular 'day off' and usually go for a hike."

He decided to tell them about his rendezvous with Rachel Brooks on the anniversary of Jonty's accident. They listened with apprehension, unsure if Tom was setting himself up for further disappointment, but wisely keeping their misapprehensions to themselves.

"It's good you have spoken to her, I suppose," remarked Peg, thoughtfully. "But be guarded, Tom, when you meet her again. Think carefully about your response."

Tom busied himself around the apartment during the daytime. A hired help arrived each morning to attend to the household chores, so Tom was only needed to 'hold the fort 'and see to Peg's meals. Each afternoon Madame Levigne arrived to assist Peg into the lounge. During this time Tom took the opportunity to take a stroll around Lyon. The wintry days were not conducive to sightseeing, but Tom enjoyed wandering around, absorbing the culture of the French town.

One afternoon, about a week into his visit, he returned to find Madame Levigne's friend had joined her. Peg, lying on the chaise, made the introduction. "Tom, this is Madame Martin, a retired midwife to whom I am greatly indebted."

Tom shook hands with the smartly dressed lady, who bore no resemblance to her friend's matronly stance. She was small in stature and her figure was trim; only her greying hair and lined face, giving hints to her age which Tom assessed as being in her fifties. He attempted to use his scattering of French vocabulary to convey his grateful thanks to Madame Martin, for her help when Peg collapsed, but his French was rudimentary.

The lady smiled. "Monsieur Smallwood, I understand you better if you speak English," she commented.

Tom was taken aback – Madame Levigne spoke little, if any English – yet her friend spoke English with barely an accent.

"Where did you learn to speak English so well?" asked Tom.

Madame Martin averted her eyes. "In London before the war," she replied then moved towards Peg, clearly reluctant to engage in further conversation.

Peg asked Tom to leave them for a few minutes while Madame Martin examined her patient.

After the two French ladies departed, Tom asked Peg, "Did you say Madame Martin lives in Bordeaux?"

Peg nodded. "Yes, but I understand she is recently widowed and spends several weeks at a time with her friend. I suspect she is enjoying having a patient to nurse," chuckled Peg. "The official sage femme, that is midwife, visits regularly, but Madame Martin is only on the floor above if I need assistance."

Pierre was delighted to spend time talking to Tom and arranged for Madame Levigne to sit with Peg one evening, so he could show his brother-in-law his place of work and the surrounding area. Tom found it fascinating and noted the seniority his brother-in-law held in the police station.

Peg went into labour in the early hours of the morning, ten days after Tom arrived. The sage femme was summoned, and Madame Martin assisted her. It was the following evening when the doctor was called to oversee the birth. To everyone's relief, Peg delivered a tiny but healthy baby boy, just before midnight. Peg was exhausted, the birth was difficult, but with three professionals in attendance, mother and baby were in good hands. Tom paced the floor with the expectant father, hating Peg's cries and making endless cups of coffee for Pierre. But the wonderful sight of his sister holding her newborn son brought tears to Tom's eyes, especially when the proud parents named him Jonathan Pierre, in honour of the uncle he never knew.

Tom's remaining vacation time surrounded the needs of the new arrival, but he was in his element. He seemed to possess a unique knack of hushing baby Jonty's stressful cries and delighted in helping when required. Two weeks to become acquainted with his nephew was not enough, especially when Tom realised, he would not see the family for many months.

"Mother and Father are coming over in March," announced Peg, reading a letter from Lilian. "You must tell her all about him, To-To, she will want all the details."

Tom smiled. His sister was beginning to look like her old self and appeared to be recovering well.

Two days before Tom's departure, Madame Levigne and Madame Martin insisted on providing a farewell meal. Over the weeks Tom had enjoyed chatting to the two ladies and felt reassured knowing they would be 'on hand' to help his sister during the early days of motherhood. They brought the food, ready cooked, down to Peg and Pierre's apartment. Tom had sampled many dishes from Madame Levigne in the weeks since his arrival, but the offering that evening was 'magnifique'! Peg was excited as

Madame Martin brought in the dessert.

"Tom, this is the 'pièce de résistance' – I guarantee you have never tasted anything like this before," she declared.

Tom's eyes widened and he tensed as he ate his serving of the dessert. It tasted every bit as delicious as the last time he'd eaten it…in Malhaven!

"Verdict, Tom?" Peg enquired.

"Splendide!" he exclaimed, observing the pastry chef with curiosity.

Chapter 21

"**M**aybe I am adding two and two together and making five...but Madame Martin mystifies me," exclaimed Tom to Pierre later that night. The two men were enjoying a drink before bed. Peg was feeding baby Jonty in the bedroom.

"The coincidences are stacking up, Pierre."

Tom's brother-in-law looked perplexed.

"In what way, Tom?" he asked.

Tom was sitting forward on his chair, nursing his drink in his hand. "That dessert, Pierre. Peg indicated it was unique...but I have eaten it before, in my own home," he insisted, staring into the glass. "It was uncanny...it was identical."

Now Pierre was scratching his head, looking totally bewildered.

"Uncanny – I don't understand the word?"

Tom often forgot Pierre was French. His command of the English language was excellent, but using a colloquialism threw the Frenchman.

"Sorry, Pierre...I mean it is strange, weird, too much of a coincidence. The dessert we ate tonight was identical to a one prepared by Rachel Brooks at the hotel, the Easter weekend she organised the guest activities. They

307

were called *canele* or *caneltes*, something like that. They are little cakes with a custard filling, they are shaped by the copper moulds in which they are baked. They smell of burnt sugar, rum and vanilla – even the decoration on the top was the same."

Pierre considered Tom's comment. "Mon, frère...your mind plays the tricks with you," he responded. "The dessert we ate tonight is very popular in France. It is a delicacy originating from the Bordeaux region, where Yvette Martin lives. Perhaps Miss Brooks had travelled to Bordeaux and seen the dessert...or maybe a friend gave her the recipe."

Tom listened then shook his head. "No, Pierre, the filling was the same and the decoration was the same, the size and shape were the same...a skill passed down from a mother to a daughter, perhaps?"

Pierre's eyes widened with realisation. "Non, non, Tom...it is impossible, it cannot be. You are saying what?"

Tom stood up and stood in front of the fireplace. "I am saying, Pierre...that Yvette Martin could be Philomena Shackleton – Darcy Shackleton's birth mother...in other words, Yvette Martin could be Rachel Brooks' birth mother!"

Pierre was shaking his head in disbelief.

"Consider this, Pierre. I think Yvette Martin is English. The first day I met her I commented on her excellent English. She said she spent time in London before the war, but I'm convinced it is her mother tongue. Next... she is in the right age group. Darcy's mother will be in her fifties now...Madame Martin is that age...do you agree?"

Pierre nodded.

"Philomena Shackleton's occupation on her marriage certificate was 'midwife'...a sage femme. Do you see my comparisons, Pierre?" Tom was on a roll; the more he verbalised his theory...the more real it seemed.

Pierre was trying to follow Tom's reasoning. "Yvette Martin's hometown is Bordeaux; hence she makes the famous *canelet* desserts from that region. But if Yvette is your Darcy's mother, how would she know about a Bordeaux dessert and teach the skill to her daughter in England?"

Momentarily Tom looked stumped.

"Perhaps she travelled to France before the war and stayed in the Bordeaux region or knew someone who lived there. No, Pierre, there are too many coincidences...I think my theory might be correct." Tom rubbed his brow deep in thought. "Could you in your capacity as a detective, check a birth, a death, marriage or even a census record for Madame Martin in Bordeaux – to see how long she has lived there?"

Pierre shook his head. "I have no jurisdiction in Bordeaux, Tom – and I would need a reason to make enquiries of that nature."

Tom looked thoughtful. "Then perhaps Peg could help by creating a little scenario," he suggested. "If the name 'Darcy' were to crop up in conversation, Peg may detect a reaction...something along the lines of 'if Jonty had been a girl, we were considering the name Darcy – do you like that name, Yvette?'."

Pierre laughed. "Oh, mon frère, you have a vivid imagination. I doubt if Philomena Shackleton – if that is who she is – will fall for that. If...as you are suspecting, she and her husband Percival left England to live in France to avoid something serious – so serious they leave their teenage daughter behind, then I think she will have developed…how do you English say…the 'poker face'."

Tom raised his eyebrows. "Well, Peg could give it a try," Tom added.

"I could give what a try?" asked Peg, walking into the room. She sat down and Tom relayed his suspicions and suggestions to his sister.

***

Six weeks later

"Good evening, Meckleridge House Hotel, how may I help you?" Tom spoke, answering the telephone.

"To-To, Peg here."

Tom greeted his sister – it was six weeks since his return from France and he'd received two letters from his sister during that period – so he was surprised she was telephoning. After initial comments, catching up on baby Jonty's progress, Tom sensed his sister was eager to share something.

"We're onto something with Madame Martin, Tom." He waited expectantly as she continued. "Your little plan about the baby's name produced no reaction, I'm sorry to say. However, a few days later she was wiping the dishes as we were washing up in our kitchen. I was deliberately talking about Aunt Dora and her home in Llandudno in

Wales. I referred to an occasion when a girl called Darcy joined us. I explained she was the goddaughter of Uncle Bart's sister. I sensed a tension in her, Tom."

His jaw dropped and he stared wide-eyed.

"I mentioned how beautiful and full of life this young girl was with her bouncy, blonde curls and how sad it was that her parents travelled abroad so much, leaving her to be cared for by friends and family. That comment threw her off balance – she dropped the dish and it fell to the floor, shattering on the tiles." Tom gasped.

"Interesting," he commented.

Peg continued. "There's more Tom," she added, speaking quickly.

"Slow down, Peg," Tom warned, knowing how his young sister was always in a hurry to pass on an item of interest.

"Pierre was asked to go to Bordeaux to interview a witness for some case he's working on…how fortunate was that? Well, he used his time after the interview to check out the *recensement de la population*' – that's what we call the census. Monsieur and Madame Martin have been residing at an address in Bordeaux since before the war. Georges – Madame Martin's husband – was listed as a factory worker, and his wife, Yvette, was a sage femme. Pierre made a note of their ages. That was all he could check."

Tom let out a low whistle. "Thanks, Peg – I think Monsieur and Madame Martin could well be Darcy's parents. Of course, it's flimsy evidence. The sad thing is, Peg – if Rachel will admit to being Darcy – she thinks her parents are dead…but if we are correct…then her mother is still alive. I have no idea how to proceed with this information, Peg. I meet Rachel again in August, so I guess I've got plenty of time to dwell on it."

"We are planning to visit England in August, Tom – it will be good to see you again. Jonty is changing every week – you will not recognise him. Mother and Father arrive next week so I am going to be busy, but I promise Pierre and I will try to help you decide what to do about informing Rachel of the fact that her mother may still be alive."

The hotel season began with the Easter house party and Tom was so busy he hardly had time to do anything except work, eat and sleep. Deborah Hogarth came up trumps! She listened to Winnie and Tom recalling the guest events when Rachel Brooks had organised them. "I could organise some activities," she suggested.

Tom was delighted. The previous Easter house party had fallen just after the court case – so the activities were low key. Deborah set about her task and the result was a huge success. During the Easter weekend Tom introduced Deborah to his friend Zac. It was obvious to Tom from the pair first meeting, that an attraction was sparked. Zac's visits to the northeast increased over the next few weeks and by July it was no secret – Zac and Deborah were an item! Tom was so pleased for his friend, but hoped he wasn't going to lose Miss Hogarth's services.

On a rare solo hike in July, Tom realised he had finally turned a corner. He felt at ease with himself again and even the looming August rendezvous with Rachel appeared less daunting. He'd given a great deal of thought to his response and knew he was ready to forgive her…no matter what she had done…she'd told him she was sorry, and he must show a forgiving spirit.

He'd been right to give himself space – last year he was still too raw, but now he felt peaceful. He would tell her she was forgiven. Tom had come to this decision weeks ago, but in recent days he had begun to ask himself – was forgiveness all he wanted to offer Rachel Brooks? He knew he still loved her – he couldn't bring himself to look at another woman in that way. Forgiveness was one hurdle to overcome…he was ready for that step…but what about the next step…reconciliation? It was a leap…but then forgiveness was a leap this time last year. Reconciliation to Tom meant the re-establishing of a friendship. Could the gulf between them be bridged? He felt sure she would keep their rendezvous; her attendance was one thing…her demeanour would be another…and then her response? Yet she was the one who was seeking his forgiveness…so she should be amiable. He dared to hope they could meet again afterwards – go out for dinner perhaps? A one-off event to underpin the end of their hostility. Was he being a fool to think this way?

Peg, Pierre and the baby arrived in August. Pierre could be called back to France at any point, but Peg would stay. A room was provided for them at the hotel and each day Tom relished spending time with his nephew. Lilian was on cloud nine showing off her grandson to all and sundry. As the weeks turned to days, the days turned to hours and now the rendezvous at Lasham Cragg was only a day away. Was Tom ready – physically? Mentally? Emotionally? Peg suggested a walk in the grounds of the hotel, when Lilian was entertaining some friends with the baby.

"Well, Tom…are you ready to meet Rachel?" Peg enquired.

"Yes, Peg, I am. I'm at peace with myself at long last and I need to show a forgiving spirit. But I'm also hoping we can take a further step...the step of reconciliation with a view to recovering a sort of friendship."

Peg gasped and shook her head. "Oh, Tom...be careful, you know how dangerous she's proved to be in the past," Peg warned.

Tom turned to face his sister as she added, "Will you tell her about Yvette?"

Tom scratched his head. "I sense your caution, Peg, but you know how I feel about her. All I'm going to do is to ask her out for dinner to show we have put the past behind us. If she refuses my invitation...then so be it. If I don't ask the question, I will never know the answer. If she doesn't accept my invitation, then I will keep the information concerning my suspicions about Yvette Martin, to myself."

***

Peg's warning rang in Tom's ears as he arrived at the viewing point at Lasham Cragg the next day. He was early again. He spent the first ten minutes looking over the edge and remembering the brother he'd loved. He remembered the happy times...the fun times. Then pulling himself from his memories he turned and sat on the famous rock – the one he'd sat on a year ago, full of turmoil, hurt and bewilderment as to what Rachel wanted. Thankfully he was not in that state of mind today...he was relaxed.

Would she turn up? Had she forgotten? Some legitimate duty may have prevented her attendance – had she formed a friendship with a suitor, and it would be inappropriate for her to keep this arrangement? He was so preoccupied with his misgivings he failed to hear Rachel approach. The waterfall was noisy today – the result of recent heavy rain. He turned suddenly, aware of her presence. He stood, admiring her beauty...their eyes connected; a smile spread slowly across her face. His heart lurched and he experienced an overwhelming urge to pull her into his arms in a tight embrace – but he resisted.

He was standing well back from the edge. She stepped towards him. Sensing the preciousness of the moment, he reached out his hands and she took them. A tingle of delight sparked through his body at her touch.

Eyes locked, Rachel spoke first. "Your answer, Tom... please," she begged, urgently.

Something was there, he was sure...a simmering of hope overwhelmed him. His gaze was spellbinding.

"Rachel," he began, running his thumbs across her fingers on both hands. "Of course I forgive you," he responded, his voice crackling.

A flush spread from her neck up to her cheeks and her lower lip trembled.

"Thank you, Tom...thank you so much," she whispered.

He tilted his head slightly, still grasping her hands and asked, "Can we...possibly...be friends again?"

Her eyes glistened. He noticed tears shimmering in their grey blue depths. An ache gripped his chest, almost strangling his breath – so much depended on her reply.

"Oh Tom...are you sure? Is it possible? It would mean so much to me...for us to be friends...after everything that's happened."

He pulled her towards him and felt no resistance. Her head rested against his chest as he gently breathed the delicate scent of her hair. He reached out, rolling a lock of her bouncy blonde hair in his fingers and realised she was sobbing. The sobs deepened and her petite body heaved as she gave in to their release. "I...I...I'm...so...so...sorry, Tom," she gulped. As the heaving quelled...he pulled back and placed his hands on her shoulders, looking down into her tear strewn face...searching...searching...for truth.

It was a pivotal moment. He was holding his breath; he felt his lungs would burst if she withheld the words he longed to hear. She lifted her eyes upwards, out of his penetrating gaze. Her brow puckered; he sensed her trembling; tears spurted from the edges of her eyes and her lips parted.

"I...I...I...am...Darcy," she whispered faintly, then closed her eyes.

The pent-up tension released from Tom's chest; he reached out and grasped the back of her head, embracing her tightly. He was speechless, words felt inadequate; the relief was overwhelming; time stood still; they stood locked in their embrace. "It's over, Rachel," he uttered, lifting his head.

Before him was the woman he loved. He was gripped with a sensation of something powerful...something wonderful...something beautiful...and something else... slowly it unfurled...it was truth! He saw a yellow rose, its petals unfurling...to reveal its magnificence...and he knew...he had witnessed...the blossoming of truth!

He cupped her damp chin and gazed adoringly into her sparkling eyes. "It's over, Rachel; it's behind us. Let's make a pact here and now to forgive and forget all that's happened. Can we make a fresh start?" he asked pleadingly, searching for confirmation. She reached out and touched his cheek, lovingly.

"Oh, Tom...I don't deserve you, but yes...yes, Tom... let's make a fresh start," she whispered.

Momentarily he hesitated, then bent forward and gently brushed his lips against hers. Pulling back, he searched her face for a sign of encouragement – he caught a sparkle in her eye...and this time their kiss was tender and loving as she melded into his arms.

Standing hand in hand they shared some personal moments of reflection, overlooking the spot where Jonty had lain, two years previously. The arrival of fellow walkers dragged them from their reverie. They turned and began the descent. On the way, Tom learned that Rachel's summer duties afforded her several free weeks while her employer and family travelled abroad. Tom told Rachel about Peg and Pierre's new arrival and their visit to Malhaven. She expressed her delight for them.

"They are travelling back home in a few days – would you like to come over and see little Jonty, before they go?" Tom asked, but Rachel was hesitant.

She stopped and looked into Tom's eyes. "I'd love to see them, Tom...but will they accept me? Not only did I hurt you, but I hurt your family also...they may not forgive me. I think it best not to involve your family at this stage."

He brushed a stray lock of blonde hair from her cheek. She was right, he was too eager. His family needed to accept Rachel first, before meeting them.

"I understand. Do you have to go back to Durham straight away?" he asked as they approached the car park.

"No, I'm free for the rest of the day," she informed him.

"Shall we take a late lunch together?"

Rachel's eyes lit up with a smile. "I'd love that, Tom," she replied.

***

Tom replayed the events of the day as he drove back to Malhaven later. He could never in his wildest dreams have foreseen how the day would pan out. At best he'd hoped… because there was always hope – that Rachel would accept an invitation to dinner at some future date. But not only had she done that, she had agreed to spend time with him that afternoon. They'd driven a short distance from Lasham Cragg into a small village. He was acquainted with a local hotel and although it was well past lunchtime, the manager provided a pot of tea and sandwiches. Their conversation covered the time from the end of the trial, as if an unseen line had been drawn demarking 'before' the trial and 'after' the trial.

They enjoyed the privacy of the hotel lounge, letting the pleasing ambience provide a backdrop to their necessary catch up. Eventually, they prised themselves away and parted – Rachel to Durham and Tom to Malhaven, but not before Tom lifted Rachel's hand to his lips. "Goodbye, Rachel, thank you for your honesty, see you on Tuesday."

"Thank you for your forgiveness, Tom," she'd added.

He'd placed his finger on his lips. "Shhh…It's forgiven and forgotten, Rachel," he winked.

Chapter 21

Not only had there been forgiveness, but they had taken a step of reconciliation. Dare he consider the possibility of renewed romance? When she admitted to being Darcy, there were no barriers left for him. But he was running...before walking...he must be patient.

Rachel entered her employer's empty home. She'd found the quietness disconcerting since the family left for their holiday but now, she welcomed it. Today had brought relief. Meeting Tom and hearing his words of forgiveness and making her confession, felt like a balm being soothed onto raw flesh.

Since arriving in Malhaven, Tom Smallwood had been a thorn in her flesh. She'd recognised him instantly and at first, she thought he accepted her denials about being Darcy. The difficulties began when she found herself being drawn to him. She found him attractive and as their friendship continued, she found herself falling for him. It was reciprocated and for that wonderful summer they'd listened to each other, shared their likes and dislikes; their fears and failings; their aspirations – they were travelling a path leading to commitment...until he said those words 'I love you, Darcy'...and a chasm appeared. Would things have been different if he'd said, 'I love you Rachel'?

She shook her head, as she tucked her feet under her body, relaxing in the elegant lounge where she'd lived for almost a year. No, Tom wanted the truth and even if his use of her former name had been a slip of the tongue...it would always be there between them. With Tom there was too much to live up to and so to keep her secret...she had to reject him. She looked back to those days after their breakup – she'd developed a hard heart; she was overtaken by disappointment and dissatisfaction, and she sought a diversion in the unrealistic Jonty. The older Smallwood brother wasn't looking for love or commitment, just fun. She blinded herself to Tom and enjoyed the playfulness and the distraction Jonty brought...for it all to end so tragically.

Could she the betrayer, transform into the beloved? With honesty, a willingness to commit, sincerity and integrity...yes it was possible. I wonder how things will develop between us, she pondered.

***

Autumn 1928

Many townsfolk in Malhaven regarded the romance between Tom Smallwood and Rachel Brooks as a big mistake. It was a whirlwind romance and sensationalist. It would all end in tears, many said, but it kept the gossip mongers occupied for weeks.

For Tom and Rachel, it was a pairing of hearts and minds. They thrived on the power of a touch, the locking of eyes, the surprising call, the unexpected note, the bouquet of flowers. They wined, dined, walked, talked and when, six weeks after they met at Lasham Cragg, Tom took her in his arms and said...'I LOVE YOU, RACHEL' it was a loving commitment to which she responded wholeheartedly, "I love you too, Tom Smallwood."

At the end of October, they drove to a local inn they'd visited previously. Tom had taken the host into his confidence and as they finished their meal, Tom reached across the table and lifted Rachel's left hand. He caressed her ring finger and gazed adoringly into her eyes. "Rachel, my darling…will you do me the honour of becoming my wife?"

She squealed with delight, clasping her hand to her mouth. "Yes, Tom, yes, yes," she exclaimed.

He reached into his pocket and pulled out a ring box, then stood, walked over beside her and bent down on one knee. He slid the tiny diamond solitaire ring on her finger, as the proprietor of the inn strode into the small dining room from his hiding place behind the door. He was carrying a silver tray, on which stood two flutes of champagne and a small vase containing a single full bloom yellow rose. They stood together and Tom bent forward and kissed his fiancée. The staff erupted with loud applause as Tom and Rachel toasted their engagement.

Tom lifted the rose from its holder, dried the end with his napkin and reaching to his inside pocket retrieved his penknife. Cutting the stem short, he placed the rose in Rachel's hair…reminiscent of that day in the Rose Garden…long before his world turned upside down.

The wedding of Tom Smallwood and Rachel Brooks took place a few weeks later, between Christmas and New Year. Zac was the best man and Blanche Rossiter was the matron of honour. The bride looked radiant and resplendent, in her white lace gown. Tom thought his heart would burst – he was so happy! The Christmas house party became part of the celebrations, most were close friends in any case. Newspaper reporters were waiting alongside the photographer as the happy couple left the church. Mr and Mrs Thomas Smallwood made the front-page headline… '*FROM COURTROOM TO CHURCH*' read the caption in the Northern Echo.

Sadly Peg, Pierre and baby Jonty were unable to travel, but Tom was taking his bride to France for their honeymoon and planned to spend time with his sister and her family afterwards.

One guest travelled from Cornwall – Annie Thomas. Tom wanted to sort a passport for Rachel but needed her birth certificate – her real birth certificate.

"I don't have it, Tom," she confessed a few weeks before the wedding "…unless Annie knows where it might be."

Annie was contacted and knew exactly where Jemima had kept Rachel's real birth certificate - in a box among Jemima's belongings, kept by Annie Thomas. She posted it to Rachel in time for Tom to make the passport arrangements – legally…but her name remained Rachel; only Zac, Annie, Peg and Pierre shared the secret. Annie was invited to the wedding and surprised Rachel by accepting the invitation. Tom and Zac conversed with the once formidable Annie Thomas and found her to be very pleasant.

On his wedding night, Tom gazed at the beauty of his bride. She'd been a hard prize to win, but he'd vowed to love and honour her before God. Their union was sublime – more than he'd ever hoped it would be. The following day they travelled to London and after a two-night stay in an expensive hotel, they travelled on to France.

Their honeymoon in Paris was idyllic as they absorbed the sights and culture of the romantic city, visiting the Louvre, the Eiffel Tower, the Arc de Triomphe, the Palace of Versailles and walking in the moonlight along the banks of the river Seine, in the biting cold chill of January.

Tom and Rachel were besotted with each other... but there was something lurking in the back of Tom's mind...something he had postponed...something he must share with his beautiful wife after they left Paris and journeyed to Lyon.

Chapter 22

France

On the morning Tom and Rachel left Paris and travelled to Lyon, Tom felt his bubble was about to burst. Beside him his young bride placed her head on his shoulder. "I'm so happy, Tom...this is the beginning of the rest of our lives. After spending time with Peg and her family we can return home and settle down to begin life as Mr and Mrs Smallwood. The last few months have been such a whirlwind."

Tom swallowed, trying to divert his thoughts. "Are you going to miss your governess role?" he asked, as the train chugged onwards through the French countryside. The engagement and wedding had taken Rachel's employers by surprise, but they'd accepted her resignation from her post without any fuss and were delighted for her.

"I'm looking forward to being the 'hostess in residence' at the hotel. I already know some of what's involved, and Deborah will keep me right," she chuckled.

Deborah was currently overseeing the hotel to allow Tom and Rachel to be away for the month of January.

Rachel and Deborah had become good friends. Deborah was taking her vacation during February and visiting London where both Zac and her family lived.

"I wonder if Zac and Deborah will have some news after Zac meets Deborah's parents?" Rachel pondered.

"Hope so – they're made for each other," commented Tom, but his mind was elsewhere. Here he was stepping out into his married life with Rachel, and he was withholding something from her. Truth and integrity were important to Tom – they formed the bedrock of his 'code for life'. It was ironic that he of all people was keeping something from his wife. It hadn't been his intention to keep his suspicions about Yvette Martin a secret – but he'd been struggling how to tell Rachel. There had always been an excuse and now he was running out of excuses.

Rachel had told Tom all she knew about her parents' 'disappearance'. He hadn't probed for information: she'd offered it freely, before their engagement. "I was used to my father travelling for business and sometimes my mother accompanied him. They didn't say where they were going and I never asked – teenagers aren't interested in travel, at least I wasn't. Going with my grandfather and aunt to live in Cornwall was an adventure…in the beginning. Then when the war started, it became apparent my parents weren't returning. I felt hurt…abandoned…rejected and alone – even though I had a lovely home and two relatives taking care of me. I often wonder if my parents are still alive. My aunt told me to treat them as if they were dead and with time, I just accepted they were dead."

Tom could choose to forget what Peg and Pierre had told him. He could choose to forget his own suspicions.

He was married to the most beautiful girl in the world, in his opinion – so what good would it do to rake up the past? But within a few days of arriving in Lyon, Peg had conjured up a plan – and Tom knew they had to see it through.

Tom had opted to stay in a small hotel in Lyon, not far from his sister's apartment. He felt they needed to have space – after all, it was their honeymoon. It was a stark contrast to the opulent hotel where they stayed in Paris – the cost had been exorbitant, but Rachel was worth every penny. They spent most afternoons and evenings with Peg, Pierre and Jonty, delighting in the progress of the little boy, who was toddling and babbling and was due to have his first birthday before his English aunt and uncle returned home. No mention was made openly about Rachel being Darcy – but both Rachel and Peg were aware the other knew.

Peg informed Tom the day after they arrived, she was hatching a reunion plan. Speaking to Tom on his own proved tricky, but during snatched snippets of conversation, when Rachel visited the bathroom, Peg unveiled her plan. Madame Martin had been in Bordeaux over the Christmas and New Year, but was due to visit Madame Levigne again in January.

The day to expedite Peg's plan arrived. It was bright but bitterly cold. Peg wrapped little Jonty up in his coat, hat, scarf and gloves and tucked him into his pram. Near to their apartment was a park with a duck pond. Little Jonty loved the ducks and each day "To-To, ducks" became a refrain, Tom could not refuse. This day Peg and Jonty were to meet Tom and Rachel at the duck pond because

Peg was inviting Yvette to take a walk in the park with her. It was a feeble plan – Yvette may not accompany Peg; it might rain; Rachel may not want to go to the park...but it was worth a try.

Tom sensed Rachel knew something was 'up'. She took ages to get ready and when he asked her to hurry, she retaliated. "Why...we're only going to see some ducks. Tom, we've been to this park five days in a row...would it matter if we skipped it today and met Peg back at the apartment?"

Tom was exasperated – after all Peg's careful planning.

"I promised Jonty we would feed the ducks," he objected.

Rachel laughed. "Tom, don't be ridiculous – a one-year-old can't understand a promise," Rachel protested, but eventually she put on her outdoor clothes, and they set off for the park. Tom felt nervous...would Yvette and Rachel recognise each other? It was still all speculation on Tom and Peg's behalf, but Pierre had been busy making enquiries. In one sense Tom hoped he'd been wrong and the two would be complete strangers.

Arriving in the park, Tom felt his stomach churning. Meanwhile Peg, Yvette and Jonty were walking around the perimeter of the pond. Peg noticed her brother and his wife approaching and waved excitedly.

"Jonty here comes To-To...you can walk to feed the ducks," Peg announced, bending down to remove the young boy from his pram. All eyes were focused on the lively one-year-old babbling with excitement, as his uncle bent down. Tom reached out to take Jonty's hand. Peg took a deep breath – this was it!

"Rachel, let me introduce you to my good friend, Yvette Martin," she began.

The two women looked at each other – both were ensconced in winter hats and scarves, but their eyes locked. Yvette stared at Rachel and Rachel stared at Yvette...neither spoke. Tom walked over to the ducks with a toddling Jonty. Peg looked between the two women and felt obliged to fill the awkward silence with chatter. "Madame Martin is the sage femme who saved my life when I collapsed, she..."

Over the top of Peg's voice Rachel suddenly yelled, "How long have you known, Peg?" she demanded.

Even Tom, some distance away, could hear her angry words.

Her voice grew louder. "How long have you known, Tom Smallwood?"

Tom swept the bewildered toddler into his arms to race back to Rachel's side, but she turned and took off at speed in the opposite direction. Tom thrust his nephew into Peg's arms and ran to catch up with his wife, grabbing her by the shoulder to pull her to a standstill.

"Get off me, Tom," she shrieked. "This is a trick...a hurtful trick...how could you?" Her voice was shrill.

Tom opened his mouth to speak but failed to articulate his words. What had he done? He had withheld information, significant information from his beloved wife.

Rachel began to thump his chest with her gloved hands. Tom took the beating – he deserved it. He enveloped her in a tight hug...his precious Rachel.

"Why, Tom? Why?" she repeated. "After what happened, we said we'd be truthful. We built our courtship, engagement and marriage on being truthful –

not keeping secrets."

She was right – he'd let her down. He felt her tension ease as her body became limp in his arms. She was cold... he was cold. This was not the time or place for a reunion.

"Let's go back to our hotel," Tom suggested and waved his intention to Peg.

They walked in silence and once they reached the privacy of their bedroom he took her in his arms.

"Darling Rachel," he whispered into her hair. "This was not meant to hurt you. There was never any intention to withhold this information from you. The facts only came together slowly, and it was pure speculation until Madame Martin returned from Bordeaux a few days ago. Pierre was in possession of some information, and he needed to confront Yvette Martin in his role as a gendarme... otherwise she could have denied it."

Rachel pulled back and stared at Tom; her eyes red with crying.

"What information?" she asked.

Tom sat down on the only armchair in the room and pulled his wife onto his knee, cradling her in his arms.

"Yvette Martin was the wife of Georges Martin who died recently. They had resided in Bordeaux since before the war, but Pierre could find nothing to prove their existence prior to that date – no birth records, marriage records or census records. So, he asked her to explain. She indicated all their documents had been lost during the war – a reasonable answer." Tom paused.

"Then Pierre looked directly at Yvette and asked her if she was French by birth...she speaks both English and French perfectly. At this point she broke down. Pierre commented it was distressing to observe. After she calmed, she admitted to Pierre both she and her deceased husband were English and had fled to France before the war, for their safety. They changed their identity and became Georges and Yvette Martin. They had lived in Bordeaux since then."

"But why did they flee to France?" Rachel pleaded.

Tom shook his head.

"Pierre was only interested to learn if Madame Martin had committed a crime. She had not. She was simply a wife, obeying her husband and fleeing to a different country, in fear of their lives. Many peoples were dispersed during wartime and lost original documentation. If Georges and Yvette stayed put in Bordeaux, they didn't need to produce documents."

Rachel was looking perplexed. "But how on earth did Pierre discover who she was…and what about me?"

Tom pulled Rachel close and told her about the little *canelé* cakes Yvette served when he stayed with Peg and Pierre last year.

Rachel gazed into the distance. "I loved those little cakes and when we left London, I took the moulds they were baked in with us – it was a memory of my mother, and somehow my aunt overlooked it," she recalled. "But cakes? What else made you think Yvette was my birth mother?"

"Her age and her perfect English…I suspected English was her mother tongue. Then her occupation – sage femme. Zac looked up your parents' marriage record before we visited Cornwall. It stated Philomena Brooks was a midwife and Percival Shackleton was a wood craftsman. When they changed their identity here in France, Yvette was still a sage femme, but Georges was a salesman. So, too many coincidences, Rachel."

"So did this Yvette Martin know about me before today?"

Tom shook his head. "No, Peg suggested we arrange an accidental meeting...and wait to see if there was any reaction – which we witnessed." They sat in silence for a few minutes. "Now 'the ball is in your court', my darling. Do you want to meet her again?"

Rachel dropped her eyes. "Will she want to meet me again?" she asked. "She turned her back on me once before."

Tom did not know the answer to that question.

***

Explanations were also being made in Peg and Pierre's apartment. Yvette, Peg and Jonty returned to Peg's apartment. The older woman was stunned and remained quiet on the way back from the park, then excused herself to lie down because of a headache. However, later in the day she knocked on the door and Peg invited her in.

"Sorry I was so quiet earlier," she explained. "But that was a shock. I suspect you know the identity of your brother's wife...am I correct?"

Peg nodded. "It has been speculation, Yvette. Tom was certain, when you made those little cakes last year, but we had no way to make further enquiries. Tom and Rachel have had a troubled relationship – it's their story to tell – and it was only resolved last summer, culminating in their marriage at Christmas. When we found out they were to spend a vacation with us, Pierre decided to make further enquiries which you know about. It was then a case of recognition…hence our meeting in the park. Now, Yvette, this is your business and I think Rachel should be the one to hear your explanation, not me. So, I suggest you meet her, here, tomorrow afternoon – are you agreeable to that?"

Yvette was cautious but agreed.

Rachel spent a restless night and subsequently overslept the next morning. Tom left a note for her and went for breakfast. When he returned, she was awake but looked distraught – she'd obviously been crying – he felt guilty for leaving her alone.

"No, Tom," she responded, when he apologised. "I needed time on my own. I have cried until I have no tears left. Why didn't they write to me? Why did they let me believe they were dead?"

Tom lay down on the bed beside her and stroked her face. His beautiful bride of less than three weeks…it seemed a distant memory. Tom experienced an emotion he rarely gave way to – anger. He was angry at a man he never knew…Percy Shackleton or Georges Martin as he became. Rachel's father had caused her so much grief and pain by his actions, and now his daughter was facing it again. This should have been the happiest time of her life… her honeymoon.

"It hurts, Tom…hurts so much. One part of me wants to go away and refuse to see Yvette Martin…but if I don't meet her, I will never know her explanation."

Tom noticed Rachel did not use the term 'mother' and his heart ached for his wife – he'd experienced betrayal and that was tough, but Rachel had experienced abandonment…which was equally tough. He held her close, trying to ease her pain…once again reconciliation was needed – this time between mother and daughter.

As they walked to Peg and Pierre's apartment later, Tom tried to prepare Rachel. "The past is the past, Rachel and what's been done cannot be undone. Remember how you needed my forgiveness. Philly Shackleton no longer exists – she is Yvette Martin. Darcy Shackleton no longer exists – she is Rachel Smallwood. But you are mother and daughter, you are bound by blood. Listen to her explanation…don't judge, it will serve no purpose. Then try – it won't be easy…but try to forgive her and try to look to the future." They walked in silence for a few minutes, then before they entered the building he stopped and cupped her chin. "See it as a second chance, Rachel," he gulped and continued, "If I could have a second chance to have my brother back in my life…then I would take it."

Rachel squeezed his hand. "Thank you, Tom, that's helpful," she replied.

He gently kissed her forehead, then they stepped inside.

Little Jonty was a joy and Tom was in his element playing with the toddler, who squealed in delight at the sight of To-To. The young boy brought the distraction they needed, as they ate the lunch Peg had prepared. But after the dishes were tidied a knock on the apartment door heralded the arrival of Yvette Martin. Peg excused herself to take Jonty for a nap as Tom and Rachel sat on the chaise, and Yvette sat by the fireplace. Tom studied her closely – she bore no facial similarities to Rachel, but they were alike in build. She cleared her throat…she was nervous but in control.

"I am shocked to be sitting here today but I will tell my story." She coughed then continued. "My husband travelled to France on business frequently. His good friend, Anton, lived here in Bordeaux, and sometimes I accompanied him – we stayed at Anton's home." She smiled. "It was Anton's sister who showed me how to make the 'canelés'. We left you with my sister, Jemima – it happened several times and meant your schooling was not disrupted. I was ignorant of Percy's business dealings – in those days it was not appropriate for a wife to ask probing questions. He was a wood craftsman, but also a salesman. It was all I needed to know." She took a drink of water.

"One day, when my husband was out of the country, some men called to see him. They were persistent and I became frightened. When Percy returned, I told him, and he became concerned. The next day he told me to pack a suitcase and accompany him. He told me our lives were in danger and we needed to go to France and stay there for a few weeks until it was safe to return. I panicked. We left you with Jemima – it wasn't unusual, but I think we both sensed it was different this time. It was your birthday, and your father gave you one of his boxes as a gift."

Rachel nodded. "I still have it – it was all I had left to remember you," Rachel added, a tear escaping from her eye.

"I kept in touch – my old friend Darcy Soames, your godmother, handled the post. I sent correspondence to her – she lived in Bristol, and she forwarded it to Jemima and vice versa. We couldn't risk our post being intercepted. Your grandfather and your aunt continued to be pestered as to our whereabouts and then they received an ultimatum… to tell them where your father could be found, or you would be taken."

Rachel gasped.

"My sister and father knew you were in danger, so they decided to leave London, creating a false identity for you. Jemima's friend from her nursing days, Annie, found them a cottage near to where she lived in Cornwall." Yvette paused.

Rachel looked devastated.

"All those years…you knew about me…why didn't Aunt Jemima tell me?"

Yvette sat up straight. "The rumours of war became a reality, closing the door on our return…it seemed best to let you think we had died."

Rachel voiced the question Tom was wanting to ask: "What did my father do to be hounded out of his own country and abandon his only daughter?"

Yvette hung her head and for the first time in their conversation, Tom detected a sign of remorse. She lifted her hands in surrender.

"To this day I do not know the full details, but in those carefully crafted boxes he made…secrets were carried."

"Secrets?" Tom and Rachel, declared in unison, looking wide-eyed at Yvette.

"Industrial secrets…I don't think Georges knew the full extent of what he carried…he was just a link in a chain. He made a delivery and stayed at Anton's home until he received a payment, then he came home. This happened four or five times a year – it was deliberately random. But someone discovered what he was doing, and our lives were threatened."

Yvette sat motionless…was that it? Tom felt there was more, but perhaps it would be revealed in a future conversation.

As Tom and Rachel dined later that night, Rachel asked, "Do you think my father was a spy, Tom?"

Tom shrugged his shoulders. "I'm not sure, Rachel. It was serious though, whatever he was carrying. I suppose he was an ideal target – a regular traveller to France on legitimate business. But if these people who found out what he was doing threatened your parents' lives and then threatened to take you in return for information regarding their whereabouts…that explains why you were told to be so secretive. I expect the advent of war intervened…If it hadn't, they would probably have found you."

Rachel shuddered. "It doesn't bear thinking about, Tom…I could have been kidnapped!" Rachel was mortified.

"Explain industrial secrets, Tom?" she asked.

Tom shook his head. "I'm as baffled as you are – but it was something written down small enough to be hidden in one of your father's boxes. Plans…or a formula…perhaps, pieced together over a number of deliveries? What kind of work did this Anton do, I wonder?"

Rachel looked thoughtful. "I remember him visiting our home in London – a businessman, I recall, I liked his accent – but I didn't know the nature of his business."

"We may never know, Rachel. But I think that man was responsible for involving your father in something so serious…it tore your family apart."

Rachel looked lost in her remembrances as Tom finished his food. Somehow the magic of their honeymoon had vapourised.

Yvette and Rachel met several times during the next week, but no more revelations were made. She did, however, much to Tom's relief, say how sorry she was about it all

— but it did little to bridge the gap between mother and daughter. A gulf existed and although Rachel said she held no animosity towards Yvette…Tom was not convinced. Once they returned home, he doubted if they would keep in touch and that for Tom was so sad – not the outcome he'd envisaged.

***

The train carriage was full. Tom was standing but Rachel managed to find a seat. They were travelling to Bordeaux from Lyon. Yvette had extended the invitation for Tom and Rachel to stay at her home for two nights to allow Rachel to see where they had lived after fleeing London and to visit Georges' grave. Rachel had been reluctant to accept the invitation at first, but Tom thought it would help towards a reconciliation between the pair – what was needed, however, was a miracle.

Yvette had travelled to Lyon the day before and met them at the station.

"Why did your husband choose to live in Bordeaux?" Tom asked, as they walked from the station to Yvette's home.

"Georges and Anton met at boarding school in England. They were life-long friends. We travelled here regularly in the early days of our marriage and even after you were born, Rachel. Anton was a clever man, an engineer. He was the one who persuaded your father to carry the papers in his clever little boxes, in a hidden compartment."

Rachel raised her eyebrows, remembering the hiding place in her own box. Tom listened thoughtfully – so

Percy Shackleton's skills as a wood craftsman had been responsible for drawing him in to becoming a courier – had his actions been criminal?

"What kind of engineer was Anton?" Tom asked.

"He and his brother owned a textile factory, but Anton died just after the war," replied Yvette. "I don't know the details, but whatever Georges conveyed in those boxes helped to make Anton a very rich man. Georges always said he was only taking what rightfully belonged to Anton. He had worked on some kind of process, in England, and did not receive payment. Once we knew we could not return to England, Georges began working at the textile factory – he never made another box!"

Yvette's detached residence was substantial…a reward for services rendered, Tom wondered, but kept his thoughts to himself. It was a large property with at least four bedrooms, as far as Tom could tell. They spent a pleasant afternoon looking around Bordeaux. After a good night's sleep and a tasty breakfast, Yvette took them to the cemetery.

Gazing at the headstone for Georges Martin, who had left this earth eighteen months earlier, Rachel felt little remorse for the man who had put his family at risk and ultimately ripped them apart. The body of the man in that grave was not her father – her father ceased to exist when he became Georges Martin. The whole experience of visiting the grave unsettled her and she longed to board the train and return to Lyon – but they were due to stay until the following afternoon.

"Go and relax in the lounge, Tom, while Rachel and I prepare the lunch," instructed Yvette as they returned to her house. Tom entered the tastefully appointed lounge. The door was ajar, and he could hear Yvette and Rachel conversing as they prepared the food. They seemed more relaxed in each other's company...perhaps there was hope of a relationship between them after all.

Suddenly his attention was drawn to voices coming from outside. He stood and walked over to the window which overlooked the garden and the road. A young teenage girl was standing talking to a pedestrian. He stood and watched. She finished talking and turned to walk up the path...and Tom froze.

Chapter 25

Tom was transfixed…it was impossible – but as the figure bounced up the path, he knew his eyes were not deceiving him. He was watching an exact replica of Rachel, when she was a teenager – when he first met her in Wales.

Within seconds he heard the front door open, and a voice called out in French, "Mère, je suis a la maison."

Tom left his position beside the window and walked over to stand in front of the fireplace, just as the door pushed open.

"Pardon, je suis desole, monsieur," the girl exclaimed in surprise. Before she could exit the room Yvette appeared, closely followed by Rachel, who walked over to stand beside Tom. Her jaw dropped, as she too gazed in bewilderment at the young teenage girl. Yvette took command of the proceedings.

"Chantal…we shall converse in English – let me introduce our guests. I suggest you all take a seat." The girl sat down heavily on a chair near to the door; her body language oozed impatience. Rachel grabbed Tom's hand and they sat on the settee beside the window. Yvette remained standing but moved towards the fireplace. Tom sensed she was about to give a well-rehearsed speech.

"Chantal – this is Monsieur and Madame Smallwood from England, Tom and Rachel." She hesitated as the girl looked across at the couple. "Tom and Rachel, let me introduce you to my daughter Chantal Martin." Tom felt the tension in Rachel's body as she clasped his hand tightly. Chantal stared at the English couple and in typical teenage fashion blurted out a comment to her mother in French.

"English, Chantal," Yvette reprimanded the girl sternly, but did not give a translation. Rachel was dumfounded as realisation began to take root. "This will come as a surprise to all of you…so let me explain," continued Yvette. She lifted her hand towards the young girl.

"Rachel…this is your sister, Chantal," then repeating the gesture she held out her hand towards Rachel. "Chantal… this is your sister, Rachel." The two stared at each other in disbelief…both were stunned. Yvette waited then spoke.

"When Georges and I came to France it was always our intention to return to England. Chantal, your father and I were English by birth and came to France before the war." The girl stared at her mother. "During the war, I became pregnant, and Chantal was born – she is fourteen years old now.

"Once we knew it was impossible for us to return to England, Georges and I came to a painful decision. My sister Jemima lost her only child as a baby…she doted on you, Rachel, and had cared for you as a mother, since we left England. We were blessed with another daughter and so we decided to leave you with Jemima and my father." Yvette swallowed.

"Rachel, you must understand your safety was paramount in our decision. I wrote to Jemima and suggested she tell you we were dead. It meant both my sister and I raised a beautiful daughter." She paused...then addressed the young French girl. "Your father and I did not tell you of the daughter we left behind...your sister. I never envisaged the possibility that one day you two would meet."

Yvette reached out and placed her hand on the mantel shelf. "To discover I was expecting another child in my early forties was such a shock, but, Chantal...you were such a blessing. We were given the chance to become parents again." Yvette paused, looking tearful. "I beg you both, now you are aware of each other's existence to see this as a bonus...you have each gained a sister and I think we must celebrate. Now, the lunch is almost ready so I suggest we eat, and you two girls can get to know one another." With that Yvette turned and left the room. Three pairs of eyes followed her in amazement.

***

Later that night Rachel lay in Tom's arms as they settled down to sleep. Tom was astounded at the way Rachel had accepted Chantal's existence. He'd expected her to want to leave Yvette's home immediately after the revelation, but instead the sisters had spent the afternoon becoming acquainted.

"She's the image of you at that age," Tom remarked. "I thought I was seeing an apparition when I looked out of the window. How do you feel about the discovery? I thought you'd be upset."

Rachel snuggled up to Tom. "I'm at ease about it, Tom; as Yvette said, I've gained a sister. I've always felt alone and now I have real, blood family. I still can't believe the chain of events. If you hadn't recognised me when I turned up in Malhaven, I would never have known I had a mother who was still alive and a French sister."

Tom squeezed her and kissed the top of her hair.

"And to think I did everything in my power to stop you from unearthing my family background!" Rachel added.

Tom pulled back and looked adoringly into his wife's eyes. "I think, Mrs Smallwood, you have been greatly blessed. Not only do you have a very handsome husband, but you have a lovely mother and a delightful sister. Embrace your new family, Rachel. I lost two family members through illness and accident…you have found two family members." He kissed her lovingly.

Rachel lay, thoughtful for a while, and just as Tom was dozing off to sleep, she nudged him.

"Tom…I have much to gain, and I must be thankful for this turn of events."

Tom sighed and cuddled his new wife…if Rachel was happy…that was all that mattered.

***

Peg and Pierre were delighted to hear about Rachel's discovery. Tom suspected Pierre already knew about Chantal's existence from viewing the census records but had wisely kept the information to himself. With only a few days before Tom and Rachel's return to England, Peg started to plan – a birthday party for Jonty's first birthday: a farewell to Tom and Rachel, and the reunion of Yvette and her two daughters – united into one elaborate celebration meal.

Chantal was a boarder at a convent school near Bordeaux, hence the reason Yvette spent so much time with her friend Madame Levigne – she was to travel to Lyon to stay with her mother and her friend. Yvette was happy her former life was no longer secretive. "I was always looking over my shoulder trying to be vague when anyone asked about my background," she told Peg. "It's such a relief to know that burden has been lifted...but I will never be able to visit England again and that will cause me sadness. However, I hope Tom and Rachel will visit me here in France."

Yvette was helping Peg prepare the celebration meal which included the little 'canelé' cakes.

"What happened to your friend Darcy Soames?" Peg enquired, knowing she had played a significant part in the correspondence trail.

A look of sadness clouded Yvette's face. "She is still alive, but she suffered a stroke many years ago, and is confined to a wheelchair. She was such a vibrant person – but her mind is still alert, and we continue to write regularly. She hid her condition from her brother. Jemima, my sister, was so grateful for her help in redirecting the letters for all those years. It was her friend Miss Thomas who informed me through Darcy Soames, of my sister's sudden death. All I knew about Rachel was her occupation."

Any apprehension on Tom's behalf soon dissipated as the celebration meal was held. Everyone was in a jovial mood, and he observed interaction between Rachel,

Chantal and his sister Peg. Chantal was enthralled with little Jonty, and he overheard Peg suggesting to Chantal they should meet sometime. Tom and Rachel's extended honeymoon ended, with lots of promises to keep in touch.

***

Summer 1929

The postie rang the doorbell and Tom answered. "My, my, Mr Smallwood you receive a lot of post from France these days," he remarked, handing Tom a bundle of letters and bending down to pat Humph.

"Well, that's because we have a lot of family living there, Bill…not just Peg. My wife has relatives living in a different part of France," he commented.

It was still a surprise to Tom how well Rachel had welcomed the discovery of her young sister. He still doubted if Rachel and Yvette would truly put the missing years behind them, but the early signs were good and, in the months since their return, Rachel had received a few letters from her mother.

It was a different story with Chantal – the young girl was so enthusiastic to communicate with her new sister and wrote frequently. Yvette had always encouraged Chantal to speak English and as a result the girl was bi-lingual, which made her letter writing easy. Plans were already underway for Chantal to accompany Peg, Pierre and Jonty when they spent their vacation in England, during the month of August. Rachel had spent weeks clearing out an attic room on the back of the hotel for her young sister. "Our families certainly pick an awkward time of year to visit," Rachel remarked one morning. "August is peak season – all the available bedrooms are full, and we need to find accommodation for family guests."

"We'll cope, Rachel – you've done a splendid job decorating that old attic room. It's been a junk room for as long as I remember it." Rachel's flair for interior design was a joy to behold. With the office tasks in the capable hands of Deborah Hogarth and Ada Beck, and Tom's time split between overseeing the farm business and acting as host in the hotel, Rachel turned her hand to interior improvements.

She was handy with a sewing machine and started with small items, cushion covers, bedspreads and armchair covers. She began a programme of restocking bedlinens and towels. Winnie welcomed her involvement, and they worked well together. In essence it was a task which had needed fresh eyes for some time, and Rachel was determined to gradually update the décor and furnishings throughout the hotel, as time and finance permitted.

August arrived and with it the French visitors. Rachel and Chantal became inseparable, finding so many things in common. Chantal helped with baby Jonty, giving his parents time to spend together. Tom, Rachel, Pierre and Peg enjoyed two evenings dining out – a luxury for the French couple.

The romance between Zac and Deborah gained momentum and they announced their engagement at Easter – plans were underway for their wedding in the autumn.

One afternoon Chantal and Rachel took Jonty for a walk. The youngster was tired, having slept little due to teething. Within minutes he was sound asleep in his pram, kindly loaned by Blanche Rossiter.

"You and Tom are such a perfect couple, Rachel. I hope I will meet someone and be as happy as you two are," Chantal commented. The young French girl was starry eyed, dreaming of handsome young suitors. "Was it 'love at first sight' for you two?" she asked and looked astounded when Rachel replied: "The newspaper photograph of our wedding carried the caption '*FROM COURTROOM TO CHURCH*'."

"Why?" asked the teenager. Rachel took a deep breath.

"Tom and I first met when I was about your age. Tom and his family were staying with their aunt and uncle in North Wales. I was supposed to be staying with my godmother, but she was too busy, and sent me to stay with her brother, where Tom and his family were staying. I vaguely remember Tom as being a shy, awkward sort of boy – his brother, however, was very attractive. I made friends with Peg, and we promised to become pen pals. Then my world fell apart." Even now, all these years later Rachel could still feel the pain of abandonment.

"I was unaware of the background. All I recall was going on an adventure with my aunt and grandfather to a little village in Cornwall, miles away from my home in London. My parents…I mean our parents, were off on their travels abroad. I thought nothing of it…until they didn't return. My aunt pretended it was a game – changing my name, calling her Mama and grandfather Papa…and never referring to my parents. We even muddled up the letters of the village where we lived. What I only learned recently was my life was in danger. Our father was being tracked down for handling sensitive documents and I could have been used as a pawn to get to him. Thankfully, none of that happened because the war intervened. I cared little for my aunt – blaming her for taking me away from my parents. I couldn't wait to leave home. I 'escaped' when I was eighteen and never went back or communicated with our aunt and grandfather…something I regret now."

Chantal was drinking in every word her older sister was saying.

"I came to this area for work and met Tom and his brother. I was astounded when I realised who they were. But I'd lived in secrecy for so long and I guarded my background fiercely. Tom and I became romantically involved and when he recognised me, I denied it. Eventually, we split up because I wouldn't admit to being Darcy Shackleton. I turned my attentions to the other brother – but it was a shallow relationship. Then on that tragic day, which you've heard about from Peg, Jonty fell and without gaining consciousness he died three months later." Rachel stopped walking. Somehow, she wanted her sister to learn from her mistakes – she needed to convey how devastating her actions had been. They were in the park and went over to sit down.

"Chantal, what I am about to tell you is something I am ashamed of; something I deeply regret. We are sisters and I hope you will keep my confidences – Tom knows all this, but no one else does. I was angry, hurt, disillusioned, confused and felt so alone and rejected. I regret to say I blamed Tom for pushing Jonty over the edge of the Cragg. It was retaliation on my behalf – I needed someone to blame. Please learn from my mistakes, Chantal. Don't let those emotions cloud your thinking. I was wrong, but once I'd made the accusation...there was no going back, and we ended up in the courtroom with Tom facing a charge of manslaughter." Rachel felt tears threatening and wiped her eyes.

Chantal remained silent absorbing the information her sister divulged. "I'm guessing Tom was cleared of the charge," Chantal remarked, after a while.

Rachel took a few minutes to compose herself. "Thankfully, yes. But I was left with a burden. I needed his forgiveness. It gnawed at me for months. I decided to contact him, and we met – at the place of the accident. It was a difficult meeting, but I made my request. Tom wasn't ready to take that step. He asked me to return to the same spot, one year later, for his answer. I knew he still cared for me...but I'd betrayed him, Chantal. Tom has a code for his life and integrity and truth feature highly in that code. During that year, I realised I needed to be truthful and tell him who I really was...otherwise I would have to walk away and forget all about Tom Smallwood." Rachel let out an audible sigh. "Tom forgave me, and I confessed to being Darcy." She paused.

"The rest, as they say, is history...a whirlwind courtship, engagement and wedding. Then on our honeymoon another bombshell was dropped...but you know all about that, Chantal."

The young girl turned and hugged her older sister. "Rachel, thank you so much for telling me. I can see it has taken courage to tell your story and I'm so happy for you that it turned out the way it did. I'm also so very, very happy that we have found each other. Thank you for the advice."

"Learn from our mother's mistakes as well, Chantal – Yvette and I have a mountain to climb. But maybe one day I can call her 'mother' – to her face again."

Tears ran down both their faces, as little Jonty stirred.

***

On Jonty's anniversary day – the day of the accident – Tom and Rachel took a trip to Lasham Cragg. Their French visitors were due to return home in a few days and Tom wanted Peg and Pierre and Chantal to accompany them. Peg, however, insisted her brother and his wife make the trip by themselves. "I have other plans, Tom; we are going to show Chantal the North Sea coast. Mother is coming to the hotel to help Winnie, which frees us all."

After spending time gazing at the view, Tom said a silent prayer thanking God for his brother's life and for directing him over the last year so that Rachel now stood at his side...as his beautiful wife.

Breaking into his thoughts Rachel asked, "Tom...why did you forgive me? I still struggle to understand why you would do that."

Tom put his arm around his wife's shoulders, making sure they were standing well back from the edge.

"The answer to that, Rachel, lies in some words my Aunt Dora used to quote. It's a part of the Bible, but my aunt wrote it down in a way I could understand it as a youngster. I learned it off by heart years ago."

Rachel looked adoringly at her husband as he began,

'Love never gives up, cares more for others than self.
Doesn't want what it doesn't have; doesn't
strut or have a swelled head.
It doesn't fly off the handle; doesn't
keep a score of others' wrongs.
It takes pleasure in the blossoming of truth.
Puts up with anything, trusts God always-
and keeps going to the end.
Love never dies.'

Tears ran down Rachel's face.

"It was love, Rachel," Tom remarked.

Taking Tom's hand, she placed it on her stomach. "I have news, Tom...we are expecting a child."

Tom gasped with delight.

"Whether it's a boy or a girl I know what I would like to call our baby."

Tom cupped Rachel's chin with both his hands and kissed her passionately. Pulling back, he declared,

"Rachel, that's splendid news...you have made me the happiest man on this planet, and you can choose whatever name you want...but I suspect it will begin with a 'D' and end with a 'Y'. It can be given to either gender...but when I used it...I almost lost you."

Rachel nodded and before Tom brought his lips to hers again, he whispered, "I love you...Darcy Shackleton Rachel Brooks Smallwood...with every fibre of my being."

Their kiss was deep and intense. As they pulled apart, Rachel reached out and touched Tom's face. She was trembling and tears threatened to engulf her.

"I'm so happy, Tom...I love you so much...I don't deserve your love; I don't deserve our happiness," she uttered.

Tom gazed at Rachel adoringly. "Let's raise our children to always value truth, Rachel," Tom added, then hugged her tightly.

***

NOTICE IN THE NORTHERN ECHO NEWSPAPER.

On the 28th January 1930.

To Thomas Ezra and Rachel Smallwood

The gift of a daughter,

DARCY ROSE.

***

Acknowledgements

A big thank you to my husband, Vic, for his ongoing support, thoughtful ideas and valuable advice. Also, for his culinary delights when my head was still 'in the book'!

Many thanks to my cover illustrator, friend and cousin, Ruth, who translated my 'vague' ideas into a coherent painting – I'm so appreciative of her artistic skill. Also, for the countless coffee sessions where she became my sounding board, as my writing ideas developed.

I'm grateful to friends and family members who read the early drafts, found the typos and gaffes and made constructive suggestions – your comments were so helpful.

Finally, thank you to the dozens of 'unknowns', who I have 'people watched' to help create and shape my characters. I will never know who you are, but that gesture, that expression, that action is in this book!

Thanks to UK Book Publishing for answering my endless questions and making this project a reality.

And lastly, I am indebted to you, the reader, for taking the time to read Tom and Rachel's story.

Susan Gray

If you have enjoyed reading 'BLOSSOMING OF TRUTH'
please leave a review on
Amazon, Goodreads or Facebook.
Please follow my Facebook Author Page
https://www.facebook.com/susangrayauthor

About the Author

As a child Susan Gray enjoyed making up stories to while away the time on lengthy car journeys. Decades later she decided to 'follow her dreams' and published her first novel 'SPANISH HOUSE SECRETS'.

She lives in northeast England with her husband and sets her books in northwest Durham. She has a son and daughter, both married, two granddaughters and a grand dog.

After a career in primary teaching, she embraced retirement, fulfilling her ambitions to travel, attend Wimbledon and write a novel. After years of encouraging young children to write creatively, she has found the tables have now 'turned'!

When not writing, she enjoys reading, walking, doing puzzles, crafting, being a Gran and catching up with friends over a coffee.

She has written six novels and 'BLOSSOMING OF TRUTH' is the second to be published.